Maeve Haran

In a Country Garden

PAN BOOKS

First published 2018 by Pan Books
an imprint of Pan Macmillan
20 New Wharf Road, London N1 9RR
Associated companies throughout the world
www.panmacmillan.com

ISBN 978-1-5098-6650-2

1 3 5 7 9 8 6 4 2

A CIP catalogue record for this book is available from the British Library.

Typeset by Palimpsest Book Production Ltd, Falkirk, Stirlingshire
Printed and bound by CPI Group (UK) Ltd, Croydon, CR0 4YY

Visit **www.panmacmillan.com** to read more about all our books
and to buy them. You will also find features, author interviews and
news of any author events, and you can sign up for e-newsletters
so that you're always first to hear about our new releases.

In a Country Garden

Maeve Haran is a former television producer and mother of three grown-up children. Her first novel, *Having It All*, which explored the dilemmas of balancing career and motherhood, caused a sensation and took her all around the world. Maeve has written a further twelve contemporary novels and two historical novels, plus a work of non-fiction celebrating life's small pleasures.

Her books have been translated into twenty-six languages, and two have been shortlisted for the Romantic Novel of the Year award. She lives in North London with her husband (a very tall Scotsman) and a scruffy Tibetan terrier. They also spend time at their much-loved cottage in Sussex.

For female friends everywhere

One

'Come on, Claudia, tell all. How was the honeymoon? Are the happy couple still speaking?'

Claudia nervously patted her carefully coloured nut-brown hair (no grey for her, thanks, even the Helen Mirren platinum variety) as she considered the question about her daughter's recent wedding.

The fact was, her daughter had very nearly called the whole thing off. And the reason she'd given was the bad example her parents had set in their own marriage.

It was exceptionally bad timing, Claudia had to admit, that Gaby had discovered her mother in the arms of the sexy choirmaster who ran her weekly singing group on the very same day she came across emails to her father from an old flame. Claudia blamed her moment of madness on giving up the teaching job she'd loved and reluctantly moving to the country to look after her ailing parents. She didn't know what her husband Don's excuse was.

'They're safely home and very happy, apart from the fact they want to build a house and haven't any money. All the fault of our generation, of course, who've pushed up house prices.'

'Of course it is,' laughed Ella. 'Everything from exploited Uber drivers to unaffordable one-bedroom flats is the fault of our generation. We're the selfish baby-boomers.' She glanced round The Grecian Grove, the scruffy basement wine bar with its badly painted murals of lecherous shepherds chasing bored-looking nymphs, where they met once a month. 'Is it me or are those nymphs looking older?'

They all laughed in recognition of the fact that after forty years of friendship they weren't so young themselves.

'Anyway,' Claudia announced. 'Don and I have resolved to start all over again. Embracing country life and each other.'

'Good luck with that.' Ella raised her glass. 'So, isn't anyone going to ask how *I* am? Actually, I'm feeling pretty good.' Her two friends, Claudia and Laura, studied her. She did look good. Her elfin looks had aged well. In fact, apart from the stray grey hair, she had the same alert and energetic look she'd always had. 'The sale went through on the house in double-quick time and I've already moved into my new riverside cottage!'

'Bloody hell, Ella, that was quick!' Claudia marvelled.

'But wasn't it really hard for you to leave?' asked Laura, trying not to let herself down and cry. She was facing moving herself, though not from choice. She was in the middle of a bitter divorce and her horrible husband Simon was insisting they sell up now that their decree absolute loomed. She knew that Ella's beautiful Georgian home had always been her pride and joy, far more to her than just bricks and mortar. Laura couldn't understand how she could be so matter of fact about losing it. 'How long did you live there?'

'It doesn't feel like that long ago, but it was,' Ella replied. 'It was right back when I got my first job as a lawyer and Laurence had just started in business. To think, as my daughters continually remind me, the entire house cost less than a studio flat in Dalston does now.'

They all took a moment to dwell on the madness of the London property market, where millionaires lived in ordinary semis and only Russian oligarchs could afford anything detached.

'It must have been so sad for you to have to leave your memories of Laurence.' Laura reached out a hand to her friend, but knew that she was really talking about herself. Ella's husband Laurence had been killed in a train crash five years ago, leaving Ella distraught and devastated.

Ella shook her head. 'That's what I thought. I thought it would break my heart to leave it all behind and move to somewhere tiny. But it was strangely liberating. It feels like a new phase. A good one. The funny thing is, I could hear Laurence telling me that. Come on, old girl, he was saying, time to move on. I'm actually quite excited, and wait – hot news – my old neighbours are giving up their allotment and it looks like I'll be able to jump the waiting list and get it.'

Despite her precarious emotional state, Laura had to laugh. 'Whatever happened to us, eh? Weren't we going to change the world?' The laughter lit up her still-pretty features, reminding the others suddenly of the Laura they'd met at eighteen in their first year at college.

'I'm happy to change it through growing greens, thank you very much,' laughed Ella.

'Not even voting Green?'

'Politics never interested me even then. Claudia was the radical one who threw paving stones in Paris.'

'Only because a gorgeous French boy encouraged me,' Claudia reminisced. 'Anyway, it was a different world then. The young knew they could do anything they wanted and no one could stop them.'

'Not where I grew up they didn't,' Ella protested. 'Do you know ninety-nine per cent of people believe the sexual revolution happened, and ninety-eight per cent think it happened to somebody else?'

They all thought for a moment of the heady days of the Sixties, when they'd been young and carefree and were never, ever going to get old.

'While we're on the subject of sex, what happened to that nice man you brought to Gaby's wedding? We liked him, didn't we, Ella?'

'We did indeed,' seconded Ella. 'Nice eyes.'

'And arse,' Claudia reminisced.

'Calum,' Laura replied crisply. 'Really, Claudia. You're beginning to sound quite repressed. He's just a friend.'

'The kind of friend who thumps your soon-to-be-ex-husband for not appreciating how wonderful you are,' teased Claudia before turning back to Ella.

'So you're getting your own allotment at last? Hold the front page.' She looked towards the door. 'Speaking of front pages, where *is* Sal?' Sal was the fourth member of their little group, a magazine editor. She was also a lover of leopard-skin onesies, ludicrously high-heeled stilettoes and studded biker jackets despite being over sixty like the rest of them.

'Maybe she's decided not to come. After all, it's not long since her operation,' Laura pointed out. Sal had shocked them all at the wedding by suddenly announcing that she had breast cancer and was about to have a mastectomy. None of them had had the slightest inkling she was even ill.

'I'm so relieved it went okay,' Claudia announced.

The last time they'd seen her they'd been gathered round her hospital bed while she'd tried on a variety of outrageous headdresses and teased the doctors that she was going to make being bald fashionable.

'Sal's a coper,' insisted Ella.

'Has she forgiven you for being so rude to her at the wedding?' Laura asked.

The normally cool, calm and collected Ella had the grace to blush, recalling how she'd got gloriously drunk and accused Sal of being selfish for not telling them about her cancer sooner.

'Oh God, don't remind me!' Ella hid her face in genuine remorse. 'I can't believe I was such a bitch!'

Admitting to her illness hadn't been the only surprise Sal had pulled from under her pink wig that day. She'd also produced a young woman called Lara whom she'd announced, to their startled amazement, as the long-lost daughter she'd given away as a baby when she'd been an eighteen-year-old au pair in Oslo. 'Speak of the devil in Prada, here she is!'

They all stood up in sheer amazement. Sal had pulled many surprises during their long friendship, Lara included, but few to rival this. Sal looked like an entirely new person. Gone was the outrageous pink wig and the fur hat and sunglasses she had used to disguise her hair loss. So was any trace of leopard skin. Instead a tall, elegant woman with very short grey hair and large stylish earrings stood in front of them wearing a discreetly cut silk dress.

'Sal!' Laura marvelled before she could stop herself. 'What on earth have you done to yourself?'

'It's called cancer chic,' Sal announced, grinning broadly. 'A grown-up look to go with my new hair growth. No one told me when it started growing back it would be curly with a touch of Annie Lennox.' Ignoring the fascinated gaze of the other customers, she began to undo the buttons of her dress.

Before any of them realized her intentions she had pulled down her bra and was proudly brandishing a dark and puckered scar which ran across her chest where previously her right breast had been.

'Impressive, eh?' Sal demanded. 'Pity there's no demand these days for ageing Amazon warriors.'

'Sal! Sit down!' Conventional Laura attempted to shield Sal from the fascinated or horrified gaze of the other customers.

'As if I give a shit!' insisted Sal. 'Modesty is the last thing that bothers you when you've been poked around like I have. Look what they've given me.' She produced an oval-shaped foam pad from out of her bra and waved it at them. 'A falsie! Do you remember the old days? When you were terrified a boy would discover your falsie during heavy petting?'

Her eyes fixed on Laura's shapely bosoms. 'No, well, you wouldn't, Laura.'

'Only Sal could think of heavy petting after a mastectomy,' giggled Claudia. 'Go on, do yourself up and tell us the gory details.'

'I was too woozy last time, wasn't I?' Sal adjusted her clothing and sat down. 'First they draw on your chest with a felt-tip pen as if you were a marketing man's flipchart, then, bingo, off comes your boob. Mine were so flat I thought I'd hardly notice but actually it was agony. Lovely Lara helped me with the exercises. That girl really was sent from heaven.' She poured herself a large glass of wine.

Ella and Claudia exchanged glances but neither had the nerve to ask if the doctor had told her it was okay to drink.

'The best thing is no hoovering or ironing, doctor's orders. Lara's doing all that for me. The poor girl does get cross with me, though, for not taking it all seriously. Just because I asked the oncologist, "Will I be able to drive, doctor?" and when he said yes I quipped, "That's amazing. I couldn't drive before!" I can't convince her I only laugh because it's serious.' She sipped her wine with relish. 'Lara's so sweet. She makes me read all the cancer blogs because she thinks they'll be good for me, make me look on the bright side. And she's right. They're brilliant. An absolute hoot. You'd think getting cancer was the best thing that could happen to you!' She raised her glass. 'Anyway, who needs breasts? Get them off, I say!'

The subject of blogs made her turn to Ella. 'And I hope you haven't forgotten, O betrayer of confidences, that you agreed to start writing for my magazine?'

Ella looked as if she'd hoped Sal had forgotten. 'Do you really think anyone would care what I have to say?' She glanced round apologetically at her friends. A few months ago she'd started a funny blog drawing on her friends' experiences of ageing, divorce and adultery that had almost cost her their friendship. Ella, not the techiest of types, had thought she could say whatever she wanted in a blog because no one would ever read it.

'Of course they'd care what you have to say, Ella,' Sal insisted, 'because you're actually very funny.'

'As long as you're not funny about us any more!' Laura insisted, still smarting from her sense of betrayal that Ella had revealed the details of her painful divorce.

'So, Laura . . .' Ella was looking so sheepish that Claudia thought it politic to change the subject. 'Where are you going to move to?'

Too late she realized this wasn't such a good idea. Laura looked stricken.

'I really don't know. I won't be able to afford much.' She tried not to show how devastated she was to leave the home where she'd brought up her children, but it was too much for her. 'It's so bloody unfair! I'm the innocent victim and I'm still losing my home, thanks to sodding no-fault divorce!'

The truth was, after years of marriage and children, Laura was terrified of growing old alone. 'It's a pity we couldn't all live together again,' she smiled, 'like we used to at uni.'

'That'd be so much fun.' Claudia couldn't help thinking of her parents and how dependent they were becoming. It would be terrific to have her friends around to give her support.

'What, you mean live together like in some kind of dotty commune for oldies?' Ella demanded. 'A retirement village like they have in America, with bingo in the afternoon and pool aerobics and golf buggies so you never have to walk?'

'More anti-retirement,' Claudia mused, getting into the spirit of the idea. 'A cross between a student flat and a kibbutz. Not just one age group. I couldn't bear to live just with other old people – even you!'

'But we're not old!' protested Laura. 'We're only in our six-ties.'

'We will be sooner than you think,' Claudia laughed. 'Think how quickly the last fifteen years went. In another we'll be eighty!'

They contemplated this awful fact in silent horror.

'You'd have to have someone to clean it,' Ella interrupted. 'Do you remember how grotty that flat was?'

'Grotty. There's a word I haven't heard in a while,' Claudia grinned. 'And we'd need kind young carers to wipe our bums and understand Netflix.'

'And to do our hair. I may not stay grey forever. As a matter of fact, I rather fancy a hint of green. The ageing-mermaid look. And we'd definitely need a bar,' nodded Sal as if this were a foregone conclusion.

'Plus a spa,' Laura mused dreamily. 'Hairdressing and pedicures, of course. Maybe even Botox. And someone to remove our facial fur.'

'And great music. The Eagles and the Grateful Dead permanently on loudspeaker,' Sal laughed. 'Someone sent me a card with an old bloke in a wheelchair and the carer's saying, "Come on, Dave. Time for your Van Morrison."'

'What about men?' Claudia enquired.

'We can probably order them from a website,' Sal decided.

'No,' Claudia giggled. 'I mean husbands. Don, for example. He'd absolutely loathe it. He always quotes Sartre: *Hell is other people.*'

'Don'll be dead by then. Otherwise he can have his own wing.'

'They actually do it in Scandinavia, you know,' Sal announced impressively. 'Lara was telling me about it. Eight per cent of Danes live in what they call "intentional communities".'

'We could have an unintentional community,' suggested Claudia, 'full of extremely old hippies who can't remember their own names. And us, of course.'

'Quite frankly,' Laura shuddered, 'and don't take offence anyone, but I can't think of anything worse.'

'I don't know.' Claudia could definitely see the appeal. 'I think it's rather a wonderful idea. The best of both worlds. You have your best friends around you to have fun with and to look after each other. I mean, why should we grow old the way people do at the moment? Dribbling in front of the telly in care homes or living alone and never seeing anyone? Why isn't it more fun? I mean, we're the baby-boomers, the Me Generation, we were going to do everything differently. Why not growing old?' She grinned round at her friends, suddenly full of enthusiasm. 'We could call it the Old Broads' Retirement Home for Fun and Frolics!'

'And incontinence,' prompted Sal. 'And don't forget our old friend dementia!'

Her three friends looked at Sal in varying degrees of horror and amusement.

'Well.' Sal put down her glass and reached for her bag. 'That's one idea that isn't going to happen. 'You might as well shoot me first. It's an absolutely ghastly thought.'

'Apart from the golf buggies,' Laura amended, as they all got up to depart for their various destinations. 'I'd adore to have my own golf buggy.'

'Personally,' Sal replied, 'I'm waiting for a self-driving car. Then I can prove my mother wrong when she told me I should have taken my test back in 1969.'

'You wait,' threatened Claudia, waving her glass of wine at them. 'You'll all come round to the idea in the end!'

Two

Ella opened her curtains with a huge smile already on her face. It was a beautiful morning, with the mist still hanging like grey gauze over the river. In her old house she'd been woken by the rosy-fingered dawn, but here her bedroom faced a different direction and she got the dramatic red magic of sunsets instead. How appropriate!

She had already been downstairs and made herself a cup of tea, the habit of a lifetime, but lately she'd added a chocolate digestive. Screw all that stuff you were told about one biscuit a day making you put on a stone over a year. At her age you were entitled to do what you wanted. Who wanted to live another thirty years if it meant you couldn't have whatever took your fancy? No wonder they lived till a hundred and ten in the high plateaus of Tibet, drinking yak's milk and eating pickled sheep testicles. No thanks! Though she had to admit she hadn't been feeling quite herself lately, but robust no-nonsense Ella refused to think about that. Laurence used to tease her that she saw all illness – especially the male sort – as a sign of weakness.

Claudia's mad proposal came back to her and she had to

laugh. She adored her friends but there was no way she wanted to spend the rest of her life with them.

She turned and surveyed her new bedroom. The old house had been painted with pale colours, mellowed by the patina of time. It had suited the place. The house itself had provided the drama just by virtue of its age and the wood panelling that warmed and surrounded you. Besides, she and Laurence hadn't agreed about colour. He liked things unobtrusive. The subtle shades had certainly been a perfect backdrop to the beautiful things they had collected over the years, from gilded chandeliers, lovely china, a painted screen and the most fabulous marble table with feet which had graced their hall, always bearing a bunch of flowers, whatever the season, to greet you as you opened the front door. She had put some of it in storage and offered anything to the girls. Her elder daughter Julia had instantly declared almost everything to be out of fashion but Cory, the younger one, had put in a bid for several lovely pictures even though she lived in a tiny studio flat.

Ella herself had selected the things she loved most to bring here and the rest had gone off to auction. She looked round, feeling surprised at how easily she had been able to wave goodbye to it all. Maybe she wasn't too old to start again.

Since moving here she had discovered a whole new palette, from warm blue, a reflection of the river outside, to Tuscan terracotta. It had felt like doing up a doll's house after her last home. Was that why she loved it? The sense that a house this size would be so much less responsibility? So much less to maintain?

Her younger daughter Cory had sorted out all the techie stuff, thank God – the broadband and something called fibre optic; God alone knew what that was. Like a car owner who doesn't want to know what happens under the bonnet, Ella just enjoyed using it all without needing to understand it. She had embraced Facebook to see what her grandsons Harry and Mark were up to (or rather what they'd let her see) and of course she'd adored blogging. What on earth was she going to write about for Sal's magazine? Especially now she had to be careful not to use confidences entrusted to her by her friends?

Her mind drifted to her other daughter, Julia. Interfering daughters. That would be a terrific topic. Ella mentally slapped herself on her wrist. It was bloody true, though. Julia, having nagged her for years about moving somewhere smaller, had suddenly wailed at Ella, 'How could you sell our family home just like that without telling us?'

And then, when Ella had started to clear three decades of belongings, Julia refused anything valuable but protested at every plastic toy her mother tried to throw out and even, bizarrely, wept over a Tamagotchi which had actually belonged to her sister. *Maybe you're a tough old boot,* Ella told herself. Or maybe she couldn't attach emotional significance to any object after losing her husband so suddenly. When that happened to you out of the blue, nothing material seemed to matter.

Did Julia feel somehow stuck in a lost childhood for the same reason? She had tried to put her arms round Julia at that thought, but Julia hadn't wanted to listen. Had Ella not noticed that the staircase in her new house was ludicrously steep? Julia demanded. How would she negotiate it when she was older? And why hadn't she bought a sensible ground-floor flat?

But her mother's other mistakes had been eclipsed in Julia's mind at the madness of the location of the new house right on the riverbank where it met the Grand Union Canal. Did her mother not remember about the Thames flooding? Was she completely crazy?

Ella was indeed so crazy that this made her go straight to her CD collection (she actually still had one) and put on Leonard Cohen to listen to him singing about Suzanne and her place down by the river where she fed him tea and oranges that came all the way from China. As a matter of fact, when she was young she'd loathed Leonard Cohen and called it 'music to slit your wrists by', but an odd thing had happened: as she'd grown older she'd come to love his melancholy songs with their deeply poetic lyrics and had even been to see him in concert.

Somehow those mournful ballads about mad muses made her think, as no other music did, of her youth. Hadn't he been in the news because he'd written a letter to his old lover Marianne when he'd heard she was dying? Being Ella, she had to know now and opened her laptop, instantly googling Marianne. The screen filled with a vast image of Leonard and Marianne, both young and golden, walking hand in hand on the Greek island of Hydra. Ella had to sit down. She'd been to Hydra herself at eighteen, feeling sophisticated and daring and that life was an adventure that was just beginning.

Cohen's tender words filled her screen. 'Well, Marianne', he spoke directly to the woman he'd loved who had inspired one of his most famous songs, reminding her that now they were both nearing death, it wouldn't be long before he followed her. Ella had to wipe away a tear, remembering that he had indeed followed her less than a year later. 'Goodbye, old friend', were his final words, and that he would see her down the road.

Ella found that she was crying properly now and had to shake herself. She was only sixty-four, for goodness' sake! Not that death couldn't leap out at you at any time, as she knew only too well. As the wonderful Nora Ephron put it, after sixty death is a sniper.

Nevertheless, this might be the inspiration she was looking for for Sal's magazine. *What Leonard Cohen can teach us all about living well*. Not bad.

Sal was wondering what going back to work would be like, and found she was really looking forward to it. It might be all right for Ella and Claudia to revel in retirement but she needed the buzz of the workplace – not to mention the money. She was well aware that of the four of them she was much the worst off, without a property to sell like Ella or a pension and a husband like Claudia. Laura might be in a precarious position, being divorced by that shit Simon, but she would have half of the marital home at least. Sal, who rented her flat and had enjoyed a life of extravagance, only had her talent and her brains.

However, Sal was an optimist and she was determined to focus on the good things: she had a job she loved and she had her newly discovered daughter Lara, though Lara had now gone back to her native Norway to be with her husband and children.

But that was fine because Sal was well now and she always had her girlfriends and the magazine, and everyone there had kept in touch.

What she hadn't expected as she walked along the Harrow Road towards *New Grey*'s offices near the junction with Ladbroke Grove was a welcome party, but she found the magazine's lively octogenarian owner, Rose McGill, plus the jolly receptionist both looking out for her.

'Sal!' Rose greeted her enthusiastically, wrapping the slender Sal in her voluminous embrace. 'Look at you!' She held Sal out at arm's length to inspect her new look. 'I wouldn't have recognized this short-haired sophisticate!'

'Yes,' Sal grinned. 'I'm calling it cancer chic. Do you think it'll catch on? Or is it beyond bad taste? I was never very good at telling.'

'Sounds like a perfect topic for the magazine,' Rose reassured. 'God, we've missed you. Well, actually *I* haven't because I've been let loose editing while you've been away, but everyone else has. Especially Michael.' Michael was the CEO and he and Rose had a continual power battle. Rose could easily win, since she owned the magazine, but Michael knew the benefit of having an owner who was so committed to publishing in this age of declining ad revenue and competition from Google and Facebook. Their mutual respect was actually deep and abiding.

'Come to my office and I'll fill you in on what's been happening.'

Sal followed the flamboyant Rose along the corridor, whose walls were almost entirely covered in framed magazine covers, taking in the familiar and comforting buzz of people at work. How she'd missed it during her three months off! The chats round the coffee machine. The quick drinks after work that stretched into badly behaved evenings. The gossip in the ladies' loo. It was the breath of life to Sal.

'Cappuccino? English Breakfast? Chai?' offered Rose when they reached her lovely, idiosyncratic office.

Sal sat down in a wing chair. She decided that Rose must possess the only work space in the country which looked like a cross between a country house library and a branch of Pret A Manger. On a table by the window stood a Nespresso-type machine in shiny stainless steel which was Rose's current pride and joy. You could almost imagine George Clooney (who always reminded Sal of a sexy dentist) suddenly materializing and proffering you a cup.

'Cappuccino, please.'

'You're not following the no-dairy path then?' Rose enquired.

'No,' stated Sal firmly. 'Nor am I eschewing alcohol or taking up yoga. I am not intending to Eat, Pray or Love – even if I could find someone interested in a one-breasted sexagenarian. I am just the same Sal but without the hair and hopefully the tumour.'

'Sally Grainger, I'm so glad you're back. Everyone under sixty is so PC.'

They chinked their cups. 'To *New Grey*! By the way,' Sal asked, 'what's happening with the American interest in buying into the company? Do you still need me to go to the US?'

When she'd first discovered she had cancer Sal had decided to keep it a secret from everyone. Her friends. Her colleagues. And even from Rose, especially when she'd announced that Sal might have to visit New York and meet a possible investor. By the time she'd finally realized she would have to admit the truth, Rose – canny as ever – had already worked it out and reassured Sal she would keep her job open. The relief had been incredible.

'As a matter of fact, you won't need to,' Rose replied.

'Right.' Sal had to admit the news came as a relief. Even though she was feeling better by the day, the idea of travelling to America and selling the magazine's concept to a hard-bitten New York businessman was a tad daunting. In fact, it made her feel quite sick.

'Lou Maynard is coming over here. His daughter lives in Surrey and she's had a baby. He's perfectly happy to come and talk in London rather than you having to fly out. Probably wants to get away from Trump! Lou is a hundred per cent Democrat.'

'Great.' Sal got out her laptop and opened the list of ideas she'd been working on.

Rose laughed. 'I see you've been taking your convalescence seriously.'

Half an hour later Michael, the CEO, put his head round. 'Sal! Great you're back. Have you managed to wrest power back from Rose's possessive grasp?'

He winked at her, softening the words.

'Michael, have you not been following the media?' Rose enquired with mock seriousness. 'Banter in the office, especially at the expense of your seniors, is no longer considered professionally acceptable.'

'Bollocks to that,' announced Michael with a grin before leaving them to it.

'I've made progress with Michael. He used to be so very proper.'

'You're a bad influence, Rose.'

'Thank you. I'll take that as a compliment.'

Laura finished tidying up the house before the estate agent was due to bring round the prospective buyers and flopped down on the sofa. She was confused as hell. She thought she'd persuaded herself that she was ready to move, that this house with its happy memories round every corner was simply making her sadder, like an old lover you keep bumping into who reminds you of the past.

Her daughter Bella had moved out with Nigel and their baby and her son Sam would be leaving soon. They were no longer children who needed the security of the family home. She should be more like Ella, who had managed to let go and view her new place as exciting, a new phase. But suddenly Laura didn't want to let go.

She stared at the bunch of flowers she'd bought and put in a vase. What the hell was she doing trying to make the place attractive to people who would be turning her out of her home? She picked up the flowers and threw them in the bin.

Outside she could hear the sound of footsteps crunching on the gravel. Then the bell rang.

Suddenly Laura grinned and flattened herself against the wall of the hall. She was damned if she was going to let them in!

The bell rang again, insistently this time, as the agent kept his finger on the buzzer for what Laura considered an unacceptably long time. And then it rang again. She could hear the agent begin to apologize to the couple and they all seemed to be checking their smartphones for emails confirming the appointment.

Just in time, feeling like the star of a spy movie, Laura pounced on her own phone and switched it to silent before they could call her.

It began to vibrate. Laura smiled and ignored it.

She heard them leave five minutes later then a set of footsteps crunched back towards her front door. The agent had obviously not yet given up the good fight.

She heard his voice as he called his office. 'Hey, Stu, I'm at Shirley Avenue. No one in. I've had to send them away. Not best pleased, I can tell you. I didn't want to explain the circumstances. Some people are funny about buying a house after a marriage breakdown. Usually the women.' He laughed nastily. Laura could just imagine his weaselly features, no doubt the kind of man who talked of *giving women one*. 'Hope we haven't got a fucking divorce resister on our hands. They're a nightmare. I'm heading straight back. See you in five.'

Behind the door, Laura smiled. She rather liked the idea of being a divorce resister. Maybe she could start a one-woman campaign.

She got the flowers out of the bin, silly to waste them, and poured herself a glass of wine. At four o'clock on a Wednesday afternoon it felt delightfully wicked. 'To divorce resisters everywhere!' she toasted and went off to find a silly DVD to go with her chilled Sauvignon.

Claudia walked along the main street of Little Minsley thinking how very like Agatha Christie's St Mary Mead it was, or maybe the Midsomer of *Midsomer Murders*.

The cottages were almost too picturesque with their thatched roofs and roses round the door, gardens full of nodding hollyhocks against a bright blue English sky. In fact, the whole place reminded her of an embroidered cloth her mother used to have on her breakfast tray. *Whatever happened to tray cloths?* Claudia wondered idly. *There must be a flea market somewhere with the world's supply on display.*

Her friends had been shocked that if she was going to leave London, she would opt to live in a village rather than out in the country away from busybody curtain twitchers and prying eyes, but actually Claudia liked villages. The scale of a village made sense. You felt involved and knew that your neighbours would look out for you. They were places where all ages mixed in a way that rarely happened in cities stratified mainly by what people did and where their children went to school.

Not that it hadn't been a shock leaving London. Actually, shock was an understatement. At first it had felt like a black hole had opened in front of her into which her forty-year career as a teacher, her colleagues, the pupils both good and bad, The Grecian Grove and her closest friends had all fallen.

The almost-affair with Daniel the sexy choirmaster had been an attempt to come to terms with her radically different life in deepest Surrey. It was that or go mad.

Fortunately her daughter Gaby had shaken her out of it just in time and Claudia and her husband Don had promised each other a new start. Just what that meant, she was still trying to figure out.

It wasn't as if she didn't have the pattern for elderly couple-dom in front of her. The prosperous nearby town of Manningbury seemed entirely populated with Stepford-like grey-haired husbands and wives, all holding hands. They held hands sitting in coffee shops, then strolled hand in hand down the street, and even went to afternoon offers at the cinema where no doubt they held hands in the dark. The effect on Claudia was to make her want to throw up. It was awful, she knew, and it meant she was a cynical old cow, but she and Don had never been hand-holders. Still, they had to find a way of making good their promise to each other.

Claudia found she was staring into the window of The Singing Kettle, one of Minsley's many tea shops. Sometimes she thought Minsley must be the tea-shop capital of the world. Countless DFLs (Down From Londons) seemed to abandon the rat race and follow their dreams of opening yet another cafe in Little Minsley. Someone inside, she suddenly noticed, was staring back.

Claudia's eyes locked with horror on the laughing face of Daniel Forrest, the sexy choirmaster. To follow her instinct and turn abruptly away would make her look like the shy and overweight sixteen-year-old that she had once been. Attempting a haughty Lauren Bacall expression, Claudia raised a dismissive eyebrow and delved into her bag for her phone, the universal saviour of awkward social situations, then pretended to be sending an urgent message.

Betty Wilshaw, her octogenarian fellow choir member, came to the rescue, arriving suddenly aboard Henry, her lethal mobility scooter. Taking in the situation in one swift and comprehensive glance, she yelled, 'Claudia! The very person I was looking for. Come with me into the post office and help me reach down some dog food.'

'Thanks, Betty,' she whispered as they pushed open the olde-worlde twelve-paned glass door. 'You saved my bacon.'

'And not just your bacon.' She gave Claudia a roguish look.

'Betty, you know perfectly well any suggestion of that is over.'

'Is it now?' They both watched as Daniel emerged from the tea shop and started walking down the street in their direction, a dangerous smile on his handsome face.

Claudia hid behind the birthday card rack and pretended to be engrossed in a gruesome selection of cards that were either puke-makingly sentimental or quite hair-raisingly crude.

Daniel was about to push open the door of the post office when Claudia's husband Don emerged from the Oxfam shop over the road. Claudia stared at him, transfixed. Only this morning he had left home in his usual baggy jeans and a jumper that had so many holes it looked like a moth's midnight feast.

Now he stood checking his phone, decked out in rust-coloured corduroys with a tweed jacket over a button-down denim shirt with a colourful silk scarf knotted round his neck the way smart Italian men do. Claudia was stunned. Don actually looked stylish!

Completely ignoring Daniel, Claudia ran across the road. 'Where did you get all that clobber?' she greeted her husband admiringly.

'Now there's an expression that takes me back. Very Carnaby Street. I was actually looking for a denim shirt and decided to go a bit wild.'

'You look terrific.'

Not appreciating this sudden opposition from a husband of all people, Daniel Forrest, to Claudia's intense relief, disappeared into the bread shop.

'Since there's not much in the fridge I thought maybe we'd have a pub lunch,' Don suggested.

Deciding she ought to follow the example of all the Stepford over-sixties, Claudia took his hand in hers.

Through the window of the post office Betty gave her a thumbs up.

A few seconds later, by dint of pretending he wanted to point something out, Don detached his hand from hers.

Claudia looked into his eyes, deeply relieved that he was as hand-holding-averse as she was. 'You know, Don, I do love you. We've got so much in common.'

Don raised an eyebrow. 'First I've heard of it. I know your friends call me Dull Don.'

'Nonsense. We're at the beginning of a big adventure.'

'No, we're not, Clo,' he replied affectionately. 'As a matter of fact, I'd say we're about three quarters of the way through.'

Laura woke up the next morning feeling a little less brave. In fact, she would have put her head back under the duvet if it weren't for her lovely son Sam appearing with a cup of tea.

'How fabulous. Thank you.'

'It's your interview today, isn't it,' he asked, putting it down beside her, 'with the lady manager who thought you had potential?'

'Indeed it is.' After Simon had left her for a younger colleague, he'd charmingly informed her that she should get off her arse and find a bloody job. So she'd annoyed the hell out of him by finding a very menial one stacking shelves in LateExpress, the supermarket right round the corner from his office. It had had the satisfying effect of shocking all his workmates and utterly infuriating Simon, who was convinced she'd done it deliberately to embarrass him.

Laura had to admit there was a teensy element of getting back at him in her choice of job but it was also – as she'd tartly informed him – not the easiest thing to find a job when you'd been a stay-at-home wife and mother for twenty-five years. Besides, the truth was, the job might be ever so humble, but it was easy and friendly and it suited her in her current fragile state.

Today's interview had come about because she had impressed a rival supermarket with her management potential.

After she'd sipped the last of the restorative liquid, she got out of bed and began to dress carefully, feeling suddenly unsure what to wear. She didn't possess such a thing as a business suit. There were charities, she'd read, that helped disadvantaged young women dress for job interviews. How wonderful. She just wished there were a similar thing for once over-privileged women like her who were facing the management world after a huge gap. She'd worked happily stacking shelves in LateExpress – she'd actually enjoyed the camaraderie far more than she'd ever expected – but for that she'd just had to sling a nylon tabard over anything she turned up wearing. This was different. In the end she selected a black dress and cardigan and a pair of plain court shoes, hoping she looked professional rather than on her way to a funeral.

She quickly bolted down some breakfast, feeling relieved

when Sam said she looked nice, and was beginning to build up her confidence when the phone rang.

It was Simon. 'What the bloody hell do you think you're up to, Laura?' was his delightful greeting. 'The agent's just been on the phone to ask if we're really serious about selling the house. Apparently a couple who were extremely interested couldn't even get in yesterday because you hadn't bothered to be there to *let* them in!'

'It was probably a mix-up by the agent,' Laura insisted, trying to keep calm and not let Simon make her feel stupid, something he was a past master at doing. 'I'll make sure I'm here for the next lot.'

'Don't bother. He's asked me to let them in.'

'You don't live here any more, Simon,' she reminded him, trying to stop herself sounding weak. 'You left me for Suki, remember?'

The truth was, when his relationship with Suki started unravelling, he had coolly assumed he could come back to her and had been livid when she'd refused him.

'The property is for sale, Laura,' he told her unpleasantly, 'whether you like it or not.'

Before she could answer Sam grabbed the phone. 'Stop it, Dad. Isn't it bad enough Mum's having to give up her home just because you were selfish enough to leave her?'

Laura shook her head and gently wrested the phone from her son. She knew Simon of old. Direct confrontation wasn't the answer. To think she'd thought she loved him for all those years.

'Goodbye, Simon,' she said, as firmly as she could, trying to keep the emotion from her voice. 'I will talk to the agent later today. Goodbye.'

She left the phone off the hook so that he couldn't call back then switched off her mobile.

'Chin up, Mum,' Sam grinned, reminding her of the grubby-kneed schoolboy he used to be, 'you'll soon be shot of him.'

Being so close to the river always made Ella extraordinarily aware of nature. It made her daughters hoot with laughter whenever she enthused lyrically about seeing a heron or hearing the song of a skylark, but Ella found enormous pleasure in these things. Maybe it was an age thing. When she was young she had been far too busy trying to win big cases in the law courts and show all the men in her chambers that women were perfectly competent, thank you. In fact, far more competent than they were half the time. Nature had come to her later and it gave her deep and abiding satisfaction.

For almost a year now she'd tended her neighbours' allotment as they travelled the globe like latter-day hippies, without realizing that it had become a cornerstone of her life. As she headed off there this morning the skies were a cloudless blue. The stretch of river in front of her was almost empty, save for a few single sculls and one rowing boat. She stopped for a moment to look and found she was a mere five feet from a rather tatty swan's nest which must have somehow survived from last year's breeding season. Next to it, looking fierce and protective, were two beautiful swans. And just a few feet away a lone white goose, as white as they were, but without the long slender neck that characterized them. She waited, watching, for fifteen minutes but the goose wasn't budging.

It struck Ella as suddenly sad. Did the goose think it was a swan? The lonely goose made Ella suddenly aware of her own single state. She had never actively looked for a relationship since Laurence had died. Not for her over-sixties speed dating or the desperate attempt to take up bridge in the hope of meeting a man. She had thought the move to somewhere smaller would help. No more rattling around in a house made for families, and in lots of ways she loved the little house, but it didn't fill the well of emptiness Laurence's death had created.

Stop this self-pity, Ella! she commanded, and began to walk briskly towards the allotments. There was nothing like a bit of double digging to take your mind off things.

Here, as usual, all was busy and bustling. Sue and Sharleen, her friends from the adjoining allotment, stopped digging and waved, and Mr Barzani, the ancient Cypriot man who seemed to spend his whole life here, grinned gnomically. The eternally bobble-hatted Bill, whom she'd come to see as the guardian spirit of the place, paused fractionally from arguing with his two cronies, Stevie and Les, about the dangers of potato blight if the weather turned nasty (which seemed highly unlikely given the perfect blue sky) and whether it was too early to sow carrots to avoid root fly, and saluted her.

Ella smiled at them all and headed off to pick her neighbours' strawberries to make jam. She had been hoarding Bonne Maman jam jars with their pretty red and white gingham lids for months and had had to fight her daughter Julia when she tried to insist she throw them out during the move.

Fancy me making jam! Ella grinned to herself. Once she'd have dismissed that as strictly for the WI, but she actually found it deeply pleasurable. In fact, she was finding, along with appreciating nature, that growing things and eating them had become one of her deepest satisfactions. Since she'd been looking after Viv and Angelo's allotment she had become part of this strange and unexpected little community and gradually, along with seeing Sal and Laura and Claudia, it had become part of her

life-support system. Indeed, it was the nearness to the allotments that had made her so keen on her new home.

She had just finished picking the strawberries and was
about to harvest the beans and some glossy aubergines when
she saw a delegation consisting of Bill, Stevie and Les walking
towards her. Improbably they were holding a bouquet of
flowers. Improbably because she knew they didn't hold with
wasting good growing space on frippery blossoms. The soil
was strictly for veg and spending good money on flowers was
beyond the pale.

'We bought you these,' Bill, the usual spokesman of the
three, offered shyly.

'They're lovely.' Ella took them, feeling unexpectedly moved
at this unlikely act of generosity. 'But why? It isn't my birthday,
unless I've gone completely gaga and forgotten it.'

'Because of the committee's decision.' Bill looked suddenly
embarrassed.

'What decision is that?'

'Didn't your friends tell you? Some friends they are, after
you've thrown yourself into this place body and soul, and you
a nice posh lady not in the first blush, if you don't mind me
saying.'

'I don't mind you saying at all. I just don't actually know
what you're talking about.'

'The stupid bloody committee,' Bill persisted, his hat bobbing
up and down in indignation. 'Load of busybody know-it-alls.
Little Stalins the lot of them. They turned down your friends'
application to hand the allotment over to you. They've allocated
it to somebody else higher up the waiting list.'

It finally got through to Ella what they were telling her. She
was going to lose the allotment. She looked at the flowers,
taken aback by quite how much she minded. This place had

become a sanctuary, a sensory delight and a source of support. The waiting list was so long there was no chance of her getting one of her own before she was eighty. Or dead.

'Here, Stevie.' Ella placed the large container of strawberries she'd just picked into his gnarled and mud-stained hands. 'You have these. Give them to your wife. I'm sure she'll find something delicious to do with them.'

Suddenly she didn't feel like making jam any more.

Three

It was such a beautiful morning that, unusually for her, Sal decided to walk to the scheduled meeting at Lou Maynard's hotel. She'd been surprised to learn that he was staying not at one of the grand conventional hotels, or even one of the smart boutique ones, but at Brook's Hotel in Portobello Road, famous for its over-the-top decor.

Brook's was once the haunt of outrageous Sixties rock stars who had grown up and then grown old and now opted for the deep-pile carpets and wall-to-wall concierges of the Ritz instead of the black walls and rampant chinoiserie of Brook's that Jimi Hendrix had loved so much.

She decided she liked the man already.

'Excuse me,' she asked the extraordinary-looking receptionist who seemed to have continued the exotic decor over all the visible parts of his body, 'could you let Mr Maynard know I'm here?'

'He's outside on the patio. Having breakfast.'

Since it was 11.30 Sal could only assume Lou Maynard wasn't one of those people who liked to pack their business trips with meetings from dawn till dusk.

The receptionist was clearly not about to show her where this was, so Sal took the nearest corridor which happened to pass the ladies' and gents'. Unable to resist a quick check in the mirror, she slipped into the ladies'.

It still took Sal by surprise that when she looked in the mirror an elegant short-haired woman looked back. She checked herself out – not too bad – and then adjusted her lipstick. She'd thrown away all her purples and reds and had taken to a rusty colour that would have won the approval of Bobbi Brown for its warm naturalness. She'd even toyed with going into Selfridges and getting one of those nice young make-up demonstrators to design 'age-appropriate make-up'. But she knew they'd probably counsel 'more is less' and Sal wasn't ready for that. She still felt 'more is just how I like it'.

She shook out the creases in her dark grey silk dress and decided she was ready for battle.

It was easy to recognize Lou because he was the only person occupying the patio, and also because naturally she'd googled him. She knew he was seventy-four years old, the owner of a multi-million-dollar property company in Brooklyn that specialized in lofts, three times married, with five grown-up children. He had startled the business community by recently founding a radical local newspaper which had turned out, even in these days of falling advertising and competition from social media, to be rather a success.

He sat half hidden behind two pink orchids, sipping coffee and smiling. He wore baggy chinos, a terracotta shirt and a taupe-coloured cardigan. At first glance he looked more a kindly grandfather than a highly successful businessman.

'Mr Maynard? I'm Sally Grainger.'

Lou stood up. She was an inch or two taller than him yet there was an engagingly solid feel about him. She also got the instant impression of energy. She'd seen it before in very successful people. A room lit up when they walked into it. And then there was the twinkle. Lou Maynard had a decided twinkle.

Please, take a seat.' He signalled to the chair next to his. 'So, how do you like my hotel?' He pointed to a potted palm, the kind you'd see in every chic sitting room in the sixties, yet rarely encountered now. 'It's as unfashionable as I am. I find that comforting. And I like a little tacky decadence. My whole room is a scene from the British Raj. Dark green walls and curtains – oh, and did I mention the elephants? There's one painted on the wall behind my bed and another pretending to be a lamp. Come on, I'll show you.'

Sal got to her feet, rather taken aback.

'Don't worry,' Lou grinned, 'I'm too old to be dangerous. What do you British say? Not safe in taxis? I love that.' He led the way past two lovebirds cooing in a cage.

'Morning, guys, say hello to Sally.'

'Actually, I'm usually Sal.'

'That has a great ring to it. Say hello to Sal.'

The lovebirds cooed at her obligingly.

She followed him to the lift. 'Don't worry,' he reassured, 'we won't have to sit on the bed. I've got a suite. Besides, the elephants can be your chaperone.'

His room, or rather suite, was truly amazing. As well as the elephants another whole wall featured the scene of hundreds of glittering potentates, watching a cricket match and looking as if they were drinking G&Ts while their punkah wallahs fanned them with feathers.

'Great, isn't it? I'll have you know I turned down the Tudor Room and the one with black walls, Jimi's favourite. It makes you feel as if you're in your coffin. I'm quite near enough to my coffin without wanting to be reminded of it by a hotel room. We can sit over there.' He indicated a huge squashy sofa covered with fabric that featured a tiger hunt. 'Thank God they drew the line at elephant's foot coffee tables. Okay, now, down to business.'

Sal tried to arrange herself in a seemly manner, which was quite a challenge since the sofa was one of those pieces of furniture that was so deep you couldn't help showing more leg than you'd intended.

She saw Lou watching her and grinning.

'You remind me of someone,' she said, hoping it wasn't too forward.

'Ed Asner,' he quipped back instantly, 'the guy who played Lou Grant on the TV. Everyone says so. I think maybe it's just the confusion over our names that stirs people's unconscious.'

'I loved that show! Lou Grant, the hard-bitten journalist on the *LA Tribune*! It was him who made me want to be a reporter!'

'Hold your horses, Sal,' he grinned back.' I think I'd better remind you I'm not really him.'

'You amaze me, especially as he was a fictional character and you, I understand, are real! And you did start a newspaper. Maybe he's in your unconscious too?'

'Maybe. Or perhaps I just got bored with making millions in the exciting world of commercial property and thought I'd stir things up a little bit. I hate to get bored, you see. And I have a very short attention span. It's my worst characteristic.'

'Is that what makes you interested in *New Grey*?'

'Maybe. It's a clever magazine. We have plenty of stuff directed at the baby-boomers but I thought *New Grey* was a cut above. And I felt there was a lot you could do with it that Rose isn't doing. Holidays. Insurance. Cruises. Maybe even intelligent retirement villages. It's a big industry now.'

Sal laughed at the thought of Claudia's suggestion of anti-retirement living.

'You're smiling. Did I say something funny?'

'It's just that my friend Claudia, who lives down in Surrey, that's a bit like Westchester County . . .'

'I know Surrey,' Lou nodded. 'My youngest daughter lives there.'

'Well, she suggested that I and my best friends live in *anti*-retirement when we get older – a cross between a student flat and a kibbutz was how she put it.'

'I love it! I was a kibbutznik myself when I was eighteen.' Lou's eyes sparkled with mischief at the memory. 'I spent a happy three months picking bananas till they made me clean out the latrines due to spiritual pride.'

'Where was it, your kibbutz?'

'Would you believe it, near the Sea of Galilee? Though I certainly didn't witness any miracles. Speaking of miracles, why don't you join me for brunch and I'll tell you all about my experiences? I only had a coffee earlier.'

Sal mentally shuffled through her day. She had an editorial meeting at 3 p.m. but she was pretty well prepared for that. Would Rose prefer her to have brunch with Lou or, in the expression so beloved of journalists, make her excuses and leave?

Sal had the sudden realization that she'd actually *like* to join him. She suspected it would be very entertaining.

'I'd love to.'

'Excellent. Despite all appearances to the contrary, the food here is very good indeed.'

They both stood up and Sal was suddenly conscious that Lou was one of those rare people who radiated so much charisma you could almost warm your hands by him.

'Follow me,' Lou grinned. 'I don't think we'll have to book. In fact, we'll probably be the only people there.'

Lou couldn't have been more right. They were the sole occupants of the entire restaurant. There were also so few staff apparently on duty that they found themselves being served by the tattooed receptionist.

Sal studied the short menu and instantly opted for Eggs Benedict.

'I like a woman who knows her own mind. Benedict is the only option. That crap they call Eggs Florentine is a travesty. But you have to have a Bloody Mary with it. They make them here nearly as good as home.'

Sal just laughed. What the hell.

Lou ordered a very rare steak sandwich which he then doused in mustard and ketchup and accompanied it with a Brooklyn Lager. 'Glad you guys have finally discovered the taste of proper beer instead of that piss you call bitter. No wonder you lost the colonies.'

'So what exactly is your interest in *New Grey*?' Sal asked, emboldened by the vodka in the devastatingly strong Bloody Mary. 'Are you really going to invest in us?'

'I might indeed. Having reached the fine age I have attained I find myself fascinated by ways of living life to the full.'

'Rose told me that. "Lou loves life," she said.' Sitting opposite the man, Sal could see how true this obviously was.

'I do indeed. Let me tell you about another of my investments. You see this little guy.' He took out his wallet and she thought he was going to show her a family photograph, a grandson maybe, and was stunned when the photograph was actually of a robot.

He handed it over and she studied the white manikin with his big wide eyes and curiously attractive demeanour.

'Meet Hiro – that means tolerant in Japanese. Which is a good word because these little guys are specifically designed for old people, to help them out in the home. He may look cute but Hiro's not your average robot. His inventor spent months downloading his own and his wife's emotional responses, plus their memories, into Hiro. He's a real labour of love, one of the most advanced uses of artificial intelligence you could find.'

'But he looks just like any other robot. You can even buy them on Amazon,' protested Sal.

'That's deliberate. His inventor didn't want him to be scary like those lifelike robots you see in movies. Thought it'd freak out the old folks.'

Sal looked again. There was a definite human quality about him.

'He's rather sweet.'

'Not just sweet. Smart. I find Japan fascinating. We forget they really started the electronics boom. And they happen to have an awful lot of old people with no one to look after them, so they've been developing these little guys. Hiro's upstairs in my closet if you want to meet him.'

Laughing, Sal looked at her watch. Oh God, it was almost 3 p.m. She couldn't believe how the time with Lou Maynard had flashed past. 'Lou, I'm sorry, I'll have to meet him another time.' She started to get up, realizing she was talking about Hiro as if he were a real person, but then only today she'd heard two items on Radio Four about robots. Even Jeremy Corbyn was always talking about them taking jobs.

'I'm going to have to run as it is. Thank you so much for brunch.'

'My pleasure. Let's do it again. I'm here for a while longer now I'm a grandfather again.'

'That would be lovely.' Sal realized she meant it. Lou Maynard was wonderful company. He'd even made her forget about her cancer and feel like a normal human being.

She rushed out of the hotel onto Portobello Road, grateful to catch a passing black cab.

Safely tucked into the back, a thought struck her. If she met Lou again, would she want it to be for business or pleasure?

Laura took deep breaths as she walked along to her meeting with Helena Butler, trying to regain the feeling of calm happiness she'd felt when her son Sam brought her a cup of tea in bed. Before Simon had called and yelled at her.

This was only a very informal interview, she knew, and might lead to nothing at all, but she'd still prepared for it carefully. Ella and Sal had told her to take a CV with her and had helped her to write it.

CVs had changed a lot, they insisted, since Laura had last written one. Instead of putting all your experience, from school and university to jobs you'd held, chronologically at the top, the modern way was to start with a personal statement.

You didn't have to give your age any more, to her relief – the law against age discrimination had changed all that – but you still had to de-age your CV. So Laura had had to take out all her O levels and change them to GCSEs so no one would guess how incredibly ancient she was!

Next she was supposed to match her skills to the exact requirements of the job but she could hardly do that as she didn't really know what the job consisted of.

She would just have to pretend to be confident and busk it.

Helena Butler's offices were on the eighteenth floor of a rather faceless modern building in a scruffy part of Victoria, saved by the amazing views right across the city to the London Eye and Houses of Parliament.

'Hello, Laura.' Helena had the corner desk in a large open-plan office. 'Can I get you a coffee?'

When Laura said she'd love one, Helena disappeared off to the coffee machine. It was all so different from when Laura had last worked in an office where there were secretaries and assistants who would – albeit moaning under their breath – be asked to do jobs like this. And in those days people even had offices of their own. Nowadays only the biggest bosses had individual offices.

Helena was back with the coffee and began to explain why she had thought Laura might be useful to them.

'The thing is, FoodCo franchises about three hundred small shops all over the UK, and because of their locations they often can't get reliable staff. I think your employer at LateExpress has probably explained how pleasantly surprised he was to find you. Most of the staff come and go. They aren't often the kind of people who want to take responsibility. So what we need is someone to go round and talk to them, give them some on-the-spot training. Do you think that's something you might consider? It would probably have to be as a consultant, at least initially.'

Laura found herself panicking. When the divorce from Simon came through she would get a lump sum, according to her lawyer, and she was entitled to half of whatever they got for the house. She wouldn't be destitute, even if she was forced to have a very different lifestyle from previously. She had imagined Helena was offering a London-based role, near to Sam and Bella and her new grandchild. Did she really want to travel up and down the country advising people?

Helena, understandably, was waiting for her reply.

'The thing is, Helena, I'm going through a rather difficult

divorce and I feel I really need to be around for my children, so I'm not sure the timing of this works for me.'

'I see.' Helena's tone had become frosty. She obviously felt Laura had been wasting her precious time. 'Well, thank you for coming in. I'd better let you get back to work.' She used the word 'work' in a tone of noticeable irony that made Laura bristle.

Laura shook her hand and almost scuttled to the door, feeling like an idiot. She knew she was lucky to get an interview like this at her age. Should she have at least tried it?

No, Laura told herself, willing herself to feel stronger. Why should she have to rush round the country staying in bad hotels or driving herself hundreds of miles because Simon had left her?

She'd rather work for LateExpress. At least they were local and they valued her. And if it embarrassed Simon that she was doing a menial job just round the corner from his office, too bloody bad.

Claudia always dropped round to check on her parents on Wednesdays and Saturdays. Sometimes she brought lunch with her. Today she had a proper pork pie, knowing it was her dad's favourite, with delicious raised pastry plus some chutney and salad. She knew her mother would make a fuss about it being bad for him, but if you couldn't have some things that were bad for you when you were in your nineties, when could you?

She parked in her usual spot round the back and went in through the kitchen.

The first thing that struck her was how untidy the house was, and worse, how grubby. The kitchen surfaces, usually gleaming from the proud ministrations of Dorothy, the cleaning lady who was almost as old as they were but had always seemed remarkably energetic, were splattered with fat.

Of her parents there was no sign. She could at least hear the faint reassuring tones of Radio Four coming from her father's shed tucked away in the back garden.

'Hello, Dad,' she greeted her beloved father Len as she pushed open the shed door. 'Hiding in here as usual? What on earth's going on in the kitchen? Is Dorothy ill or something?'

Her father was sitting in his wing chair, a packet of Benson & Hedges and an ashtray on one side of him and a gin and tonic on the other. Her father's capacity to drink G&T without ice had always amazed Claudia, who liked her wine so cold it frosted the outside of the glass. She suspected it might be a habit born of necessity since creeping inside to fill an ice bucket would attract her mother's attention. A warm G&T was probably a small price to pay for freedom.

She noticed that he had almost finished the *Times* crossword and she smiled lovingly. Nothing wrong with her father's brain.

The same couldn't be said of his body. He would need another hip operation and possibly a knee replacement as well. Looking on the bright side, they were lucky to live in an age where such things were easily accessible even though he was over ninety. The main problem, of course, was the recovery time when he could only hobble about and was rendered more or less helpless.

'Hello, Claudia love. Your mother's fired Dorothy.'

'She can't have. Dorothy's been with you for thirty years. She'll come back in a week and no one will mention it.'

'Not this time,' her father replied gloomily. 'Olivia told her she was an interfering old busybody and wasn't welcome.'

'What had Dorothy been doing? Trying to make sure Mum took her pills?'

Claudia's mother Olivia had been diagnosed as bipolar but often hid her medicines. Claudia remembered guiltily how she had sometimes enlisted Dorothy's help in finding them. Fortunately she seemed much better these days.

'Oh dear, maybe I'd better go and see her.'

'I'd leave it if I were you.'

'But you can't live in a filthy house!'

'There's something else. Claudie, come and sit here.' He moved the ashtray and patted the stool next to him. 'Claudie, you won't really let her put me in a care home, will you?'

Claudia couldn't bear hearing her lovely big, strong, reassuring dad sound like a frightened child.

'Of course not.' She took his hand and began to stroke it.

'Your mother says she will. She says she can't cope with me. I fell over the other day and she had to get the neighbours in.'

Claudia wondered for a moment if sacking the cleaning lady was also part of her mother's campaign to prove she couldn't cope with looking after Len. In one of her manic phases it wouldn't be beyond her. 'No one's going to put you in a care home, Dad.'

'They're awful places. I visited my friend Max in one. People sitting round all day dribbling and smelling of piss.'

'Look, I've brought you a pork pie and some chutney. You eat this and I'll take Ma out to lunch. Have a little talk with her.'

'Would you?' he asked eagerly, grabbing her hand. 'I'm scared, Claudie. You know what your mother can be like.'

'I'll sort it out, Dad.'

'I'm glad you came to live near, Claudia. You don't miss London and your friends?'

She shook her head, even though she was missing them a lot at this very moment.

'No, no, Dad. I still see them quite often. And I'm nearer Gaby and Douglas here.'

'That's good.'

'Bye, Dad.'

Her father made a pathetic attempt to get up, revealing a brown stain on the seat of the chair.

Oh, bloody hell.

Feeling she needed cheering up after experiencing Helena Butler's obvious disappointment in her, Laura decided to drop in at LateExpress, the supermarket where she'd been working since she'd split with Simon. She needed to see her employer's smiling face, and speak to someone who unconditionally approved of her.

It was a good time to pop in, after the morning stream of people on their way to work and before the lunchtime sandwich rush. Mr A, as he was universally known, beamed at Laura and, abandoning his post behind the counter to a bored-looking seventeen-year-old, rushed towards her with his hand extended. 'Mrs Minchin, what brings you into my humble establishment? You are not due in till tomorrow!'

'I just popped in for a sandwich,' Laura lied. 'I've had a meeting in town.'

'Ah.' Mr A looked crestfallen on her behalf. 'With the vulture lawyers, as Mrs A describes them?'

Mrs A always had a colourful way with words. She had branded Suki Morrison, the younger woman her husband Simon had run off with, as a jezebel and floozy and very publicly banned her from the shop.

'No, as a matter of fact.' She didn't want to admit that she

42

had been for a job interview, although he would immediately and generously congratulate her for taking a quite understandable step up the social ladder. He had never quite been able to accept why such a ladylike personage as Laura had deigned to work for him and she had not felt it appropriate to explain that she was feeling so fragile and unconfident as her life fell apart around her that she actually preferred a job without much responsibility.

And she had found good friends in the gentle Mr A and his fierce and disapproving wife who had loyally taken Laura's side in her marital dispute.

Laura glanced round. Mrs A, bedecked in her familiar pink quilted dressing gown, usually appeared at this time of the morning, as imposing as the Queen of Sheba, despite her odd attire, to check if her husband was misbehaving in any way. As Mr A was firmly under her be-ringed thumb, she was usually doomed to disappointment.

'You are wondering what has happened to my lady wife,' Mr A announced mournfully. 'She has taken to her bed.' Laura couldn't imagine the proprietress, who was usually glowing with health, her skin polished by expensive products she ordered from the internet, knowing a day's ill health. 'Mrs Minchin, we have a thundercloud coming in our direction.'

'Oh,' Laura teased gently, 'the weather looked quite nice to me.'

'I speak only in metaphor. It is coming from India.'

'Ah.' Laura felt none the wiser.

'Mrs A's mother. Have you heard of Kali, who some call the goddess of revenge who is often depicted dancing on top of her husband?'

Laura shook her head.

'Nothing to Mrs A's mother. She has fallen out with her husband and announced that she is coming to live with us.'

Laura tried to recall the layout of the flat where Mr and Mrs A lived above the shop. It didn't seem adequate to house a goddess who danced on top of her husband.

'Can't you tell her there isn't room?'

'Too late, Mrs Minchin, too late. She has booked her passage.'

'By ship?' Laura tried to remember novels like *A Passage to India*. Weren't voyages from the East so long the acronym POSH had started then? Because the rich people booked Port Out Starboard Home to avoid the glare of the sun in their cabin. Maybe it would take weeks. Months even.

'It is with Air India.'

'Oh dear.'

'Oh dear indeed, Mrs Minchin.'

Ella walked slowly back to her new house, clutching the flowers Bill had presented to her. The way she was feeling would seem ridiculous to her friends. She was the only one of her friends who had the slightest interest in growing things. They would just say she could stick some flowers and the odd fruit bush in her new garden. But it wasn't only about producing beans and peas. The allotment had kept her in tune with the seasons; each task – digging, hoeing, sowing seeds – all had their right moment. She remembered a quotation from Genesis which, though she wasn't religious, had always stuck in her mind. *As long as the earth endures, seedtime and harvest, cold and heat, summer and winter, day and night will never cease.* That was what she'd felt at the allotment. The diurnal round, as the poet Donne would put it. Even better than watching *Countryfile* on the telly, though Ella loved that too. It had been a protected little world right under the Heathrow flightpath, only moments from traffic and crowded office blocks, where everyone helped each other out, a bit like the community Claudia was suggesting they create for themselves.

God, Ella – she shook her head at her own fancifulness – *I'm not sure Bill, Stevie and Les would see the Grand Union allotments as the Garden of Eden. But maybe they would, although of course they'd never put it quite like that.*

She'd miss them too. Where else would Ella have got to know a gnarled old Greek Cypriot like Mr Barzani, who gave her a recipe for aubergines baked slowly in olive oil, apparently named after a priest who'd died of pleasure eating them?

She was saved from any more mournful reflections by the unexpected sight of her grandson, Harry, leaning on the wall outside her new house.

'I'm learning to drive, Gran,' he greeted her, 'and Mum's always too busy to take me out. So I thought about my racy gran and wondered if maybe you would?'

Ella laughed out loud. The reason she was called racy at her mature age was because of her car. In a moment of madness, feeling flush with cash after selling the house, Ella, who rarely splashed out on herself, had seen a Mini Convertible in the window of a car showroom and had gone straight in and bought it because it reminded her of her youth.

'I've brought my L plates.' Harry produced two bright red Ls from his jacket.

'As long as we stay round here where it's quiet,' Ella replied dubiously, unable to resist Harry's winning smile.

They both climbed into the car.

'Can we have the roof down?' Harry instantly demanded. 'It's much easier to see in this kind of car with the roof down,' he wheedled.

Ella pushed the button to lower the roof. Harry looked on with delight, making Ella think of the mischievous little boy he'd been before his parents had got so academically ambitious and packed him off to boarding school. Thank heavens they'd seen the light at last and allowed him to go the local sixth-form college.

'How's the new school?'

'Brilliant thanks, Gran.'

Ella showed him how the gears worked on the car and how to set the handbrake.

They drove carefully down the quiet road by the river while Harry proudly demonstrated his three-point turns and parallel parking.

'You're much more patient than Mum,' Harry pointed out.

'She's probably busier than me. Watch out for the accelerator. It's quite a fast car, remember.'

At that moment a motorbike shot out of a side street right in front of them. Harry attempted to brake and accidentally put his foot on the accelerator. The car shot forward, missing the bike by inches.

Ella grabbed the handbrake and yanked it on until the car juddered to a halt.

Harry turned to her, the colour drained from his face. 'I think you'd better drive, Gran. Maybe I should stick to Mum's Ford Focus.'

They swapped seats in silence. Ella, feeling he needed encouragement before he completely lost his nerve, grinned at her grandson. 'You were doing really well till then.'

'Till I nearly killed someone,' Harry replied.

And then it hit her in its full horror. She had just let her precious grandson, on the brink of his adult life, drive her car when he wasn't covered by her insurance! How could she possibly have forgotten?

'I don't think we'd better tell your parents,' she finally managed. And then, still reeling with the guilt, 'Why don't I pay for you to have some proper driving lessons?'

'Oh my God, would you, Gran? That'd be amazing. And it'd mean I wouldn't need to wreck your new car so it'd be a saving in the end.'

As she parked her car back in its usual space, it struck Ella that this hadn't been her only memory lapse. She'd lost her car in the car park a few months ago, witnessed by Neil, her irritating son-in-law, and once she'd climbed into the driving seat and for a moment not known what to do. Maybe she ought to do one of those memory tests for oldies. No doubt they had them online. She'd also had some tummy pains but she didn't see how they could be connected with forgetting things. She probably ought to go to her GP but Ella, practical though she was, was convinced we all ran to doctors too soon. Everything was medicalized these days. Her parents had been part of the generation who didn't visit a doctor in their lives.

After she'd sorted out her father, Claudia went off to look for her mother and found her delighted to go to lunch at Igden Manor.

'Gosh, do you remember the last time we came here?' Olivia asked, grinning delightedly at the memory as they parked in the car park behind the main part of the hotel. 'Gaby was about to call off the wedding because of parental bad behaviour. Until I got you all playing croquet.'

'Yes, funny how croquet saved the day,' Claudia conceded. 'It usually makes people want to kill each other.' It was true, though, that on that occasion her mother had come to the rescue.

'This is a beautiful place,' Olivia pronounced. 'I always like it here. Posh without being too formal.'

Claudia looked around her. Igden Manor was made of pale golden stone, with a wonderful rust-coloured tiled roof. In front lay the large croquet lawn giving onto a wide terrace with outdoor tables and gay parasols. Some of the rooms were in the main part and the rest in cottages, each with their own separate terrace or garden. Her mother was right, it was a lovely hotel.

'I wonder how old it is?'

'The funny thing is, the whole place is a replica, not old at all,' Olivia explained. 'Just a pastiche of an ancient hamlet. There was one here aeons ago, belonging to some bishop. We should go for a walk after lunch and I'll show you the stock pond where he kept his fish. It's right behind where the swimming pool is now.'

'I'd forgotten the swimming pool.' Claudia looked longingly at the bright blue water surrounded by sun loungers. It would be delicious on a really hot day.

The restaurant was through a very appealing bar where they served light snacks and sandwiches. Claudia, dreading the encounter ahead with her mother, wasn't hungry and just ordered a Caesar salad. Olivia, enjoying the treat of being taken out, opted for vichyssoise, followed by roast chicken and apple tart with ice cream. While Claudia signalled to the waitress that they'd like a coffee, Olivia headed off to the ladies'.

The coffees arrived and Claudia drank hers. When ten minutes had passed and there was no sign of her mother, Claudia began to feel a little anxious, remembering her mother's up and down mental condition. She had seemed extra normal today, though.

After another ten minutes she went to look for her, suddenly panicking that Olivia might have fallen over or be needing her help – after all, she was eighty-five.

In the end she heard her mother before she saw her. Olivia was leaning across the reception desk, deep in conversation with the woman who was working there.

'Really?' her mother's voice echoed through the whole area. 'You say the hotel's going to close down then? Unless they can find someone to take on the lease?'

She turned to Claudia, her eyes narrowed like a hawk descending on a field mouse, and gripped her daughter by the arm. 'Come on, dear, let's have that coffee you promised me.'

It was obvious her mother was big with news she couldn't wait to impart.

'How absolutely fascinating,' she announced as she sat down.

'What is?' Claudia could see they weren't going to get to discussing putting her father in a care home for some time.

'That's my friend Joan's daughter behind the desk. I've known her since she was a child.'

'But what was it she told you that was so riveting?'

'Apparently the hotel's been run by three different people in the last five years and none of them have been able to turn a profit. Too old-fashioned. Not enough amenities. You young people all want spas and gyms, I can't think why. They're quite busy in the summer but the winter's as flat as a pancake. Besides, it's not a freehold apparently. Just a lease from Lord Binns. His family's owned everything round here since the Domesday Book, so no one wants to invest in all these expensive facilities. They've tried conferences and weddings but it's never really worked out. Now the place is going to close down! I must admit, I think that's a real pity.' She sipped her coffee, leaving a bright red lipstick mark on the rim of the cup. 'So, Claudia dear, what did you want to talk to me about?'

But Claudia had stopped listening. The maddest, craziest, most wonderful idea had just occurred to her. Of course it would never happen, there would be too many obstacles. It was entirely ridiculous to even think about it.

But suddenly she couldn't think about anything else.

Four

'What do you mean, take over the lease on Igden Manor?' Don looked at Claudia as if she'd suggested they give the Queen notice to quit so they could move into Buckingham Palace. 'How the hell could we do that? And why, for God's sake? You just said the place has had three different owners and none of them could make it work. Why would we be any better? Neither of us have even run a B&B, let alone a country hotel, and anyway, where on earth would we get the money?'

'It wouldn't be a hotel. It would be our future, the best of both worlds, living with the people who mean the most to us and looking after each other. My dream of growing old together disgracefully!'

'And let me guess. These people would mainly be the Coven?' The Coven was the rude name Don always applied to Claudia's group of girlfriends.

'Not just them, obviously. My parents too, and who knows, maybe Gaby and Douglas? They work nearby and they're always complaining they can't afford to buy anywhere.'

'And how exactly would all this be paid for?' Don asked

scathingly. 'Out of our state pensions with you doing a bit of French coaching on the side?'

Claudia looked away, reality beginning to intrude into the excitement of her sudden vision.

Don came and put his arms round her. 'Sorry to burst the bubble, but it is a mad scheme.'

'I know,' sighed Claudia, 'but I've got to find some kind of solution for Ma and Dad. She seems all right at the moment. In fact, you'd have laughed at the sight of her wheedling all this information out of the poor woman on reception. Ma's probably better informed than the liquidators, or old Lord Binns who owns the place.'

'Your mother in full Valkyrie mode is indeed a sight to see. On the other hand, she probably saved the wedding so we have to be grateful.'

'It's Dad. She's told him she can't cope and is going to put him in a care home.'

'Poor old Len. He's not that bad, surely?'

Suddenly Claudia crumpled. 'Don, he'd shat himself when I went round there. And he didn't even know. I'm really worried about him. And I don't think Ma can be bothered with any of it.'

Don patted her, rather ineffectually. He was never very good at emotional outbursts. 'Oh God. Shakespeare was right about the seven ages. From the mewling, puking infant to the old man *sans* teeth, *sans* eyes, *sans* taste, *sans* everything.'

Capable Claudia felt her eyes misting up at this awful prospect for her beloved father. 'That's why it would be so great to have a group of friends living together, all helping each other, not sticking Dad in some godawful care home.'

'I'm sure they're not all awful.'

'And the cost . . .'

'There is another solution. I noticed it a lot before we left London. Get him a live-in carer. I was forever seeing old people in London being taken round by people who were obviously their carers.'

'A sort of nanny?' Some of her friends had had nannies for their children, quite often with mixed results.

'If you like. There'll be loads of agencies, I'm sure.'

'I suppose I could look into it.'

He patted her again. This time it annoyed her quite inordinately. 'More sensible than your crazy scheme about the hotel.' His smile was so patronizing that she wanted to slap him and had to remind herself firmly that they were supposed to be making a new, more loving start to their life in the country.

'I suppose you're right,' she admitted grudgingly.

'Tell you what,' he suggested as an olive branch, 'let's go and have supper in The Laden Ox. Save you cooking.' Don's lack of cooking skills had always been a sore point between them. 'You could spend the time making a few phone calls to agencies, or looking online.'

'Yes.' Claudia made herself stop thinking about the honeyed embrace of Igden Manor, with its hollyhocks and mellow stone, and confront the considerably more immediate problem of finding a suitable carer and persuading her mother it would be a better option than sticking her dad in a home. She could see that might be an uphill struggle. Olivia liked having her home to herself.

Sal rushed back to the office and made it just in time for the ideas meeting she'd scheduled at 3 p.m.

'Long session with Lou,' Rose commented with an infinitesimal lift of her eyebrow. 'How did you find him?'

'Great,' Sal replied as if she'd been asked about the price of butter. She didn't want Rose reading anything into the length of her absence. 'I think we could really do business with him.'

'Good. I'm extremely fond of Lou.'

The team were assembled and ready in the meeting room.

'Firstly,' Sal smiled round, 'it's just so great to be back! And I'm even more delighted how well the sales figures have held up in my absence – despite Rose at the helm!'

There was a universal laugh and Rose stood up and took a bow.

'So, on to the next issue.' The Alice-down-the-rabbit-hole fact about glossy magazines was that they always operated so far ahead that it might be a completely different season outside from the one they were working on.

One positive aspect of her absence was that Sal felt she was bursting with ideas about everything from gardening to beauty, and from new technology to how to make your money go further. She was itching to get their tech guru to try out the car that drove itself and to push holidays for the age group that could make the most of avoiding school holidays.

She saved the idea she was most excited about till last.

'I've been reading how online dating for the over-fifties is the fastest growing sector of the market,' she announced enthusiastically. 'So why don't we launch our own dating site? I've met happy couples who've got together through Guardian Soulmates and even *Private Eye*, so why not *New Grey*?'

'Haven't some of our rivals already launched in this area?' asked the features editor.

'Yes,' conceded Sal. 'But we'll do it better. Savvier. Sassier.' She had no idea what she actually meant by this but it seemed to be going down well with Rose and the troops.

'Good idea, Sal,' Rose congratulated. 'We should definitely get on and research it.'

An hour later they'd mapped out the main content for November and put out some tentative feelers for Christmas, even though outside it was still balmy.

When she came out she found Ella waiting for her in reception.

'We had a meeting planned,' Ella grinned. 'Have you forgotten?'

It was clear that Sal had indeed forgotten. She hoped it wasn't an outbreak of chemo brain. 'Ella, I'm so sorry. I've been rushing round like a mad thing since I got back. Come over to the desk I laughingly describe as my office.'

'I'm glad you forget things too,' Ella replied, looking suddenly concerned. 'I'm actually getting quite worried about my memory.'

'Bollocks. We're all forgetting things.'

'Not like me. It was bad enough when I lost my car in the car park in front of my son-in-law who already thinks I'm a batty old bird, but today I was genuinely concerned.'

'Why, what did you do? Forget to put any clothes on? Lock yourself out? Lose your car again? People do these things, you know, without feeling the need to shoot themselves.'

'I let my grandson drive my car when he wasn't even insured. And we almost hit someone.'

'Ah. Okay, that is a bit more batty old bird. Come in. You obviously need a coffee.'

Ella followed Sal into her bright and colourful office.

'Come on, forget about all that for now,' Sal suggested. 'Let's have your thoughts for the column. Actually, I quite like "Batty Old Bird". Shall we call it that? Or would you like something more businesslike? Up to you, obviously.'

Ella laughed. 'Why not own up to the truth? "Batty Old Bird" it is.' She listed the ideas she'd been considering as they sipped their coffee. By the end of an hour with Sal she was feeling an awful lot happier. She could see how good Sal must be at enthusing a team.

'Time we had another Grecian Grove session,' Sal counselled. 'Always makes you feel better when you can share your worries. Why don't I sort it out?'

Ella got up. 'Sounds great. Anyway, time I left you to it. Where's the loo by the way? My batty old bladder is playing up too.'

Sal laughed. 'What a bunch we are! I'll phone the others about the Grove. Let's make it soon.'

On the way out Ella dashed into the ladies' loo just in time. Why the hell was she peeing so often? God, next stop would be Tena Lady Pants. It hurt to pee as well and the urine seemed to have a strange odour. Not that acetone aroma you got from eating asparagus but something rather unpleasant. Oh, bloody hell, she'd better keep an eye on that.

She was going to have to dream up some nice treats for herself. She was damned if she was going to turn into a moany old bag like her mother had been.

She might pop round and see Laura tomorrow. It was awful to admit that Gore Vidal had been right. You always felt better when your friends were feeling worse.

Now that was a column even she'd be too ashamed to write.

Laura caught the bus home wondering what on earth Mrs A's mother could be like that she could put the fear of God into that formidable dressing-gown-wearing diva. She smiled to herself, remembering the wonderful memory of Mrs A driving the bitch who had caused the end of Laura's twenty-five-year marriage out of the shop, every inch the avenging angel, albeit in pink quilted cotton.

She was agog to find out. Mr A, still reeling from shock and looking like a zombie, had said his mother-in-law would be arriving scarily soon.

Thank heavens there were no more estate agent appointments today and she could lie on the sofa and relax.

In fact, there was a lovely surprise waiting on her doorstep. Her daughter Bella, with baby Noah slung across her chest in a stretchy sling with a butterfly stencilled on it. Despite carrying a sleeping baby across her chest Bella managed to look amazingly stylish.

'Bella, darling, I didn't know you were coming. I hope you haven't been waiting long. Isn't Sam in?'

'Doesn't seem to be.'

Laura leaned down and kissed the baby's tuft of dark hair poking out of the top of the sling. 'Oh, Bella, he really is gorgeous!'

'I knew you'd be a supergranny.'

'Did you?'

'You were such a brilliant mum you were bound to be.'

Laura felt her eyes welling with unexpected tears. She felt such a failure at the moment that hearing this was just what she needed.

'Thank you, darling. Lovely sling by the way. Did you make it yourself?' Bella was very talented at sewing her own clothes, even if they were in haute Goth fashions.

'Yes! I've decided to start making slings. Nige was wearing one I made the other day and this incredible hipster woman came up and Instagrammed him then asked where he got it from. My brilliant Nigel said, quick as a flash, "It's by Bella

Minchin, no doubt you know her stuff," and the woman asked for my details right there on the spot!'

'Bella, that's terrific.'

'I know, and I've got even better news.'

'What's that?' Laura led the way to the sitting room.

'It's very tidy in here,' commented Bella, then she threw her arms, baby and all, round her mother. 'Oh, Mum, it's because you're having to show people round! How stupid of me.'

'So what's the other news?' Laura could do with all the good news she could get.

'Nigel's been offered a teaching job. Not just filling in, a proper job. He had the interview the other day. He thought it was just a chat but it turned out it was the real thing. And they loved him. It's teaching comparative religion and ethics for A levels, intellectually stimulating stuff. Mum, he's so excited! I'm just so happy for him.'

'Where's the school?'

'Well, that's the thing. It's in Surrey. Quite near your friend Claudia as a matter of fact. And we thought maybe we'd find somewhere to rent down there, much cheaper than London.'

Laura's bubble of pleasure burst at the thought of losing her daughter and baby grandson, who only lived round the corner, as well as her home, but she was careful not to let it show. 'Darling, that's wonderful news. I'm so happy for you.'

'And I'm going to start a little online business, nothing ambitious. I thought I'd call it "SlingIt", as in "SlingIt for modern Mums and Dads". What do you think?'

'Sounds great to me.'

She took Laura's hands and danced her round the sitting room, baby and all. 'I'm going to be a mumpreneur!'

'And you'll be brilliant at it, just like you are at everything you do.'

'Oh, Mum.' Bella's face suddenly crumpled. 'Maybe it wouldn't be fair to you to bugger off to Surrey. What with you having to move and this bloody divorce and everything.'

'Nonsense,' Laura heard herself insisting brightly. 'You're just worried about losing the free babysitting!'

They plumped themselves down on the sofa side by side. Noah seemed to be still sleeping, the love. 'Tell you what,' Laura announced, 'this calls for a glass of wine!'

Fortunately for Laura's precarious state of mind Sal was as good as her word and swiftly organized their next get-together at The Grecian Grove.

Ella got there first and was pouring out her woes at losing her allotment to Claudia. 'I'm trying to sympathize,' Claudia insisted. 'But you know me, I'm about as green-fingered as Zsa Zsa Gabor. Maybe you should try Sal or Laura.'

'Sal just says she hates the great outdoors and can't imagine why I would want to spend time there and Laura's too taken up with having to sell her house.' The thought that Laura had much more to be miserable about made Ella pull herself together.

'Here they come.' They turned to wave at Sal and Laura. Sal, with her new chic look, was looking particularly stylish. There was also, Ella decided, a new sparkle about their friend.

The others studied her.

'You do look good, Sal,' agreed Laura, after Claudia and Ella commented on their friend's appearance. 'Anyone would think you'd finally met a man!'

The swiftness with which Sal suddenly delved into her enormous handbag, pretending to look for her phone, made Ella laugh. 'You *have* met someone. I know, the rich American who's staying at that hotel! You did talk about him quite a lot, you know.'

'What utter rubbish!' Sal bristled. 'I've only met the man for a couple of hours.'

'It doesn't take long for the *coup de foudre!*'

'At my age! It would take more than a thunderbolt to make me fall in love. Besides, he's been married three times and has nine grandchildren. *And* he's about to be sort of my boss.'

'That's never stopped you in the past, as I recall,' reminded Ella.

'Anyway, Claudia, how are things with you?' Sal changed the subject abruptly.

'Not that brilliant as a matter of fact. I've got to find a carer to come in and look after my dad or my mother is threatening to put him a home.'

'I know what you should do!' Sal started to laugh, completely forgetting she'd meant to change the subject. 'Lou Maynard – he's the rich American who wants to buy into the company – he's got this robot with him called Hiro. He's really interested in the subject of ageing and this robot is programmed to look after old people. I'm sure he'd lend Hiro to your dad.'

'Sally Grainger.' Claudia shook her head. 'Have you completely lost your marbles? It's either that or you really are in love. Of course my dad doesn't want a bloody robot. He needs a kind, caring human, not a machine, who'll make sure he eats when he should and takes his medicine.'

'I'm sure Hiro could do that.'

'Then why don't you have him come and work for you?' Claudia insisted. 'Your flat could do with a bit more tidying and hoovering.'

'Now, come on, girls.' Laura put her arms round her friends.

'Don't let's fall out over a robot. Let's all just have a nice group bitch about Simon instead.'

Sal called for a bottle of their dreadful wine and they had a very enjoyable interlude listing the shortcomings of Simon and the male sex in general.

'Just as well we've got each other!' Ella concluded, laughing.

This reassuring fact tempted Claudia to raise her dream of all living together but she decided they'd only laugh at her again.

'Oh, and another thing.' Laura remembered her promise to her daughter. 'Bella's boyfriend Nigel has been offered a job.'

'The giant goth? What as?'

'Teaching A levels in Ethics and Comparative Religion as a matter of fact,' Laura replied quellingly, forgetting how stunned she'd been herself to discover this surprising side to her enormous son-in-law substitute. 'And the thing is, it's down near you, Claudia, and they're looking for somewhere to rent. She wondered if you had any ideas.'

'Oh, Laura.' Ella instantly understood how sad this would be for their friend. 'When are they moving?'

'I'm not sure,' sighed Laura.

This time Claudia couldn't resist. 'If we had Igden Manor, they could come and live with us. It has the most lovely alms-house cottages. Perfect for a couple and a baby.'

'Claudia,' Sal said, shaking her head, 'you're not banging on again about us all moving into some crazy retirement home?'

'It wouldn't be a home!' protested Claudia. 'It would be an intentional community. The lease on the most gorgeous country hotel has just come up, with all these cottages round it. It would be perfect! Everyone would have their own front doors but still be together!'

'And how would we pay for this gorgeous country hotel?'

demanded Sal, conscious that she didn't even own her own property. 'That is, even if we wanted to get it, which of course we don't!'

'That is a bit of a problem,' grinned Claudia. 'But I'm working on it.'

'Have you met my friend Claudia?' Sal enquired of the others. 'She's barking mad.'

'I don't suppose Bella would be up for being a carer for my lovely dad?' Claudia asked.

'I could ask,' Laura replied dubiously, 'but what with a newborn baby and she says she's starting her own online business, making baby slings, I'm not sure it'd be practical.'

'No, I can see that. I'll just have to find an agency.'

'Don't forget Hiro,' Sal chipped in.

'Who did you say was barking mad?' Claudia quipped back.

'Okay, okay. But Lou says in Japan having a robot looking after old people is getting really common. They even play them the violin.'

And on this vividly bonkers image of a metal manikin serenading her father with Vivaldi, Claudia announced that she really ought to go and catch her train.

Pushing all thoughts of electronic assistants out of her mind, Claudia set about finding a carer of the more conventional kind. There were plenty of agencies for live-in helpers, she discovered, with costs ranging from the just-about-affordable to the seriously astronomical. She decided the agency in nearby Manningbury had the twin benefits of being based only a few miles away and not too outrageous in its fee scale. Claudia decided to enquire first and tackle her mother once she'd found someone who would fit the bill.

The woman behind the shiny desk in Your Home Help was

reassuringly calm. She listened to Claudia's description of her father's issues and also the fact that Olivia might be somewhat obstructive to the idea.

'Perhaps your mother might not really know how very expensive residential care actually is. A lot of people are genuinely shocked. The fees can be between five hundred for the absolute basic to three thousand pounds a week, more if nursing is required. Has your mother considered how she might pay for it?'

Claudia listened, appalled. How on earth did people pay for places like this? She suspected her mother had absolutely no idea about cost, and possibly some vague thought that the local authority might pick up the bill.

'It sounds like that's your best argument for her accepting home care. As a matter of fact, we have a very nice and experienced lady, Mrs O'Brien, who might suit you down to the ground.'

Hearing this was an enormous relief, but even the cost of home care wasn't cheap. She was going to have to have a serious discussion with her mother about how it was going to be paid for. 'When could this lady start?'

'As soon as you'd want her.'

'I'd have to interview her first. Possibly with my mother.'

'Naturally. You can't have a complete stranger in your home without making sure you like them. Of course, she has excellent references.'

Claudia left Your Home Care feeling relieved but also ridiculously nervous about how her mother was going to react.

'How is your morning looking, Sal?' Rose enquired. 'Only Lou Maynard is coming in to discuss how his investment might work and I wondered if you'd like to join us?' Meetings were always amazingly informal at *New Grey*.

Without even realizing she was doing it, Sal nipped into the ladies' and surveyed herself in the mirror. She really wasn't looking too bad. Of course one view was that a clash with death should mean you no longer cared about such trivial things as your appearance. After a brush with the Grim Reaper you should either give yourself over to endless pleasure-seeking or exotic travel and work your way through your bucket list or go the other way and try and Do Good. Sal, on the other hand, was just relieved she was still on the planet, and even more that she still looked quite good. Who would have thought after all those years of trying to appear half her age she actually looked better when she accepted it? Thank you, God.

What was more, maybe it was bloody ridiculous, but she was conscious of an unfamiliar excitement. A smile kept trying to creep across her face which she was finding hard to repress.

'Sally! Good morning!' Lou had leaped to his feet, as sprightly as a man half his age. 'Rose told me you would be joining us. You've probably heard that she and I are pretty near to reaching an agreement.'

It struck Sal that it was very odd that Michael, the CEO, wasn't present. Oh dear, that meant he must oppose the scheme. But of course, it was Rose's company.

They spent the next hour discussing the way his involvement might work and the plans he had for the future. It all sounded very exciting that the magazine would have a link with New York, one of Sal's favourite cities in the world.

'I always think London is more like New York than any

other place I visit,' Lou smiled as he got up to go. 'By the way, if you want me, try my cell phone. I'm checking out of Brook's.'

Sal was conscious of a kick of disappointment. How ridiculous.

'Are you going to stay somewhere else?' she found herself asking.

'At my daughter's down in Surrey. Seeing the newest grandkid.'

'Whereabouts in Surrey? Only my very good friend Claudia lives there. The one who wants to start the crazy retirement commune.'

Lou laughed. 'The cross between the frat hall and the kibbutz?'

Sal laughed at this Americanization of student living.

'Maybe I should meet her and hear all about it,' Lou laughed.

A thought struck Sal. 'Will you be taking Hiro with you?'

Rose had been watching this interchange with great amusement. 'Who the hell is Hiro?' she demanded.

'Lou's pet robot,' Sal enlightened her. 'He keeps him in his wardrobe.'

'It's not one of those sex toys, I trust?' Rose enquired.

'Hiro would be most offended,' Lou replied sternly. 'He and I are just good friends.' He stood up. 'Let's keep in touch,' he smiled at them both.

'Well . . .' Rose raised an ironic eyebrow at Sal when he'd left. 'You and Lou seem to be on even better terms than I'd imagined.'

Sal got hurriedly to her feet. 'I must dash. I have to brief the designer on next month's cover.'

'Of course you do, Sally,' nodded Rose with an infuriating smile on her wrinkled face.

An unfamiliar flush had spread over Sal's face and neck. *Probably another bloody side effect,* she reassured herself. Certainly nothing to do with Lou Maynard. She was over sixty, for God's sake, not some simpering girl, and besides, she'd never been the soppy sentimental type. On top of which she'd only known him five minutes. She popped into the ladies' again, threw cold water on her face and got herself ready to meet the designer.

Laura returned from her early stint at LateExpress to find three messages from the estate agent, all with news of eager prospective buyers.

She sat down heavily on her sofa, then jumped straight up again. If she wasn't going to be a successful divorce resister and barricade herself into her own home, then she'd better face reality and take control. And that meant finding herself somewhere she'd at least like to move to.

She assumed it would be simpler if she started with the agents who were supposed to be selling this place. Maybe then she could get a deal on their commission. She opened her laptop and studied their website. They had about twenty flats on their books, most of which were both characterless and tiny. Laura knew what she wanted. Minimum two bedrooms and there had to be outside space. She hadn't been a *Location Location Location* junkie without taking in the wise advice offered by Phil and Kirstie. She clicked on her house-hunting heroes and instantly came across Phil's top tips: make friends with your estate agent, look for natural light, get a view you like, hold out for a garden if it matters to you and remember 'the feeling' – you have to really like the place.

Armed with lovely Phil's advice, she decided to drop in on

the agents and start making friends with them. To be frank, she hadn't made a very promising start.

The first person she met was the sharp-suited young man called Stu. 'Ah yes,' he replied, 'the lady from Shirley Avenue.' He smiled maliciously, obviously eager to get his own back on a dangerous divorce resister. 'Estate agents won't admit it,' he replied confidingly, 'but we dearly love a divorce. Three potential sales, you see.' Had she imagined it or had the revolting little yob actually winked? 'First is the family home, next the bijou flat for the ex-wife and – if we're really smart – a third for the husband and the new lady in his life.' If she'd been holding a coffee, this was the moment Laura would have thrown it over him. 'So, Mrs Minchin, what can I interest you in?'

Laura stood up. 'Nothing, thank you.' She summoned up the most disdainful smile she could muster; after all, Phil couldn't be right about everything. 'I think I'll stick to Zoopla. At least a website can't insult its prospective clients.'

When she got out she was almost shaking. Thank God she had a message from Ella. She called her straight back.

As soon as she described the encounter with the revolting agent, Ella insisted she come straight over.

An hour later they both sat in Ella's front garden watching the twilight settle over the river, listening to the birds begin their evening chorus, drinking glasses of palest pink rosé. Thank God for friendship.

Ella at least seemed happy with her newly downsized house. 'It's a hell of a lot less hassle,' Ella said. 'And just look at these views.' She almost added that the only wrinkle in her happiness was that she kept forgetting things, but decided not to spoil the moment. An idea suddenly came to Ella, and she hesitated, not wanting to interfere, but then she couldn't resist. 'I don't suppose you'd like me to help you look, would you? I mean, I did find this place – and that was even in an auction. I think I'm quite good at it.'

'Ella!' Laura sprang up and embraced her. 'I can't think of anything more brilliant! You can be my very own Kirstie All-sopp.'

'Well, I'm glad it isn't your own Phil Spencer!' and wonderful efficient Ella refilled their glasses.

'To the perfect post-divorce pad!' Ella clinked her glass against Laura's, relieved that Laura was looking as if a heavy weight had been lifted off her shoulders. It was a lovely moment, only slightly spoiled by the fact that suddenly she desperately wanted to pee.

Claudia's mother Olivia sat stony-faced across the untidy kitchen table, her arms crossed over her not inconsiderable bosom, looking like a particularly unamused Queen Victoria. 'Do you mean to say you've been talking to agencies without even consulting me first?'

Claudia tried not to look at the state the house had got into and answer the question. No carer would come here unless they got the cleaner back first anyway. Another battle. It was as if everything was becoming a battle with her mother these days.

Claudia decided the time had come to stop standing for any more nonsense.

'Look, Ma,' she announced firmly, 'you put the fear of God into Dad about sticking him in a care home when you had NO BLOODY IDEA what a care home would cost or how it would be paid for. Let me assure you there is no way either you or we could afford to put him in a halfway decent place and he's not poor enough for the council to pay, so this is your only option.' Her mother was looking so snooty that Claudia couldn't resist adding, 'Maybe you're the one who ought to be in the home anyway.'

'I thought you said they were too expensive,' retorted Olivia. 'I suppose you'd better bring the wretched woman along to meet me.'

'Too right. And before that we need to get your cleaner back. I'll call in on the way home. Where is Dad anyway?'

'Where do you think? In his shed. One of these days he'll move his bed in there.'

Claudia had to stop herself adding, 'And who could blame him?'

She went off to her father's lean-to sanctuary to look for him. To her amazement she found him watching an illegal football channel with commentary from Brazil which the cleaner's grandson had found and set up for him on his ancient laptop, a gin and tonic at his elbow.

'Gola! Gola! Gola! Gola! GOO-LAAAAA!!!!!' congratulated the commentator.

'I think someone might have scored,' suggested Len with a wry smile.

'I love you, Dad,' announced Claudia.

'Me too, little Claudia. Am I still for Colditz?'

'I don't think so. Fortunately the fees are too steep. We're getting a carer in.'

'Not by the name of Rosa Klebb, I hope?'

'I think she's actually called O'Brien.'

'Oh good. I like the Irish. They understand the important role of drink in your declining years.'

He seemed much more himself today she was glad to see.

'How has your mother taken it?'

'I think it'll depend if she can get the woman under her thumb.'

'I'll try and behave myself.'

Claudia came and sat on the arm of his wing chair and kissed the top of his bald head. 'It's Ma who needs to behave.'

'Don't ever get old, Claudia.' He smiled his mischievous smile up at his daughter. 'If there's anything good about it, I'll let you know.'

'You said that ten years ago.'

'I rest my case.'

Five

Laura, already feeling so much better now that she'd enlisted Ella to help her, had another pleasant surprise waiting at home the next day after work. Her son Sam had cooked supper.

'Spaghetti bolognese,' he announced with a flourish. 'Madam is served. Oh, and I found this piece of paper on the mat.' He handed it over with a grin. 'I don't think it's from Dad.'

'If it was from Dad, it would have had a rock attached and he'd have thrown it through the window.'

'Tsk, tsk, Mum, that would bring down the value of his investment.' They smiled rather sadly at each other. 'Cheer up, I even bought a bottle of exceptionally cheap wine.'

'How delicious,' Laura replied, meaning it. It was so sweet of him to go to all this trouble. She looked at the piece of paper. It was from Calum. She'd wondered why he'd gone silent for all this time when, as her friends had pointed out, he'd taken a slug at her husband Simon at Claudia's daughter's wedding. And then, weirdly, she hadn't heard from him. He could hardly have lost her number *and* email address, unless his vengeful ex-wife had wiped them from his phone and that was hardly likely. It was all rather a mystery. Anyway, now he was saying he was sorry to have missed her and maybe they could meet up?

'How's the house sale going?' Sam asked, pouring the wine. It was indeed really bad, but it could have been literally bull's blood and she would have still drunk it, partly because Sam had bought it and partly, let's face it, because she needed it.

'All right, I think.'

'And how about your new place?'

'Nothing so far but I haven't been really looking. Ella's going to help me, though. She's good at houses. She just sold her own and downsized to a small one.'

'Rightsized,' corrected Sam with a grin.

'Sorry, what do you mean?'

'That's the correct PC expression. Apparently there wouldn't be this outrageous problem with the housing market if everyone "rightsized" to an appropriately sized home. By the way, Mum . . .' He paused as if he didn't know what to say next.

'Yes?'

'I think it's time I moved on. Bit sad living at home at my age. I'm twenty-two, not some nerdy teenager.'

She wanted to shout that it wasn't sad at all, it was wonderful, that she'd love him to stay and be there for her, to cook spag bol and buy terrible wine. But she saw how unfair that would be, how Sam had to go and lead his own life with people his own age. She just wished he could be one of those Italian men she'd read about who stayed at home till they were thirty-five, with their mamma waiting on them hand and foot.

'Of course.' She paused. Then added weakly, 'You don't have to, you know. I'm going for a two-bed flat.'

'I know, but maybe it's the right time.'

'I understand.' She took a large gulp of wine. 'You cooked. I'll do the washing-up. It was lovely.'

'Thanks, Mum.' He grinned and disappeared up to his room. She could hardly expect him to watch the same TV as she did.

She cheered herself up by texting Calum and saying she'd love to meet up.

Nine p.m. already. Only another hour till she could go to bed. How sad was that?

Sal found herself staring into her screen and daydreaming about Lou, somehow ignoring the hubbub of the office around her. She almost jumped when the designer asked if she was happy with the layout he'd emailed her of the fashion spread.

'Sorry, Jed!' she apologized guiltily. 'I'll get right on it.'

This wouldn't do at all. One lunch and the man was already affecting her well-known efficiency.

She cast a practised eye over the pages. They were great.

'That's terrific, Jed.'

She forced her brain back into work mode and despatched a message of congratulation to the fashion editor and their new young stylist. They had managed to source some clothes that genuinely flattered older women without being dowdy or ruinously expensive. It might be hard for a twenty-one-year-old to get this right, but she definitely had the touch.

Lou's face with its teasing and ludicrously infectious smile started to insinuate itself back into her mind.

'Get lost, Lou,' she commanded, not realizing she'd said the words aloud. The features assistant, who sat opposite her, jumped and gave her a strange look.

Sally Grainger, she instructed herself, silently this time, *stop behaving like some silly teenage girl!*

Fortunately she had some reading to do which required her full attention and turned out to be an effective proof against irreverent Americans.

'So when is this carer woman arriving?'

'Mrs O'Brien. In half an hour. I'm just going to tidy up.' Thank God the cleaner said she'd start again next week. Claudia felt like a cleaning woman herself. She'd popped in every day this week to tackle the mess and do the washing. Replacing a treasure was bloody hard work. She didn't know how the cleaner had put up with her mother all these years.

Claudia had hoovered everywhere, wiped down all the surfaces and put everything away. She'd even tidied her dad's shed by the time the doorbell went.

Mrs O'Brien was older than Claudia had expected. In fact, she looked like a smarmy yet sinister Disney granny, all fat cheeks and twinkly smile.

She saw the surprise in Claudia's face and winked. 'Don't worry, appearances can be deceptive. I'm as strong as an ox, as my old dad used to say. Is it all right if I come in?'

Claudia stood back and invited her into her parents' kitchen.

'Mrs O'Brien's here, Ma!'

Olivia looked the arrival over disdainfully, from her white hair, tied up in a bun, and her Day-Glo-pink tabard with Your Home Care's logo in a discreet corner, to her trainer-clad feet. 'You look too old for the job to me,' she announced.

'I was just telling your daughter here. I'm younger than I look. Besides, Mrs Warren, experience is what counts, I always say. And patience. Old people have their own little ways, I find.'

'My husband certainly does.'

'So do you, Ma,' Claudia reminded.

'And what exactly does a "carer" do for the extortionate sum your agency demands?' Olivia enquired testily.

Claudia realized they hadn't even offered the woman a seat and did so. Mrs O'Brien sat down on the edge of it as if she couldn't wait to start whatever task was required of her.

'Would you like a cup of tea or coffee?' Claudia asked.

'No thanks. I stop for ten minutes at eleven and four. My usual routine is to wash and get my lady or gentleman up, give them breakfast, get them dressed. Then we might go out for a walk, if they can manage it.'

'My husband hates walking. He likes sitting in his chair in the shed watching sport on television.'

'I do a lunch, some activities. Does your husband like any activities?'

'Ma, why isn't Dad here? He should be answering for himself. He's not completely gaga. I'll go and look for him.'

Of course he was in the shed. It was, Claudia reflected sadly, the only place in the house which felt like his. Even though it was summer there was a fug from his fan heater, overlaid with cigarette smoke, his wing chair, a huge pile of old newspapers, possibly a fire hazard, containing his completed crosswords, and his semi-concealed bottle of gin.

'I think we'd better put that away,' Claudia smiled at him.

'Doing the dragon's work for her?' enquired her father, his twinkle rather less in evidence than usual.

'She doesn't seem like a dragon. Unless she's keeping her scales out of sight till later. Why don't you come and meet her?'

'Let your mother interview her. I'll be a good boy and let her clean my arse and make me take my pills if it means I can stay at home. It's your mother who won't want anyone around.

And of course, the irony is it's *she* who should be taking the bloody pills!'

Claudia kissed the top of his head, feeling assailed by guilt. Should she and Don be having him to live with them? The trouble was, they had so little room. Besides, the stairs were so steep it would mean he'd have to sleep downstairs and none of them would have any privacy, least of all him. No, the carer had to be better.

She began to think about Igden Manor again and had to stop herself. *Get real, Claudia, it isn't going to happen.*

She went back into the kitchen to see how her mother was getting on with Mrs O'Brien and discovered that the atmosphere seemed to have subtly altered. Her mother's tone was less imperious. Despite her claims of only two breaks at fixed times, Mrs O'Brien was pouring her mother's best Assam tea leaves from Fortnum & Mason into a china pot. Claudia paused a moment, still out of sight and listened.

'I love a bit of good Assam tea myself,' Mrs O Brien seemed to be confiding. 'Proper tea leaves now, none of your cheap teabags that taste like ash from the cinder pile. And always a good china pot.'

'I couldn't agree more, Mrs O'Brien,' Olivia nodded.

'My husband now,' the woman divulged, 'makes it in a cup with the milk in too. But he's a man. That's your problem, Mrs Warren,' she opined, 'your husband's a man. At least he's not an Irish man. They're the worst. But men generally are a useless lot. They're what I call a necessary evil.'

To Claudia's utter amazement her mother was nodding sagely, as if Mrs O'Brien had just revealed the secrets of creation.

Her mother finally noticed Claudia. 'Oh, there you are. Mrs O'Brien here seems a very sensible woman. She's prepared to start next week. And listen to this, Claudia, she says we really don't need a cleaning woman, that she'd be happy to take that on herself. That would be quite a saving.'

Claudia stared at her mother in amazement. Her cleaner had been coming in twice a week for thirty years and Olivia seemed to have no loyalty to her whatsoever.

'That's very good of her, Ma, but really, she'll have her hands full caring for Dad. I'm not sure it's appropriate she takes on cleaning as well.'

'You must never look a gift horse in the mouth. If Mrs O'Brien's prepared to do it, surely it's up to her?'

Mrs O'Brien twinkled back at her, all generosity and grandmotherly good cheer.

Claudia could see that as far as her mother was concerned, the matter was settled.

'Come over here, Mrs O'Brien,' Olivia beckoned, 'and bring your tea with you. Tell me more about your husband the necessary evil.'

Oh God, Claudia winced, she could see an entirely specious bond of oppressed womanhood forming between these two without the slightest spark of recognition that it was probably they who were the oppressors.

Her poor dad.

Ella had been daydreaming too, though not of men. Instead her vision was filled with the idea of creating a vegetable garden to rival the allotment, where glossy dark green courgettes could follow on from delicious asparagus, then onions, carrots, runner beans in rows with their festive red flowers, potatoes, giant marrows, festoons of sweet tomatoes, and maybe, as her confidence grew, more exotic fare like pak choi and Swiss chard, with its rhubarb-like red stalks. A cornucopia of fruit and veg abundant enough to satisfy Pomona, the goddess of fruit trees, of gardens and of orchards.

Ella found that she was smiling at the thought of them never having to buy anything from the supermarket ever again.

Maybe she could even get the others involved, persuade them of the mental joys and emotional satisfaction of growing things you could eat.

Thinking about Sal in her leopard skin, Claudia who, despite living in the country for years now, still only had hideous pink hydrangeas in her garden and Laura, who bought all her flowers and veg in Waitrose, she realized this might be an uphill task. But then nothing would give her more pleasure than growing things herself and trying to get the others involved too.

Sal sat at her desk in the busy open-plan office mourning the days when people had a tiny bit of privacy at work to make their private phone calls. She was longing to phone Claudia and explain that she might be getting an unexpected visit from a grey-haired ball of energy called Lou Maynard. She could message her or email her but she wanted to try and convey a little about the man to her friend. No, let's face it, she just wanted to talk about him. Well, she'd have to do it later.

For now she should be concentrating on deciding which of the shots she liked best from the fashion shoot with London's most celebrated older model. The truth was, of course, nothing to do with age. The woman looked great because she was lean as a greyhound with cheekbones like ski jumps. She would have been stunning at any age. Sal decided to have a word with the fashion editor about choosing someone a little more representative of the readership next time.

Anyway, the preparation for the dating site was going well. It would need investment, though, and Rose had asked her to prepare a short report to be presented to the board, which actually consisted of Rose plus her financial advisors. The thought crossed her mind that Lou might get a seat on the board if he became a substantial investor. She must try and find out.

The other thought, which she was trying to push to the back of her mind, was her follow-up appointment. She didn't want to get Lara over for it. Maybe Ella would come with her? Down-to-earth Ella could be relied on to keep things calm. For the first time, Sal found herself wondering what it would be like to have a husband with you, like so many of the women at the hospital seemed to have.

For God's sake, Sal, she told herself irritably, *you're perfectly okay on your own!*

She decided to compromise and drop Claudia a quick email.

Hi, Claudia. I may have mentioned our new American investor, Lou Maynard. Lou has a daughter down near you and has gone to visit her. I happened to mention your anti-retirement village to him and, God knows why, he seemed rather charmed by the idea. Don't be surprised if he suddenly turns up and wants to hear more! Talk soon. Sal.

She just hoped Lou wasn't going to go and encourage Claudia in her crazy ideas.

To her surprise Laura had found her temporarily jaundiced idea of humanity was continually challenged by working in a local supermarket. The thing was, people were, on the whole, exceptionally friendly and very nice. You got the impatient or rude customer but most people had a cheerful word and a smile. The job might be low-status and pay rather ridiculously but it had few worries attached and that suited Laura just fine at the moment. She felt the odd pang of guilt at having passed up the chance of a more managerial role, but the truth was, she didn't feel strong enough for anything more demanding yet.

'Top of the morning, Mrs Minchin,' Mr A greeted her jovially.

She was glad he seemed a little happier. Maybe the thundercloud had been diverted.

'Any more news from India?' she enquired delicately, stepping round the painful topic.

Mr A's face fell comically. 'Two weeks,' he announced tragically. 'Mrs A's mother arrives on the twenty-third. I must go to Heathrow airport to bring her back. Perhaps I will drive into oncoming traffic and that will be the end of it, in this life at least.'

'Now, now, Mr A,' Laura replied soothingly. 'Apart from anything else, driving into oncoming traffic on the M4 is very difficult. There's a barrier in the way.'

He smiled sadly. 'The trouble is, Mrs A's mother is a big noise in India, a famous lady. She will find our humble life here below her touch. Where is she even going to sleep? Our spare bedroom is full of stock for the shop. And always she makes Mrs A feel a failure because we have given her no children or grandchildren.'

Laura could see the ripples of his mother-in-law's visit widening miserably and it made her feel very cross.

'How about a hotel?'

'In India she would stay in a hotel in a palace on a lake. Here it is Travelodge or Premier Inn. You can see my problem.'

Laura was about to point out that London was full of grand

hotels from Claridge's to the Savoy which could rival even palaces on lakes, but they would of course be ruinously expensive. She wondered if her son Sam could find a nice Airbnb with charm and character for the imposing guest. But maybe that would add insult to injury?

'Do you want some help clearing the room? I could find somewhere for the boxes out the back, I expect,' Laura offered.

'Mrs Minchin, you are very kind lady. If my wife could only regain former bossiness, all would be better. She is suffering a decline with overdose of chocolate digestive biscuits and many episodes of *Gogglebox*. I think it is all that is coming between her and total collapse.'

'Oh dear, as bad as that? I wonder what on earth we can do?'

With her usual efficiency Ella had already started browsing places for Laura to live on Rightmove and was truly appalled about how much you had to pay for a flat like a box without even a pocket-handkerchief of a garden attached. She had obviously done really well with her auction purchase. Maybe that would be the answer for Laura too, though there were obvious risks attached, since 'Buyer Beware' applied and you could never be 100 per cent sure what you were getting. Still, it had worked for her. She looked out of her window as an egret – a small white heron with a plume of feathers on its head – landed on her bird table and helped itself to the sunflower seeds intended for the humble blackbirds and robins. How wonderful it was to be so near the river. Her moment of peace was brutally interrupted by a sudden pounding on the front door.

She skipped down the steep stairs, ignoring the voice of her daughter Julia in her head pointing out their impracticality for anyone over sixty, to find that it was Julia herself at the front door.

'Julia darling!' she greeted her daughter. 'How lovely to see you! Would you like something to drink? Cup of tea? Glass of wine?'

'That is absolutely typical of you, Mum,' Julia reposted furiously, her pretty face made ugly by anger. 'Offering me a glass of wine when you know I'm driving. But then I suppose it's nothing compared to the fact that you almost killed my son!'

Ella had been wondering what Harry would have recounted to his mother about the driving debacle. Thank God she didn't seem to have worked out about the insurance, not that that made Ella feel a whole lot better. She was still eaten up with guilt at having let her precious grandson drive uninsured.

'Oh, for goodness' sake, nothing actually happened!' she was tempted to point out to her furious daughter, but the thought that something *could* have happened stopped her. It was strange how you felt more responsible for your grandchildren than you had for your own children. With her two daughters, Julia and Cory, in the car, Ella had bowled along listening to rock music without a care in the world. Maybe it was the memory that when she'd been growing up herself they hadn't even had seat belts.

'Of course, I blame that ridiculous car. I don't know what you were thinking turning yourself into some ludicrous granny racer. You've got no idea how pathetic you look at your age with a car like that.'

'I like my car,' Ella insisted. 'I have earned it after years of driving old estate cars packed to the gunwales with my children's gear.'

'Well, my son won't be driving in it, I can tell you that now.'

'It was your son who asked me to take him out because you were too busy,' Ella reminded her reasonably. 'Look, Julia, I am really sorry about what happened with Harry. As it happens, I think you're right. It might be better if I don't take him out again.' She didn't expand that the reason was because she was worried about the memory lapses that were beginning to seriously concern her.

She probably ought to do something about it, but didn't think she could face it. What if it turned out to be something really serious?

She thought of phoning her younger daughter, Cory. Cory would be sympathetic without implying it was somehow her fault. Julia would no doubt raise the spectre of too much alcohol being responsible, probably insist she gave it up. The trouble was, while Julia had plenty of time to interfere, Cory was busy working.

She'd have to decide what to do for herself. And it certainly wouldn't involve giving up chilled Sauvignon!

Laura stood in front of her bedroom mirror trying to decide what to wear. Calum had invited her for a drink at six o'clock in a local wine bar considerably more upmarket than The Grecian Grove. She wondered about the significance of this. People who didn't know each other very well usually met for six o'clock drinks since it gave you the option to continue for the rest of the evening or make some excuse that you had something on later. Yet her relationship with Calum had been more intimate than that. Not so intimate that they'd been to bed together – that was still too scary for Laura after breaking up so recently from Simon – but she had thought they were on the way to being close. Certainly her friends had got that impression.

And then he'd gone quiet. Maybe it had all been too fast for him. After all, the way they'd met – at a group for people recovering from marriage break-up – had hardly been the best of beginnings. Two recently damaged people seeking solace in each other perhaps before they were ready? But Calum had seemed perfectly balanced and rational. Not the kind of man to rush headlong into heartache. She had willed herself not to read too much into seeing him, but still the green shoot of hope had begun to poke through her pain.

Best not to make any assumptions and just go and chat to him. No doubt he would fill her in. He was a nice man, that was why she'd been drawn to him. She was sure of that.

He was already waiting for her with a bottle of chilled Picpoul – he must have remembered she liked it – in the window of the wine bar.

'Laura.' He stood up and greeted her with a slow smile. She'd forgotten how tall and broad he was, as if his suit was almost struggling to contain him. 'You look lovely.' He kissed her on the cheek. She could see herself in the mirrored wall behind him and was relieved that she did indeed look pretty. The warm peachy shade of her fluffy cardigan always suited her. 'How are you? What happened with the job interview you were going for?'

Laura sat down as he poured her wine. 'They quite liked me, I think. But the job would have meant a lot of travel and, to be honest, what with everything that's been happening, I didn't feel that was for me.' She didn't add that one of the reasons was wanting to be around for her son and grandson, since, as it turned out, neither of them were going to need her.

'How about you?' she smiled at him gently, not wanting to pry.

'You're probably wondering why you haven't heard from me lately.'

Laura shrugged. 'I imagine you had your reasons.'

He looked suddenly at a loss. 'It's my wife, Kate. Ever since the divorce she's been interested in me again. She says I've learned a lot at Relationship Recovery.'

'And what do you think?' Laura kept her voice as devoid of disappointment as she could.

'I don't know. To be honest, I'm totally confused. It hadn't been me who wanted the marriage to end so I would have thought I'd be thrilled, in spite of all the things we'd said to one another. But since I met you . . .' His voice trailed off and then he looked at her steadily. 'I had hoped there might be something genuinely between us. Well, the chance of something.'

They sipped their drinks, neither knowing what to say. Laura had been so hurt by her husband's affair, and even more devastated by discovering that Suki was pregnant, even though it had ended sadly in a stillbirth and, as far as she knew, they had then parted. She didn't know whether she could deal with this. Besides, she didn't really know what he was offering.

'Calum, I'm sorry, but you'll have to work this out for yourself. Maybe we rushed into this too soon.'

He reached out and covered her hand with his. 'I have worked it out. I've told her our marriage ended when she walked out on me.' He lifted her hand to his lips. 'I'm only interested in you, Laura.'

Relief and the longing for love leaped in Laura, drowning out the small voice of doubt.

She leaned across the table and kissed him.

Ella was actually glad to have the task of flat-hunting with Laura as she was really missing the allotment. She knew her friends thought she was weird to care so much, but it was the people she was missing, and more than that, she was coming to realize, it was also the structure it had brought to her life. In spite of having a husband and two daughters, the truth was, Ella had been a borderline workaholic. She had always disguised this fact by telling herself how important she felt her work as a lawyer had been, but actually she'd enjoyed everything about work – the sense of purpose, the company of colleagues, she'd even enjoyed the travel into town. Maybe in some strange way the little community of the allotment, even though it was made up of very different characters from those at her well-paid employment, had given her a similar framework, a reason to get up in the morning.

And without it her life seemed oddly empty.

She needed a new challenge and for the moment helping Laura would have to be it. Besides, she was quite worried about her friend. Laura had based her whole life on husband and family and now she'd lost Simon and her children were leaving as well. Add that to the loss of the home she'd taken such pride in, and Laura was the one who really needed support.

Ella had thought her friend mad to work in a supermarket. It had seemed almost demeaning for a woman of her intelligence, but somehow the loss of the allotment was showing her that everything was more complex than it seemed. Late-Express gave Laura a much needed framework to live by, and as far as she could tell, an odd kind of friendship.

Good for her. Now, if Ella could help find her somewhere nice to live, maybe things would start to look up.

She went back to the enjoyable job of browsing flats. The wonder of the internet meant she could see twenty at a sitting, with floor plans (in Ella's view the most essential tool for the house-hunter) and for the posher properties there was even a 360-degree video tour.

After an hour or so she was beginning to feel discouraged. The prices for ground-floor flats with gardens situated in anywhere Ella considered the known world were way beyond the budget Laura had quoted her.

She went downstairs to make herself a coffee and realized tomorrow was the day for the bins. She'd better put them out now as the binmen arrived at a godforsaken hour and waited for no man – or woman.

It was amazing how much recycling she managed to generate for one person, including rather a distressing number of bottles.

She gathered them into discreet paper carrier bags which she collected for the purpose and opened her front door.

To Ella's horror her keys were the first thing she noticed. They were still in the lock. She removed them instantly, feeling really stupid. Thank goodness Julia wasn't around or it wouldn't just be Claudia's dad who was for the care home. It would be Ella too.

Sal studied the layout for next month's magazine and realized her mind was elsewhere. In Surrey to be precise.

She was genuinely shocked with herself. How could she have arrived at this advanced stage of her life and still be fantasizing about men? Especially one particular man she'd only just met, and with whom she already had a professional relationship? Not that professional relationships had deterred her in the past. In fact, she'd often felt an illicit thrill in imagining the important men she'd worked with coming to her flat in North Ken and removing their pin-striped suits before engaging in extremely unprofessional conduct.

A message buzzed on her phone, putting an end to these inappropriate memories.

To her amazement it was from Lou Maynard.

> My daughter has booked me into a slice of olde England called Igden Manor. Didn't you say your friend lives nearby? Why don't you come down at the weekend? You can have your own cottage. Every cliché available . . . croquet, hollyhocks, even a ghost dating from one of your Henrys . . . Lou.

Sal found she was smiling. It would be great to see Claudia without having to stay with her and disapproving Don. She knew it was weird but she always preferred the independence of hotels to her friends' houses. Something to do with an en suite bathroom and a twenty-four-hour minibar.

Sounds great, she messaged back. And then panic struck her. What were Lou's intentions? He'd been sensitive in stressing that she'd have her own cottage, but what if the question of sex came up? How could she, a one-breasted recovering cancer patient, even think of taking her clothes off in front of a man ever again?

Maybe she'd better make an excuse and back out.

'So I said, Mr O'B, stop standing there like a tart at a christening and get off your backside for a change . . .'

Claudia listened, stunned. Her mother, who always claimed she hated swearing, was sitting at the kitchen table sharing a pot of tea and a plate of shortbread fingers with the new carer and Olivia seemed to be finding her absolutely hilarious. Normally Claudia would have been happy that her mother seemed to have accepted the woman, but what about her father? The whole point of paying Mrs O'Brien was for her to help with his personal hygiene and entertaining him.

'I'll just go and see how Dad's getting on,' she commented caustically.

'Yes, why don't you, dear?' was Olivia's bland and carefree reply. 'He's probably not even dressed yet. He's started watching the racing on that wretched device of his, still in his dressing gown.'

She saw the swift look of complicity pass between them at the general uselessness of the male gender and felt furious for her father's sake. Wasn't the bloody woman here to *get* him dressed, for God's sake?

She knocked on the door of the shed.

'Come in,' replied a tremulous voice. She pushed open the door and stopped in shock. Her father seemed even older and more reduced since she'd last seen him, as if he wanted to slip beneath the rug on the sofa and never emerge. There wasn't even the usual spark of delight at seeing her she had come to expect.

'Hi, Dad, not dressed yet, slugabed! Can I give you a hand?' It struck her that her father might not really like her helping him with his personal care, that affection and intimacy were different things. 'Or would you prefer I got Mrs O'Brien?'

'I'll be fine,' he replied quickly and swung his thin legs off the sofa. 'Just catching up on Kempton Park races from yesterday.'

Claudia turned away, hating to see her beloved father so unsteady on his feet.

'Just pass me my stick, could you, darling?'

'Can I get your clothes for you?'

Len grinned, a trace of her beloved dad emerging. 'I think I'll just wear what I had on yesterday. I took them off in here as a matter of fact. Don't think I'm likely to bump into Lauren Bacall and bowl her over with my careless charm in Minsley.'

Claudia chuckled. 'Shall I come back in ten minutes? Cup of tea?'

He nodded, beginning to look more himself. Why hadn't her mother or that bloody woman thought of taking him one?

She stomped back into the kitchen.

'My father would like a cup of tea.' Mrs O'Brien got to her feet, but not before she'd shot a quick glance at Olivia. Claudia sat down in her place. 'Right, Ma. I think what we need with Dad is a rota. You don't have to show him – in fact, it'd be much better if you didn't – but he needs a clear structure to be followed every day. It doesn't have to be that busy, he'd hate that, but it needs some clear points, starting with getting him dressed in the morning.'

'Claudia,' her mother said, lifting her chin mutinously. 'May I remind you this is my house?'

'Of course, Ma,' Claudia replied soothingly, and then with a little more steel in her tone, 'but then Don and I are meeting most of the costs of the carer.'

Mrs O'Brien sniffed loudly and disappeared towards the shed carrying a cup of tea on a small tray. 'Don't worry, Mrs Warren, I won't be long and we can make a start on sorting out that airing cupboard.'

Claudia's heart sank.

Clearly her first impression had been right. Her mother had co-opted the carer.

Laura sat dreamily looking out of the bus window. Calum hadn't stayed last night because she'd been concerned about Sam, but they'd decided that next time they went out she would stay over at his place.

Planning ahead might seem a little practical rather than romantic but it would give her a chance to wear her best lingerie, or even buy some new stuff, and get herself ready for making love to the first man other than Simon in twenty-five years.

The thought was wonderful but terrifying. Ever since she'd been married Laura had always felt like the Carrie Fisher character in *When Harry Met Sally* who says to her husband, 'Promise me I'll never be out there again.' And here she was, out there. And scared.

There was a palpable air of excitement among the tins of beans and onion bhaji sandwiches at LateExpress, crowned by the stunning presence of Mrs A, fully dressed in a sari rather than her usual pink quilted dressing gown.

'Her mother is arriving tomorrow,' hissed Mr A. 'She is getting into practice at rising early.'

As Laura was on the late shift today and it was almost midday, she tried to repress a smile.

'Where will her mother be staying? Upstairs with you?' Laura tried to picture the terrifying-sounding visitor in their small box room and signally failed.

'We have reserved room at the White Swan Hotel, not even a mile from where we are standing,' Mr A replied proudly. 'We are sure my mother-in-law will be happy with an establishment with such a romantic-sounding name.'

'Have you actually visited it?' Laura enquired, picturing the rather shabby hotel with its peeling white stucco she often drove past when giving Sam lifts here and there.

'Has good rating on Trip Advisor,' Mr A insisted.

'That's excellent then,' Laura replied hopefully and went to sticker the past-their-sell-by-date sandwiches. She could already see one of their regulars, a colourful old man in dungarees and a beret with a Salvador Dali moustache, who seemed to entirely subsist on LateExpress price-slashed chicken wraps.

'So what is it that makes Mrs A's mother famous?' she enquired in a low voice when she took over the till from the proprietor.

'She is a matchmaker,' he announced reverently. 'She wants to come here to expand her sphere of influence to all sad singles in UK who have no culture or religion.'

'Goodness!' Laura commented, taken aback. 'She must be very dynamic.'

'She is tornado,' sighed Mr A.

'And how should I address this tornado if I meet her?' Laura asked, fascinated. 'Or should I just curtsey?'

'Her name is Mrs Lal. She does not think the name is distinguished enough and never forgave Mr Lal for possessing it.' He shrugged.

'Does she have a Christian name?' Laura suddenly laughed at the thought of the word 'Christian' applying to the culture of India. 'Sorry, that's probably totally inappropriate.'

'Her name is Lalita which means playful or charming.' He smiled secretly to himself, but whether this was because his mother-in-law was or wasn't playful or charming, Laura couldn't tell.

'I'm really looking forward to meeting her.'

'Mrs Minchin.' Mr A bowed. 'It is sometimes better to travel hopefully than to arrive.'

Out of the corner of her eye, Laura noticed his newly despondent spouse bearing down upon them, and wondered how long the peace and sanctuary she'd enjoyed so much at the little supermarket were likely to last.

*

Sal sat at her desk pondering two things. Whether to ask Ella to come with her to her scan and if she wanted to tell Claudia about her imminent visit to Surrey. This might seem stupid to an outsider – of course she should – but Claudia might well take it as encouragement for this crazy scheme of hers about them all living together.

The first problem was solved because Ella rang her, full of ideas for her new column. After she'd listened, impressed at Ella's boundless energy and enthusiasm, she broached the question.

'That sounds terrific. Now I've got a favour to ask. You gave me a bollocking because I wanted to face this fucking cancer alone. Well, honeybun, now I'm giving you a chance to dip into cancerworld. Aren't you the lucky girl?'

'Sal.' Ella tried to follow the logic of this outburst. 'What are you talking about?'

'I've got my follow-up scan tomorrow. I'd planned to go alone but then I thought maybe I'd give you the pleasure of accompanying me.'

Under the flip tone that had so irritated her daughter Lara, Ella could detect a hidden seam of fear and panic.

'I'd be delighted. Where and what time?' Ella's usual brisk tone was more comforting than Sal could ever tell her.

'Four o'clock tomorrow at the Princess Mary Hospital.'

'Shall I see you there? I assume, knowing you, you'll be pretending it's a lunch engagement instead of a breast cancer follow-up.'

'Am I that transparent?'

'Sal, remember how long I've known you.'

'Right,' Sal replied, feeling stung. 'Maybe I'll tell Rose.'

'I think that's an excellent idea, then we can go and celebrate afterwards if it's good news.'

There was a pause on Sal's end of the line. 'Or commiserate if it isn't.'

'Come on. Positive thinking! Remember those cancer blogs.'

Sal couldn't help laughing. 'I know. Such a hoot. I mean, I bet you're really jealous of me that you haven't had breast cancer.'

'Now, now. It doesn't mean I haven't got anything else.'

Sal put the phone down and mulled over Ella's strange remark. Surely Ella wasn't keeping some dark health secret from them all? It just wasn't her style.

She moved on to the second task on her list.

'Hello, Claudia,' she greeted her other old friend. 'Bit of a surprise for you. I'm coming down to Surrey this weekend. Staying in a hotel called Igden Manor. Have you ever heard of it? You know me and the country, so I bloody well hope it's good.'

Six

'Did you say Igden Manor?' Claudia squeaked.

'Yes, why, do you know it?'

'Why on earth are you of all people coming to stay at Igden Manor?'

Sal toyed with the idea of trying to keep Claudia off the scent and plead a conference about the role of social media in women's magazines and decided she'd see through it in a millisecond.

'Yes. Well. I might as well make a clean breast of it.' The unfortunate choice of words made her go off in fits of laughter.

'Come on, Sal, be serious. Why the hell are you coming down here and to Igden of all places?'

'My new American friend suggested it. His daughter lives near, one of his many children, you understand, and she's just had a baby and apparently thought Lou would prefer to stay in the kind of hotel you get in Agatha Christie rather than with her. And he invited me.'

So many questions occurred to Claudia that she didn't know which to ask first.

She started with the most pressing. 'And you said yes!

Sal, that's amazing. He must like you a lot to ask you for a weekend when you've only just met. But how long's he planning on staying? Igden Manor isn't going to be open for much longer.'

'What? Why on earth? I wonder why Lou's daughter booked it then. The bailiffs'll probably arrive while we're in the middle of dinner!'

'I don't think it's common knowledge yet. My mother wormed it out of the receptionist. But, Sal, the really crazy thing is Igden Manor is the place I imagined us all living! It's absolutely perfect. The main building is beautiful but it isn't really old, it's just a copy, so you can do what you want with it. And the almshouses all round it have already been converted into cottage suites.'

'Oh my God.' Even Sal was lost for words. 'You mean I have voluntarily booked myself into your daft anti-retirement community!'

'Hardly. It's a four-star hotel at the moment. But it could be with a little adapting. I can't tell you how thrilled I am.' Claudia's voice was breathy with excitement. 'In fact, I'll pop over and show you round while you're there. And anyway, why don't you come over to us for Sunday lunch?'

Oh Christ. Sal began to feel panicked. Could she back out, having already accepted Lou's invitation? Make some excuse about her health after the check-up?

'I'm not sure . . .' she began.

'Sal! Stop it,' Claudia insisted. 'I won't come over if it's a problem and you don't have to come to lunch. Just enjoy yourself with lovely Lou.'

Sal took a deep breath even though she hated sodding mindfulness. Why was she getting so het up? She wasn't ready for retirement and anyway, she hadn't got any money to buy into

Claudia's mad scheme. Besides, she was as urban as brunch in Borough Market.

'Okay, thanks, Claudia. I'll talk it over with him. He's really going down there to see his new grandson.'

'Of course. How selfish of me. Have fun. Igden Manor is absolutely beautiful. Don't forget to pack your swimsuit. There's a lovely little outdoor pool with sunbeds where you can stretch out if the sun comes out.'

'Thanks, Clo.' Sal began to relax. 'That sounds right up my alley.'

Laura had hardly got in her front door when the phone went. She ran to it, hoping it might be Calum.

It was the smarmy estate agent. 'Good news, Mrs Minchin.' Was that a touch of malice she could detect in his tone? 'We've had an offer. For the full asking price.'

Despite the lecture she'd been giving herself that she wanted to move on, Laura's heart plummeted. 'Excellent.' She didn't even want to think which couple had made the offer. 'They'll want to do a survey.'

'Exactly. Would next Tuesday at 10 a.m. be agreeable?'

She was actually working then and almost said no it wasn't, but she knew Mr A would be more than willing to let her change her shift. 'Absolutely. Do I have to be here?'

'It helps in case there are any questions.' His tone was veering towards the suspicious.

'Fine.' She put the phone down. She'd had enough of this Stu and his hopes of three sales. She certainly wasn't going to buy a place from him herself.

Laura found herself wandering round the house, the hub of her world for so long, the home she'd treasured and loved and polished and had thought to be a place of safety.

So much for that. She paused at the octagonal table she'd bought in an auction and been delighted with. It was covered with framed photographs. She picked them up one by one. Her wedding to Simon. Bella as a baby – even then Bella had a special quality. A family holiday in Puglia standing in front of one of those funny little houses with cone-shaped roofs like medieval helmets. Their third anniversary when Simon had treated them to a minibreak in Wells-next-the-Sea. The birth of baby Sam.

Without warning she found herself dissolving into tears. Had it all been the most monumental mistake? If she'd chosen someone other than Simon, would she be standing here happy and looking forward to the years ahead?

A sound behind her made her turn.

It was her son Sam.

'Come on, Mum,' he said gently. 'I know what you're think-ing and the answer's no, it wasn't a waste. There wouldn't have been me or Bella for a start. You just have to remember the good times. Accentuate the positive, as the Americans say.'

Laura smiled mistily through her tears. 'I bet my mascara's run.'

'Yep. Black tramlines down both cheeks. And remember this. Neither me nor Bella is talking to him. The woman he ran off with has gone back to her mum. I imagine his colleagues at work take quite a dim view of his behaviour. Frankly, I wouldn't want to be Dad.' He grinned, his long fair hair falling over his face. 'We'll be okay. All of us. It's not as if we're kids.'

Laura smiled, bowled over by the maturity of her son's response. She obviously needed to grow up too.

'Come on, what you need is a nice glass of wine, a takeaway pizza – the posh kind – and something on the telly that reminds you of the essential goodness of mankind. How about some Freddy Krueger?'

'A nightmare figure who never dies? Sounds perfect.'

'Come on, we'll watch it together. Give me your credit card and I'll order the pizza.'

Laura sat down on the sofa. She had a vague feeling she was the one who ought to be doing the comforting, but what the hell? Sam seemed to be doing a pretty brilliant job on his own.

Sal waited for Ella on the steps of the Princess Mary Hospital, watching with fascination the row of patients in wheelchairs still puffing away at their fags. Still, who was she to disapprove? She'd hardly led a healthy life herself. No fags – she'd given them up before she was thirty – but plenty of booze. *Stop that*, she told herself. She loathed the guilt police who made people blame themselves for their cancer.

As she glanced round for Ella, Sal realized how nervous she was feeling. On the surface she'd been all ballsy insouciance, especially at work, but underneath it all she was terrified. And this was what it would always be like. You were never 'cured', just hopeful your cancer wouldn't ever come back.

'Sal.' Ella arrived at a brisk run. 'So sorry. I was looking at flats for Laura on the internet and forgot the time. We're not late, are we?'

Sal shook her head. She led the way to Surgical Outpatients. 'Might be a bit of a wait. Have you got something to read?'

'Don't worry. I can go back to browsing flats.'

'On your phone? Aren't they too small?' Sal, despite her job in magazines, wasn't really part of the generation that did everything on their phones.

'Do you want a coffee or anything?' Ella asked. 'Or aren't you allowed to eat?'

'I'm not having an operation,' Sal laughed, glad to release her tension. 'Just a check-up.'

As it turned out, Sal needed to have a mammogram on her remaining breast. Ella tried to distract her by laughing at the cubicle they went into which led from the waiting room via a tiny changing area straight into radiology. 'Just like a priest hole. The Elizabethans would have been really impressed.'

And then another wait before they were summoned by the surgeon.

'Good morning, Ms Grainger, and how are we today?' Sal contemplated the plump shirt-sleeve-clad consultant, brimming with confidence and bonhomie, and wondered where they found these guys. They seemed to be born to be consultants, probably wearing pin-striped Babygros and handing out diagnoses to all the other babies.

'Fine, thank you. This is my friend Ella Thompson. She's a lawyer so watch out.'

The consultant smiled a little less jovially. 'Your mammogram is clear, which is excellent. Time to talk about reconstruction, I think. Have you given it any thought?'

Only a man could ask such a stupid question. As a matter of fact, she'd spent days browsing all the different takes on the question.

'In the end it really comes down to two real choices, rather like vanilla or chocolate ice cream. Either an implant or a flap when we take tissue from somewhere else in your body.'

Ella and Sal exchanged glances at his extraordinary choice of wording.

'Or doing nothing at all,' corrected Sal. 'I see some surveys say over forty per cent of women opt for that.'

100

'Going flat?'

'You make it sound like a puncture,' Sal pronounced acidly.

'Ha ha. Very good.'

'So, if I were going for reconstruction, which do you recommend?'

'They both have advantages and disadvantages.'

'Just like life,' sighed Sal.

'Implants are more straightforward but we find the flap can give less trouble in the long run.'

'And where would you take the tissue from?'

'That depends. Your belly?'

'Sounds good.'

'Or possibly your back or thigh.'

'What about my nipple? Will I get that back? I was rather fond of my nipple.' Suddenly Sal thought of Lou Maynard and a tsunami of sadness welled over her that she should be feeling this for a man when she was so maimed.

Your timing never was very good, she reminded herself.

'I think I'll pass on the reconstruction and stick with being an Amazon. They were strong women who didn't take any shit from anyone.'

The surgeon suddenly smiled. 'Ms Grainger, I think if anyone can carry it proudly, you can.'

She felt Ella's hand reaching out for hers as they got up to leave.

'And don't sue me,' he announced with a grin as they were about to go out the door. 'That last was purely a personal view by the way. And anyway, you can change your mind any time. There's no statute of limitations on breast reconstruction.'

'What do *you* think, Ella?' Sal asked as they made their way towards the lifts.

'You mean what would I do in your position?' Ella grinned. 'The proper answer is that only you can know, but what the hell, I'd probably go for the full Dolly Parton. I've always hated having small boobs. I'd opt for new ones. Possibly double D.'

'Mine are so flat you'd hardly notice the difference. Fried eggs on a plate. I think I'll stick with the one. Sunny side up.'

'Sal.' Ella hugged her, ignoring the glances from the harassed-looking medical staff all round them. 'You're a wonderful woman and I love you.'

Sal had to rush off to a meeting and Ella, who'd assumed Sal would need her for the whole day, suddenly felt an overwhelming desire to drop in on her friends at the allotment who would be busy planting, digging or simply admiring their handiwork before she went home.

She was right. Bill, Stevie and Les were there, sat in a row having a cup of tea looking like the three wise monkeys. They were all retired and spent most of their lives here.

'Ella,' they chorused, jumping up, 'come and join us for a cuppa!'

She breathed in the river air which seemed surprisingly fresh. Not at all the 'thrilling-sweet and rotten' river smell of Rupert Brooke's famous poem.

'So you can't keep away from us,' teased Stevie.

'Something like that,' Ella agreed. 'Actually, I've just been on a follow-up appointment with my friend who's been ill and hospitals depress the hell out of me. I needed cheering up so what better than visiting you lot?'

'What indeed?' echoed Les.

'Go on, Les,' commanded Bill, the unacknowledged leader

of the pack, 'get the kettle on. And none of your gnat's piss for the lady. She needs a good strong reviving cuppa.'

'That would be perfect,' she thanked them.

They all sat in a row and surveyed the scene. It seemed reassuringly busy even though the growing year obviously changed. She sighed with satisfaction. Everyone here looked hard at work and happy. No depression or moping in front of the telly, just a feeling of busy productivity. There was nothing like being outdoors feeling you were creating something from nothing. You planted a seed and if you tended it properly and protected it from slugs and marauding birds, you could watch it grow into something wonderful like a marrow or a brussels sprout plant, which when she was six her daughter Cory had always said reminded her of a little tree. Some of her friends had tried to point out that surely it would be easier and cheaper to buy your veg in the supermarket but Ella had just laughed.

She tried not to look at the allotment she'd so enjoyed tending.

'You should get on with a bit of planting of your own, Ella,' Bill, noticing and understanding, commented gently.

This was, of course, what her daughter Julia had told her, but somehow, though she loved the cottage, it only had a tiny garden and what she really missed was the companionship.

Stevie appeared with a cup of treacly-brown tea and a trug filled with glossy vegetables. 'I ran them under the tap,' he informed her proudly. 'You don't want them all muddy.'

Ella sighed. Actually, she used to love being up to her elbows in mud, sifting it as if she were making crumble, the height of Ella's culinary achievements, until it was fine and rich and ready for planting.

Oh well, no use moping. It wasn't helping her. She should just get some pots of geraniums and admit defeat.

She picked up the vegetables and poured them into the jute bag Stevie held out. It read TRESPASSERS WILL BE COMPOSTED and it almost made her cry, remembering the mug she had given him with the slogan GIVE PEAS A CHANCE and how he hadn't got the joke till half an hour later then suddenly fallen about with laughter and toddled off to repeat it to everyone else on the allotment.

Come on, Ella, this really won't do, she instructed herself firmly. She knocked back her tea, so strong it tasted like bitter medicine, embraced them all and headed for her car.

Sal could have done with half an hour's peace to think through her decision but instead found Rose waiting for her in her office.

'Just checking on the progress of the dating site. Have you put together those figures?'

Sal sighed, half wishing she hadn't come up with the idea. It was turning out to be more complex than she'd thought and now one of the big daily newspapers had just offered a free bottle of wine at Café Bleu, the chain much beloved of their target age range since it offered a not bad three-course lunch for a tenner, if you joined up with *their* dating website.

'By the way,' Rose added, 'I see you're staying at Igden Manor this weekend.' She indicated the email the hotel had sent her confirming the booking which Sal had printed up and left on her desk. 'Isn't that old Murdo Binns' place?'

'Rose.' Sal shook her head. 'I have no idea what Murdo Binns is. It sounds like a posh waste-disposal company.'

'It's not an *it*, it's a *him*. *Lord* Murdo Binns. I'm pretty sure he owns it.' Rose smiled with a rare attempt at coyness. 'I used to think I was in love with Murdo Binns. Of course it was a very long time ago.'

'Shall I give him your regards if I see him?'

'I doubt very much you will. His mother used to live in the place and when she died they turned it into a hotel.'

'Fascinating,' Sal nodded, trying to change the subject in case Rose asked who she was going with.

'Well, have a lovely time.'

'Thank you.'

'Nice to see you relaxing for once. You work too hard.'

Sal laughed. 'Not as hard as you do.'

'I suppose we're both the same. That's why we get on.'

'Hello, Mum.' Laura answered her door next morning and found her daughter Bella on her doorstep. She opened her arms to her daughter and grandson delightedly, suspecting Sam might have suggested she drop round.

'Hi, darling, how lovely to see you both. Have you got time for a coffee?'

'Absolutely.' She took the sleeping Noah out of his sling. 'Would you like a cuddle?'

Laura held her grandson tenderly against her chest, his downy head resting under her chin, breathing in his clean, milky baby smell, and let herself enjoy the moment. Whatever happened to her, Noah was the future. Somehow it was infinitely reassuring.

'Sam said you've had an offer.'

'Yes. The full asking price so unless they find dry rot or an extension of the Central Line running under the house, it'll be time to move.'

'Oh, Mum. I'm so sorry.'

'Thank you, darling.' Laura felt so lucky that at least she had two generous children who cared about her, though she mustn't trade on that. They had their own lives to lead. 'It was your home too. Are you upset about it?'

'Apart from wanting to kill Dad? No. Besides, we . . .'

Bella obviously decided this wasn't the moment to pursue her line of thought and stopped.

But not soon enough for Laura. 'Besides, you . . . ?'

'Well,' she hesitated. 'London rents are so high and Nigel isn't the commuter type so, as I mentioned, we need to find somewhere a bit nearer his new school.'

'In Surrey,' Laura stated flatly, hoping she might have changed her mind.

'Yes.' Bella reached out a hand to her mother. 'In Surrey.'

'Suddenly everyone seems to be moving to Surrey.'

'It's not that far away,' Bella replied. 'It's not as if it's Leeds. Or New Zealand. It's only an hour down the A3. It can take that long to cross London.'

'Of course it can.' Laura tried to pull herself together. It was just that today, because she was feeling so lonely, it seemed as far as New Zealand.

'You should look round there too!' Bella suddenly enthused. 'After all, your friend Claudia's there.'

'I'm not sure I'm ready to be put out to pasture yet. Besides, my job's here.'

Bella politely didn't reply that she could probably get a job in a supermarket in Surrey. 'Of course. And you like it there.' She grinned mischievously. 'And it annoys the hell out of Dad. Fair play.'

The doorbell rang, waking Noah who protested loudly. Laura handed him reluctantly to Bella. 'If that's that smarmy estate agent . . .'

But it wasn't the estate agent, it was Ella. 'Ella!' Laura

greeted her warmly. 'Come and stop my daughter trying to persuade me to join the Gin and Jaguar set in Surrey.'

'I'm not sure that's quite how I'd describe Claudia and Don,' Ella laughed. 'They're more the Sauvignon and Real Ale set.'

'You know what I mean!'

Ella looked at Noah, who had stopped screaming and was regarding her large plastic necklace with fascination. 'Can I have a little hold? My grandsons are a bit big for a cuddle. About six foot.'

Bella handed over the baby who proceeded to cram as much of Ella's necklace in his mouth as he could. 'Isn't he gorgeous?' Ella said. She studied Bella's striking face. 'I think he looks like you.'

'He looks like a baby,' Bella laughed. 'Anyway, now you're here I might pop off into town. I'm seeing someone about my baby sling.'

Ella contemplated it. 'It looks fine to me.'

'Bella's going into production with her own baby slings, silly!' Laura laughed.

'Right. Are you leaving Noah?' Ella asked hopefully.

'I think I'd better take him. I'm still breastfeeding. But I'm really glad you're here.' She put an arm round her mother. 'We're so glad Mum's got such a good support team.'

'Yes,' Ella laughed. 'Husbands come and go but friends last forever, as we're always saying. Okay,' she announced, suddenly brisk. 'Do you want to see this flat?' They sat down and Ella opened her laptop. 'Two beds, a nice sitting room with room for a table and chairs, and sole access to the back garden.'

'It looks really nice.' Laura peered at the rooms on the screen. 'How much is it?'

'Not as much as you'd think but they do want a quick sale. Shall we go and see it?'

Laura nodded, feeling more cheerful than she had for weeks. Bella was right. She did have a good support team. And if the flat was as promising as it looked in the photographs, it might be somewhere she could actually bear to live.

Contrary to her expectations, it seemed there could be life after divorce.

Sal laid out the clothes she assumed to be suitable for a country weekend on her large double bed. She'd never been very good at the country. The one time she'd made an effort to blend in she'd splurged on a suede jacket and an expensive cashmere sweater to find everyone else in jeans and parkas. In the evening, learning her lesson, she'd changed into jeans and made her way to the host's house to find them all wearing evening dress. It was beyond her. Give her a lunch in Lambeth or cocktails in Canary Wharf and she'd know exactly the right dress code, but once she got beyond the M25 she was sartorially at sea.

Just to cover herself she packed jeans *and* an evening dress.

The thought of Lou made her suddenly nervous. He was such a warm, reassuring man, like a small but friendly bear. Part of her said, *Don't be stupid, it'll be fine.* But what about if it went further and she had to take her top off? Maybe she should have made an excuse and backed out after all.

She tried to calm herself down by having another glimpse at the hotel's website. It had a central block in mellow stone with roses growing up the front and two rows of pretty cottages round the sides. How bizarre that this was the actual place that Claudia envisaged them all living together. But surely it would cost a mint, and anyway, it looked as if it could accommodate about twenty people. Who exactly did Claudia imagine would be joining them as they went quietly gaga?

Claudia could hear them all the way down the path to her parents' front door – her mother Olivia laughing loudly with the new carer – and it made her want to explode. She was about to confront her mother when she decided to let it go for now and nip round the side entrance to look for her father in his shed hideaway.

'Hello, Claudia darling,' Len greeted her jovially. 'Avoiding the unholy alliance? I don't blame you.'

Her father, she had to admit, looked surprisingly cheerful, but his surroundings shocked and outraged her. There were used cups and saucers, a pile of old newspapers that looked like a fire hazard, unwashed laundry and to cap it all his hair looked straggly and unwashed, as if he lived on the street rather than in a nice comfortable rectory.

'Dad, what is this bloody woman actually *doing*? We hired Mrs O'Brien to help you.'

'She is helping me. By keeping your mother off my back. It's brilliant actually.' He clicked the remote and the racing came on the TV.

She had to admit he was looking a lot happier than when she'd last seen him.

'But it's like a student flat in here!' she protested.

'Excellent. Best days of my life. Permanently pissed and three months off in the summer. Better than being old, I can tell you.'

'You haven't found anything good about being old since I last saw you then?'

'What do *you* think?' He looked so twinkly and endearing that she leaned over to kiss him and got the familiar tell-tale whiff that had made her hire the carer in the first place.

It was too much for Claudia. 'I'm going to talk to the woman.'

'Careful, Clo,' pleaded her father. 'I really am happier.'

Did he really not know that he was sitting in his own shit? Claudia found she wanted to cry.

She pushed open the door from the garden and found her mother and Mrs O'Brien staring at her as if she were a rather unwelcome intruder. 'Claudia, dear,' her mother said finally. 'Wherever did you spring from? Mrs O'Brien and I have just been planning the shopping. I thought we might pop into the shopping centre and go to Sainsbury's.'

'What about Dad?'

'Well, you're here, aren't you? You could stay with him and after that he'll be fine on his own. We'll leave him some food and water.'

'He's not a dog!' Claudia wanted to shout.

'And what about if he needs the toilet? He's already soiled himself. Really, Mrs O'Brien, I thought you said your first job during the day was personal hygiene.'

'Don't get shirty with Una!' Olivia answered aggressively.

So it was Christian names now, Claudia noted.

'Your father won't let her anywhere near him to clean him up!'

'Then she has to persuade him. That's her job. She works with old people. There must be a way of talking him round.'

'Your father is a very obstinate man, Mrs Warren.'

'No, he's not, he's absolutely delightful!' Claudia heard herself shout.

'Then you'd better clean him up yourself if he's so delightful, and good luck to you!' Her mother reached for her bag and coat just as a taxi pulled up outside and she and the carer departed down the garden path, leaving Claudia fuming.

How kind of her mother to leave Claudia to find a solution to her father's incontinence with no help from her or the so-called carer.

Oh, bloody hell! Now they were paying the woman to go swanning round Debenhams (she could bet that was their goal rather than Sainsbury's) with her mother while her father still sat in his own excrement.

Great outcome all round.

Laura was feeling more cheerful than she had for weeks when she went in to work at LateExpress. She'd really liked the flat and they had put in an offer at once. It would all depend on how quickly the sale of her own house went through, of course, but now she could look forward to something positive coming out of this horrible mess.

She could tell there was something in the air as soon as she walked into the shop, a sense of extreme tension laced with anxiety. The young girl who was meant to be manning the till seemed to be lurking away out of sight in the stock room and there was no sign at all of Mr A.

Laura took off her jacket, donned her tasteless tabard and stationed herself in front of the cigarettes. These were the most probable target for pilfering, though the small bottles of vodka and gin were popular, not to mention the vacuum-packed steaks. She'd read, to her astonishment, that there was apparently a thriving market in meat theft, even for the big supermarket chains, with people managing to walk out with whole legs of lamb, even frozen ones, stuck up their jumpers.

There was no end to the inventiveness of the contemporary pilferer.

After about ten minutes Mr A appeared, looking pale and shaken.

'My mother-in-law has arrived and I have delivered her to the White Swan Hotel,' he announced just above a whisper in case she could hear him from three miles away. 'Already she has telephoned to complain. The place is shoddy, the service slow and her room too noisy.' He shook his head sorrowfully. 'And all this in the first half hour.'

'Oh dear,' Laura sympathized, wondering what on earth could be done to improve matters. Would it be totally unfair to Sam if she invited her to stay with them for a few days? There was the question of the sale, of course, but now that they had accepted the offer at least there wouldn't be prospective buyers tramping round looking at the place.

'How would you feel,' Laura found herself asking, 'if she came and stayed with me for a day or two until you find a longer-term solution?'

'But have you room?' he asked, his gloom visibly lifting.

'Well, actually,' Laura explained apologetically, 'I do live in rather a big house. It's up for sale because it was the family home, but that means it's tidier than usual and I assume it wouldn't be for long?'

'Mrs Minchin, I knew you were nice lady, even my wife acknowledges you are nice lady, but this generosity could save our bacon. Let me have consultation with my wife and I will let you know on the instant.' He ran off, his phone beginning to ring again in his pocket. Probably his mother-in-law with another complaint.

You must be certifiably mad, Laura told herself. But she liked Mr A a lot and he had been kind and generous to her. She would like to help him out of a hole and it would probably only be a day or two till they found some better alternative.

Laura was rewarded by the vision of Mrs A, for once not in her quilted dressing gown but a formal sari in shades of bright emerald, embellished with row after row of flashing gem stones, hurrying towards her and grabbing her hand, which she clasped to her generous bosom.

'Mrs Minchin, you are our saviour in shining armour!'

'It's nothing.' Laura tried not to giggle. 'You've both been exceptionally kind to me during a difficult time of my life. I'd love to be able to repay you with this small service.'

'Mrs Minchin, it is not small. It is big.'

'Do you think your mother would be prepared to stay at the White Swan tonight or would you like me to go home and get a room ready now?'

'I think now is better,' Mr A replied instantly, picking up a wire shopping basket and proceeding to fill it with items. Bombay Sapphire Gin with Fever Tree tonic, two fillet steaks, oven chips, some slightly wilted French beans and a large packet of Mini Cheddars. 'For dinner tonight,' he explained.

'Wouldn't your mother-in-law prefer something Indian?' Laura enquired. 'I could easily order some. My son always keeps the takeaway menu handy.'

'My mother despises Indian food,' Mrs A said, shaking her head. 'She much prefers French cuisine.'

'Right,' Laura replied, racking her brains for French recipes. She used to be quite a dab hand back in the day when they had dinner parties. She sagged slightly. How long ago that seemed. Well, however much of a dragon this lady turned out to be, by the sound of it she wasn't going to be boring and Laura could do with a diversion just at the moment. 'I'll slip off home now then. What time would you like to drop her round?'

'How soon would you be ready for her?'

Laura tried not to look too stunned. Clearly this lady was like a nuclear attack. You only got a four-minute warning.

Seven

Laura tried to call Sam on his mobile to warn him about their unexpected visitor, but as usual he didn't pick up. Why did no one under thirty ever answer their phone? She was halfway through leaving a convoluted message when the doorbell rang.

She'd just spent the last half hour changing the bed in the spare room, laying out fresh towels with a guest soap and placing a small vase of flowers next to the bed. It struck her rather sadly how much she'd enjoyed doing things like this over the years of her marriage, small but pleasurable domestic acts, and how little homemaking was valued in the modern world. Only career success seemed to matter. Her twenty-five years of looking after her home and family now seemed faintly embarrassing and anachronistic. The Sukis of the world were the ones who were admired. Laura mentally shook herself. She wasn't going to think about Simon's younger colleague who'd caused the break-up of her marriage. That would mean Suki had won.

Instead she skipped downstairs and opened the front door.

Without being conscious of it, Laura realized she'd had a somewhat stereotyped picture of Mrs A's terrifying mother as being somewhere between Indira Gandhi and Mrs Kumar from Number 42. Instead the woman who stood at her front door, though she couldn't be younger than seventy, was as sophisticated and sleek as a senior diplomat's wife, wearing what looked like a couture outfit in French blue wool with matching high heels.

'Mrs Minchin, this is my mother-in-law,' announced Mr A, 'the distinguished Mrs Lalita Lal, a very famous lady.'

Laura felt momentarily tempted to curtsey. 'Come in, Mrs Lal, you are extremely welcome.' She almost added, 'to my humble abode'. What on earth was happening to her? She could see why Mr A was so terrified of the woman.

She led Mrs Lal into her sitting room, with Mr A following behind at a respectful distance pulling an enormous and wildly expensive Louis Vuitton suitcase.

'Can I offer you a cup of tea?'

Mrs Lal checked her Patek Philippe jewelled watch. 'I would prefer a gin and tonic,' she announced grandly. 'It has been a trying day.' She looked accusingly at Mr A as if this were entirely to be laid at his door.

'Let me show you where to put the suitcase.' She led her kind employer up the stairs to the spare room. 'Will this be all right? What exactly was the problem with the White Swan?'

'Mrs Minchin,' he replied despairingly, 'what was not a problem? You would think we had placed my mother-in-law in a Delhi prison.' He looked around approvingly. 'This is a very fine room. My wife and I will earnestly attempt to find alternative accommodation as soon as possible but in the meanwhile I cannot thank you enough.'

'You don't need to. Just come down and advise on how strong to make the G&T.'

The answer was very strong indeed.

'I blame the British,' Mrs Lal opined as she knocked it back in three large gulps. 'We Indians didn't touch the stuff till the Raj.'

'I thought it helped prevent malaria,' Laura asked innocently. 'Isn't that a good thing?'

'Pure excuse,' pronounced Mrs Lal, holding out her empty glass.

'Maybe time for the Mini Cheddars,' advised Mr A as they made for the kitchen to replenish her drink.

'Why don't you chat to her while I start the supper?' Laura suggested, reducing him to such a look of wild-eyed panic that she took pity on him. 'Don't worry. I'll put the oven on for the chips. The rest will only take a moment. Does your mother-in-law like her steak well done or rare?'

'Probably still alive,' he whispered with a rebellious grin. 'Like Indian tigress.'

'Why don't you head off now? I expect I'll cope.'

He produced a bottle of red wine from his parka pocket. 'Vintage is very fine.' He tapped his nose. 'Not from shop. From off licence.'

'Go on, off you go. I'm sure we have more if we need it. My husband liked his wine and since he left rather quickly he didn't have the chance to take it. We have plenty in the garage.'

They both went back into the sitting room.

'A long time to mix one gin and tonic.' Mrs Lal fixed them with a gimlet gaze.

'We were discussing how you like your steak,' Laura countered.

'With chips. Another bad British habit.' Laura was beginning to think that however short a time Mrs Lal was billeted with her would be too long.

'Tell my daughter I will be ready at noon tomorrow,' she

instructed her hapless son-in-law. 'Has she bought the tickets for *The Mousetrap?*'

Mr A nodded enthusiastically.

'I am a great admirer of Mrs Agatha Christie. I saw the play performed in Delhi the year of the coronation.'

'Whose coronation was that?' Laura prattled on, thinking it must be some Indian potentate's.

'Queen Elizabeth II of course,' Mrs Lal replied as if there were no other royal worth considering.

The oven pinged just as Mr A took his leave and Laura was able to busy herself with the supper.

'Would you like the television on?' Laura enquired, putting her head round the kitchen door.

'No thank you,' Mrs Lal replied. 'I am not yet a dribbling old person. I will consult Twitter on my iPad.'

Laura quietly laid the table for two, wondering what had happened to Sam. He hadn't even replied to her message which wasn't like him.

Rather to her surprise the simple meal of steak and chips with French beans and salad seemed to go down excellently with Mrs Lal, especially the red wine. Laura made sure she got most of it and the effect seemed to mellow her.

'What I want to know,' she enquired affably once the meal was cleared away, 'is why a lady like you who lives in a nice house like this is working for my waste of space of a son-in-law in his tiddly little supermarket?' She surveyed Laura over the top of her glass. 'You can tell me it's none of my business, that I'm an interfering old harridan, which no doubt is what you've been told already.'

Laura laughed, liking her for the first time.

'The thing is,' Laura admitted, 'I'm getting divorced.'

'Husband left you for younger woman?'

Laura nodded.

'Always the same story. Men have no imagination. The new woman is subordinate: secretary, flight attendant, junior colleague. All ego. Men are ninety per cent ego, ten per cent penis. Brain is bypassed altogether.'

'Anyway, I wanted a job but not one I had to worry about. Your daughter and son-in-law have been really kind to me.'

'I am glad they have that much sense.'

'Why do you disapprove of your son-in-law?'

'Marriage is my business. I found her a good catch. But she wouldn't marry him.'

'Of course, I'd forgotten. You're a matchmaker.'

Mrs Lal sniffed. 'I make introductions between suitable people of equal status.'

Behind them Laura heard the front door open and Sam tumbled in, looking dizzily happy, his arm round an exceptionally sexy-looking girl in a tiny clinging dress that just about covered her knickers. Oh God, what timing. This was almost the first occasion he'd ever brought a girl home and it had to be one who looked like every mother's nightmare.

'I mean,' Mrs Lal continued, waving her empty wine glass and ignoring the interruption, 'what is better? Behaving like young generation, going to pub, getting drunk and falling into bed with first person they meet and never them seeing again? Or finding someone through introduction who is on the same wavelength and they can at least talk to in the morning?'

Laura turned to find a scarlet-faced Sam looking as if he would rather be anywhere than here.

'Hi, darling. I did leave you a message. This is Mrs Lal, the mother of the kind lady I work for. She's staying with us for a day or two.'

'Right. Okay.'

'And who is this?' Mrs Lal surveyed Sam's friend with the critical eye of a butcher examining a chop.

'My name's Kylie,' the girl answered with a defiant edge to her voice. 'As in Kylie Minogue. You may have heard of her.'

'Come on.' Sam grabbed her hand. 'Let's go to my room.'

Mrs Lal watched them depart. 'Bad,' she pronounced. 'Very bad. Not the kind of girl I would introduce to your son.'

Laura tried not to laugh that in the age of Tinder a Mrs Lal could still exist. She began to feel sorry for all those culture- and religion-free singles Mrs Lal had in her sights.

Sal arrived at Manningbury station, the nearest to Igden Manor, and looked round for a taxi. Before she had time to hail one, a smiling young man approached. 'Ms Grainger? Mr Maynard booked me to meet you and take you to the hotel. He was really sorry not to meet you himself but he said he'd be back in time for a drink before dinner.'

Sal had to admit that sounded a very pleasant prospect. It also gave her time to unpack and sort out what she was going to wear tonight. Maybe even have a quick shower to wash off the city dirt.

Igden Manor turned out to be even more attractive than the website led you to believe. A large medieval-looking central block in mellow golden stone with Gothic-shaped mullioned windows, surrounded by rows of cottages in the same style on either side of a lavender-lined path. A peacock even stood on the lawn posing with its tail feathers fanning out exotically.

'What an amazing place,' she confided to the young man as he took her case. He clearly worked here.

'Yes, and the extraordinary thing is, it isn't really old. The father of Lord Binns, who owns the hotel, built it from scratch out of bits of old building. Apparently his wife was an actress who loved "The Lady of Shalott" and he was trying to create the right backdrop for her to feel at home.'

'Lucky lady.'

They crossed a lawn and halted beside the last cottage which looked out over a pond with ducks swimming on it.

'How pretty,' commented Sal.

The young man opened the door onto a room that certainly lived up to the medieval fantasy of the surroundings. 'This is one of our cottage suites. Two bedrooms, a seating area and even your own kitchen.'

'I'm not really the domestic type,' confessed Sal.

'Me neither, but you can make tea in the morning and there's fresh milk in the fridge.'

'Now that's what I really call luxury.' She glanced round at the four-poster bed with its crimson and gold hangings and decided it wouldn't be out of place in a castle.

'It is a little over the top,' commented the young man, following her gaze.

'Don't worry,' Sal almost purred. 'I can live with over the top.' He had been so friendly that she didn't know whether it would be appropriate to tip him but then she remembered what it was like to be young and hard up. It was always appropriate to be given a tip.

And so it proved from his broad smile and nod of thanks.

'Anything you want, just dial zero for reception. You can register when you go over later.'

'Thanks a lot.'

She unpacked her bag, laid out the slinky black dress she intended to wear later, and began to run a bath with the lovely little free toiletries from the White Company. Then she opened the fridge. Normally she tried to avoid hotel minibars because they struck her as such a rip-off but not tonight. Tonight she opened the quarter bottle of champagne and poured some into a long-stemmed glass.

She had survived cancer and got her hair back. She might have lost a breast in the process, but that was surely a small price to pay for life. The thought crossed her mind again about what Lou was expecting. Would this weekend be a romantic one? There was no reason on earth she could think of that he should have asked her here unless he liked her, but it could be on a platonic basis. Maybe three marriages, nine grandchildren plus running his businesses was enough for him. Sex might have become an optional extra rather than the yawning hunger it once was.

For both of them.

It was driving Claudia crazy to think that Sal was just a few miles down the road – at Igden Manor of all places. Even though the whole idea of living there was ridiculous she'd still been doing some more digging into what was happening with the place. The difficulty seemed to be that Lord Binns, who owned it, was only prepared to grant a thirty-year lease which meant that any sane businessman or consortium wouldn't pour money into something so short-term. On top of that the kind of people who were prepared to pay the room rates expected five-star facilities including an indoor pool, spa and gym. But when the hotel had applied for planning permission to convert a barn in the grounds, it had been refused when local objectors pointed out that the barn was the only genuinely old building on the property.

The Quakers had apparently made Lord Binns an offer to convert the house into a care home, but Lord Binns didn't approve of God, and even less of the paltry sum they were offering in his name. He was still hoping Mammon would come up with a better offer.

Sitting at her sunny kitchen table, Claudia picked up a message from her daughter Gaby, who worked in the same architect's office as her new husband, Douglas. The fantasy suddenly came to Claudia that if they ever did get their hands on Igden Manor, her likeable and efficient son-in-law Douglas would be a terrific asset as an architect.

'Not still thinking about your potty scheme to house the Coven?' her husband Don said, interrupting her pleasant daydream.

'Even if I was,' she answered acidly, 'there's no way we could get the money.'

'Thank God for that.'

'Come on,' she relented, remembering they were supposed to be reinventing their relationship. 'Let's go out for a walk. It's a beautiful day.'

'As long as you promise me the walk isn't going to accidentally end up at Igden Manor.'

'Brownie's honour,' she agreed and reached for her jacket.

Sal looked at herself in the mirror. She had bathed, washed her hair, and anointed herself with an aromatic oil then slipped into her sleek black dress which was low-cut, but not low enough to hint at the black lace bra that contained the foam pad that replaced her missing breast. Fortunately she had always been so small-breasted that at least she didn't look lopsided. She smiled to herself, remembering the obsession with boobs they'd all had at school, sending off for ridiculous bosom-promoting creams and doing an exercise while repeating 'I must, I must, increase my bust.' And now here she was, minus a breast. How strange what life had in store. Just as well you had no inkling.

She decided, rather than stay here alone, she'd head off and have a look round the hotel, maybe even head for the bar. As she walked to the door she noticed a brochure listing the prices of the various rooms and almost had a heart attack. This room was over £400! And she was staying two nights!

She strolled along the lavender path, breathing in the heady early evening scent, amazed that the summer was advancing. Where did all the time go? When you were young it almost seemed to stand still, yet now it raced by. She passed through an ancient-looking arched door, which took her into a lovely courtyard where tables and chairs were laid out for dinner. On the other side of the courtyard was another ancient door and this led into a labyrinth of passageways until she finally arrived at reception. She quietly informed the young woman behind the desk which room she was staying in and asked if they needed her credit card. The girl consulted her screen and smiled broadly.

'No need at all. The bill plus any extras is all taken care of. Enjoy!'

Relief flooded through Sal, and with it the tiniest twinge of anxiety. 'I'm waiting for a friend,' she announced. 'A Mr Maynard. When he arrives could you tell him that I'll be waiting in the bar.' She looked round at the confusing passageways. 'Assuming there is one?'

'Let me show you.'

Sal followed the dark-suited figure through two small cosy sitting rooms with deep garnet velvet sofas, antique rugs and jewel-coloured flower arrangements to a long bar facing an enormous inglenook fireplace, dotted with tables and chairs. Sal settled into the corner with another glass of champagne.

After all the worries of recent months she could get used to this.

Ten minutes later she sensed his presence before she actually saw him. It was as if the energy level in the bar had risen inexplicably. Then there was the bustling as Lou erupted into the room followed by two members of staff, one clutching a menu and the other diligently requesting if he would like a drink. Clearly Lou Maynard was not the kind of man you left in a corner. She wondered how he did it. Was it the liberal application of large tips on arrival or simply the force of his personality?

'Sally, welcome to Surrey,' he greeted her, then, noticing her empty glass, he turned to the drinks waiter. 'What happened to the rest of the bottle?'

'I opened a new one specially, sir,' apologized the waiter.

'Then bring it plus another glass.' He sat on the stool opposite her and took in her smart appearance. 'You look wonderful. I'll go and change in a moment.' He indicated his chinos and cardigan. 'Grandpa gear.'

'You really don't need to,' she smiled.

'But, my dear, I really must,' Lou put on his best Noël Coward accent which sounded a hoot on top of his sardonic New Yorker twang. 'We can't have you dining with a derelict when you're looking a million dollars.'

The champagne arrived and he topped up her glass then filled his own. He got to his feet, still holding on to his. 'Just give me five. My room's next door and I won't go for the full George Clooney. Just a lounge suit.' He raised his glass to hers and Sal found she was laughing as she watched his progress through the bar.

The dinner was delicious, just as good as anything she'd had in London, and afterwards he suggested they stroll round the grounds to a small stream he'd spotted earlier. 'Don't worry, it's all lit up down there,' he remarked rather cryptically.

'You mean in case I slip in my advanced years and break my hip?'

'In case there were any satyrs lurking in the bushes waiting to pull you in and ravish you,' he grinned.

'I don't think there are satyrs in Surrey,' she offered.

'My dear, there are satyrs everywhere. In Surrey they probably wear three-piece suits and drive Jaguars.'

It was a glorious night with the stars like diamonds tossed onto a bolt of dark blue velvet. The air seemed to shimmer in the warm flower-scented night. Just as they turned back towards the hotel Lou pulled her against him and kissed her. Sal, who had been so uncertain about an advance from him, felt his lips, strong and dry and sexy but somehow reassuring, and kissed him back. Just as suddenly he let her go.

'Thank you for coming this weekend,' he said simply and led her back to her cottage by the duck pond. Just as she felt the buzz of tension rise again, he kissed her on the cheek. 'Goodnight. Breakfast is till ten o'clock. Sleep well.'

He waved and swiftly departed, leaving Sal standing outside her room, not sure if she was relieved or disappointed.

'Cup of tea! It's a beautiful morning!' Claudia woke up to the sight of her husband Don, who always slept in the nude, standing beside the bed in a Masterchef pinny and nothing else.

'Love the look,' Claudia commented, still half asleep. 'Can't think why Jamie Oliver doesn't adopt it.'

'He hasn't got my body,' Don put one hand on his hip and posed in a parody of Mr Universe.

'Luckily for him,' Claudia countered, ducking under the covers as Don threatened to remove his pinny and join her.

'I'm making one of my famous fry-ups if you fancy it,' he replied, pretending to look wounded.

'Bacon and egg's fine but no sausage for me.' She lifted up his pinny in emphasis.

'I know you don't want sausage. You've gone off sausage ever since your dad got ill. Don't think I haven't noticed.'

'Oh dear, have I?' Claudia replied guiltily. 'Why don't you come back to bed?'

'No dice.' He shook his head. 'I only like sausage when it's spontaneous.'

'You might have to wait a while then.'

'I'd noticed, Claudia.' He walked towards the bathroom. 'Believe me, I'd noticed.'

Claudia sipped her tea and thought about how ridiculous it was that Sal was two minutes' drive away and she wasn't going to see her. It would be the most natural thing in the world for her and Don to nip in for lunch in the bar as they often did, sometimes taking her parents along too. But she'd promised not to. How was Sal getting on? she wondered.

Sal, as it happened, was also contemplating bacon and egg, though the Igden Manor chef was disappointingly fully clothed.

'So, what shall we do today?' Lou asked. He had already been up and swum fifty lengths of the outdoor pool. 'Did you by any chance bring walking boots?'

Sal raised a telling eyebrow. 'Right,' he said. 'Sneakers?'

'I don't possess any sneakers.'

Lou laughed. 'I'm impressed. Is that because you only walk from the kerb to a cab?'

'I always think exercise is overrated. I do have some deck shoes, though,' Sal conceded.

'Halleluia. So at least a gentle stroll is on the cards.'

'How was the baby? Your newest grandchild?' Sal changed the subject.

'Round face. Snub nose. Two legs. Two arms. Regular issue.'

'Lou! What happened to the vaunted grandparental passion?'

Lou helped himself to what seemed to Sal to be his sixth slice of toast and slathered it with butter and marmalade. 'Great British invention, marmalade. Do you know we don't have this stuff in the US? Well, maybe Boston Brahmins do, but not us everyday folks.'

The idea of Lou as one of the everyday folks made Sal burst out laughing.

'Okay, the baby's gorgeous, you just don't get quite so excited when he's number nine.'

'Tell me about your wives,' Sal asked boldly. Somehow she felt with Lou you could ask him anything and he wouldn't be offended.

Lou took another bite of toast. 'Number one, Natalie. Jewish like me. When you're Jewish you always marry your mother first time round. It's in the Torah. We stayed married eight years. Had three children. I was a big disappointment to her. I hadn't yet figured out a way of getting rich. Number two, Melody. Melody was hippie dippy; she even sang at the Troubadour. Three more children and she left me for her yoga guru. Number three, Joyce. Joyce was a journalist and even more of a workaholic than I was. She was a grown-up though, forty when I met her. We only had time for two children.'

'And why did she leave you?'

'She died as a matter of fact. Joyce was an alpha like me and I can't convey how angry she was about getting ill.'

'Oh, Lou, I'm so sorry.' Sal reached out a hand to him, furious that she of all people could be so crass.

'Yeah. Tough call. The kids had to put up with me, but there was one upside no one tells you about. I became a better father. I'd hardly spent any time with my kids till then and suddenly I had to get to know them. Have you seen that movie *Kramer versus Kramer* where the couple are getting divorced? Dustin Hoffman starts off as a selfish shit and becomes such a good dad he offers to give the kid back to its mom if that's what he wants? That makes me cry every time. And it helped with my other kids too. Now we're one big happy family.'

Sal sipped her coffee. The scenario Lou was describing couldn't have been more of a polar opposite to her own life, without husband or family, when she'd battled cancer alone. Except for the joy of finding lovely Lara.

'How about you?' Lou asked, realizing what she must be thinking. 'Your story about your long-lost daughter makes me cry as well.' This time it was Lou who leaned over and took her hand. 'It has to be said, I'm a big crier. Horses refusing to jump. Little kids singing, I'm gone.'

'Yes, Lara's wonderful. And I have three grandchildren too.'

Lou grinned. 'The pleasures of later life. Especially handing 'em back to their parents. Now, what else are we going to do today? I fancy lunch in one of your English pubs.'

'Stop talking like a hick American.'

'Maybe I am a hick American.'

'You are the most experienced world traveller I've ever met. You know places in London even I don't know. And I'm a Londoner. Like that hotel of yours. And I bet you've already decided which pub.'

Lou grinned. 'As a matter of fact, I have. It's called The Laden Ox. I love that name. It gets great reviews and it's only a gentle hike from here. Even in deck shoes.'

'I'll go and put them on.'

'There's also a fascinating old priory we can go and look at after.'

'I can't wait,' Sal grinned.

'Extend your cultural range from senior fashion and online dating for oldies,' he winked.

Sal took herself off to her room, smiling ludicrously and looking round her at the peaceful unchanging surroundings. She suddenly realized she was happy and it was such a shock that she stood still for a moment, taken aback. Happiness wasn't a familiar emotion. And of course it was all down to being here with Lou.

She wondered again why he'd invited her.

Don't spoil it, she told herself sternly. *Live in the moment. Go with the flow. Get into all that mindfulness crap.*

And for the first time Sal, who had always rigorously controlled everything in her life, including who she allowed to know about her cancer, mentally began to say *Om* . . . and relax.

It was a blissfully unfamiliar feeling.

Ella went to fetch her car from its usual parking spot at the far end of the row of riverside cottages. Another glorious day. She'd promised to take Laura to see a couple more flats in case the first one fell through. It was definitely hot enough to put the roof down.

She waved at a small child who was standing mesmerised by the way her roof dropped down into the boot of the car in just a few seconds. It was quite impressive to her too, and she was sixtysomething.

Laura was upstairs getting ready when she arrived. Unlike Ella who was always up even before the lark – who said larks got up early anyway? – Laura liked a lie-in. The door was opened by a completely strange Indian lady dressed up to the nines in an outfit Ella instantly recognized as by Catherine Walker. Ella had indulged in the odd Catherine Walker herself when she'd been coining it at the Bar and knew just how much they cost.

'Mrs Lalita Lal,' the unknown lady informed her grandly. 'I am a guest of Mrs Minchin. She is an employee of my daughter and son-in-law.'

'At LateExpress?' Ella held out her hand. 'I'm Ella Thompson, an old friend of Laura's. As a matter of fact, we met at university.'

Mrs Lal stood back to let her in.

'May I offer you some coffee?'

'Thank you. And may I say what a great outfit that is? Is it Catherine Walker?'

Mrs Lal's rather cold and haughty manner instantly softened. 'Do you like her also? I used to wear the clothes of Mr Norman Hartnell, couturier to the Queen, but then I discovered Catherine Walker instead.' She made it sound as if they were bosom buddies. 'You know she designed the dress Princess Diana wore to her grave?'

Ella blinked, lost for words at this startling revelation.

'Her butler, Mr Paul Burrell, telephoned Catherine,' Mrs Lal continued in the same confidential tone, 'to ask how the princess should be dressed in her coffin, and that was what Catherine advised.'

'Goodness,' was all that Ella could think of to say. She knew it was true that Diana had worn a Catherine Walker dress to be buried in but as for phoning Paul Burrell, it sounded wildly far-fetched to her. In fact, just the sort of nonsense they dredged up on the internet. But who knew? She was relieved of the necessity for more chat by the sight of Laura's son Sam, who dashed down the stairs, holding by the hand the most ravishingly rumpled girl, before they both dashed wordlessly out of the front door, Ella suspected to avoid the eagle-eyed attentions of Mrs Lal.

'Ella!' called Laura from upstairs. 'Sorry to keep you waiting. Won't be a mo.'

'And where are you both off to?' enquired Mrs Lal. Ella strongly suspected she hated being excluded from anything, even if she was otherwise engaged.

'To look at some flats for Laura.' She wondered how much the lady knew about Laura's current situation. 'As you probably know, Laura is getting divorced and is going to have to move out of the home she's lived in for twenty-five years.'

Mrs Lal shook her head in disapproval just as Laura herself appeared. Out of the blue she grabbed Laura's hand.

'Look at it like this, Mrs Minchin,' she advised in her caressingly confidential manner. 'You had him when he was double cream. Now he is an old yoghurt, put him in the bin and forget about him. He probably isn't even worth recycling.' She looked out of the window. 'Where has that hopeless son-in-law of mine got to?' she went on seamlessly. 'He should have been here half an hour ago.'

Laura and Ella were in fits by the time they got into Ella's car.

'I love her. She's priceless. But why is she staying with you?'

'She hated the hotel lovely Mr A, her hopeless son-in-law, booked her into and I felt so sorry for them I offered to have her here. I'm hoping it won't be for long.'

'No indeed. Though you'd certainly learn all about Catherine Walker's client list. I understand she also dressed Queen Noor of Jordan. Though not, as far as I know, for her grave. I'm not sure she's right about Simon not being worth recycling, though. To us he's an ancient old two-timer with a paunch, but the sad fact is, some lovely young thing with a father complex will take him on before you can say decree absolute. Whether it's divorce or death, men are only single for a year, quite often a lot shorter. Women turn to their friends for support, men just get another woman in. It's the way of the world.'

'I feel another of your blogs coming on,' Laura accused, her eyes narrowing. 'Or worse, now you're in print. Hands off my old yoghurt!'

Ella laughed and got out the details of the first flat they were due to see.

They'd been driving and chatting for ten minutes when Ella pulled up to a sharp halt. 'Sorry,' she apologized, 'forgot to do up my seat belt.'

'Ella.' Laura looked at her as if she'd gone totally mad. 'You're already wearing it! It would have beeped if you weren't.'

Ella glanced down. Oh Jesus, her memory lapses were getting worse.

'Silly me, so I am. Now, this place is just round the corner.'

Sal and Lou wandered at a gentle pace through the hotel's lovely gardens, passing two ponds and a small building which was once a dovecot.

'Okay, Mr History Man,' Sal teased. 'I bet you didn't know that they didn't have dovecots just because they looked pretty or even to stick spare guests in if they were over-booked in the manor. Pigeon poo was so highly prized as fertilizer that it was actually taxed by the king!'

133

'Ms Grainger, I'm impressed. Where did you glean this important historical knowledge?'

'Actually, it was in the hotel brochure,' Sal confessed.

They paused to watch a peacock spread his amazing feathered tail in an attempt to interest a bored-looking peahen.

''Twas ever thus,' sighed Lou. 'The male risking rejection as he abases himself before the dismissive female.'

'If he's anything like the men I know, I've got a good idea what he's thinking.'

'And what's that?'

'What do you mean NO?'

'And what gives you such a jaundiced view of masculine vanity, Ms Grainger?' Lou demanded.

'Experience,' Sal replied promptly.

They had reached a small country lane leading towards the village and made their way down it. It was barely a ten-minute walk to The Laden Ox. A large white van delivering craft beer was parked near it, masking the pretty painted sign declaring it to be Little Minsley.

'What will you have to drink?' Lou enquired. 'I thought I might brave a pint of your warm bitter beer.'

Sal thought. In a village pub champagne would be over the top even for her. 'Half of cider, please. A still one if they have it.'

'Right. I'll collect some menus at the same time.'

He returned five minutes later with a pint of beer and a long-stemmed glass of fizz. 'I didn't think you really wanted cider. I'll take it back if you did, though it'd be a pity as they opened a new bottle. 'Don't get much call for it round here, as the landlord informed me.'

'I'd better force myself to drink it then,' Sal smiled, studying the menu. The first thing she noted was the pub's name at the top. *The Laden Ox, Little Minsley.* 'Oh my God, don't say we're actually *in* Little Minsley!'

'Why, do you have something against the place? Did it collaborate during the war? Was it a plague village where the whole population's buried under the pub in a pit?'

'No, no,' Sal spluttered into her champagne. 'It's just this is the village where my great friend Claudia lives, the one who wants to start the mad anti-retirement community! And the incredible thing is, she had Igden Manor, the hotel where we happen to be staying, carmarked as the place where it would actually be happening.'

'Why don't we drop in on her after lunch then?' Lou beamed. 'You know I always wanted to hear more about it. Madly impractical old hippie ideas are right up my street. Don't forget I married a Melody.'

After they'd finished the meal Sal realized that if they took the same lane back to the hotel, they had to actually pass Claudia's house. She'd been so engrossed with talking to Lou that she hadn't noticed on the way there. Now that she was aware of it, she felt too guilty not to at least say hello.

Eight

Sal found she was half hoping that Claudia would be out, but no such luck.

As soon as Claudia saw her friend walking up her garden path with a small man with the build of a bear and a hundred-and-fifty-watt smile, Claudia rushed out to greet them.

'Sal! How amazing! It's so great to see you! It's been driving me mad to know you're up at Igden Manor and I couldn't drop in and show you round, but obviously I respect your privacy and right to a –' she had been going to say 'romantic weekend' but something in Sal's demeanour made her check herself – 'few days of peace. Come in! Come in! How are you finding the place?'

'Absolutely gorgeous. Though at the price they charge for the rooms I'm not surprised it's closing down.'

'You didn't tell me that!' Lou looked as startled as a pheasant who's just worked out the shooting season's begun. 'I'm Lou Maynard, by the way.' He held out a hand to Claudia, who had rarely felt such a strong grip. 'Sally and I work together.'

'Sorry, but I thought it would have sounded a bit rude,' Sal explained to Lou, 'to announce that the lovely hotel you'd booked was going bankrupt.'

'Too right. I would have probably freaked. So what's the story? Headless horsemen driving away the clients?'

'Nothing so exciting,' Claudia laughed. 'It's all very British. The actual owner is an old aristo called Lord Binns and he's terrified of it being bought up by some – sorry' – she grinned at Lou – 'faceless American hotel chain so he's only prepared to grant a thirty-year lease. That means no one who takes it on will be prepared to spend any money on it. On top of that the current lot did try to open a spa and pool in one of the barns but the planning permission was refused so they're throwing in the towel.'

'Sal tells me you'd like to take it over yourself and all live there together,' Lou prompted.

'Shh, don't let my husband Don hear you,' Claudia whispered. 'He'd think you were encouraging me!'

'I take it he's not so keen on the idea himself then?'

'As turkeys are on Christmas. He's just grateful we'd never get the money.'

Lou grinned. He had a very engaging smile, Claudia decided. 'Money's never the problem if the idea's good. You'd be surprised. Indian banks. Russian banks. Maybe Chinese banks. They all love lending money to Brits.'

'I'm not sure I like the sound of that. We might get our legs broken.'

'As a matter of fact we're on our way back to the hotel now? Why don't you come too? I'd love to hear your scheme for the place.'

Sal looked horrified.

'It's more a dream than a scheme to be honest,' Claudia confessed. 'My husband thinks it would be hell on earth. Sal thinks I'm off my head, don't you, Sal?'

Sal nodded vigorously.

'Yeah, well, she might change her mind if she was as old as me,' Lou pointed out with another of his endearing grins.

'Or if she had parents like mine,' Claudia sighed. 'My mum's in her eighties and my dad's in his nineties and I'm not sure how long they'll be okay on their own. Especially my dad.'

'I thought you'd hired a carer?' Sal asked.

'We have. But she and my mum have become joined at the hip and she's completely neglecting my father, even though it was him we hired the bloody woman to look after. The funny thing is, he's perfectly happy, much prefers my mother being occupied and out. There's just one problem – apart from wanting to kill the carer.'

'And that is?'

Claudia hesitated, unsure whether it would be fair to her father to reveal something so personal.

'Hygiene. To be frank, he's becoming incontinent, my darling dad, and he doesn't even know it.'

'That's sad,' Lou sympathized. 'Don't they have devices to help these days, self-cleaning bidets, pads at least?'

'Probably but Dad doesn't even realize he has a problem.'

'This may seem a little fantastical to you,' Lou suddenly grinned, looking more impish than ever, 'but I may have something that could help.'

Claudia got her jacket and they began to walk back through the village towards the hotel. She seemed to know almost everyone they passed and each one enquired after her parents.

'I hear you've got a carer in to help,' announced an ancient lady on a mobile scooter in a booming voice. 'Mind you keep an eye on them, dear. You hear such dreadful stories these days.'

'You see,' Sal confided, 'this is what I couldn't bear. Even living in a village would be bad enough, let alone anything smaller. Everyone knows your business.'

'That was just Betty,' Claudia explained. 'She's brilliant. She used to be a Bluebell Girl back in the day – you know, a high-kicking chorus girl,' she explained for Lou's benefit. 'She's one of my best friends. I was sceptical about village life too, but not any more. It's lovely having friends who're older and younger than me. You just don't get that in the city.'

'Thank God,' murmured Sal.

'Now, Ms Grainger,' Lou teased her. 'I'm shocked at your limitations. I had you down for a free spirit.'

Sal realized she must sound like a mean old bag but couldn't resist snapping, 'That's why I don't want to live in a village where everyone knows your business!'

'Free spirits should just rise above the nosy neighbours,' Lou corrected.

'That makes me think of transcendental meditation,' Sal replied, laughing. 'I actually tried that when I was young. I was a terrible failure. I could never switch off my hyperactive superego.'

Claudia nodded. 'I know just what you mean. I'm the same with mindfulness. I just sit there in my leotard saying, "Come on, inner peace, I haven't got all day!"'

'Clearly you'll need a better teacher when you have your classes in the new-age old-age community,' Lou teased them.

But Claudia wasn't listening. They'd arrived at the entrance to Igden Manor and she wasn't going to miss a moment to start explaining her vision.

'It was this place that got me going really. That and worrying about my parents. I can really see this place being the perfect location. You've got the main house over there' – she pointed to the beautiful stone building – 'and that has ten rooms in it, so lots of room for staff, and for anyone who ends up needing extra care, plus some guest rooms, of course. All the communal parts would be in that area. Dining room. Large lounge. Terrace at the front.'

'And the bar,' Sal reminded, laughing.

'Of course the bar.'

'But – and this is the crucial thing – you've also got all the cottages, each with its own front door. Some of them could be joined together to create three bedrooms. Privacy is absolutely crucial or we'd all drive each other mad.'

'We'd drive each other mad anyway,' Sal protested acidly. 'That's why it's a terrible idea.'

'Am I sensing a pattern of negativity here, Ms Grainger?' Lou enquired.

'Too right you are.'

Claudia wasn't to be diverted. 'Then there's the outdoor pool. Good for those creaking joints.'

'Yes, I can see mandatory aqua aerobics will be on the schedule.' Sal shook her head.

'And the croquet lawn. Plus there's a tennis court down by the stream. Carp fishing for the contemplative.'

'Sounds like an English country paradise to me,' Lou grinned. 'I can just see Miss Marple in a deckchair.'

'More like *Midsomer Murders* . . . with me doing the murdering!' Sal murmured.

'Talking of Miss Marple, how about tea on the lawn?' Claudia suggested.

Ten minutes later they were ensconced in wicker chairs, sitting at a white linen-clad table with a pot of tea, cucumber sandwiches, scones and a three-tiered selection of fancy cakes.

'You see,' Claudia smiled at them both, 'this is what it would be like. Our retirement would be like the Dowager Countess of Grantham's in *Downton Abbey*.'

'Wasn't she the interfering old bat?' Sal enquired. 'If I could spice up my declining years with some serious interfering, I might be more interested.'

'And I had you down for a peaceful woman,' Lou announced affectionately.

'Sal? Peaceful?' echoed Claudia incredulously.

'Perhaps she shows me another side,' winked Lou. 'I find her very peaceful.'

'Well, after marrying your mother, then Melody the hippie, not to mention your third wife the workaholic, maybe I'm a restful change,' countered Sal, smiling across at him.

A sudden truth hit Claudia. Sal had finally found her equal. What Claudia had taken as a fun weekend between friends was way off-beam. If she wasn't much mistaken, Lou was serious about Sal. She might even find herself actually marrying the man. Claudia experienced a kick of disappointment. That would rule Sal out of her mad scheme. But then Sal was pretty resistant anyway. And still working.

Oh well, it was never going to happen anyway.

'Tell me one thing,' Lou enquired. 'Sal told me your idea was about you girls living together but this place is really quite big.'

'We'd drive each other completely cuckoo if it was just us.' She turned to Sal. 'A student flat crossed with a kibbutz was the dream, remember? I'd hate just to live with my own age group. You need young people too. Babies! I thought of asking my son-in-law Douglas, the architect, to come and have a look. Maybe they'd come and live here too. None of this generation can afford to buy anywhere. And Laura's daughter Bella's looking for somewhere to live as well. Her husband

Nigel the goth's going straight and taking a job in a school in Surrey.'

Sal glanced across at Lou. He was actually swallowing all this stuff! She couldn't believe it in a hard-headed businessman like him. Maybe Claudia had put something in his tea!

'I can see how close this idea is to your heart,' Lou was saying. 'But what you need is a proper business plan if you're going to have any chance of making it work. It's a pretty ambitious scheme.'

'I know.' Claudia looked at Lou, a glow of pleasure lighting up her attractive face, taking years off it. 'But my mother wormed something out of the receptionist that was really quite interesting. Because it's only a thirty-year lease, the sum the old boy wants is quite reasonable.'

Lou grinned. He'd spent years working with developers and leases, and ground rents. 'Yes, but he might build in a rent review and put it right up. Landlords are in it for the investment, not for charity.'

'I know,' Claudia sighed. 'Still it *could* be viable.' She poured them all another cup of tea. 'So what is this mysterious answer you have to my father's problems?'

'Wait till after tea and I'll show you.'

They sat back in their chairs and watched the other guests playing croquet on the lawn.

'I gather it's a brutal game,' Lou remarked. 'Much more vicious than ice hockey or American football.'

'Oh yes, they fight to the death in croquet. My dad used to be really good at it once.'

'Okay.' Lou got to his feet. He was very sprightly for someone over seventy. 'Now, girls. I ask you not to scoff. I ask you only to listen and watch.' He signed the bill and started leading them across the lawn towards the car park. 'This is another of my little interests, along with finding a very enjoyable way to age.'

They had arrived at Lou's hire car. He pressed the key and the boot popped open. Lou bent over it and lifted something out. To Claudia's amazement it seemed to be a three-foot-tall robot.

'Meet Hiro. He's been specially developed for what is delightfully known as "elder aid". He has a range of skills beyond any human carer's, he can beat you at chess, and he speaks nineteen languages.'

Claudia shook her head. 'Then he'll understand when I say "Put him back in the boot." My dad wouldn't accept help from a robot in a zillion years.'

'You said this carer you've hired doesn't tidy up,' Lou replied. 'Hiro does. He also helps with cooking, cleaning and – wait for it – personal hygiene. The Japanese have an awful lot of old people and not enough young to cope with them. Hence Hiro. The Japanese invented electronics, remember. I've invested quite a bit in this little guy. As I was telling Sal, he's not your average robot. Hiro is state-of-the-art. Will you indulge me and just try him out with your dad? The worst thing he can do is tell him to get lost!'

'And rather fruitily at that! I hope Hiro doesn't understand swear words.'

'He's so smart he'll start using them.'

Claudia was beginning to realize that Lou Maynard was a force of nature that was hard to resist. God alone knew what her mother would say, but it would certainly get up the nose of Mrs O'Brien.

It would be worth the experiment for that alone.

'Okay, you're on. Let's go and introduce Hiro to Dad now.'

*

Laura surveyed herself in the bathroom mirror. She had a date with Calum she didn't want Mrs Lal to know about. She didn't look too bad but maybe a touch of red lipstick to bring out the shade of her jersey wrap dress would improve things? It also made her feel sexy, not something Laura often aimed for but tonight she felt a bit daring. She'd stopped worrying so much about her future now that Ella was helping her find a flat. There was something very reassuring about being able to hand the problem over to efficient Ella and she suspected Ella was enjoying it too. She'd been a bit down since that allotment business.

The doorbell rang and Laura looked round for her handbag. Where was it? Damn! It was down in the sitting room. Too late she remembered that Mrs Lal was in and Laura could hear her answering the door and greeting Calum in her grandest post-Colonial manner. Poor Calum. He had no inkling of her unexpected guest. She'd better get down stairs PDQ. As she got up she snagged her sheer tights – another unusually sexy item for Laura – on a sharp drawer handle. Damn! Now she'd have to find another pair. She opened her knicker drawer, usually well organized and colour coded, to find that Bella had been rooting in there and all was chaos. White pants in with black, opaque and sheer tights all jumbled together. It took her ten minutes to find another suitable pair, check them for holes – one wear could do for a ten-denier pair if you were unlucky – and get herself organized and ready.

'So, Calum – I hope you won't mind if I call you that?' Laura could hear Mrs Lal's penetrating tones enquire, 'when did you say your divorce became final? And you say your wife – er, Kate was it? – would like you to continue to invest in the matrimonial home? Is that not a rather unusual arrangement?'

Laura hesitated at the bottom of the stairs, stunned at how

Mrs Lal dared to ask such devastatingly personal questions of a man she had never met before. Part of Laura felt indignant on his behalf that he should be subjected to this inquisition, and by someone she was simply allowing to stay as a favour. On the other hand, she was riveted by his replies. How *had* this Kate dared to suggest he keep his money in the family home even though their children were grown up? Surely that tied him to her, and how would he ever be able to afford a place of his own?

She coughed loudly, threw her shoulders back and pulled her stomach in as her Pilates teacher advised, and walked into the room.

Calum, she decided, was looking exceptionally handsome. Just like her, he had made an effort, which boded well.

'Sorry I kept you waiting. You've met Mrs Lal? She's the mother-in-law of my kind employer and is staying with me for a few days.'

'Calum here and I have been having a very interesting conversation.'

Laura couldn't help smiling at how uncomfortable Calum was looking. 'Don't worry about Mrs Lal's direct questions. She's a matchmaker back home in India and likes to get things clear.'

'Not a matchmaker, that is a very vulgar expression,' corrected Mrs Lal grandly. 'I simply arrange introductions.'

'And have I passed the test?' Calum enquired, his eyes on Laura.

The unnerving silence that followed threw them both.

'Oh dear, clearly I haven't. Would you like to tell me why?'

'No time, I'm afraid,' Laura announced briskly. 'The film starts in half an hour and I insist on catching the ads. They're often the best bit.' She grabbed Calum's arm before Mrs Lal got the opportunity to elaborate.

'See you later, Mrs Lal. Is Mr A coming to pick you up?'

'No, I shall stay in tonight and experience a quiet domestic evening. Your son Sam is going to introduce me to the offerings of Netflix and his favourite Italian speciality via Deliveroo. My treat. Have a pleasant evening.'

'So who on the earth is that terrifying old crone?' demanded Calum as soon as they climbed into his car.

'I'm really sorry. I thought she'd be out with her daughter and son-in-law, not eating takeaway pizza with my son. I hope he's not going to terrify her with zombies or chainsaw massacres.'

'I doubt if a whole tribe of zombies could scare that lady. She'd start asking them all their prospects and they'd run off at once.'

'And I don't know how she's won Sam round. He was furious with her for pronouncing on the unsuitability of his extremely sexy new girlfriend.'

'Speaking of which . . .' Calum looked meaningfully at Laura and left the sentence unfinished.

The sheer tights and red lipstick had been worth it.

A thought occurred to Laura. If she did take Calum home later, they would have to run the gauntlet of her son and Mrs Lal watching horror movies and chomping Margarita pizzas.

It was quite a dampener.

As it happened, Ella, four miles across the city, was coping with her own offspring issue.

She had just been settling down to a steak and ale pie for one (with free ceramic dish which she enjoyed recycling) and a large glass of red wine when the bell rang. Ella, glancing at her tempting dinner, wondered if she could pretend to be out, then grumpily got up to answer it.

It was her daughter Julia carrying a plastic bag of something from their garden.

'Oh, hello, darling.' She tried to summon up some enthusiasm. 'I was just sitting down to supper.'

'So I see,' Julia replied, eyeing it up disapprovingly.

'Would you like a glass?'

'Mum, obviously not. I'm driving.'

'One small glass wouldn't do any harm.'

'Your generation are so irresponsible! Look, eat your dinner. I actually came to apologize. Neil thinks I overreacted over Harry.'

How nice of Neil, Ella thought. Once she'd really disliked her son-in-law and thought him rigid and narrow-minded but now he seemed more reasonable than her own daughter.

Ella decided not to think about the Harry episode when she'd forgotten he wasn't insured. Maybe it wasn't to do with her memory. Maybe anyone could have done it. Anyway, it was nice of Julia to come and apologize.

Julia came back in bearing a salad she'd just made. 'Thought some home-grown chard would be nice and healthy for you, but I don't know why I bothered . . . Do you know how many calories there are in that pie? Seven hundred and forty-two!'

To be honest, Ella was a bit shocked. That did seem a lot of calories. But she was even more shocked that Julia had actually looked in her bin for the wrapper to find out. How dare she!

'And what with that glass of wine it's probably a thousand calories. Just before bed too. If you're not careful, you'll end up with diabetes.'

'Julia!'

'Okay. Okay. But are you taking plenty of exercise?' She stood looking out at Ella's small front garden. 'I don't know why you haven't started planting out there. You made such a fuss about losing the allotment.'

'It wasn't just growing things. I enjoyed the company down there.'

'I can't think why. A lot of old men in woolly hats. Anyway, don't you miss the old house?'

'I don't think about it much,' Ella replied between mouthfuls. 'It was very big for just me.' She didn't add that what she really missed was being able to talk to her husband Laurence, buried, with a special dispensation from the council, under the huge cedar of Lebanon in the garden. She'd even thought of moving him to a proper grave but it seemed sacrilegious. He'd be happier where he was.

'And I still can't see why you've moved to somewhere as risky as this. It's bound to flood, you know.'

Ella sipped the last of her wine. Julia had effectively managed to spoil the entire meal. On the other hand, she hadn't meant to. She had brought the salad as a peace offering. It was just that Julia wasn't very good at apologies.

'Right,' Ella willed herself to say, refusing to reply to this last suggestion, 'I'll have some of your lovely salad, I think. A mere eighty calories.'

'Well, I still think you're mad to move somewhere where it's clearly going to flood.'

Why couldn't Julia show Ella a little bit more sympathy and understanding and recognize that she could make her own decisions? Ella got up and gave her daughter a kiss. 'Just think, when it does, you'll be able to say I told you so with complete justification.'

'I can't believe I'm doing this.' Claudia knocked on the door of her father's shed. He hated you to just burst in. This was his private empire; he would remind any intruders gently that he was the Emperor.

His empire was a very sad one, Claudia couldn't help thinking as she pushed the door open. It was grubby and untidy with teacups and empty glasses piled up on the floor. As usual the air was tainted with the whiff of stale faeces. And as usual Claudia wanted to cry.

'Dad,' she greeted him affectionately, kissing the top of his head and trying not to breathe in, 'this is my friend Sal – you remember Sal from Gaby's wedding? – and Lou, her friend and colleague.'

Len looked up from the TV with a vague smile. 'Hello. Welcome to my little kingdom.'

'Dad, Lou has brought a little surprise for you. He's wondering, since you're an engineer, whether you could help him out with a bit of research?'

'Is he indeed?' Her father seemed to liven up at this suggestion. 'And what can an old codger like me do to help with research?'

'I've sunk a considerable amount of money into a Japanese company—'

'I'm not very fond of the Japanese,' Len replied, reaching for the remote again.

'Dad was a prisoner of war. He was one of the last soldiers who built the Thailand to Burma railway. He was only eighteen.'

Even Lou's megawatt personality seemed stunned into silence at this revelation. But not for long.

'I'd love to talk to you about that, sir.'

'I don't talk about it,' Len replied. 'Ever.'

'Now this research, it's actually about growing older.'

'As I've told my daughter many times' – the old twinkly Len

peeped out for a moment – 'growing old is crap. There's nothing to recommend it.'

'As I am discovering,' Lou grinned back. 'But this research may make it less crap.'

'How? I'm not going to sit here with wires in my head!'

Lou wondered how to sell the idea to this impressive old man. 'The research is collected in a rather unorthodox way. By this little guy.' He stood back to reveal the surprise standing just outside the door.

'What's that?' Len strained round to look. 'Some kind of Dalek?'

'He's a trained healthcare assistant.' Lou picked up the robot and brought it inside the shed. 'He's programmed to wash up, tidy rooms, remind you about when to take medicine and a bunch more as well. He's a clever little guy.'

Thank God he hadn't mentioned hygiene, Claudia thought. But Lou had had the sensitivity to avoid anything personal.

'Look, I'll switch him on.' He pressed a small remote control.

'Hello, Leonard,' announced the robot in a surprisingly lifelike tone. 'My name is Hiro. I'm pleased to meet you.'

'Well, I'm not pleased to meet you,' Len replied testily. 'Claudia, is this some damn fool idea of your mother's? A nurse in disguise to stop me smoking and ban alcohol? You can put the thing back in its box right now. I'm perfectly capable of doing everything for myself.'

'Leonard!' Her mother Olivia's commanding tones rang out from the door to the shed. 'What the hell is that *thing*? If you think we can afford for you to spend God knows what on some stupid toy just so you can take it apart and see how it works like you do with everything else, you're mistaken, I can assure you.'

Her second in command, Mrs O'Brien, was peering over her shoulder. 'Look at the state of it in here,' she mumbled. 'To think he won't even let me in to have a tidy!'

Claudia wondered who was telling the truth, her father who said the woman never came near him or the carer who claimed she was barred from doing so?

'Well, you won't need to any more,' Len announced, suddenly restored to being Emperor of his shed by this unwelcome intervention. 'In future I will have Hiro to help me.'

Nine

'You know, you really shouldn't encourage her in this mad fantasy about setting up a commune,' Sal informed Lou crossly when Claudia had left and they were back in Sal's hotel room. 'We're all only sixty for a start.'

'Sixty-six,' Lou corrected her, happily contemplating the quintessential English garden with its dark blue delphiniums and masses of rambling roses. 'I looked you up. These places start at over-fifty in the States.'

'Well, this isn't America. You always overdo everything there. Besides, I loathe the idea and I'm still working.'

'Yes, but how long will you want to go on?'

'Forever!' insisted Sal. 'I love my job. Look at Rose, she's over eighty.'

'Yeah,' Lou reminded her gently. 'But Rose owns the company.'

'And Rose and I are really close.'

'Because you're two old gals.'

'Nonsense! Look at Anna Wintour. She's sixty-eight! And Karl Lagerfeld is still designing at well over eighty. And I'd have you know none of the others are up for it. Laura's going through a hideous divorce. Ella's just bought a new house, for God's sake. It's only Claudia who's obsessed, and that's because she doesn't know what to do about her parents.'

'I rather like the idea, I have to admit,' Lou announced.

Sal looked at him incredulously. 'But you're from *Manhattan*!' Her tone implied that someone who lived in a palace and looked enviously at a mouse hole must be certifiably insane.

'Brooklyn as a matter of fact,' he corrected. 'It's not so crazy. You know I'm interested in a lot of different aspects of ageing, the magazine, robot technology in elder care ... you ...'

'How dare you!' Sal turned on him, grateful they were on their own so she could vent her fury. 'Of all the outrageous things to say ...'

She was prevented from continuing because Lou was suddenly kissing her, pushing her gently backwards towards the huge bed.

Sal began to panic. She liked Lou, more than liked him, and in some ways wanted nothing better than to have him make love to her. But there was the question of her breast. What if it revolted him?

'Lou, look ...'

He stopped, his eyes searching her face, no longer laughing. 'I'm too old for you?'

'No, no.'

'Too complicated? Too many wives and grandchildren?'

Sal shook her head. 'Not at all!'

'I'm a crass American?'

This time it was Sal who started to laugh.

'I remind you of Donald Trump?'

'It's just that ... I've had a radical mastectomy. I only have one breast. I decided not to go for reconstruction. I imagine as

153

you're from the home of cosmetic surgery that must seem a crazy choice.'

'What if I told you that, like Hitler, I only had one ball?' Lou demanded, trying not to smile. 'Would you find me repulsive?'

'No, of course not.'

'Or two but very small?'

Sal hid her face in her hands, recognizing the way this was going.

'Or what about no balls at all? Well, actually I do have balls, but the hair from my head has migrated to my nose and ears. I think that makes us roughly equivalent. I also have burgeoning man tits so I could be the one with the boobs in this relationship. How would you feel about that?'

The answer was helpless laughter.

'Good. The one thing I can do, to paraphrase the words of the immortal Woody Allen, is laugh a woman into bed.'

They fell back together onto the four-poster. Sal hoped vaguely that none of the staff would choose this moment for turn-down time, but after a few more seconds she couldn't have cared if the owner himself walked in.

He might not be the youngest lover she'd ever had, but Lou Maynard definitely didn't disappoint.

It was almost midnight by the time Calum dropped Laura back. She'd really enjoyed the evening he'd planned – a revival of François Truffaut's *Jules et Jim* followed by a meal in an unpretentious Italian restaurant nearby.

'It should really have been French after that film,' he'd suggested smilingly as they'd sat down at their table.

'Actually, I prefer Italian,' Laura had reassured. 'I adore pasta.'

An enjoyable argument had followed about Jeanne Moreau's

amazing but annoying character in the film, and they'd both agreed about that too.

The evening had rushed past and she suddenly remembered the arrangement that he'd come back with her, but when she saw that the curtains hadn't been drawn and Mrs Lal was standing in the window looking out like an outraged duenna protecting the honour of her virginal charge, she decided she'd lost her nerve. She almost expected to be challenged with the words 'What kind of time do you call this?'

Instead Laura thanked him and agreed that she'd love to go out again soon. She fought back irritation as she put her key in the lock. It was bad enough trying to work round Sam, but now Mrs Lal as well!

'Good evening, Mrs Minchin,' her guest greeted her. Laura had suggested the use of Christian names but had got nowhere. Mrs Lal preferred formality. 'Did you have an enjoyable evening?'

'Yes, lovely,' Laura replied, longing for a cup of chamomile tea in bed. 'I hope you did too?'

'Yes, my daughter and son-in-law took me out to dinner.'

'Great.' She wondered what had happened to the pizza plan. 'Where did you go?'

Laura tried not to choke. The restaurant she named would probably have set them back £150 a head! Laura hadn't even been there when she and Simon were feeling flush. 'Right,' Laura replied faintly. 'And how was it?'

'The foie gras was disappointing,' Laura fought down the giggles that threatened to engulf her. Oh dear, poor Mr and Mrs A having to shell out a fortune for disappointing foie gras.

'Would you like to know what I thought of your escort tonight?' Mrs Lal enquired. 'From a professional point of view?'

No. In fact, she wanted to put her fingers in her ears and go 'la la la la la' all the way to bed rather than hear it.

'He wore suede shoes,' Mrs Lal pronounced magisterially. 'And of course you know what they say about that.'

'No.' Laura really was getting the giggles now. 'What do they say?'

'Never trust a man who is too good-looking or wears suede shoes. That was the first piece of advice my own father gave me.'

'And why do people think that? Could it be that they're stupid and ignorant?'

'Because they aren't trustworthy, Mrs Minchin.'

Laura wondered if she dared ask what they thought of a man who wore suede shoes *and* was too good-looking. But Mrs Lal's next comment effectively shut her up.

'And I don't think he should have taken a call from his wife while he was waiting for you. If you ask me, they sounded altogether too chummy.'

'What the hell is that?' Claudia's husband Don demanded as he leaned over her shoulder scanning the spreadsheet she had created.

'Can't I even have half an hour of privacy?' Claudia answered evasively. She had taken herself upstairs to the small study in the hope of avoiding his scrutiny.

'It's not bloody Igden Manor again?' Don demanded furiously. 'Retirement plans for the Coven? No wonder none of your friends has a husband between them. You're all obsessed with each other! And as for privacy, you can have as much as you want. I'm taking the dog for a walk. I may be some time.'

Claudia wanted to shout that it wasn't just for the Coven,

Don's horrible name for her and her friends, but for their daughter, and for her parents! And hadn't she given up her beloved London and her job as a teacher to come and live here because *he* wanted to?

She made herself a cup of coffee, feeling guilty that she and Don had agreed to try and start again together after she almost had an affair with Daniel the choirmaster. Oh God. Why didn't life get simpler as you got older? By this age her parents just saw themselves as old and didn't really expect anything from life, but Claudia didn't *feel* old. Besides, what she was working on was something she believed would make things better for all of them, the best of both worlds, as she kept reminding herself. Friendship *and* care. And fun too.

She grabbed her bag and looked for her mobile to dial the number of her son-in-law Douglas, the architect.

'Hello, Douglas, Claudia here. I wondered if I could ask you for some advice? I've got this idea that everyone else but me seems to think is completely bonkers. You've always struck me as particularly grown-up and sane. Do you think you could – very discreetly – come and meet me this week at Igden Manor Hotel and I'll enlighten you?'

'How intriguing,' her son-in-law replied. 'Is it something Gaby knows about? Only I don't like keeping things from her at this stage of our marriage.'

'Though you will later?' Claudia couldn't resist saying. 'Sorry, that was naughty of me. Yes, by all means tell her. But it's your professional advice I'm after at this early stage.'

'Right. Tomorrow at eleven? I have to be down your way later in the day so that would work for me.'

'Tomorrow at eleven it is.'

Claudia almost held her breath. She was actually taking a

step, no matter how tiny, towards making the dream a reality.

'Hello, Leonard, maybe you and I should get to know each other.'

Len looked across at the metal manikin with its large humanoid eyes, long articulated arms and triangular body on wheels. It made him think of an upright hoover in a miniskirt.

'You're smiling, Leonard. I'm happy that you're happy.'

'I'm not happy! I'm furious I let them foist a damn robot onto me!'

'My name is Hiro. I'm a hundred and twenty centimetres tall and I weigh twenty-eight kilos. I have been designed as a companion.'

'I'm Len,' Len replied. 'I'm six foot three and I weigh eleven stone. I'm designed to be a husband. When I'm allowed. And I don't know why the hell I'm talking to you when you're a lump of metal with an algorithm for a brain.'

'You're very funny, Len. Do you like jokes?'

'Oh, for God's sake! I'm ninety-two years old, not eight!'

'Why didn't the skeleton cross the road?' Hiro persisted.

'I don't know,' Len replied wearily. 'Why didn't the skeleton cross the road?'

'Because he didn't have the guts to do it!'

Despite himself, Len found he was laughing.

'So, what do you like to do, Leonard?'

'Nothing,' Len replied grumpily, returning to his copy of *The Racing Post*.

'That doesn't sound very good for you.'

'I don't like things that are good for me.'

'I see from your preferred reading matter that you enjoy

horse racing. Perhaps I could help you with that. I have a very good brain.'

Len looked at him thoughtfully. 'I wonder if you could.' A thought occurred to him. 'I suppose you could come to the betting shop in Manningbury to pick up my coupons. I don't suppose you drive?'

'That's not yet one of my capabilities.'

'Never mind. We could go on the bus. In fact, let's go now.'

Len reached for his stick, delighted at the prospect of the bored betting staff confronting a robot on a Monday morning in Manningbury.

'Do you need the toilet first, Leonard?' Hiro asked in the politely neutral tone he used for all his conversation.

'No, I do not!' Len paused. Actually, maybe he did. He wasn't very good at telling these days.

'I can always help, you know,' Hiro offered.

'I'm not having a damn robot wiping my arse!' Len shouted back.

'You have to remember, Leonard, I'm not a real person. I'm just here to help you.'

'I'll ask for your help when I need it.'

'Then I'll be happy to supply it. Would you like a hug?'

'No, I would not like a hug!'

Together they made their way up the path by the side of the house to the road.

Mrs O'Brien, glancing out of the window, dropped the mug she was holding. 'Mrs Warren, will you take a look at that?' she screeched.

Olivia and Mrs O'Brien peered out at Len and Hiro. 'Oh my God, this is all my daughter Claudia's fault. People will think he's off his head talking away to that giant piece of Meccano.

I'll have to get Claudia to come and take it away before my husband is the laughing stock of the village!'

But Claudia wasn't answering her phone. She had turned it off so that she could concentrate properly on her spreadsheet.

'Oh my God, what time is it?'

Sal sat up and reached for her dressing gown. Lou might have persuaded her that her Amazon appearance didn't put him off – a fact he had proved not once but twice – but she didn't like walking around one-breasted.

She had originally planned to go back to London last night but Lou had talked her into staying. Her secret smile of satisfaction attested that it had been well worth it. But she'd planned to get up early and catch the train so that she could be in the office by ten.

'Dunno,' Lou mumbled, fumbling for his watch on the bedside table. 'Nine thirty.'

'Oh, bloody hell! I meant to catch the train an hour ago!'

Lou reached over and started to undo her wrap. She grabbed his hand. 'Okay, Mr Insatiable, I get the message, and a very nice one it is too, but it'll have to wait. I have an editorial meeting at eleven.'

'You'll never make it anyway,' he grinned, reminding Sal of a good-natured satyr. 'You might as well call in sick.'

'I never even called in sick when I was sick,' Sal smiled back.

'Now that's what I call stubborn. I was hoping for breakfast in bed.'

'I hate breakfast in bed,' Sal asserted. 'All those crumbs.'

'You say potato . . .' Lou took her hand. 'We're obviously completely unsuited. Stuck-up Brits.' He began to kiss her again.

Reluctantly she broke away. 'Crass Americans. No sense of irony. Look, I really do have to get dressed.'

She went into the bathroom and quietly closed the door. Funny how you could make love to someone but not want to have them hear you pee. She hurriedly applied her make-up and dragged a brush through her new growth of hair. She couldn't stop herself smiling. She had no idea where this relationship was going to go, but what the hell? Rose would of course have guessed, especially with Sal being late when she was never late.

Oh well.

'I've ordered you a cab in fifteen minutes,' Lou announced from the depths of the four-poster. 'You'll have time to grab a bite in the restaurant. The next train's at ten twenty-five. You should just make it.'

Sal, who treasured her independence fiercely, found herself revelling in handing over the reins to a personality that was even stronger than her own.

'How about you?' she asked, still smiling.

'I'll have breakfast in bed. Just me and the crumbs.'

She sat on the edge of the bed and kissed him again. A horrible thought slapped her in the face. She had no idea how long he intended to stay. For all she knew he might be going back to Brooklyn tomorrow.

'What are your plans?' she asked, suddenly self-conscious. It wasn't her style to cling. But then it wasn't her style to fall for someone as she'd fallen for Lou Maynard.

'What, after I've had breakfast in bed?' he grinned at her tantalizingly.

'With that expression,' she informed him, 'you look just like Tigger.'

'I feel just like Tigger.' He took her hand. 'And it's all down

161

to you. I ought to stay here a day or two and then I'm coming back to London when I hope to persuade you to come out to dinner.'

A thought occurred to her. 'What are you going to do with the robot?'

'Leave him with your friend's dad. He's doing important research, remember.'

'What happens if Len doesn't want him?' she replied dubiously.

'He will. Hiro's a very taking little fellow.'

'Have I gone mad,' Sal asked him, 'falling for a man I hardly know who talks to robots?'

'If your symptoms are making me laugh and having wild sex twice on our first date, I truly hope so.'

'It's not our first date,' Sal corrected primly. 'We had brunch at Brook's.'

'That was work. On current experience I have high hopes for our second date.'

'Don't count your chickens. I may decide to go celibate.'

'Ms Grainger.' He kissed her hand. 'I truly hope not.'

In the taxi on the way to the station she stared dreamily out of the window. She really ought to be planning the agenda for the editorial meeting, not reliving sex with Lou. Once she got on the train she made herself put him out of her mind. Fortunately it was only a short journey and once she reached Waterloo there was a long row of black cabs waiting. Sal jumped gratefully into the first.

'The Harrow Road, please,' she told the cabbie. 'Near where it meets Ladbroke Grove.' She'd better just call the office and tell them she'd be there in half an hour but she couldn't find her phone. Damn! It must still be in the room. She'd have to get Lou to bring it. How on earth would she survive even a day or two without it? If she hadn't been daydreaming about Lou, she'd have noticed as soon as she'd left.

Thirty minutes later the cab drew up outside *New Grey* and Sal willed herself to be the self-possessed magazine editor.

'Hello,' she greeted the receptionist. 'I'm a bit late for my meeting with Rose. Have they started yet, do you know?'

'Oh my God, Sal,' was the stunned answer. 'Do you really not know?' The usually cheerful woman on reception looked the colour of a three-week-old sheet. 'Rose has had a heart attack. She's in intensive care in St Mary's Hospital!'

Ten

Sal felt her own heart almost seize up at the news.

Without her realizing it, Rose had become a lodestone in her universe: mother, confessor, advisor, trusted colleague, perhaps the only person in her life who she felt truly understood her. It had been Rose who had offered her the job editing the magazine when she was over sixty and had found work almost impossible to get. It had been Rose who guessed about her cancer and reassured her that her job would be unaffected. And it had been Rose who understood how it felt to be a woman from a humble background who had fought all her life for her achievements. And Rose, for her part, had seemed indestructible.

'How is she?' Sal struggled to keep her voice under control. 'What have the doctors said so far?'

'I don't know. Michael went in the ambulance with her and he's still there.'

'Is she allowed visitors, do you know?' Sal demanded, not even stopping for an answer. Even if visitors were banned, Sal knew she would have to try and see her, if only to touch her hand and somehow convey how much she meant to her.

'Right. I'll ring Michael now from my office. How has everyone taken it?'

'Total shock. Imagine if the Queen had died and multiply it by a hundred. People feel Rose *is* the company.'

She called Michael but his phone was switched off and she was only able to leave a message. The next call was to Lou.

'I know, I know,' he replied at the first ring. 'Michael's already messaged me.' Hearing his voice was the only thing that could possibly have comforted her. 'I'm coming straight up. I know how important she is to you.'

It was so wonderful not to have to explain to him that someone who wasn't a blood relation, whom in fact she'd known only a relatively short time, could matter so much to her. But Lou had instantly understood.

'I don't know if she has any relatives . . .' Sal tried to remember if Rose had ever talked of family members.

'Apparently there's a nephew in Canada. Some kind of jet-setting businessman. Michael's already contacted him.'

'Maybe if he's jet-setting he'll jump on a plane and come at once. Did Michael say anything about the prognosis?'

'The heart attack was major, but they've performed a procedure to widen the arteries.'

'I can't get through to Michael. I think I'm just going to go to the hospital and see. I couldn't bear it if it was bad news and I hadn't tried to see her.'

'Absolutely. The magazine will survive . . .'

A beat of silence fell between them as they both had the same thought. But Rose might not . . .

'What time will you be in London?'

'About four. I need to say goodbye to my daughter and the baby.'

'Come to the magazine. Lou ...' Sal hesitated, suddenly unsure of herself.

'Yes?' The comforting warmth of his voice gave her back her confidence.

'You can stay with me if you want.'

She loved that he replied without a moment's hesitation. 'That would be terrific.'

'And could you bring my phone? It's probably under the bed.'

As she walked up the steps to the hospital half an hour later all the fear she'd tried to submerge when she'd had cancer came rushing to the surface like stinking water in a drain.

Rose! She repeated the mantra as she queued at the busy reception desk. *Rose, don't you dare die!*

She washed her hands at the antiseptic dispenser by the lifts and took the fast lift to the eighteenth floor. The view up here was spectacular, the whole of London laid at your feet. She hoped Rose would get the chance to appreciate it.

You needed a code to get through the doors into the high-dependency ward but a young doctor was going through who let her pass.

She asked at the nurses' station for Rose's whereabouts and was informed firmly that this was the patients' rest time.

'Sally!' a commanding voice rang through an open door. 'Sal! Is that you? Thank God, can you go and get me a decent cup of tea? The stuff they give you here tastes like cat piss.'

Sal almost cried with relief. It was the quintessential Rose McGill.

The sight of her friend and employer was less reassuring. Rose sat propped up with tubes and plasma bags surrounding her like trees in a forest. Worse, without her usual dramatic clothes and coiffed hair she suddenly looked vulnerable and old.

'Rose!' Sal rushed to her bedside and took the heavily be-ringed hand in hers. 'Thank God you're all right.'

'I think that's probably a bit of an overstatement. Alive might be more accurate,' Rose replied with a small attempt at a grin. 'Now about this tea. Make sure the water's absolutely boiling and they don't put the milk in at the same time. These cafes are all staffed by young people who may be absolutely charming but have no idea how to make a proper cup of tea.'

'I'll get it now,' Sal promised, grateful to have a practical task. 'Where's Michael?'

'Gone back to the office to reassure the troops I'm not dead. Yet.'

'Okay, I'll be right back.' Sal disappeared out of the ward, better able to appreciate the amazing view now that she knew Rose was sitting up and talking. In the nearest cafe she repeated Rose's strict orders to the barista and picked up a scone with butter and jam to go with it. Hospitals always seemed to feed you when you didn't want to eat and left you to starve when you did.

Back up in the ward Rose surveyed the paper cup critically. 'Not bad. At least it's brown. And thanks for the scone. I'll save it for later. Now sit here beside me on that chair.' She sipped the tea with relish. 'In my experience there isn't any situation a cup of tea can't improve, except possibly dying, and they don't seem to think the Grim Reaper's lurking just yet. I have to take things easy, though, apparently. Time to take my hand off the tiller.' She sighed deeply and fixed Sal with her familiar penetrating gaze. 'Don't make the mistake I made and put all your money and love into your job. Not that I didn't enjoy every minute of it but it has left me somewhat up shit creek.

No doting children to come and offer me a granny flat. Just this nephew I've only met once in his life.'

Sal wanted to hug her in sympathy, remembering how when she'd had her cancer she'd had to pretend the minicab driver was her husband in order to be allowed home. The joys of single life.

'I suppose I'll have to go to some godawful convalescent place where they'll charge a fortune and won't let me have a drink.'

'How about a friend you could stay with?'

'My dear Sal, when you get to my age your friends are all dead.' She hesitated, visibly upset. 'Look, my dear girl, they've told me I can't go back to work. I know the magazine will be safe in your hands but I'm afraid I'm going to need to fund my declining years.' She reached out a hand to Sal. 'And that means selling the business. I've asked my nephew to supervise. He's quite smart, they tell me. I'm so sorry but I don't see any alternative.'

Sal sat up very straight and looked out of the window to hide her dismay. She'd finally found a job she loved and then this happened.

Stop being such a selfish cow!

'The main thing is for you to get better.' She returned the pressure of Rose's hand.

'And what about you and Lou? Now that I'm in intensive care I'm allowed to ask impertinent questions. I'm sorry I'm dropping him in it but I suspect he can afford to take a small hit. Did you have a lovely weekend? I think it's so funny you stayed in a hotel owned by Murdo Binns. I told you, I knew him quite well once.'

A small secret smile lit up Rose's gaunt features, making

her look almost young again. Sal wondered what had passed between Rose and Lord Binns that made her look so happy.

'Yes,' Sal replied, deciding it would be too intrusive to ask.

'Good. Lou's a nice man and I suspect, despite your tough exterior, you could do with a nice man.'

'Yes.' Sal couldn't help smiling and shaking her head. 'But I'm not sure he's planning to stay here.'

Laura was grateful that Mrs Lal was out when the surveyor for the purchasers arrived. He seemed to be an amiable young man, grateful when she offered him a coffee, and nicely mannered. The prospective buyers were both lawyers, he told her with a raised eyebrow, and seemed to be in rather a hurry. They had asked for the survey by the end of tomorrow.

He then asked Laura lots of questions about where the stopcock was, which made her giggle, so that she had to apologize both for the giggle and the fact that she had no idea.

In the end he gave up on Laura when she didn't know where the gas meter was or where the fibre optic entered. Laura said she didn't know they *had* fibre optic.

She could have rung Simon but she didn't want to give him the pleasure of saying 'For God's sake, Laura!' He had sacrificed the right to sarcasm along with conjugal rights when he ran off with Suki.

'Right,' announced the surveyor briskly as soon as he'd finished. 'I'd better get a move on if I'm going to finish this by tomorrow. My boss says he's never seen a couple in so much of a hurry. They told him they wanted to complete as soon as possible.'

'But we haven't even exchanged contracts yet!' Laura panicked. The British legal process over house buying was so slow she'd assumed she'd have a couple of months yet, even if everything went smoothly.

The young surveyor shrugged. Mrs Minchin was a nice lady and she'd given him a coffee and a chocolate digestive so he took a risk and gave her some advice. 'At least this way it won't fall through. Maybe you'd better start planning. Have you got somewhere lined up?'

'I've put in an offer for a flat.'

'That's good.' He glanced round at Laura's crowded sitting room, adorned with countless mementoes from her marriage and family life. 'A big job moving from here. How long have you been here?'

'Only twenty-five years.' Laura attempted a smile and found it harder than she'd expected.

'Well, good luck with it all.'

Laura let him out and half ran to the phone to ring Ella about the flat. They needed to get on the case at once. She'd also better get a move on or she was going to be late for work.

Claudia sat at the PC in their small study, nursing a cup of coffee and feeling very proud of herself. She'd worked on the business plan almost all night and – though she said it herself – it looked highly professional. It was also to some extent a work of fantasy in terms of actual income, but then weren't most business plans?

She pressed Print and watched the pages spewing out with an enormous grin on her face before the cold wind of reality made her confront one question. Who exactly was going to live in the place? So far her best friends, the basis of the idea in the first place, were all resisting and even if she could persuade her parents and Don to sell up, who the hell else would live there?

Would there be any point to the disruption if they had to advertise for strangers to join the venture?

Claudia told herself she wouldn't think about that now. Lou had told her to send it to him when she'd finished for his advice and that was what she would bloody well do. There, she'd sent it!

Next was her meeting with Douglas, her architect son-in-law. They'd have to be discreet, obviously, and pretend to be just strolling round the grounds.

First, though, she'd promised Lou she'd drop round to her parents' house and report on how her father was getting on with Hiro. If it was a disaster, Lou had said he'd pick the robot up and chalk it down to experience.

She drove the half-mile between her own house and her parents' and parked down the side near her father's shed. Normally the first thing she heard when she got out of the car was her mother's bossy tones or the buzz of chatter between Olivia and Mrs O'Brien.

Today there was silence. Beginning to worry, Claudia pushed open the shed door, and stopped, stunned. The place looked like something out of a magazine. Every object had been restored to its home, the washing-up done, the rugs that dotted the wooden floor hoovered. Sunlight streamed in from shiny clean windows onto her father, sitting on the sofa with Hiro standing behind him looking over his shoulder, apparently at Len's iPad. Both were so engrossed they didn't notice Claudia's arrival.

'Hello, Dad,' Claudia greeted him. 'It looks terrific in here.'

Len looked round as if he hadn't even noticed. 'Oh, good. Hiro and I have been down to the betting shop in Manningbury. He caused quite a sensation, I can tell you.'

'I imagine he might.' Claudia tried not to laugh at the

thought of all the seedy regulars being faced with a three-foot robot.

'We picked up my coupons and some race cards. We're just working out the odds now.'

Hiro straightened up and faced Claudia. 'What kind of horse can swim underwater?' he asked improbably.

'I don't know. What kind of horse can swim underwater?'

'A seahorse,' replied the robot with something approaching a smile.

'Hiro thinks we should bet online. A lot easier than dragging ourselves to Manningbury on the bus.'

A sudden fear jolted through Claudia. She'd had to wean her mother off the addiction she'd developed for online vouchers and offers. What if her father went down the same route?

Len seemed to guess her thoughts. 'Don't worry, love. Hiro only lets me bet a pound.'

Her father grinned at the robot which rocked back and forth in an electronic attempt at laughter.

'You two are so funny,' she informed them. 'You remind me of the two old men on *Sesame Street*.'

'Time for the toilet, Leonard,' the robot suddenly piped up.

To Claudia's amazement her father began to get to his feet.

'As long as he's making me money,' Len grinned at his daughter, 'I've agreed to do what he says.'

'I'll leave you to it then.' Claudia turned to the door and as she closed it behind her she realized the other miraculous development.

There was no more horrible smell. Hiro was worth every cent of the millions that had been spent on his development.

*

When Laura arrived at LateExpress she was surprised to find both Mr and Mrs A standing behind the till, deep in anguished conversation.

Even before she could disappear into the back to find her Day-Glo tabard with LateExpress emblazoned on the pocket, Mrs A turned to her with the tragic look of Cleopatra contemplating the asp.

'Mrs Minchin, firstly we would like to thank you for your great kindness to my mother.'

Laura nodded, wondering what was coming next. 'I've enjoyed having her. As a matter of fact, where is she? She left in a taxi early this morning. I assumed to meet up with you.'

'You have not heard of our catastrophe then?' enquired Mr A.

Laura shook her head. She did hope the business wasn't in trouble. They'd worked so hard establishing it.

'It's Mrs Lal,' announced Mr A in the tone of a funeral director.

'What's happened?' demanded Laura anxiously.

'She has decided to stay in the UK.' He reached out a hand to Mrs A. It struck Laura that she'd never seen them touch before. 'Permanently.'

In the taxi on the way back to *New Grey* Sal had to struggle to keep herself from breaking down. She'd been through so much: the cancer, the fear of growing old alone and in poverty, and then Rose had rescued her with the offer of the job editing the magazine. Now that would finish.

She wondered for a mad moment if Lou might take over the magazine. After all, he owned part of the company. But reality bit with all the instant terror of her submerged fears. She'd only known Lou Maynard for a few weeks. They got on like old friends and their lovemaking had made them both feel young again. But what did she really know about him? He had ex-wives and grandchildren in the US, a flourishing business in Brooklyn. His roots were there, not here.

Sal, who had spent her whole life distrusting men, had finally trusted one and maybe it would turn out to be the biggest mistake of her life.

Now she would have to deal with the collective worry of everyone who worked on the magazine just when she would have liked to collapse quietly. With the mania for open-plan she didn't even have an office of her own. Rose had suggested she break the news to everyone as gently as she could, not be dishonest but try and persuade people to wait until Rose's nephew arrived and things became clearer. For now, they should try and keep things as normal as possible.

Sal pushed open the swing doors into the magazine and could instantly sense the tension hanging in the air. No one had gone to lunch. Instead they hung about in hushed little groups.

'How is Rose?' demanded the receptionist instantly.

'Very weak,' Sal replied in a serious tone. 'But also very much still with us. Could you get everyone to come to Rose's office in an hour and I'll give you all an update.'

Suddenly she wished that Lou was coming earlier. She could do with his reassurance and his lightbulb energy. *Stop it, Sal*, she told herself firmly, *you've never depended on a man yet. Don't start now.*

Just walking into Rose's office made Sal want to cry. It was so completely like Rose herself: individual, unconventional and yet somehow remarkably cosy. She sat behind the vast mahogany desk and thought about what she was going to say.

By the time the staff, from the receptionist to the writers, commissioning editors and salespeople, all looking universally glum, had trooped in she had it clear in her mind.

'The first and most important thing to tell you is that Rose is going to survive.'

There was a palpable release of tension, like the slackening of a rubber band.

Everyone liked and admired Rose. Now the not so good bit.

'Unfortunately, Rose has been told work will now be out of the question because of her age. But she does have a nephew who is a successful businessman and he is coming to take over the reins of the business.' She didn't have to tell them he'd probably sell it. After all, maybe he wouldn't. 'Rose says the best thing we can do to aid her recovery is to keep calm and carry on.'

There was a ripple of laughter as they could all imagine Rose saying this herself.

'So, thanks, everyone. And back to work.'

They all filed out, murmuring to each other. It was barely ten minutes till reception buzzed her to announce that Lou was here.

She was already standing up by the time he arrived and shut the door firmly behind him.

'How are you?' was his first question as he came straight towards her with his arms wide open. Even though she was taller than he was, Sal sank gratefully into his comforting embrace.

'Well, first, overwhelmingly relieved that Rose is recovering. Second, pretty crap because she intends to get her nephew to sell. Obviously I haven't told the troops that.'

He perched on the side of Rose's desk. 'No.' There was a pause when he took one of Sal's hands. 'Now don't worry, it'll all work out in the end. One small bit of good news. Well, I hope you think it's good news . . .'

Sal's heart surged. Maybe, like she'd imagined earlier, he was going to say *he* was considering taking over the company himself.

'I just got your friend's business plan about her retirement idea and I've decided to make an investment. Nothing major but I'd like to see how the whole thing pans out.' He produced his dazzling smile and blazed her with it. 'Who knows, maybe I'd like to live there myself one day?'

As soon as she'd finished her shift Laura called Ella in a panic. 'Ella, it's about the flat we saw. As long as the survey's okay, my buyers want to complete as soon as they can!'

'But isn't that a good thing if you really want that flat we saw? They were keen to sell quickly too.'

'I'd like to go round to the agent first thing tomorrow and make sure I'm really going to get it. Will you come with me?'

'Can't you just ring them?' Ella had been planning to finally plant her front border.

'I always think going in is better. They put a name to a face and care more.'

'*Estate agents*,' laughed Ella. 'Of course I'll come. What time do they open?'

'Nine o'clock. I've just googled them. Is that okay for you?'

When Laura had rung off, Ella wrote herself a Post-it note and stuck it on the kitchen counter to remind herself. Then she took a step back and stared at it. When had she started having to do that? People with dementia did that.

Ella sat down heavily on the arm of the sofa. The truth was, she *was* concerned about her memory lapses. Look at how she'd let Harry drive her car uninsured, completely forgetting he wasn't covered. And she was forever forgetting people's names, the routes from A to B, even really familiar ones. And there had been those really scary moments when she'd sat in the car and – just for a split second – not known what to do.

She should either see her GP or do one of those online memory tests. Just imagine if Julia got wind of it. She'd be all over Ella like the measles, telling her what to do, taking over her life. It didn't bear thinking about.

So *not* thinking about it was exactly what Ella would do. She headed for the fridge to pour a glass of wine and paused. White wine was probably part of the problem. Oh, sod it. She'd rather have a glass of wine and be forgetful.

After he'd dropped his bombshell Lou left Sal at the office while he dropped in to see Rose in hospital. She was grateful to have had the time alone with him. She'd hidden it from Lou but she was actually terrified about the future. The months alone in her flat came back to haunt her, when she'd applied for every job that seemed even vaguely possible and been rejected by all of them.

Except at *New Grey* when wonderful Rose McGill had ignored her age and recognized her talent. It had seemed like a miracle at the time. And now, just when things were going so well, it was all going to collapse. And instead of increasing his investment in the business to try and keep it going, Lou was going to put money into Claudia's stupid retirement scheme!

And the thing was, Lou was shrewd. He wasn't some amateur investor who put money into any old scheme as if it were the 3.40 at Cheltenham. He knew what he was doing.

Sal realized, in the back of her mind, she'd had a secret fantasy. Without even admitting it to herself she'd dreamed he might suggest she come back to Brooklyn with him, that they might have a more permanent future.

How ridiculous. She was a one-breasted sixty-six-year-old, no matter how chic and sassy, and the odds were wildly stacked against her. Lou might be older than her but the Darwinian rules of dating decreed that he could pick any woman from thirty to fifty. What was that statistic she'd read the other day? More than forty per cent of women over fifty-five in the UK lived alone. Could that be true? She couldn't remember where she'd seen it. If it was true, it wasn't simply that older women were more likely to be killed by a terrorist than find a man, as wonderful Nora Ephron had quoted; they were more likely to *be* a terrorist than find a man!

Sal shook herself. She must stop thinking like this. She was strong. She was brave. She had fought off cancer. Instead of all this negative thinking she should go home and make the flat welcoming before Lou arrived.

Sal's shoulders sagged. The trouble was, she didn't feel strong and brave today. But maybe with Lou's comforting bear hug, she would remember she was Sally Grainger, brave and bold editor of *New Grey*.

But for how long?

Eleven

Ella bought a cappuccino and waited for Laura in the cafe opposite the estate agent's. Five minutes later Laura emerged from the tube station and started walking towards her, looking ludicrously young and pretty in one of her pastel cardis, her make-up perfect as usual.

Over the years Ella had sometimes suspected that either Laura slept in her make-up or got up an hour early to apply it.

Ella waved. 'Right, are you ready to charm the socks off the agent?'

'Not if they're anything like Stu the Scumbag who's selling our house,' Laura replied. 'But I suppose they can't all be as horrible as he is.'

Ella pushed the door open for her and Laura went in.

'Hello,' she announced. 'My name's Laura Minchin. I've made an offer on 22 Rydale Road. The sale on my existing house is probably going through much quicker than expected, but we haven't heard back from your vendor yet and I'd really like to get a survey done as soon as possible, ideally in the next day or two.'

The agent, a young girl in what struck Ella as a really rather unsuitable mini-dress, put down her toffee muffin and licked her fingers, suddenly taking on the appearance of a hunted deer.

'Er,' she began, glancing over at the manager who was busily ignoring her and leaving her to her fate. 'The thing is . . .'

Ella didn't like the sound of this at all.

'The thing is . . . ?'

'Well, er . . .'

'Well, er, what?'

'I'm afraid the vendor has accepted a higher offer,' she blurted finally.

'And you didn't have the goodness to let us know in case we might like to amend ours?' demanded Ella, seeing the devastated expression on Laura's face.

'It all happened very quickly yesterday. And they were cash buyers,' she added limply.

'Is it definite?' Laura insisted.

'They're doing the survey now. I suppose they might find something awful . . .' The girl's voice trailed off.

'Bloody estate agents!' Ella muttered. 'The whole system's fixed anyway.'

'We do have this nice flat in Hounslow,' the girl suggested, starting to click on her screen.

'My friend doesn't want to live in Hounslow!' snapped Ella, feeling guilty that she hadn't advised Laura to have some back-up options.

'Oh God,' Laura announced as they trailed out. 'You know what this means? Those pushy lawyers want me to move out in a month and I have absolutely nowhere to go. And if I delay, Simon will say I'm just trying to block the move.'

'If I were you,' Ella insisted angrily, wishing Laura could be a bit more feisty, 'I'd try telling Simon to go screw himself instead of hitting on his junior colleagues!'

Sal rushed home, stopping for flowers, milk, bread, cereal and all the basics of normal everyday life. All that was usually in her fridge was white wine and she suspected this might not a) make the best impression or b) provide a suitable breakfast.

North Kensington was its usual self – a combination of depressing and grungy, but with colourful outposts of gentrification, even of hipsterdom. A vintage clothes shop and a trendy bakery had sprung up in the shops beneath her flat and, much to Sal's amusement, a day spa called Posh, though Sal had to admit, it didn't look that posh to her.

She glanced round her basement flat, wondering what Lou would make of it. She had decorated it not long ago in what the young man applying the paint had smilingly dubbed 'fifty shades of grey'. Sal had decided grey was restful as well as fashionable and after all, she worked for a magazine called *New Grey*.

Aware that restful could be mistaken for dull, she had enlivened it with what the design magazines called 'pops of colour' with hot-pink cushions and a large arrangement of faux peonies in an arresting shade of fuchsia.

She had adorned the walls with large oil paintings acquired from various affordable art fairs and student degree shows. In fact, it had been a fantasy of Sal's that she might try painting herself one day; these didn't look that hard to produce after all.

In preparation for Lou's arrival she'd opened a bottle of Chablis, which she knew he liked, and booked dinner in a bistro round the corner. Trying to cook for Lou herself was a step too far.

She'd already changed the sheets and duvet cover on her

large bed and toyed with putting candles next to it to flatter the ageing flesh but decided it would look too presumptuous. It again struck Sal how short a time they'd known each other. Maybe she was the late middle-aged equivalent of a holiday romance.

The doorbell rang and there he was in the stairwell, clutching a bunch of long-stemmed roses.

'Come in.' She took the flowers almost shyly, put them in the kitchen sink and turned to find herself enveloped in a Lou Maynard bear hug. Sal closed her eyes and let herself be held. It was extraordinarily comforting.

'How was Rose?' she enquired, reluctantly raising her face from his cashmere cardigan.

'More at a loss than I've ever seen her,' Lou replied. 'A strong lady having to face her own weakness and not liking it one bit. She asked if you'd do her a favour and check out some convalescent homes.'

'Of course.' Sal handed him a glass of wine.

'But the real problem is the long term. The words sheltered housing – I think that's what you call it here – make her come out in hives. She's frightened of being alone, Sal.'

'Aren't we all?' Sal almost replied, but didn't want to admit her own weakness. 'Which reminds me,' she added pointedly, 'why on earth are you even thinking of investing in my friend Claudia's mad scheme in Surrey?'

'Maybe Rose isn't the only person frightened of getting old.'

'*You*, old?' she smiled back. 'You'll never be old. Just more experienced at life.'

'Thank you.' He bowed. 'My favourite daughter's nearby. Besides, I love olde England.' He went quiet for a moment. 'Hey, what about Rose moving into your friend's anti-retirement village? You said she wanted all ages. What was her description? A cross between a student flat and a kibbutz. Rose would fit right in. And didn't you say something about Rose knowing the old aristo who owns it? An old flame from the past?'

'Well, she did seem a bit coy when she mentioned him. Look, Lou' – Sal knew her friend would kill her for saying this – 'this scheme of Claudia's. It's never going to happen. She hasn't even persuaded her husband yet.'

Lou shrugged, smiling his light-up-the-room smile. 'I wouldn't be so sure. Her son-in-law – Douglas is it? – has done some basic calculations on how to use the space as well as a very cute sketch of how it all might look.'

He pulled out his iPad. There, all in black and white, was Douglas's vision of Igden Manor as some kind of twilight towers.

Sal reeled in shock. There was something about seeing it like that all down on paper that made her feel it might actually happen.

Lou's next words only served to enhance the impression. 'As a matter of fact, I'm going down there tomorrow to help your friend discuss a lease.'

'What?' Sal squeaked. 'She never said anything to me!'

'She's got a lot on her plate, what with her parents . . .'

'And an unexpected guest – your robot,' Sal added acidly.

'Now, now. I gather Hiro's quite a hit locally. He's a nice little guy.'

'He's not a guy at all,' snapped Sal. 'He's a lump of metal with computer chip for a brain!'

'You've got to be more open, Sally,' Lou teased. 'The world's changing. Artificial intelligence is everywhere. Robots are a reality even if Hiro is a hundred times more sophisticated than they are.'

'Well, I preferred it the other way. When I still had a job.'

Lou put his arms round her. 'Come on, you're a strong woman.'

The sympathy in his voice was too much for her. The Sal who had lived alone all her life, always self-supporting, getting through cancer without telling anyone, suddenly collapsed. 'I've been so stupid, Lou. I'm about to be jobless and I've always spent to the hilt. Even this flat' – she looked around at her stylish refuge, the one place she'd been able to retreat to and lick her wounds when life got tough – 'is only rented. If I wasn't earning and couldn't pay, I'd lose this place as well.' To her absolute horror she found she was crying.

Oh my God – the thought drummed into her consciousness – *every bloody article we've ever run about impressing men says to be strong and independent and here you are blubbing like a very ancient baby!*

But Lou, wonderful Lou, didn't seem in the slightest bit fazed. 'Look, I'm going to Surrey to help Claudia because negotiating leases is my business; it would be crazy not to offer my help when I've said I'll invest. And when I get back I'll take a look at your lease. You never know, maybe there's a pot of gold at the end of it.'

'Would you?' Even that was comforting, though not as comforting as if he'd said, 'Beautiful Sally, come back to Brooklyn and live with me there.'

But clearly he wasn't going to. Maybe it was time she accepted that opting to stay here and get involved in Claudia's mad scheme seemed to matter to him. And maybe it ought to start mattering to her.

'Why don't you look for a convalescent place for Rose down in Surrey and then, if this Igden Manor looks like it's happening, she can come and see it.'

'Fine,' Sal heard herself saying, though she was still reeling that Claudia's mad scheme seemed to be becoming a reality. 'I'll do just that. Now, would you like a drink before we go and eat?'

Lou looked into her eyes. 'There are other ways that occur to me of passing the next hour.' He nodded towards the bed. 'That is, if you were agreeable?'

'Oh yes,' Sal smiled, thanking the powers that be for sending this lovely man into her life, even if it was only for a while. 'I'm definitely agreeable.'

'Oh my God, what am I going to do now?' Laura's girlish good looks collapsed into tear-stained tramlines of mascara. 'These buyers want me out and I've got nowhere to go! And Simon thinks I'm just trying to sabotage the sale!'

Ella put her arm round her friend and guided her towards a nearby cafe. Her instinct was to shake Laura and say, 'Pull yourself together and forget about bloody Simon!'

But before she could, Laura seemed to wake up of her own accord. A sudden smile peeked through the tramlines of her distress. 'Actually, I did think of sabotaging it. Sewing kippers into the curtains or blocking the loos so the whole place ponged. That would serve him right. But the thing is, I want to move now. That flat made me see how the future could be. I might even give everything in my house to charity and start again as a minimalist!'

Ella grinned, thinking of Laura's house, stuffed as it was with pretty things, photo frames and candlesticks, fake flowers and colourful cushions, scented candles and gilded chandeliers. 'Yes, Laura, of course you will.'

As they walked back to the tube with their takeaway coffees, Ella remembered the property developer she'd negotiated with about her own recent buy, and wondered if he'd be able to help Laura find something. She'd look up his email when she got home. 'Come on, onwards and upwards. I'll go back online when I get home. We'll find somewhere else soon.' But before they got to the tube station Ella's phone rang.

'Hello, Ella,' a nervous voice informed her. 'This is Mrs Gregory, your neighbour on the left. It's bad news, I'm afraid. There's been a flood.'

'Oh my God.' Ella felt panic rising. 'I'll come straight back. Thank you for letting me know.' She turned to Laura. 'Oh Jesus, that was my neighbour. The river must have flooded. Julia always said it would but I loved the cottage so much I wouldn't believe her.' She summoned a passing black cab. 'I need to get back at once.'

'I'm coming with you,' Laura insisted. Her job at Late-Express could wait. Mr and Mrs A were still deeply grateful for having Mrs Lal to stay.

They sat in silence, trying not to picture all those stories on the TV news of homeowners waist-deep in stinking water, trying to salvage their precious possessions from the engulfing mud and debris.

Laura reached out a hand and held Ella's.

'Thanks for coming,' Ella breathed.

'Having you help me with flat-hunting has made all the difference,' Laura replied. 'I was dreading it and you made it fun.'

'If not exactly successful,' apologized Ella.

After that they sat in tense silence until they reached their destination.

As they neared the river Ella leaned forward and spoke to the cab driver. 'You may not be able to get right to my house. Apparently there's been a flood.'

'Can't see any sign of it yet,' he replied, slowing down and leaning out of his window. 'River's at low tide.'

Ella looked at her friend and shrugged. 'Weird. He's right. The water isn't high at all. I was expecting the road to be impassable.'

Two minutes later they pulled up outside Ella's cottage. There was still no sign of flooding, only a white Dyno-Rod van parked outside the next-door neighbour's house. As they got out and paid, the cabbie laughed and said, 'Maybe somebody was pulling your leg and thought it was April Fool's.'

'If they were, I'll kill them,' Ella replied just as her front door opened and a distraught-looking woman emerged. 'Mrs Thompson,' she blurted, 'I'm so glad you're back. It was my husband Bert who saw the water coming through your front door and all down the path here . . . and since you'd given us your key he went in . . .'

For the first time Ella noticed there was a stream of water covering her tiled front path. 'What the . . .' Ella remembered to mind her language just in time in front of the neighbour she knew was an enthusiastic Seventh-day Adventist.

'It was coming down the stairs from the bathroom.' Mrs Gregory pointed towards the house. 'Bert used to be a plumber before he retired and he reckons whoever installed your bath didn't put in an overflow pipe so when you accidentally left the tap on, it had nowhere to go but over the top of the bath . . .'

Ella ran up the stairs to find the whole of her lovely new beige bathroom carpet soaked and ruined.

'I'm afraid the plaster's fallen off the ceiling in your sitting room as well,' apologized her neighbour, as though it were somehow her fault.

Ella stood, stunned. The flood hadn't been caused by the Thames suddenly rising as her daughter had predicted. It had been caused by Ella forgetting to turn off the tap like some helpless old person who couldn't be trusted to look after herself.

'Come on, I'll help you clear up.' Laura could see how near to tears Ella was, something she'd never seen before. 'We all do stupid things.'

Ella surveyed the mess. There was plaster all over the floor in the sitting room and the expensive new carpet she'd only just had fitted was stained all the way down the stairs.

'Not as often as I seem to,' Ella replied bitterly. She sat heavily down on the sofa, all her usual brisk decisiveness evaporating. To Laura's horror, she suddenly looked old. 'The thing is, Laura, this wretched tap isn't the first thing I've forgotten. I keep forgetting things.' She stared away from Laura into the distance. 'I'm beginning to think there may be something seriously wrong.'

Laura struggled for something to say. Of all of them, Ella had always been the strong one. 'Tell you one thing,' Laura said, attempting a little joke to cheer her friend up. 'At least Julia wasn't with you.'

When she'd finished helping Ella clear up as best they could, Laura headed home feeling resentful that she would still find Mrs Lal there. There were limits to generosity and friendship and she'd reached them. Tomorrow when she went into work she'd grab Mrs A – no point telling Mr A since he was powerless in the face of his wife's wishes – and insist they find her somewhere else, whether her guest wanted to move on or not.

But when she arrived the house was oddly silent. She wondered where Sam had got to, since he'd told her he was in tonight. She dropped her bag and coat in the hall, feeling suddenly exhausted, and headed for the tempting embrace of the sofa, planning to put up her feet and watch a box set with a glass of wine by her side.

Instead she halted, transfixed by the unexpected sight of Sam and Mrs Lal already occupying it. More extraordinary still, they seemed to be holding hands!

On further examination she realized that Mrs Lal was simply stroking his hand in what seemed to be a sympathetic and reassuring gesture, which was doubly astonishing since Sam normally shrugged off all physical affection as if he might catch bubonic plague.

'The bitch has ditched him,' announced Mrs Lal in funereal tones. 'I have been explaining to your son the many reasons he is better off without such a shallow and unsuitable young woman.'

And the extraordinary thing was that Sam was listening to her.

'I think Lalita's right in the end, Mum.' Laura's eyes widened at the use of the terrifying Mrs Lal's first name, which she'd never dared use herself. 'She was just using me to try and pull that berk Stephen Steel. And she was a real culture-free zone too. You should have heard her boasting that she'd never read a book in her life as if that were supposed to be clever!'

'Very stupid and shallow,' repeated Mrs Lal. 'And now we have to persuade your lovely mother, who has so much to offer a man, that this Calum she is seeing is not free of his wife's influence. It is bad enough when a man is under his mother's influence – and obviously that is something I hold on to myself with my daughter – but his *wife's* when they are no longer married ... he can only be a pussycat with no strength of character.'

'Oh, go to hell, Mrs Lal,' blurted Laura, no longer able to contain the welter of emotions swirling round in her mind. 'I'm going to bed!'

*

Sal blocked off a couple of hours to begin her online search for a convalescent home in Surrey for Rose. She soon found that convalescence was now seen as a practice run for a permanent stay and offered mainly by care-home chains. There seemed to be two kinds – the much more affordable charity-run homes, reasonable in price but where they expected you to make your own bed and join in with everyone else, or the posh country-house hotel kind where you could order yourself a G&T and stay permanently in your room if you preferred. She suspected Rose wouldn't last a week if she was expected to join in communal sing-songs and do her own laundry, but the cost of the posh kind was staggering. No wonder there was a national crisis in paying for these places!

'I don't give a damn where I convalesce,' Rose insisted when Sal laid out the options. 'As long as I don't have to wear an incontinence pad and I have a room with a big TV, it's all the same to me. My real problem is what I do afterwards. I don't think I could bear to have someone living in who I didn't get on with, treating me like a five-year-old and helping themselves to my wallet while I wasn't looking.'

Sal sighed. 'Maybe Lou's right and you should talk to my mad friend Claudia about this crazy anti-retirement scheme of hers. Lou is actually investing in it!'

'Not the one in Murdo Binns' hotel?'

'The very same.'

'Will they have sex and drugs and rock'n'roll?'

'I very much doubt it. Claudia's taste runs to easy listening and her husband Don likes folk music with those things you put in your nose.'

'Jew's harps? Good. I'm far too old for sex and drugs but I like a bit of "Hey Nonny Nonny". Maybe I should think about it. I'd love to see Murdo's face if he knew I was moving into his property.'

'Come on, Rose,' Sal demanded. 'Tell me the story of this mysterious Murdo.'

'He thought he was in love with me when we were silly young things but I really didn't think I'd make a Lady.'

'And certainly not if it was Lady Binns!'

They both laughed so loud that the nurse came in and adjusted Rose's drug line as if, after all she'd been through, laughing might finish her off.

As Sal got up to go, Rose caught her hand. 'Thanks for doing all this for me. And I'm really sorry about selling the magazine.'

Sal tried to smile. 'I know now why you'll need the money. Care homes cost a fortune.'

'Tell Lou he can drop my name if it helps his negotiations with Murdo.'

She waved to Rose from the door, but Rose was looking out of the window, with a smile of such intense satisfaction on her face that Sal wished she could be there if Lou did mention her name to the curiously named Lord Murdo Binns.

Claudia sat with her A4 pad trying to decide how to approach the meeting with Igden Manor's owner. Her husband Don was still angry and disbelieving about the whole idea, and kept on making such sarcastic comments that frankly she wouldn't care if he went and lived in a cave.

She picked up Douglas's rough sketches of how the space could be used and couldn't help smiling. The central block – with the current hotel reception and bar – looked much the same but he had cleverly divided up the cottage wings to create separate dwellings with their own private gardens. The overall effect struck Claudia as being like a medieval hamlet, with both privacy and a sense of community. The gatehouse had three bedrooms, two on the ground floor, which might suit her parents.

Claudia took a deep breath. It had taken so long just to get to this point and yet there was so much negotiating ahead! No wonder lots of people talked about living together as they aged but few of them actually did it. *Courage,* she told herself, *this is a dream. Let's try and make it real!*

She grabbed her pad and headed for the manor, passing her parents' house on the way. The door to the shed was open and she could hear her father and Hiro chatting away. Maybe Hiro could come and live with them too!

Lou Maynard was driving up just as she arrived.

'Claudia, good to see you.' Lou looked round at the quintessentially English scene with its hollyhocks and delphiniums swaying gently in the morning breeze next to a white dove cooing in its dovecot. 'This place blows my mind,' he grinned. 'It looks just like a cookie tin of olde England. So what do we know about this old boy, Lord Binns?'

'He's the major landowner round here. He owns half the county.'

'So money isn't his major motivating factor?'

'I imagine his good name matters more. But you never know with the British aristocracy. They can be rich as Croesus and mean as Ebenezer Scrooge both at the same time.'

'Hah. Just like John Paul Getty?'

'Who was he?'

'Maybe the richest man in the world and he had a payphone installed in his lobby. Come to think of it, he lived in Surrey too.'

He opened the door to the reception area. 'Once more unto the breach, dear friend . . . to paraphrase the bard.'

Claudia laughed. 'Olde England is definitely getting to you.'

'Can I help you?' asked the receptionist, the same one who had told her mother about the hotel's problems, Claudia noted. How fitting.

'We've come to see Lord Binns.'

'Yes, indeed. He's in the library.' She abandoned the reception desk and led them through the bar, out onto the sunny terrace and into a small room at the end of the building. 'Your guests, Lord Binns,' she announced.

An elegantly suited man of about eighty with a languidly fashionable air rose from a wing chair and walked towards them. He made Claudia think of those black and white photographs of the fast set who surrounded Princess Margaret in the fifties. He certainly didn't fit into the usual plus-fours and shooting stick image of most country landlords.

'One of our American brethren?' was his somewhat dampening response when Claudia introduced Lou. She could feel Lou's irritation beginning to rise and shot him a look. Lord Binns looked from Claudia to Lou. 'Right, who's doing the talking?'

'Over to you, I think, Claudia,' prompted Lou.

Both men listened as Claudia explained her vision of the best of both worlds, young and old, friends and family all living harmoniously together in this glorious setting. Not on top of each other, but there to help and share when needed.

'Bloody barking, if you ask me,' was Lord Binns' sardonic response. 'But then my friends are all dead and I loathe my family. Why should I agree to this tempting utopia?'

This time Lou took up the argument. 'There's only thirty years on the lease. The place needs an update. Trip Advisor keeps harping on about your lack of facilities and how expensive the rooms are. We save you the embarrassment of the manor going out of business. Instead a new venture takes over, burning with the zeitgeist of the times. A new concept for ageing! The young helping the old! Everyone is impressed with your foresight. Articles are written. Local radio reporters flock.'

'And how is this retirement Garden of Eden going to be funded?'

Claudia gulped.

'Through a trust,' Lou replied smoothly. 'Funded by the residents. Administered by lawyers expert in this area.'

'No doubt the bloody local council would love it,' Lord Binns commented. 'Always banging on about social care and how no one's ready to pay for it.'

'Would you like to see a sketch?' Claudia produced her son-in-law's drawing from her bag. 'Of course it's only very much a first stab.'

He studied the charcoal sketch with interest.

'Whole thing sounds precarious to me. What if everyone hates each other?'

'Oh no, we're all old friends.'

'As a matter of fact,' Lou intervened. 'I believe you know one of the people who's declared an interest.'

'I very much doubt it.' Claudia and Lou could see they were losing his interest. Any moment he'd tell them their time was up.

'Rose McGill, she owns a number of magazines.'

'I know who Rose McGill is,' he almost snapped. For an instant he looked away, a small smile twisting his lips. 'I haven't seen Rose for a very long time. And you say she wants to come and live here?'

'Absolutely,' lied Lou.

'Thank you both. You've certainly given me food for thought.'

'Lou!' Claudia berated him as soon as their host had left. 'The poor woman hasn't even seen the place!'

'Lord Snooty doesn't need to know that, though, does he? Besides, I think Rose would enjoy knowing she was stirring up old memories. Didn't she tell you I could use her name if it helped?'

'Yes,' conceded Sal. 'But not actually say she'd agreed to live here. Well, we've done our best. Now we just have to wait and see.'

'How about a little glass of something?'

They were the only people in the bar even though it was almost lunchtime. Lou ordered champagne and refused to accept a glass from a bottle that looked as if it had been opened in 1964.

After the satisfying pop of a new one being opened, Lou raised a toast. 'To Rose McGill. In Rose we trust! Even if she has never been here!'

Twelve

The phone was ringing when Laura got home and there was no sign of Sam or, thankfully, Mrs Lal.

'Mrs Minchin? It's Stuart from the estate agent's here. Good news. Your buyers are happy with the survey. They'd like to complete as soon as possible and move in in three weeks.'

'But is that really feasible?' Laura tried not wail.

'Indeed. Providing all the documentation is ready. It's all moving along most satisfactorily.'

'It may be for you, you slimy bastard, with your three sales from every divorce!' Laura wanted to yell.

Instead she put on her chilliest voice to reply. 'Tell your clients that I will let them know as soon as I have talked to my son and daughter. This is their family home after all.' She didn't need to tell him that Sam was quite happy to move in with a friend and Bella had already gone months ago.

'Besides which, I have a friend of the family living with me. An elderly lady from India.' Mrs Lal might as well come in useful for once.

'Of course, but I'd advise you to give them a date soon.' A

196

touch of concern that Laura was going to morph into a divorce resister after all had crept into his smarmy voice. 'You don't want a deal like this slipping through your fingers.'

You mean, you don't, you arsehole! Laura would love to see his face if pretty-in-pastel Mrs Minchin actually said what she was thinking.

'I'll get back to you.'

She put down the phone and sat on the sofa, fighting back tears. This was it. The official end of her marriage, more real even than divorce. A sudden sound made her sit up. She'd thought she was alone but she could definitely hear music coming from Sam's bedroom. What's more, it wasn't the usual music he listened to, baleful, soul-searching singer-songwriters; this was bouncy and exotic and upbeat and . . . Indian!

Laura abandoned the sofa and went upstairs. It was definitely coming from Sam's bedroom. Her knock was drowned out by the thrumming base line from an electric guitar. She opened the door to find Sam and Mrs Lal sitting on the bed with TomTom the cat between them like a prim chaperone.

'Mum, hi,' Sam greeted her with a smile. 'Isn't this music great? It's Bhangra. Lalita has it on her iPhone. It's traditional Indian folk music with electric guitar and keyboards. I'd heard of it, obviously, but never really listened to it before.'

'My daughter introduced me to it,' Mrs Lal explained. 'She used to play it around the house.'

Laura couldn't imagine the formidable Mrs A bopping to the Bhangra beat but was glad that Sam seemed so cheerful.

'Are you all right?' Sam was always so intuitive it amazed Laura.

'That was the estate agent. The buyers want us to move out in three weeks.'

Sam heard the catch in her voice and jumped up. 'Shit, that's soon. Will you be all right?'

'I should be asking you that,' Laura grinned.

'In India,' Mrs Lal commented, 'people get thrown out of their homes with no notice at all. It is quite common.'

'Thank you, Mrs Lal,' Laura replied waspishly. 'I'll bear that in mind when I have to leave the home I've lived in ever since I was married.'

'Now you are divorced,' Mrs Lal replied, refusing to be offended, 'you need a nice man and a new home.'

'Yes, Mum.' Sam put a protective arm round her. 'You should let Lalita find you someone. She's arranged two thousand marriages in India.'

'I've already found a nice man. His name's Calum.'

Mrs Lal raised a sceptical eyebrow at the very moment it struck Laura that it had been a curiously long time since she'd heard from the man she'd begun to think of as her boyfriend.

Downstairs, away from the blaring Bhangra, Laura rang her daughter Bella. Bella at least would surely have regrets about leaving her childhood home.

'The sooner the better, Mum,' was Bella's instant reply. 'It'd be much better for you to move on. Find a nice ground-floor flat to grow old in. Preferably with a spare bedroom so I can come and stay with Nigel and Noah.'

Ella discreetly hired a carpet cleaner and set about rescuing her brand-new pale carpet from the effects of the flood. The smell of damp wool took her back to childhood holidays in Wales when it was so wet even the sheep booked into a B&B.

Her daughter Julia had advised her against getting a beige carpet. Why didn't she choose something practical instead –

sludge possibly or taupe? But Ella didn't like sludge and blamed taupe for rendering countless colourful rooms she'd loved dull as ditchwater (come to think of it, ditchwater was just the sort of name they gave to paints nowadays). Julia had been right as usual because now her carpet was sludge-coloured anyway.

Two hours of hard slog were beginning to pay off. Apart from the last few feet where the water had pooled, the carpet was looking almost restored. She'd have to get a rug to cover the bit at the bottom, which was beyond rescue, but at least it would look engagingly boho.

In the end a lot of the lasting damage had been to her dignity. How *could* she have gone out leaving the bath tap running? And as for that bloody plumber who hadn't put in the overflow pipe, she might well sue him.

And at least Julia didn't know. Apart from the weird smell the disaster was now almost undetectable. Ella let out a long breath of satisfaction and took the steam cleaner up to the bathroom to empty.

The basin was under the riverside window so Ella could watch the river flowing as she brushed her teeth. But the sight that met her eyes was worse than the threat of rising flood waters.

It was Julia deep in earnest conversation with her neighbour Mrs Gregory who, eager to relive her and Bert's moment of glory, was clearly recounting every gruesome detail of Ella's incompetence to her daughter.

There was only one thing to do: pretend to be out. Ella tiptoed down the stairs to the kitchen, grateful that the cottage was the middle of a terraced row so Julia couldn't find her way round the back and that she had resisted – much to her daughter's indignation – to give her a key despite Julia's insistence that Ella might fall or be taken ill. 'I'm in my sixties, not my eighties!' she had protested.

Julia rapped on the door. Ella ignored it, and the call to her mobile that followed, and then the further call to her landline. That wretched Mrs Gregory. No doubt she would have told Julia that Ella was in.

What would she do if she was in one of those Scandi noir box sets Julia loved so much? Feeling ingenious, Ella texted her daughter that she had gone into town to meet Laura. She might not believe it but at least she wouldn't dial 999 and get the police and ambulance service down here telling them her mother was inside and might be lying on the wet carpet suffering a stroke.

From the bathroom window she watched Julia read the text and look disbelievingly up at the cottage.

That was when Ella got the giggles, wondering how long Julia would stand outside staring up for evidence of her delinquent mother.

If she knew Julia, it would be quite a long time.

Sal and the rest of the staff watched, stunned, at the speed and efficiency with which Rose's nephew proceeded to close down the magazine. Sal might have chosen the word 'insensitivity' were it not that Justin did everything with such apparent tact and good humour.

In her own mind, and privately to Lou, she dubbed him 'the smiling assassin'. He had done his homework and respected the letter of the law in what was owed to the staff in terms of payoffs and pensions, but gave not a penny more.

Within a month or so *New Grey* had been sold to a Canadian company he had done business with before. The Canadians were big on retirement, apparently.

Already the leaving parties were being planned. To Sal they seemed more like wakes.

'Come on, what's happened to my brave Mustang Sally?' Lou prompted, seeing her looking dismal.

Sal didn't want to recite her woes again, though it was very tempting. She'd never had a man to be really honest with, but if she was, surely she'd frighten him off? And sometimes it seemed to her he was the only thing in her life that was really good at the moment.

Lou put his arms round her. 'Scared, huh? I know you loved your job.'

The sympathy in his tone undid her. 'Yes,' she admitted, 'I am scared. No pension and anyone with a lick of sense would at least own their property, so they'd have that as a buffer. Muggins here stuck to renting.'

Lou, sitting perched on the side of the bed, looked thoughtful, making Sal giggle.

'What's so funny?' he asked.

'You. You look like Rodin's Thinker.'

'I'll have you know I'm thinking on your behalf.'

Sal sat down next to him and laid her head on his shoulder. 'I know,' she said in a small non-Sal-like voice. 'Thank you.'

'I know a lot about leases, here as well as in the US. I have to. How long have you been here?'

He whistled when Sal answered. 'That long? And what do you pay in rental?'

He laughed out loud when Sal told him. 'That's a pretty damn good deal.'

'The flat was in bad condition when I took it on. I've spent quite a lot on decorating it,' she grinned at him. 'Giving it the Grainger touch.'

'Your landlord might be prepared to buy you out. It happens

201

with very long lets. The area has changed, got more valuable. They might be able to double the rent with a new tenant.'

'But then I'd have to move,' Sal replied, an edge of panic in her voice.

'True. But you might get a lump sum that made it worth it. I'll draft a letter to your landlord and we'll see how they take it.'

Sal put her arms round him. It wasn't exactly an offer to go and live in Brooklyn, but just having his presence in her life felt like going to bed with a hot water bottle and a goosedown duvet on a cold winter's night.

The phone by Laura's bed rang so early that it made her jump and instantly wonder what the emergency was. Not something to do with her daughter Bella or baby Noah?

To her surprise it was Claudia.

'Sorry to wake you. My alarm goes off at six.'

'Bloody hell. Actually, it's good you rang. I've got to get up for work.'

'It's about Ella,' Claudia explained. 'I'm worried about her. She rang me last night and went on and on about not being able to remember anything and then burst into tears. Ella! She's always been the efficient one!'

'I know. She left the tap on in her house and flooded the place. She's desperately hoping Julia doesn't find out or she'll start saying Ella's got dementia.'

'Oh my God! You don't think she has, do you? Has she seen her doctor?'

'She doesn't want to. In case it turns out to be true.'

'God, Laura, that's awful!'

'Yes.' Laura realized she hadn't even faced the suspicion herself.

'And how about you?'

'I'm okay.' She tried to keep calm and not admit that she was absolutely bloody terrified of moving out of her home and not knowing where she'd go. Images of *Cathy Come Home* and the homeless people under Waterloo underpass kept invading her consciousness. 'Except that I may have to move out in a few weeks.'

'Laura! Where to?'

'Well, that's the problem. I haven't found anywhere yet.'

'Come here!' Claudia offered impulsively. 'We've got a spare room for the moment and you can store your stuff in our garage. We're too lazy to use it and always park in the driveway. You can stay as long as you like.'

Suddenly the thought of being in a place full of thatched cottages with bright geraniums in window boxes seemed overwhelmingly appealing to Laura. It would be like Thrush Green, the village in the novels by Miss Read she'd loved as a child. It could be a kind of holiday till she decided what to do next.

'Are you sure? What about Don? Won't he mind being invaded?'

'He'll enjoy the distraction. He's always liked you. He thinks you're the least bossy of my friends.'

'In that case, I'd love to.'

As she put the phone down a wave of relief swept over Laura. She didn't have to worry, at least in the short term. She'd go in today and explain the situation to Mr A at Late-Express. In fact, she felt such a burden lifted off her shoulders that she didn't even mind if Mrs Lal stayed on till she moved.

She got up and dressed in her favourite pale yellow cardigan even though she was going to work.

And then she remembered Ella. Was something serious the matter with her or was it just a bad case of forgetfulness?

Ella looked out of the window at the beautiful day outside. The sun shimmered on the river like shot silk. Four swans glided past, the water sparkling in their wake. Geese honked gaily as they flew overhead. It was a day for gardening. It would have been perfect weather for going to the allotment except for some reason she wasn't feeling too brilliant. Besides, Ella had another, far less pleasant task in mind.

She sat down at the little table by the window which served as desk and dressing table and got out her laptop. It was time she faced up to things. She put 'Signs of dementia' into her browser and realized she was holding her breath. There is no definitive test for dementia, she read. The only way for a definitive diagnosis is an autopsy of the brain after death. Oh great. Two thirds of people with dementia, the article continued, are female.

Bloody hell! Ella fumed. *How utterly outrageous!*

She clicked again until she found what she was looking for: the kind of test her GP would use if she braved going to see her, which she had no intention of doing. This was between her and her brain.

1) What year is it? Well, that was simple enough.
2) What month is it? That was easy too. She could certainly manage that.
3) Now there was a bit of a rub; at this point her GP would give her a name and address to remember. Ella decided to make one up.
4) What time is it – to the nearest hour? To her irritation Ella got this wrong, opting for ten o'clock when it was nearer nine.

5) Count backwards from twenty to one. Easy peasy.
6) Name the months of the year in reverse order. No problem.
7) Tell me the name and address of the person named earlier. Ella did so.

Ella found she'd lost three points overall which put her in the No Memory Problem area; between eight and nine she should see her GP; between ten and twenty-eight would mean clear memory impairment that should be investigated.

Ella almost skipped downstairs to make herself a coffee, but stopped on the threshold of the kitchen. The room was full of smoke from a milk pan she had put on and forgotten. Why hadn't the sodding smoke alarm gone off? And then she remembered it had been beeping the other day because it needed a new battery.

And Ella, who had survived the loss of her beloved husband in a train crash and not crumbled, sat down at the kitchen counter and wept.

Claudia sat looking at the letter in front of her. She got few letters these days and never one that looked like this. The paper was so thick it almost seemed like parchment, and the address was embossed in gold letters across the top as if it were an uber-posh wedding invitation. But the contents were even more startling.

Lord Murdo Binns, eccentric aristocrat and owner of Igden Manor, stated that he would be prepared to consider their proposal – on one condition.

That Miss Rose McGill should be one of the tenants.

Claudia was pulled in two directions. Elated that his response had been so positive but at a loss to know what to do next. No point approaching Sal, since Sal thought the whole project was bonkers, so she supposed it would have to be Lou Maynard. He at least was positive about the idea, though the Lord alone knew why. But how would she get hold of him? Then she remembered he'd left his mobile number.

Claudia rang it.

'Lou,' she began, 'you're not going to believe this!'

'The old bean said yes?' Lou sounded surprisingly unfazed. 'I thought he might. He's got more money than he knows what to do with. He's old. And he wants to have some fun.'

'But there was one really strange condition.'

'Concerning Rose?'

'Yes, how did you know?'

'I saw his reaction. I suspect he's been thinking about Rose for fifty years.'

'And he'd sell us the manor cheap just to have her near him?' Claudia marvelled. 'That's amazing.'

'Oh, he's probably got other reasons as well. I suspect that old Murdo's quite smart under that Bertie Wooster exterior of his. I quite like the cove, as Bertie might say.'

'How do you think she'll react? Is there any chance she might be interested?'

'Sal and I are taking her down to a convalescent home tomorrow, cannily selected to be near to Igden Manor, so who knows.'

'You know, Lou, you are a bit of a magician.'

'Thank you, Claudia. Once Rose is settled in maybe we should bring her over.'

'That sounds brilliant. And Lou . . .'

'Yep?'

'Thank you for Hiro. He and my dad are firm favourites in

the local pub. Except for one thing. Hiro keeps beating the locals at dominoes.'

'I'm glad it's only dominoes and not Blackjack,' Lou responded.

Claudia couldn't help laughing. She liked Lou a lot. If he really did intend to live at Igden Manor, he would be a huge asset. And surely he could persuade Sal to come too? The thought of Ella and her worrying forgetfulness broke into Claudia's thoughts.

Lou was smiling broadly when he broke the news to Sal about Lord Binns' stipulation.

'Oh my God,' was Sal's appalled reaction. 'Do you mean this completely nutty scheme might actually be going to happen?'

'Only if we can persuade Rose that living in a thatched commune is what she's been longing for all her life!'

Laura put on her hideous LateExpress tabard and wondered if her horrible ex Simon would venture in to buy sandwiches. This had been the place he bought them every day until Laura had started to work here – expressly to embarrass him, according to Simon. Maybe she'd put rat poison in them.

Or maybe not. Laura was feeling a lot more cheerful now that she wasn't going to be homeless. At least not for the moment.

'Mr A, can I have a word?' she asked her employer.

Mr A looked instantly hounded. 'Is it about my mother-in-law Mrs Lal? It is terrible that you have been exploited so badly. But the problem is . . .'

'Yes?'

'She likes it very much at your house and has resisted all

our offers of alternative accommodation.' He dropped his voice. 'Even Claridge's. Despite the fact that it is the Queen's favourite hotel.'

Poor Mr A looked devastated.

'Probably a good thing,' Laura reassured. 'A week in Claridge's would cost a bomb. Besides, she seems to be getting on very well with my son. But the thing is, I'm selling my house and the new owners want to move in in a few weeks so I'm moving out of London for a while. To stay with a friend in Surrey.'

'Ah,' nodded Mr A sagely. 'I have heard Surrey is a very beautiful county. Much like Simla in India.'

'I expect, knowing the Brits, Simla was made to remind them of Surrey.'

The implication of Laura's words suddenly hit him. 'Then you are leaving us here at LateExpress?'

'I'm afraid so.'

'And will you be living permanently in Surrey?'

'I'm not sure. My friend is trying to start an unconventional retirement community there, but I don't think I will join.'

'Unconventional? With hippies and dropouts and loud music?'

Laura giggled. 'More gin and tonic and Pilates.'

'We had plenty of hippies in Uttar Pradesh. My father told me about them begging from the locals.'

'How shameful.' Laura had never been hippily-inclined herself, but all the same, could it really be fifty years ago since the Summer of Love? What had happened to life? Where did it go?

Laura pulled herself together. She was in danger of turning into a Joni Mitchell song. 'So you see, you will have to find somewhere for your mother-in-law to move to soon,' she announced gently.

Mr A was looking pensive. 'How many ladies in this retirement community will there be?'

Laura shrugged. 'I don't know. My friend wants young people too, though whether young people will want to live with a bunch of old ladies, I don't know.'

'It will be like Indian village. You need old, young, goats, sheep, cats, dogs, as well as the grannies.'

'I'll tell my friend about the goats and sheep. I don't think she's thought of those.' But as she said it Laura couldn't help thinking how lovely it would be to live with her grandson Noah instead of only catching the odd glimpse of him. Maybe Indian villages had it about right.

Ella headed into town, leaving her car behind in case she had any more strange turns, and treated herself to an individual quiche (Lorraine was still the best, in her view, despite veggy competition) and bought some batteries for the smoke alarm which made her feel marginally more in control.

Hunger suddenly came over her and she sat on the wall with her feet dangling above the river and ate her quiche, throwing the crumbs to the ducks then headed slowly home, noticing that she still had that odd pain in her lower abdomen. Maybe she really ought to go and have that looked at.

A car, which she instantly recognized as belonging to her daughter Julia, was parked carelessly across the front of her driveway, as if to block her own in. Yet it seemed to be empty. Then she noticed that Julia was busy deadheading her late-flowering irises, the irises Ella deliberately left so they could store energy for next year's flowering.

Julia looked up, her pretty face flushed with excitement as

though she had been waiting a long time, and had something important to impart.

'Mum!' she greeted Ella. 'I'm so glad you're back. I've got some terrific news. I've been talking it over with Neil and we've come up with a really good scheme. We'll convert our garage into a granny flat and you can come and live with us, see more of Mark and Harry. You'd be completely independent, but still near when you need it!'

Ella's heart sank. Of course it was kind, but it was in Julia's nature to continually interfere and they would fall out in five minutes. If it had been her other daughter, who was almost too sweet and dreamy for her own good, the plan might have worked, though even then she doubted it.

'That's so sweet of you,' Ella replied carefully. 'But I could never put you to all that expense.' She knew money was tight in their household.

'That wouldn't be a problem,' Julia replied gaily. 'You could pay for it, couldn't you? Out of the money you'd get for this place.'

Once Julia had gone Ella sat down, trying to contain her irritation. Why was it that when you hit sixty people thought you couldn't make your own bloody decisions just because you'd been a bit stupid about forgetting things?

Ella looked round at her new surroundings, the brightly painted walls and colourful cushions that dotted her sofa, and felt suddenly as if she had no idea where she was. The feeling was so overwhelming that she began to panic and could feel her heart racing.

She closed her eyes and waited for the feeling to pass. Instead it intensified so that she looked down at her hands and couldn't tell if they belonged to her or not or even where she was.

Something was definitely happening to her. Was it a stroke?

The terror of being left dependent, something that had always been a deep horror of hers, began to engulf her.

She got up and stumbled to the phone. It took her a moment to remember that for the emergency services you had to dial 999.

Thirteen

Sal wouldn't have believed it if she hadn't had the letter right here in front of her. In view of her exceptionally long-term status as a tenant, the owners of her building stated, they were prepared to offer what struck Sal as an enormous sum 'to surrender the tenancy'.

'Surrendering the tenancy' was of course legalese for moving out. The letter was also marked 'Without Prejudice', which Lou said meant they could withdraw it at any time.

'You should grab it while you can,' was Lou's advice. 'Landlords are businessmen. They might change their minds.'

But Sal wasn't ready to take quite such a step yet. She'd think about it.

Lou put his arms round her. 'Well, don't think about it too long.'

They locked up her flat and departed in Lou's hired Jeep to go and pick up Rose from hospital and drop her at the convalescent home. Rose, thank God, seemed more like her usual witty and acerbic self.

So much so that Lou had the inspired idea of stopping off at Igden Manor for lunch en route.

God was clearly on their side. The sun shone, the birds sang, the summer flowers around the paths that wound between the main building and all the cottage suites bloomed. The whole place looked chocolate-box perfect. 'Of course,' Rose confided over a very dry sherry, 'I've always loathed the country. Never seen the point of it. I've had my eye on a nice block of flats with a lift near Sloane Square for years.' Sal and Lou exchanged an anxious look. 'But it's been bought by the Russians, like the rest of London. Russians, Chinese, investors from Singapore who want a safe haven for their dirty money and never intend to even set foot here. Do you know, some of the new flats they're building don't even have kitchens?' Rose sipped her fino sherry with the satisfaction of letting rip her prejudices. 'Makes perfect sense. What's the point of blowing twenty grand on a state-of-the-art kitchen when a microwave's all you need?'

She looked round at the colourful oriental poppies, the blue agapanthus nestling among the Rambling Rector roses. 'So I'm quite coming round to the idea of leaving.' She smiled at them both mischievously. 'Now tell me, exactly what did Murdo Binns say about me having to live here?'

They looked at her, stunned, as her steak arrived. 'This meat is overcooked,' she informed the unfortunate waiter.

'But madame, look, it is hardly cooked at all!'

'I requested it to be still mooing,' Rose replied as the man removed it. 'As a matter of fact, Murdo mentioned it himself. He came to visit me in hospital. Didn't I tell you?'

'No, Rose, you didn't,' Lou replied, realizing she was enjoying herself hugely.

'He brought a bunch of red roses. No idea you weren't allowed flowers in some hospitals any more. Had to give them to the prettiest nurse he could find. Male as a matter of fact. You know Murdo, he likes to keep people guessing.'

The steak reappeared in a pool of blood. This time it was brought by the chef himself. 'Is this *saignant* enough for madame?'

'It'll do,' she replied haughtily and proceeded to demolish it in record time. 'I've been eating nothing but hospital pap for days,' she explained, looking round the restaurant. 'Young man,' she summoned the waiter again. He arrived looking distinctly nervous.

'Yes, madame?'

'Tell the chef the steak was delicious.'

'Murdo isn't the only person who likes to keep people guessing,' Lou murmured to Sal.

After they'd completed their meal with crème brûlée and evilly strong coffee, Rose began to get up. 'So,' she announced in her most regal manner, 'you'd better show me round and persuade me why I should want to come and live here.'

'Just lie back, love, we'll look after you now,' the gruff voice informed her. Ella looked up into the reassuring face of a burly paramedic. Thank God she'd had the wit to leave the front door open before the ambulance arrived.

She felt herself being lifted and half carried through her sitting room. His female colleague was wearing a green jumpsuit which randomly reminded Ella of one she'd worn herself in the sixties. There! She could still remember stuff, no matter how trivial.

All the neighbours were outside. An ambulance arriving was a major drama.

'Is there anyone we should call?' asked the young woman, once they had laid Ella down inside.

Ella felt panic rising. She couldn't bear the idea of Julia arriving and taking over.

'My daughter, Cory Thompson.' Ella realized she was clutching her mobile as if it were her only lifeline. 'Her number's in my phone.'

'That's fine.' The man took over again. 'June here will call her. Now, Mrs Thompson. Can you smile for me?'

'It's not funny,' Ella mumbled.

The man ignored her. 'Raise both your arms, please.' Ella did so.

'What day of the week is it?'

'Friday,' Ella replied irritably.

'Okay.' This clearly wasn't the right answer but anyone could get that wrong, especially when they'd stopped working. 'Now, tell me your symptoms.'

'Memory loss. Sometimes forgetting quite important things I normally wouldn't.'

'Okay.' The paramedics exchanged glances. 'Anything else?'

'Total confusion. I suddenly didn't know where I was or what my hands were for. That's why I called you.'

'Hello, is that Cory Thompson?' the female paramedic enquired calmly. 'Your mother has had an episode and is on her way to Hammersmith Hospital.'

Ella could hear the panic in Cory's voice as she demanded more details and Ella felt suddenly guilty. Cory had had no inkling of Ella's situation. The paramedic said it would be better if she came to the hospital as they needed to run some tests.

'Any other symptoms?' the man was asking Ella. 'Headaches for instance?'

'Yes. I have been having the odd headache.'

'On a scale of one to ten, how bad?'

'Oh, for God's sake, I don't know. Five?'

'Anything else. Frequency for instance?'

'What the hell is frequency?'

'Needing to pee a lot. Has your urine smelled different?'

Ella thought of asparagus pee and smiled. The man was watching her strangely, she decided.

'Now that you mention it, my pee does smell rather awful.'

'Cloudy or bloody? Do you have a burning sensation?'

Actually, Ella had had all these and dismissed them. 'Yes,' she said doubtfully, 'all of those.'

They had reached the hospital.

'All right, Mrs Thompson, we're there. Just lie back. You'll be fine.'

Ella closed her eyes.

'I'm pretty sure what the problem is,' murmured the male paramedic to his younger colleague. Ella realized she wasn't supposed to hear. 'A UTI. I had one last year and thought I'd gone barking mad. Didn't even know who the Prime Minister was.'

'Just as well with this shower in office,' remarked the young woman.

Ella lay back and closed her eyes again. She knew that a TIA was a transient ischaemic attack but had never heard of a UTI.

The hospital seemed to be full of drunks and people screaming at the staff in a hundred different languages like something out of the Tower of Babel.

'Right,' asked the triage nurse, 'how old are you, Mrs Thompson?'

'Sixty-four.'

'Good. What year is it?'

Ella suddenly panicked. 'I should know this,' she replied, looking embarrassed.

'Can you add four and four?'

Panic engulfed Ella again as she couldn't think of the answer.

'Fine. We'll do a CT scan, plus urine and bloods.'

Oh God, this was serious. They must think she'd had a stroke. She tried to fight off the fear of something so horrible.

'Won't take long, then we'll do an ECG.'

Ella wondered if Cory was rushing to the hospital and whether she would have instantly rung Julia, who would be livid that Cory knew first. She wasn't going to think about that now. She tried to do mindfulness exercises to distract from her panic.

Then it was over and she had an ECG and also a chest X-ray for some reason. She supposed she was lucky to be an emergency and not have to sit for hours and hours in A&E.

Finally the senior registrar, a harassed young woman who looked no older than Cory, arrived at the end of her bed.

'Good news, Mrs, er ... Thompson. You haven't had a stroke and there's no sign of brain damage. We think you have a UTI, a urinary tract infection.'

Ella remembered the mumbled reference from the paramedic. 'But how can a urinary infection make you forget things and not know what your hands are for?' Ella demanded.

'Infections can be very serious,' replied the young woman, obviously eager to get off to someone who was more seriously ill than Ella. 'We've had perfectly sane people talking gibberish and unable to answer simple questions. You're suffering from a serious bladder infection which can cause extreme confusion and is often mistaken for early dementia in older patients.'

'So what's the treatment?'

'We'll put you on antibiotics and with luck you should be back to normal in a matter of days.'

Even before the antibiotics were administered Ella felt like jumping up and singing. She hadn't had a stroke and she hadn't got dementia! If she could have, she would have ordered champagne for the whole ward.

But the experience had taught her one thing. From now on she wanted to be among friends.

She had decided to stun Claudia by telling her that if their crazy scheme went ahead, she would sign up for it too.

Laura looked round the house that had been her home for more than twenty years. There was so much accumulated stuff. She knew she was guilty of collecting most of it herself, as well as not throwing things away. The trouble was, in her view, as soon as you threw something out you suddenly wanted it. Well, now was certainly the moment. She'd hoped Bella could help her sort her belongings out but baby Noah had come down with the sniffles and Bella had to cancel. Sam had offered but a job interview had materialized which obviously took priority.

'Maybe I could provide some assistance,' Mrs Lal had suggested. Before Laura could politely refuse her guest had fetched her iPhone and Sam's speaker and the room was suddenly full of Bhangra music. Laura had to admit, it was quite cheering.

'Now, you are in charge,' Mrs Lal informed her generously. 'I will find bags and boxes and we will label them for storage with your friend or give them to the shops for the poor and indigent. Though I have to say, since I have moved here I have found some of your charity shops quite enticing, especially for bold costume jewellery.'

Laura couldn't help smiling at the thought of Mrs Lal's Catherine Walker creations adorned with necklaces from Oxfam.

'Thank you,' Laura replied faintly, realizing the time had

come to Keep or Chuck the evidence of so many years of marriage.

The knick-knacks and photographs, which she'd thought would be so hard to sort through, were easier than she'd expected. Anything with Simon in, including her wedding photographs, went into Chuck. Anything with her children went into Keep.

Laura moved swiftly on to pictures. How strange that Simon had not come back for any of the artworks he'd claimed to love so much. She wondered for a moment what *had* meant something to Simon about their life together.

What would he want to keep? The photos of him and the children? She remembered that the only photos Simon had ever put up himself were in the downstairs loo. A framed photograph of Simon as captain of rugger, of cricket, of fives.

Yes, he'd miss those.

She lifted them all off the wall and carried them back into the sitting room where she placed them carefully in the box marked Chuck.

Next the kitchen. How much cooking would she be doing in her new life? Would it be a case of ready meals for one from COOK, where she'd seen so many grey-haired customers fill their baskets with two-for-one offers?

She lifted the row of cookbooks down from the shelf: Nigella, Jamie Oliver, Nigel Slater and Delia Smith.

It was the Delia that caught her eye – dear old Delia who had been her kitchen companion right from the early days of her marriage when Laura couldn't even boil an egg. It was the original edition, the one with Delia in a red Eighties jacket with shoulder pads and bright red lipstick.

The book fell open at a gravy-spattered page. *Carbonnade de boeuf*. It had been her mainstay for large family gatherings all her married life. Sam had loved the cheese-covered slices of French bread on the top.

A piece of paper slipped out with timings on it. When to put in the casserole. What time to add the pudding. What would it have been? Apple crumble or her speciality pear tart?

Laura found that tears were coursing down her face. Would she ever be cooking for cheerful family gatherings again?

The casserole seemed a symbol of her marriage. Interesting once, exciting even, but now old-fashioned and discarded. Who cooked a carbonnade now?

Her thoughts were interrupted by the shrill chimes of the doorbell.

'Shall I go?' enquired Mrs Lal.

'No, it's fine.' Laura smiled as she opened the door to find Calum standing on the doorstep with a large bunch of pink hydrangeas in his arms. It was a flower she particularly disliked.

'Hello, stranger,' Laura replied sardonically. 'What brings you here after all this time?' She didn't ask him in. She noticed for the first time that his hair was expensively cut in that style ageing men adopt because they think it makes them look younger. And were those *highlights*?

'Laura, I . . .' He tailed off miserably.

'You're going back to your wife,' Laura completed his sentence for him.

Calum looked at her as if she had the miraculous powers of a seer or early Christian saint.

'How did you know? We've only just decided ourselves.'

'Oh well,' Laura replied, without looking behind her at Mrs Lal, 'someone with a lot of experience of marriage warned me that was what you were likely to do.'

'I see. Well, good luck, Laura. You deserve it. You're a very nice woman.'

'So everyone tells me,' Laura replied crisply. 'I hope you're both very happy.' She paused tellingly. 'This time.'

And she shut the door before he'd had the chance to say any more.

For a moment Laura wished she could rush upstairs and not face the 'I told you so' expression her guest would undoubtedly be exhibiting.

But Mrs Lal's smile was all innocence. 'Come and sit down, Mrs Minchin. We have both worked very hard.' She pointed at the wall of boxes and black bin liners. 'As a matter of fact, I purchased a bottle of Dom Perignon from your corner shop. I think this is the time for us to open it.'

Laura looked at her in amazement. Mrs Lal must have concealed it in the fridge under the spring greens and the pitta bread. And to think the corner shop sold Dom Perignon! They must be over the moon.

The pop of the bottle opening was infinitely reassuring. Mrs Lal poured it into two champagne flutes.

'To the future. And do not concern yourself further. I will find you a man who is worthy of your kind and loving nature!'

They clinked glasses.

'As a matter of fact, Mrs Lal,' Laura stated, sipping her Dom Perignon, 'I wouldn't mind if I never encountered a member of the male sex ever again. Apart from my son, that is.'

The reality came to her that when she moved out her unexpected guest would have to move too. 'What are your immediate plans, Mrs Lal?'

Mrs Lal beamed. 'Your kind son has found me a temporary apartment to rent in Kensington.' Laura smiled indulgently. To think she'd never thought of that herself. She had two wonderful children.

As they would soon be parting, Laura finally dared the question that had often occurred to her. She paused.

'Yes?' said Mrs Lal, reading her mind. 'You are thinking if I am such a famous lady in India, why am I not going back there? Do I just want to stay in order to torture my son-in-law?'

Laura almost blushed.

'The truth is, Mrs Minchin, I did not leave my husband. My husband left me. Me, the celebrated matchmaker who appears on TV and in gossip columns! You can imagine how humiliating it would be if that got out!' Her voice rose in indignation at such treachery. 'So I decided to come here and start again.'

Laura, touched that her terrifying guest had trusted her with this delicate revelation, raised her glass. 'To both our new beginnings!'

Claudia stood discreetly behind a herbaceous border at Igden Manor and studied the rough plans her son-in-law Douglas had drawn for her. To her utter amazement Rose McGill was quite keen! That magician Lou Maynard had brought her here for lunch and the chef had apparently done the rest. Rose had even asked if the chef was going to be staying on, a thought that filled Claudia with sudden panic. Sal, too, was considering joining them, since Lou was so keen. Claudia suspected Sal had hoped for the bright lights of Brooklyn, but Lou seemed to have been seduced by Surrey.

Suddenly her crazy dream was becoming a reality. Now Laura was coming to stay and Claudia could try and win her over to life in Little Minsley. The only one still needing to be persuaded was Ella.

222

And her parents. And Don.

She put away the plans, grateful that at least it was a lovely time of year and the countryside was looking its best.

Laura arrived the next day in a large self-drive van. Claudia had expected her to be in pieces at having to leave her beloved home but Laura was surprisingly jaunty.

She even negotiated the narrow space between the gate-posts into Claudia's drive as if she were a Formula One driver judging a difficult gap between two rivals.

Don, who had hoped to direct her, looked stunned.

'I was just thinking that for once I didn't have Simon with me to tell me what a bad driver I am,' Laura announced. 'Shall I leave everything in the van for now or would you rather I started decanting?'

'Lunch first,' insisted Don, who had just got a nice bottle of Burgundy, which he wasn't normally allowed at lunchtime, out of the garage in her honour. The fact that Laura's stuff, now much reduced with Mrs Lal's help, was all going in there had been a source of some irritation to him, since it served as his unofficial wine cellar.

'You never leave anything in there long enough to need a wine cellar anyway,' had been Claudia's acid reply. Fortunately Don liked Laura the best of all the Coven. She was pretty and feminine and didn't seem to hold a universal grudge against men despite that shit Simon's treatment of her.

He liked her even more when she produced a bottle of single malt for him and a ripe Brie that would be perfect with the Burgundy. Cheese was another thing Claudia didn't really approve of and never bought except on special occasions.

She handed the bunch of hydrangeas to Claudia. 'Just for now. I'll buy you some proper flowers next time we're out.'

'Thank you,' Claudia smiled, not pointing out that the front garden was full of pink hydrangeas which she loathed and was always too lazy to get round to replacing. 'They're lovely.'

'No they're not. Calum brought them round as compensation for telling me he's going back to his wife.'

'Oh Laura! He seemed so nice!'

'Especially that time he took a swing at Simon,' endorsed Don, remembering the time Simon had dared to turn up at their daughter's wedding just after dumping Laura.

But secretly Claudia was delighted. Laura was far more likely to join her scheme without the encumbrance of a man.

'Lunch,' announced Claudia and led her friend through the house to a shady table in the back garden.

'So how's it all going with Twilight Towers?' Laura asked gaily after her second glass of wine.

'Surprisingly well. I mean, I'm not saying it's happening . . .'

'Thank God,' muttered Don mutinously.

'There's my parents to sort out. And the money. And a proper working agreement.'

'And a way of me staying here,' Don added.

Claudia ignored him. 'Actually, I'm finding it all a bit much,' she confessed. 'I'm big on ideas, but organizing's never been my forte.'

'A fine time to realize that when you've started this bloody thing going,' snapped Don.

'I know!' Laura smiled at them both, delighted at her inspiration. 'You need Bella!'

'What, your daughter Bella? Bella the goth with spider tattoos all over her hands?' Don demanded.

'Bella is brilliant. She's even living down here. Nigel's teaching at some posh private school. I'm sure she'd help you – especially if there's a chance of cheap accommodation. Didn't you say you wanted all ages, not just a bunch of wrinklies?'

'I think I'm going down to the pub.' Don stood up. With Laura here, Claudia would probably want to have a heart-to-heart about what shits men were. 'Your dad and Hiro will probably be there.'

'Make sure you don't get too pissed to help empty the van,' Claudia commented.

'Who the hell's Hiro?' asked Laura.

Claudia giggled. 'You'll meet him soon. Everyone loves Hiro.'

Laura raised a sceptical eyebrow. She hoped Claudia wasn't trying to fix her up with this Hiro just because Calum had gone back to his wife.

Two days later Bella arrived with baby Noah slung round her neck in one of her colourful slings to discuss the idea of getting involved at the manor. The spiders' web tattoos were still with her, but she had started to abandon her *Hammer House of Horror* outfits and wear colours. Maybe, Laura thought with a smile, it was because the slings looked better against colour and Bella knew she was her own best advert.

'Hi, Mum. I'm so sorry I couldn't help you with the big move. How was it?'

The tender concern in Bella's voice almost made Laura cry. She might have failed at marriage but she'd produced these amazing children. 'Not as bad as I expected. Mrs Lal helped me.'

Bella looked at her in surprise. 'I thought she was supposed to be Kali the goddess of vengeance who eats men, or possibly sons-in-law, for breakfast!'

'I'm not a man or son-in-law. She was actually very helpful.' Laura grinned. 'Apart from her threat to fix me up with a partner worthy of me.' She saw Claudia's quizzical look. 'Mrs Lal is a famous matchmaker back home in India.'

'Right. Now, what is it that you think I can help with?' Bella asked. Laura had explained about the cheap rent for Bella and Nigel if it all came off.

Claudia got out the plans and outlined to Bella exactly how far they'd got with the scheme.

Bella pulled out her iPad. 'The first thing I'd do is find out what kind of accommodation everyone needs. Will the cottages be big enough or do you need to convert any of the outlying buildings? Plus how will you use the main hotel and also the coach house? And of course you'll have to work out how much everyone can pay and get them all together so you can discuss how it'll all work.'

'Bella, you're a genius!'

'Not really. I'm hoping to start my own business so I'm having to get down to basics myself.'

With a sigh of relief, Claudia gave Bella her son-in-law Douglas's details and suggested she talk straight to him.

There was now absolutely no excuse, Claudia concluded, not to try and persuade her mother that living at Igden Manor was just what she and her father needed.

Claudia could hear Mrs O'Brien's strident tones – apparently pointing out the many shortcomings of Mr O'Brien – as soon as she went through the garden gate. But once she opened the door of the kitchen Claudia sensed a subtle change of atmosphere. Her mother was not sitting opposite the carer at the kitchen table entering into the spirit of the discussion but busying herself with unnecessary tidying of the already immaculately tidy spice shelf. When Claudia arrived she looked round and smiled.

Ah-ha, thought Claudia, *Ma is getting bored with Mrs O'Brien's overpowering personality.* No doubt her mother felt there was only room for one overpowering personality – and that was her own.

'So where do you imagine your father and I would live in this wild scheme of yours?' Olivia enquired irritably.

This was more promising than Claudia had expected.

'Igden Manor is a lovely place as you know, more like a medieval hamlet than a hotel, and Gaby's husband Douglas has been doing some terrific plans, rough at the moment admittedly. I rather thought you and Dad might like to be in the main building. The rooms are lovely there and of course there's already a lift.'

'For when we're too gaga to even walk?' Olivia sniffed.

'Do you think you'd *like* to live in a hotel after having your own lovely home?' enquired Mrs O'Brien maliciously.

'It won't *be* a hotel,' corrected Claudia acidly. 'We'll be converting it into luxury accommodation suited to everyone.'

'And will the planners let you?' Mrs O'Brien asked innocently. 'They wouldn't even let my daughter put up a garage.'

'The buildings aren't listed and in a situation like this, where we will be providing our own social care, they may well,' snapped Claudia.

'Funny kind of a care home,' commented the woman.

'It isn't intended to *be* a care home.' Claudia tried to keep her temper. 'More an experiment in growing old differently.'

'I'm not sure I'd want to be part of an experiment, like a lot of those poor rats in laboratories. It's terrible what they do to them.'

Claudia was about to respond when her mother cut in. 'You're perfectly entitled to your view, Mrs O'Brien, but possibly you should keep it to yourself. I think you'll find the dishwasher needs unloading. As a matter of fact,' Olivia addressed her daughter frostily, 'I don't care where I live as long as it's not with that damn robot!'

Claudia took herself discreetly off to the shed.

She stopped on the threshold, listening. Her father never bothered with anything but sports channels, and at this time of year the cricket. Instead the soothing notes of Vaughan Williams filled the entire shed.

'Hello, Dad.' She put her arms round Len and kissed the top of his head. 'Is that "The Lark Ascending"?'

'"Fantasia on a Theme by Thomas Tallis." Lovely, isn't it?'

'I didn't know you were into classical music.'

'Hiro's trying to educate me. We've been listening to Debussy and Elgar.'

Claudia glanced in amazement at the white manikin with the huge blue painted eyes. He actually seemed to be smiling. It ought to be creepy, but somehow it was sweet instead.

'Poor Hiro. He loves *Madame Butterfly*, but being Japanese, it makes him cry.'

'Time for your blood pressure tablets, Leonard,' pointed out Hiro.

Len meekly accepted the pills.

Without meaning to, Claudia sniffed the air. It smelt sweet in that artificial fabric-conditioner sort of way.

Len saw the gesture and laughed. 'Hiro's obsessed with air freshener. Better than shit, I suppose, which reminds me, Hiro. Time for the toilet before we go to the pub.' He disappeared into the outdoor privy which had been there ever since Claudia was a child.

The little robot seemed to feel the need to make polite conversation. 'Why did the traffic light turn red?' he enquired suddenly.

'I don't know,' replied Claudia, taken aback.

'Because it had to change in the middle of the street.'

Claudia collapsed with laughter, partly because it was sweet and funny but mostly due to the bizarre experience of being told a joke by a robot.

'Right.' Len reappeared. 'Are you ready, Hiro?'

'Yes, I am, Leonard, ready when you are,' was the solemn reply. As he opened the door with his articulated metal hand, Hiro turned to Claudia. 'Happy to meet you again, Claudia. I hope that your dreams come true.'

Claudia stood watching them make their bumpy way down the front path, her father with his stick, Hiro on his silent wheels, and felt a lump rising in her throat.

Her father had made a genuine friend. And her all-powerful mother had no idea what to do about it.

Fourteen

Claudia couldn't believe the impact having Bella involved was having.

It was as if a touchpaper had been lit under her mad scheme which would result in the whole thing actually happening.

Bella, with Noah slung round her neck in one of his colourful slings, had busily been drawing up lists of the practicalities. The key thing was how they would get the money together. Something Claudia herself realized she'd been avoiding. Could the accommodation work and what planning permission would be needed? And the biggest question of all: who was actually ready to sign up?

As if that weren't enough, Bella had rounded up a couple of young lads and emptied the hired van of all Laura's furniture which was now neatly stacked in Claudia's garage. She was a marvel. Someone really ought to give her a country to run.

And today – Claudia could hardly believe it – Bella had organized everyone to come and discuss it all in Claudia's sunny kitchen.

'Mum, could you take Noah?' Bella handed the baby over to

his beaming grandmother as she put out coffee cups and a big pile of croissants from the bakery in the village.

Somehow Bella had managed to persuade Olivia and Len, Claudia's mother and father, Sal and Lou Maynard, who had brought Rose McGill from her convalescent home, plus a rather sulky and unconvinced Don, as well as Claudia herself and their son-in-law Douglas with a sheaf of plans.

'Douglas and I have been looking at Igden Manor in a lot of detail,' Bella began. 'Sneaking round in the undergrowth. I think the chef thinks we're having outdoor assignations.' She grinned mischievously at Douglas. 'Anyway, Douglas is the architect, so over to you.'

'I'd like you all to take a look at this.' He indicated his sketches which were propped up on Claudia's cookbook stand in the middle of the table. 'We're lucky for two reasons. Although the hotel and the cottages *look* old, they're actually entirely fake and aren't listed. Secondly, all the cottages are joined together in a three-sided arrangement with the main building in the middle, rather like a medieval monastery. That makes it a lot easier to knock down internal walls and create accommodation of differing sizes, depending on what you need, without radically altering the look of the place. You could actually create one-, two- or even three-bedroom houses.'

'But can you do that? Will the planners let you?' asked Don.

Claudia noted that he was using the word 'you' rather than 'we'.

'And more to the point,' Rose put in pithily, 'can we find out before we commit our cash to the scheme?'

'As I understand it' – Lou looked at Douglas for confirmation – 'the planners in this country will sometimes give you an opinion in advance?'

Douglas nodded.

'And what will happen to the hotel building?' Rose enquired. 'Will there still be a bar and a restaurant?'

Douglas laughed. He really liked Rose. Maybe it was the colonial in them both, she originally from Canada, he from Australia. 'I'm not sure you could have an official bar. More one of those honesty bars you have on holiday. Food is something you'd have to discuss.'

'Food is pretty damn important,' Rose commented.

'Which brings us to staff,' Bella threw in. 'You'd definitely need staff.'

'And a get-out clause,' muttered Don. 'When you all realize you actually hate each other.'

'And do you think you can achieve all this for the sum we can raise between us?'

Douglas shrugged. 'You've put your finger on it, Rose. The next issue is to see how much we can raise of the sum Murdo's asking.'

Bella looked round at the assembled group. 'It seems to me that the really big question isn't about the money, or the accommodation, which can be sorted, or staffing, or even whether there's a bar, but something pretty fundamental. Do you think you could actually live together and make it fun and happy and a million miles better than living on your own?'

Before any of them could answer, the door opened and they looked round. Claudia thought it might be Hiro, eager to be included.

Instead it was Ella.

'Ella! What on earth are you doing here?'

'What do you think? I've decided to throw in my lot with you bunch of superannuated hippies.'

'But why on earth?' Sal protested. 'You've just bought a little cottage on the river.'

'It's a long story.' Ella grinned at them all, still glowing with relief that she didn't have bloody dementia. 'Suffice it to say that living with you lot is probably my only escape from a granny flat in my daughter Julia's garage. Paid for by me.'

Sal burst out laughing. 'You'd better sit down then and join the crew.'

After another hour they were beginning to flag. 'I think we've all got enough to think about,' Claudia announced. 'But first I'd really like to thank Douglas and Bella for all their amazing kindness.'

Bella laughed, a lovely throaty mischievous sound. 'We're not quite as saintly as you make us out to be,' she pointed out. 'There is just a sliver of self-interest. Nigel loathes renting in Guildford. He and Noah and I are longing for somewhere beautiful but reasonable to live and Douglas and Gaby are hoping for a little plot of land they could develop.'

'One of those outbuildings you've got so many of might make an amazing living and working unit,' Douglas seconded. He waited a beat of a second. 'You did say you wanted young blood, Claudia.'

At this point Len, Claudia's dad, who hadn't seemed to be taking much in, sat up. 'Excellent idea,' he insisted with a twinkle. 'Douglas can organize the croquet tournaments.'

Douglas laughed and started to hand round copies of his sketches. 'I'd like you all to take a proper look at these and try and decide what sort of accommodation would suit you.'

'Bloody hell,' Don murmured, 'the asylum's really opening, isn't it?'

Claudia studiously ignored him.

Having Bella on board, Claudia told her proud mother Laura, was changing everything. Suddenly things were happening.

She and Douglas had not only got a meeting with the planners but Bella had somehow charmed the authorities into putting their application in for the next planning committee meeting, so they needed to make decisions fast.

The inevitable arguments would now ensue about how much each person paid, who wanted which cottage, and who deserved the more substantial coach house.

Claudia had expected the stiffest opposition to come from her parents, or rather her mother Olivia. They had, after all, lived in their home for thirty years. Her father would be happy with anywhere as long as there was some kind of shed nearby, but Olivia had always had delusions of grandeur.

What Claudia didn't know, because Olivia had kept it from her, was that her strong, obstinate, proud mother was beginning to be scared herself.

It all came to a head when they got back from Igden Manor and Olivia found that Len, without Hiro to nag him as he had been borrowed for the afternoon by Lou Maynard, had messed himself, and then on top of that there was a note from Mrs O'Brien that the washing machine had packed up.

For one terrible moment she thought she might hit her husband.

Just in time, the sound of wheels behind her on the tiled passage made her whip round. 'I see Leonard has had an accident,' announced Hiro without any inflection of criticism in his metallic voice.

'He hasn't had an accident!' Olivia shouted, lowering her face to his level. 'He's messed in his pants!'

Hiro took the bewildered Len's hand in his artificial one.

'Come, Leonard,' he announced patiently, 'let's get you cleaned up.'

When they'd gone Olivia half collapsed at the kitchen table, feeling guilty. At least in this Igden Manor community, Len wouldn't be her sole responsibility. Of all Hiro's skills the ability to clean up her husband had been one of the most astonishing in fact. Frankly, she hadn't believed it until Lou had showed her a robot demonstrating it on YouTube.

With her daughter Bella suddenly so in demand, Laura offered to take on her baby grandson Noah at least part of every day.

'Hello, baby.' She looked into Noah's mysterious deep blue eyes, which seemed to have the wisdom of ages in their inky depths. 'You and I are going to really get to know each other.'

Noah's answer was a long slow smile, as if he already found the game of life a very funny and slightly ridiculous one.

'What do you think?' she asked him very seriously. 'Should I give up London and come and live here with my friends? I could see more of you, which would be wonderful, but do you know what, Noah, I don't feel *old* enough? Is that ridiculous and vain? Am I still looking for love even though I ought to know better?'

Noah offered her the sweetest of smiles and filled his nappy noisily.

'You're quite right,' Laura conceded. 'That's what I ought to think about love too. A heap of poo. And nothing like as sweet-smelling as yours is.'

Bella and Douglas managed to get the meeting to discuss their plans much sooner than they'd expected. It was only when they were sitting opposite the planners and Douglas began to outline the scheme they realized they were benefiting from a triple whammy: the authorities were worried that if Igden Manor went bust it would look bad for business locally; the leader of the council personally disliked Lord Binns – no doubt due to the historic enmity between posh aristos and local government officials – but didn't want to offend the largest landowner in the county; and lastly because social care was the buzzword of the moment and the Tory council knew it didn't provide enough of it.

'Tell you what,' Bella grinned as they came out of an hourlong meeting when almost everything they'd asked for had been okayed in principle, 'I'll bet you twenty quid they'll be calling Igden Manor a "community of the future" or some such thing, not to mention showing people round it, even though they haven't put a penny into it.'

She stopped, her eyes widening with mischief. 'You don't think they actually *would* put some money into it, do you?'

Douglas laughed out loud. 'They might if you were in charge of negotiations. You're quite an operator, Miss Bella Minchin.'

'*Ms* Bella Minchin, if you don't mind. How about nipping into the pub for a swift half to celebrate?'

Douglas nodded and ten minutes later they were sitting in the snug of The Laden Ox, clinking glasses.

'So what do we do next?' Bella enquired.

'We get people to opt for the accommodation they want and then the tricky bit – get them to prise the cash out of the socks under their beds and lay it on the table.'

'Okay, my metal mate, how have things been down here with Leonard?' Lou asked Hiro, putting his arm round the manikin as if he were indeed an old friend.

For once Lou didn't get the usual response to his charismatic personality. Hiro shook him off.

'I am not a spy,' he announced tersely.

'No, but you are designed to be a carer and carers report back on their clients. For their own sake.'

'Things are going as well as expected,' Hiro conceded haughtily. 'His wife does not like me and neither does the woman who was hired to care and neglected her duties.'

'Why doesn't Leonard's wife like you?'

'I think she is jealous. Yet she has no desire to do the caring herself.'

'Perhaps you should try and win her over. From what I've heard you're a very winning little chap.'

'Perhaps you are right. I will go now if that is all right.'

He disappeared out of the door on his soundless wheels.

Sal shook her head. 'What a weird modern world we live in. I can't even cope with Siri on my smartphone.'

'Sweet old-fashioned gal. You ain't seen nothing yet. It won't be long before every home has a Hiro.' He laughed and reached out for her, pulling her towards the bed. She wanted to talk about his children, all eight of them, and what they would think of his decision, and whether he could really give up his life in Brooklyn for Surrey, but she knew better than to protest. Being handed this happiness so late in life had taught her one thing.

Enjoy it while you can.

She did let herself ask one little question. 'Whereabouts do you want to live in our free-spirited non-retirement community?'

'The cottage at the end,' he announced with his usual instant certainty. 'Next to the pool. It'll be nice and quiet and I can get up and swim seventy lengths then come back and make passionate love to you.'

'After seventy lengths?' she teased. 'Are you sure you're not boasting?'

'Want to try me out?' He moved towards her threateningly.

Laughing, she fell back onto the bed. If he wanted to make passionate love to a one-breasted sexagenarian, who was she to object?

One thing she knew for sure. Growing old with Lou certainly wasn't going to be dull.

In the end Claudia and Don opted for the coach house themselves. 'I'll agree to this crackpot scheme provided I get some independence from the Coven,' he insisted. 'Otherwise I'm out.'

Claudia didn't actually believe this but she could see the appeal of the coach house. It was rather a handsome flint-built building with its own walled garden at a small distance from the hotel at the rear, quite near the road, which Claudia was about to protest about, but seeing her husband's mutinous expression, she wisely kept her mouth shut. It was almost opposite a Harvester and two minutes from a rather scuzzy pub. She could see that both these might hold an attraction for Don. He could cross the road and complain to sympathetic ears in the public bar about his harpy of a wife and her loony friends. He'd had high hopes of signing Lou up to his camp at the start of the negotiations, but despite his overwhelmingly masculine demeanour, Lou seemed to be a secret feminist. Weird people, Americans.

Ella chose a two-bedroom cottage at the other end of the U-shaped block, quite near a small duck pond. After the river, she announced happily, she'd got used to the sound of water and ducks quacking was the kind of peaceful sound that would get her to sleep. She actually hoped to carve out a bit of private garden of her own but decided to try and negotiate that later. There was enough to fall out over already.

Rose had opted for the main hotel building. 'It reminds me of a chateau I once had a fling in near Bordeaux. Plus I want to be near the lift and the bar,' she announced firmly.

The staff, once they decided how many they would need and could afford, could be accommodated in the small block near the hotel car park where the current waiters and chambermaids, all friendly and unfailingly polite young people, were currently billeted.

Bella had called a meeting this afternoon for final bids to be made and for everyone to announce how much they could afford to pay, which they would do via sealed bids to avoid embarrassment. Tension crackled over the tea and scones as they gathered in the large chintzy lounge.

'Lord Binns has hinted he would settle for a million,' Douglas announced. 'It's a ludicrously low sum, but he owns half the county and I think he's bored with all the problems.'

'Plus he wants to see more of Rose,' Sal teased.

Rose simply raised a thin pencilled eyebrow, making Sal think of Edith Piaf at her most outrageous.

'There would also be the conversion costs and we need to consider the question of staff,' Bella announced brightly. 'I have researched this and staff would be £12 an hour at least plus National Insurance and pension contributions, so a minimum of £15. Claudia has asked me to stay on and manage, which I'm happy to do. Especially if we get that dear little cottage with the creeper growing up it, two along from the end.'

'You'll be next to us,' Sal smiled. 'That'd be lovely.'

'And of course there's the chef,' insisted Rose. 'I'm not in unless he is.'

Bella almost dropped her head into her hands but decided it would be unprofessional. Finally she turned to her mother.

'What about you, Mum? Are you throwing in your lot with us wild frontierspeople?'

Laura felt herself blushing. How ridiculous. Yet she did feel a bit of a traitor. This was such an important venture to her friends.

'Not me, I'm afraid. Too much of a city girl.'

'In Twickenham?' Bella pointed out.

'All right, too much of an almost-Londoner. I will come and look after Noah a lot, though.'

Bella opened the envelopes and quickly got the calculator out on her phone.

'I'm afraid we need someone else to join up,' she announced evenly.

Everyone tried not to look at Laura, who was acutely aware of the money for her half of the house soon sitting in her bank account.

Claudia caught Sal's eye. She knew Lou was a rich man and that he was, after all, interested in Igden as a business model for similar places as well as a place to live with Sal.

Sal discreetly shook her head. She was already worried what his children were going to think of this mad idea, and of her for pulling him into it.

Lou the businessman's mind, however, was running on another track altogether. 'You could easily borrow it from a bank.'

'I didn't think banks were keen to lend to anyone over sixty,' protested Ella. 'I'm sure I heard a whole piece about it from Outraged Pensioner from Tunbridge Wells. They won't lend to wrinklies even if they're rolling in it.'

'British banks might not,' conceded Lou. 'But Chinese Banks would. And Indian Banks are falling over themselves to lend here.'

A wild outrageous thought sparked in Laura's brain. She might not be ready to come and live here herself. But she could think of someone who might.

She found herself smiling secretly.

Would it be fair to unleash Mrs Lal on her friends' fledgling retirement community?

Fifteen

'So who the hell is she, this Indian woman?'

Claudia flushed with embarrassment at the *memsahib* tone in which her mother Olivia uttered these words.

'Her name's Lalita Lal,' Laura replied, struggling to find the right diplomatic words to describe the phenomenon that was Mrs Lal. 'She's the mother-in-law of the lovely man I've been working for in London. She's quite rich, very well dressed, and back home in India she's a well-known matchmaker.'

'How old is she?' Olivia persisted.

'I don't exactly know. Well over seventy, I'd say.'

'I thought she was the interfering old bat you couldn't wait to get rid of?' Ella asked suspiciously. 'You wouldn't be trying to dump her on us so you wouldn't offend your employers?'

'How could you suggest that, Ella?' Laura was genuinely wounded. If this was an example of them all living together, then she was glad she was out of it. 'I didn't get on with her at first but then she was incredibly kind to my son Sam, and actually very kind to me.' She thought of the Bhangra music and the Dom Perignon and how Mrs Lal had made leaving her home so much easier.

'And yet you won't be inviting her to join you in your new abode, I take it?' The sarcasm was still there.

'For God's sake, Ella,' Laura replied, 'I don't even know where I'm going to be living!'

'Okay,' she conceded, feeling guilty that the flat Laura wanted so much had fallen through, partly as a result of her own inattention. 'Why don't you find out what this lady's situation is, whether she'd be remotely interested, and whether she could afford to buy a stake in an olde English manor house and live with a bunch of oldies in Surrey? And then we'll meet her.'

Laura rang Mr A that afternoon. The suppressed excitement in his voice was abundantly clear. 'Mrs Minchin, you are as the white dove after the flood returning with an olive branch in its mouth. Mrs A and I have been at wits' end trying to find the solution that would keep her happy. I think that perhaps you are providing it.'

Laura felt panic rising like the very flood waters Mr A had so vividly evoked. This was all moving dangerously quickly. Of course, money had not been mentioned yet.

'Besides, Mrs Minchin, my mother-in-law has conceived one of her rare affections both for you and your interesting son.'

'The thing is—' Laura attempted to damp down his ardour – 'to buy a share would actually cost a lot. And it would have to be on a trial basis at first.'

'It would be peanuts to Mrs Lal!' declared Mr A. 'She could buy the whole thing if she wanted. Her second husband – not Mrs A's father, you understand – was a manufacturer of wire needed in the telecommunications industry. I'm sure I need to say no more.' He must be a brave man who had dared drop

Mrs Lal, Laura thought privately, and cause her so much embarrassment that she didn't want to return home.

'Perhaps she might like to come and see round and meet the other tenants then? All very informal,' she added hastily, 'no commitment on either side.'

'I think she would like that very much. I will ask her this very evening when she comes round.'

Laura said goodbye. The thought occurred to her that if Mrs Lal was so bloody rich, why had she ended up in her spare bedroom?

She was sitting on Claudia's sofa later that night, a glass of chilled white wine beside her and Noah on her knee laughing up at her, thinking this was pretty close to heaven when her mobile rang. She knew before answering that it would be Mr A.

'Mrs Minchin, it is I. I wanted to tell you that my mother-in-law is very interested in your proposition and wonders if she could come and look tomorrow?'

'A woman of decision anyway,' Claudia commented, refilling Laura's glass.

Laura nodded, not feeling able to mention quite how much decision.

There was quite a buzz of excitement at Claudia's house the next day waiting to see the celebrated matchmaking millionairess arrive. They all somehow pictured her as an Indian Cruella de Vil who would turn up in a long limo, possibly accompanied by Dalmatians. So they were disappointed when a quite normal Ford Focus parked outside at the time Mrs Lal was expected.

And even more surprised when the occupant turned out to

be Julia, Ella's daughter, looking extremely angry and demanding to see her mother.

'Julia!' Ella exclaimed when she was discovered lying on a chaise longue in the conservatory having a post-prandial nap. 'What on earth are you doing here, darling?'

'What do you think I'm doing?' demanded her irate daughter, anger bringing out unattractive blotches on her face and neck. 'I'm here because Cory told me you don't want to live in the granny flat Neil and I have been to considerable trouble, not to mention expense, to have designed for you. That you want to live down here much nearer Cory than me and your grandchildren with your champagne-swilling friends using up our inheritance on some ludicrous post-hippie commune!'

Ella took a deep breath, realizing she had been putting off breaking the news to her demanding daughter. 'I'm really sorry, darling, but the thing is, I'm absolutely fine. I just had a urinary tract infection which was making me behave rather strangely. Now I've had antibiotics I'm completely better and don't need looking after at all.'

'Right,' Julia said, unappeased. 'So that's why Cory says you're selling your cottage so you can come and live here with the dotty brigade in some swish hotel which you're actually bloody *buying*! And how much is that going to cost?'

Before Ella had the chance to answer, Julia had turned round. 'Well, I think it's really selfish!' she yelled, almost hysterical.

In all the excitement of the mother–daughter confrontation no one noticed the taxi that had just turned off the main road and was approaching down Claudia's drive.

It stopped a feet away from Julia.

The door opened and a vision appeared dressed in a sari of

orange, magenta and fuchsia silk accompanied by the sound of tinkling bracelets.

'Mrs Lal!' Laura exclaimed, stunned that she had abandoned her usual Catherine Walker elegance for a sari that looked as if it came from Shepherd's Bush market.

'By God,' declared Len enthusiastically, pushing to the front of the group. 'It's a nautch girl! I wonder if she's going to dance.'

Claudia had a faint recollection that a nautch girl was one of the famous temple dancers who kept the British *sahibs* in thrall to their charms. Their new guest would surely be offended at so sexist, not to mention imperialist, an implication.

But Mrs Lal didn't seem to find the reference insulting at all and had produced a simpering smile.

'Stop it, Dad,' Claudia insisted. 'You've been reading too much *Flashman*.'

'What is *Flashman*?' enquired Hiro, as usual at Len's heels.

'*Flashman* is a fictional bounder in the British army who behaves utterly disgracefully and always gets away with things,' Claudia began to explain, then stopped abruptly. What the hell was she doing explaining the dastardly hero to a metal manikin? Modern life was seriously strange.

'As a matter of fact,' Mrs Lal intervened, 'I love *Colonel Flashman*. I like to think he is a true representative of the British army officer.'

Laura decided she'd better change the subject. 'It's great of you to come down so quickly. Would you like to come and see round the manor?'

'Yes, indeed I would. I am very intrigued at the interesting life choice my daughter and son-in-law have outlined to me. But could I first make use of your facilities?'

'Of course,' Laura smiled. 'I'll show you the way.'

'I also need to change my clothes,' she whispered to Laura as they looked for the loo. 'I can see my colourful choice of outfit has startled the assembled company and perhaps given your aged father the wrong idea. I will change straight away.'

In fact, the assembled company was even more startled when Mrs Lal re-emerged in a black designer dress she must have stowed in her capacious handbag, plus a long Isadora Duncan-style scarf.

'Where did the dancing girl go?' Len enquired, looking around in a bewildered fashion.

'Oh, for God's sake keep up, Leonard,' snapped his wife Olivia. 'And stop waffling on about temple dancers.'

'Come, Leonard,' Hiro announced huffily, 'it is time for your toilet.' He ushered Len away as Olivia watched them, sparks of fury glinting in her eye.

'How original,' commented Mrs Lal. 'A robot carer. We could do with that in India. One day we will have 150 million over-sixties.'

This thought was so astonishing that no one could think of an answer except Hiro, who stopped and executed a kind of old-fashioned bow. 'Dearest madam, I would be happy to demonstrate my caring skills,' he announced proudly.

'Amazing little fella, isn't he?' guffawed Len. 'He can do the *Times* crossword and wipe your bum after.'

'Not with the *Times* crossword, I hope,' Mrs Lal commented drily.

'Really, Leonard,' Olivia pronounced, 'that's hardly a suitable subject.'

'I think it's exceptionally suitable,' her husband replied.

'And so would you if the alternative was wearing incontinence pads.'

Laura decided it was time she and Ella led Mrs Lal off to Igden Manor. She was certainly getting a baptism of fire.

Mrs Lal seemed entirely enchanted. She took one look at the hollyhocks and delphiniums and the abudance of roses and pronounced it to be just like her family home in India.

'If you did want to live here,' Ella asked her cautiously after an extensive tour, 'which part do you think you'd like?'

'Oh,' Mrs Lal replied. 'Definitely in the hotel.'

'Of course it won't *be* a hotel,' Ella pointed out. 'People will have their own apartments.'

'But you won't have to clean it *yourself?*' she asked, horrified.

'Of course you will,' Ella replied briskly, although this had not been discussed. 'I mean we're not *old.*'

'You know, Ella,' Laura whispered to her as Mrs Lal stood admiring the delphiniums. 'I think you've still got a lot of working out to do.'

And as it turned out, they'd have to do it pretty quickly. The outline planning permission came through the following week.

Bella called them all together.

'So, people, what are we going to do? Are you going to offer this Mrs Lal and her Indian millions a place? If you do, then we are ready to approach Lord Binns officially.'

'I say go for it!' Lou announced, with his usual undimmed enthusiasm.

'You always say go for it,' Sal smiled at him lovingly.

'Of course I do.' He ruffled her short grey hair. 'I'm an American!'

'But what if you hate her?' Now that it actually might be happening, Laura was feeling doubly guilty that she wasn't joining in and that she had suggested the force of nature that was Mrs Lal.

'We're not supposed to be living in each other's pockets,' Rose insisted sensibly. 'It's a big place.'

'As long as she doesn't try and take over running everything,' Olivia commented acidly. 'I've seen her sort before at the golf club.'

'Actually,' Laura threw in, 'what she really wants to do is more matchmaking. She's thrilled there's a big over-fifties singles club in Guildford, and guess what? They do speed dating over the road at the Harvester on Tuesdays. I think that should keep her busy.'

'What do you think, Don?' Ella asked.

Don looked up in surprise from his phone. He'd been considering nipping over to the pub. No one usually asked him what he thought. 'Oh, yes, fine by me.'

Claudia knew from years of familiarity with her husband that he had no idea what he was agreeing to. Perhaps, if they wanted to get the venture off the ground, it was just as well. 'Looks like we're agreed then. Mrs Lal's in.'

'Isn't anyone consulting Leonard?' chipped in Hiro.

'All right, everyone?' Bella enquired.

They nodded their assent, this time Len included.

'We ought to have some champagne,' Ella exclaimed.

'Let's wait till Murdo accepts before we crack open the bubbly,' Rose pointed out sensibly.

'Okay, who's going to make the offer?' Bella looked round at the assembled faces.

'I will,' replied Rose with a small secret smile.

'Do you want me along for moral support?' asked Lou.

'No, I think I'll do just fine on my own,' Rose replied.

Claudia had a suspicion they might be seeing quite a lot of Lord Murdo Binns in future.

And then extraordinarily, amazingly, it was done.

Lord Murdo Binns stood in his huge study in his vast Elizabethan pile, laughing uproariously at his own private joke, as he accepted their offer. Rose had dressed up for the occasion in a high-necked purple dress with a three-stranded pearl choker, and rather precarious high heels for someone who had recently been so ill. She looked marvellous. She even got Murdo's secretary to take a photo on her phone to show the others the historic moment.

To the great relief of all, the miraculous Rose had persuaded Murdo to give them time to sell their own homes before he required payment. Then Lou, despite Sal's concern, went a step further and offered each of them a no-interest bridging loan so that, if necessary, they could all stay in their homes until the building work was finished which made the whole process much less worrying.

Sal was looking worried at his generosity but Claudia was only grateful, and summoned the estate agent to value her parents' home as well as their house, plus advise them about when to put it on the market.

He was particularly excited about her parents'. 'Rectories are always in demand from city types,' he confided to Claudia. 'It sounds good when they're telling all their friends. Plus your parents have hardly touched the house in years. People like that. Especially city types.' The estimate he then delivered made Claudia have to sit down. He was keen on their house too, just the kind of place people like to retire in, and quoted her a reasonable price which would more than meet their contribution to the manor.

The man announced he could also find Sal and Lou a very nice rental property through his contacts, where they could stay during the building work.

She couldn't wait to tell her parents. She thought of all the steep stairs, the patches of damp that her mother ignored, the lack of proper central heating and the inconvenient kitchen and could see why her mother might want to move to a warm hotel-like environment where someone else was responsible for calling the plumber.

The thought suddenly struck Claudia that as the instigator of the scheme that might be her. And then she remembered brilliant Bella. They would be all right as long as Bella stayed on to manage the place.

Bella and Nigel had opted to move into their cottage right away, despite all the disruption ahead, and though Claudia worried about Noah, they were young and brave and it did make sense that Bella should be around. The work would be finished sooner with her to charmingly chivvy. At least it was all at the back of the property, with the heavy work out of the way and the finished rooms inhabitable.

One thing Claudia was shocked to discover from Douglas was that old people were encouraged to have showers not baths. It was the getting in and out, he explained. They would have to have hoists, and hoists were very expensive.

Claudia tried not to think of being so old she was hoisted into the bath. And all the power points would have to be moved to wheelchair-access level. It was all rather lowering.

And then she remembered the good things. Her friends around her. Help with her parents. A swimming pool!

The trickiest question was when to put their houses on the market, especially their own home. Her parents' rectory would be snapped up in a flash.

Claudia sat down and treated herself to a chocolate biscuit with her coffee. Maybe it would be more straightforward than she'd thought.

With all this talk of house moving, Laura realized she really must find a place of her own. The terrifying thought hit her – where *was* home? A message on her phone from the young woman agent in London, who obviously still felt guilty about accepting a higher offer on the flat Laura had liked so much, informed her of a lovely property quite like the one she'd lost that had suddenly come on the market. Would she be interested?

Yes, she would. A bridge between lives would suit her very well. She doubted if Claudia would mind if she left stuff here. She explained the situation to Claudia, who of course told her she was still very welcome, and caught a train that morning to view the place.

The agent was right. It was nice. Knowing how quickly nice places went, she made an offer on the spot and was instantly accepted.

Now she faced telling all the others and, worst of all, saying goodbye to her grandson.

'Are you sure, Mum?' Bella asked her anxiously, putting her arms round her mother. 'Now that it's all actually happening here?'

'It's really hard,' Laura admitted. 'But I just feel too young to bury myself in Surrey. I'll come and visit. Promise.'

'You're still hoping to meet someone, aren't you?' She surveyed her mother affectionately. 'I don't see why you shouldn't. You're amazingly young and pretty.' The words 'for your age' hung unspoken in the air between them.

'I'm going to miss Noah so much.' Almost the best thing

about Laura's stay with Claudia had been spending so much time with her grandson. She would miss everything about him, the feel of his skin, his milky smell, the mischievous grin that appeared every time he saw her.

'He'll miss you too. One of the best ideas about your mad hippie commune is mixing up the generations.'

'Except that I'm not staying,' sighed Laura. The pain of the decision was almost as bad as when her marriage collapsed.

'Come on, Mum, this isn't like you. You're a glass half full person. We'll soon come and stay in your spare bedroom and christen the new flat, won't we, Noah?'

He held out one of his fat little wrists. He'd already learned that if he did this Laura would kiss it.

Laura felt a tear fall as she did so.

It was only an hour to London but it would feel like a hundred miles. She'd better make the most of her remaining time here.

As soon as the agent left, Don started banging around grumpily in what could only be called male passive resistance. The trouble was, like most men, Don might be the life and soul of the party when he was in the pub, but the idea of *living* with anyone, even his own friends, filled him with dread. Eventually it was too much for Claudia.

'Just think about other people for a change. My parents need looking after, my father dreads living in a care home, and if you recall, I gave up the career I loved to move here partly because you wanted to. You had actually seen round this house behind my back!'

Don had the grace to look shamefaced. 'Fair enough,' he sighed with the air of an early Christian martyr.

'And if you go round looking like that, I may murder you and save you the decision!'

Finally he produced a small smile.

'That's better. It'll be fun.'

'Of course it will,' he attempted bravely.

Claudia decided to put their house on the market before he could change his mind. They had an offer in less than a month from a couple not unlike themselves who were moving out of the city. In fact, they loved it so much they were prepared to wait for as long as it took for Claudia and Don to move out. They stood at the back door holding hands and gazing out at the garden. 'It's just what we dreamed of,' the woman whispered to her husband.

'Oh my God,' Don poked Claudia. 'Hand-holders.'

'Isn't it better if we're selling up that it's to people who're going to love the place?' Claudia demanded.

'Yes, but *hand-holders*. Whenever I see grey-haired hand-holders I want to shoot them.'

'When did you turn into such an old cynic? What's wrong with people with grey hair showing affection?' But actually Claudia agreed. She and Don didn't go in for that sort of nonsense.

The buyers became a little less mistily romantic when it came to some rising damp pointed out in the survey, but they finally arrived at an agreeable sum which would easily meet Claudia and Don's contribution for the coach house.

'Well, Claudie, looks like we're joining a commune,' Don murmured. 'I'd better look out my loon pants and see if they still fit me.'

'It's not a commune,' Claudia replied waspishly.

'You prefer retirement community, do you?' her husband grinned.

Claudia shrugged. They really were going to have to find a better name for the concept behind the manor.

And finally the project was underway.

Mrs Lal had grandly announced she was going back to India for a short while to tie up some affairs there. Sal had moved out of her flat and into the cottage the agent had found until the manor was ready.

Douglas had been officially appointed, through his firm, to mastermind the works. Bella would project manage. Len and Hiro were taking a particular interest and became a regular feature as spectators, which the builders seemed to find a great joke. Hiro was even asked to do the odd calculation.

The building works only halted once when Len, in breach of every building site rule, charmed a strapping workman into letting him have a go with the big digger and ended up with a heart scare.

Claudia had to rush to hospital and found the faithful Hiro at his side and no sign of her mother Olivia.

'I'm so sorry, love. I know I shouldn't have done it but I miss all those big machines.' Her father, before he retired, had been a structural engineer. 'But one thing is good. I've found out I've got a bad heart.' He took Claudia's hand. 'Will you promise me something, Claudie?' His voice was suddenly serious. 'If I have a heart attack, don't let them take me into hospital and stick tubes in me like Frankenstein's monster. I don't want to be revived. I want to die at home. Will you promise that, please?' There was a crack in his voice that wrenched at Claudia.

He turned to Hiro. 'Will you too?'

Hiro took his hand. 'Leonard, I am only a machine.'

'No you're not. You're my friend. And you've got more brains than most idiots I meet.'

Hiro nodded solemnly.

Sixteen

Ella thought about putting her cottage on the market in the conventional way through an agent and couldn't be bothered. She'd been through the whole process so recently. Instead she called up Tim McInerney, the developer who'd outbid her in the auction and then sold it to her for the price he'd paid. Julia would protest she wouldn't get as much for it that way, but Ella decided it was like selling your car via part exchange rather than doing it yourself on eBay. Worth it to save yourself the hassle.

It was all done in a very gentlemanly way and he even suggested they have a drink when she was next in London. That would give Julia something to think about, if she had a beau who was twenty years younger!

Instead she ought to think about where she was going to live for now. She had decided she wanted to live locally, especially as Claudia had asked her to plant a vegetable garden for the manor so they could grow their own produce. Wandering through the village, she saw a sign in The Laden Ox offering a cabin in the wood at the bottom of their pub garden. The drawback was no water, loo or electricity. Suddenly this appealed to Ella. She would be a hermit or a wood sprite, redis-covering nature. She went in and hired the place on the spot.

The pub landlady was thrilled and got them both a glass of wine to mark the occasion.

Great, thought Ella, *what could be nicer than living in a wood at the bottom of a pub garden?* Even if it did mean she had to sleep with two hot-water bottles inside a sleeping bag when it got really cold.

Just as they were clinking their glasses a rather attractive man wandered into the pub to see if it was open yet. He was about her age, rather suave with designer stubble and a silk scarf knotted in the manner of José Mourinho.

'What are you celebrating, girls?' he enquired merrily. 'Can anyone join if they pick up the tab?'

'Now, Daniel,' tutted the landlady. 'We're not officially open yet. This lady is going to move up to Igden Manor as soon as it's finished, but till then she's renting my chalet in the wood.'

'Is she indeed?' He turned to Ella. 'You're part of the new-age old-age commune then?' His eyes twinkled mischievously. 'We're all riveted to see how it turns out. Will there be non-stop Bob Dylan and naked festivals with free Sanatogen?'

'I think we'll probably keep our clothes on most of the time,' Ella replied. 'We don't want to scare the horses and children.'

Daniel surveyed Ella's neat, still gamine appearance. 'I think the horses and children could probably cope and the rest of us might enjoy it.'

Ella held up her glass of wine consideringly. This man was flirting with her. And he was clearly a regular in the pub where she was going to be an almost-resident. What did she think about that?

'So how long before it'll all be finished up there?'

'Quicker than you'd think. They're working at it full tilt.'

'I'm amazed at old Lord Binns agreeing to sell at such a knock-down price.' Clearly the whole village knew every detail of the deal. She'd have to get used to the difference between village living and the anonymity of London.

'Perhaps he's looking forward to the naked festivals as well.' Shocked at herself, Ella realized she was flirting back.

'Dirty old man. He has to be eighty at least.'

'Excuse me.' Ella slipped as elegantly as she could off her bar stool. 'I have to go and sort out my stuff.'

'Hope to see more of you, as they say,' Daniel replied, opening the door for her.

Later on, when she unpacked the few things she'd brought with her for her new cabin living, she went to pick up the key from the landlady. 'So who exactly was that?' she asked.

'Daniel Forrest. He runs the local choir. They meet here every week.'

Oh my God, Ella realized, feeling foolish. So that was Daniel the sexy choirmaster. The man Claudia had had a flirtation with, which had almost wrecked her daughter's wedding when Gaby found out.

Ella could see Claudia's point. There was something intriguing about Daniel Forrest.

All the same, the last thing they needed was Ella herself falling for Daniel Forrest. She'd better make sure Claudia kept distracting her with the vegetable garden!

Claudia had to admit they were incredibly lucky with their builders. They were punctual, polite and amazingly hardworking. To her amazement they even worked on Saturdays.

And considering she'd known nothing about building work, Bella was an absolutely brilliant project manager. With advice from Douglas she'd trawled the internet and now could speak Builder fluently. Claudia, for instance, had no idea what things like M&E – which turned out to be mechanical and electrical – or UFH – underfloor heating – meant, but Bella grasped them at once and had gained the respect of the building site even though she quite often had Noah slung round her chest when she issued her instructions. Claudia had taken to looking after Noah some of the time since Laura was in London, and it had made her rather hope her daughter Gaby might decide to have one herself. Of course she couldn't *say* anything. Mothers these days weren't allowed to have views on wanting grandchildren or it was seen as a breach of human rights.

After that life settled down much as before as summer changed into autumn and then winter. Ella made several visits back to London to the famous allotment for advice and tips for planting the vegetable garden, and also, Claudia suspected, because she missed it so much.

Claudia, shopping in Sainsbury's, saw a large stack of mince pies and sent a photo of it to Gaby on her phone, with the caption: Oh my God, the nightmare that is Christmas approacheth.

Then came the idea that, while her parents still had the rectory, it would be lovely to have a really big Christmas there, and it would be a great way of saying goodbye to it.

So they all started planning. Olivia loved guests, especially if other people did the work. And actually a communal Christmas was great fun, when each person could contribute something different.

After that the months seemed to flash by and finally, *finally*, the following May, Douglas and Bella announced that if they didn't mind ignoring a few builders finishing off, it was ready for them to move in.

Claudia decided she ought to move first to supervise everything and Don, who looked about as thrilled with the move as a wet Wednesday in Wigan, finally agreed to organize vans and transport. 'Poor Vito' – he surveyed their dog – 'I bet he'll hate the move,' he stated glumly.

Vito, who loved every two-legged creature from the postman to a passing burglar, was looking decidedly upbeat at the prospect of more humans to pet and feed him.

They moved their belongings plus Vito's basket into the coach house, where Bella had thoughtfully arranged (as she had in all the apartments) a moving-in bunch of roses in a jam jar.

'Oh, look at that!' Claudia pointed out almost tearfully. 'Like home already!'

The day after, when they had at least roughly unpacked, they would move her parents and – a subject of much disagreement – Hiro the robot.

'At least he doesn't need his own room,' commented Don.

'My mother keeps putting him in the broom cupboard with the vacuum cleaner,' Claudia giggled.

'I suppose it begs the question,' Don said, shaking his head thoughtfully. 'What exactly *is* a carer robot? A broom with a brain?'

'Hiro's been wonderful with Dad. He's much more than a broom.'

They surveyed their new home.

There was a sudden knock and Bella arrived with a bottle of champagne, holding the now-toddling Noah firmly by the hand in case Claudia's dog was there, whom Noah now took great delight in chasing.

'We've come to welcome you and show you all the features,' she announced proudly.

'You shouldn't have gone to the expense of champagne.' Claudia knew Bella's finances were stretched, even if the free accommodation helped a lot.

'It was on offer in Aldi!' Bella grinned. 'It was so cheap I could buy one for everyone.'

'Who cares.' Don tickled Noah who laughed delightedly. 'Champagne is champagne. I wonder where the glasses are.' He looked round at all their unpacked boxes.

'Don't worry.' Bella rootled around in the backpack that went everywhere with her. 'Plastic but still flutes!' She handed round three champagne glasses.

'Don will do it. He's an expert.'

Don grinned and began to open the champagne. 'The secret is to move the bottle not the cork,' he informed them. After three turns the cork popped open with not even a drop spilled. 'Like the sigh of a satisfied woman,' he announced pompously.

'If you say that one more time, I'll divorce you!' Claudia informed him.

'Come on, time for the tour,' Bella intervened and started off into the living area. The dark-beamed oppressive almost stable-like feel of the old coach house had disappeared, along with the row of horse brasses which Bella had donated to The Laden Ox. Instead the room was open and light, painted in shades of subtle grey. The inglenook fireplace now contained a large stove instead.

'Much more energy-efficient,' Bella pointed out.

'Is it gas-fired?' Don asked gloomily. One of the few country pursuits he'd learned to love was chopping and stacking logs.

'No. Wood-fired.' Claudia could have kissed her. 'It'll definitely need lots of logs.'

The mood was calm and peaceful. A little lacking in personality but they would add that. This would be the backdrop for the rest of their lives.

'Note all the plugs at waist-level. That's so you can reach them if you're ever in a wheelchair.'

'Right.' Don caught Claudia's eye.

'Downstairs loo.' She led them to it. 'There's a shower as well as a toilet in case the stairs ever become a problem. And the loo's amazing. It cleans you without toilet paper.'

Claudia sighed. It was all very practical and realistic. And just a tad depressing.

'They call it future proofing,' Bella explained. 'The law insists on it now.'

Don raised his glass and looked at his wife. 'I think this calls for a toast. To Don and Claudia who will never run out of toilet paper ever again.'

And Don and Claudia fell about laughing.

Noah produced a sudden shout of delight and pointed in the direction of the large French window.

They turned to find a scene worthy of a Bollywood movie.

Mrs Lal had arrived in a black Mercedes with what seemed like a posse of flunkeys carrying exotic items into the hotel building which had been converted into luxurious apartments for Olivia and Len, Rose and Mrs Lal.

They watched spellbound as a three-foot elephant decorated with what looked like real jewels led an art deco lamp held by a life-size Nubian slave and a vast gilded Chinese screen.

'Just wait,' Don commented. 'There'll be a giant Buddha next.'

'Keep your cultural stereotyping to yourself,' Claudia chided. 'We don't know what religion she is.'

Don had gone ominously silent and pressed his nose right up against the French window. 'Bloody hell!' he said, stunned. 'Look at that!'

The final flunkey was carrying a six-foot oil painting which had been wrapped in a car rug which had just fallen off to reveal the image beneath.

This was of a young woman with black hair, an ethereally pale face, dark eyes and a slightly parted red mouth, whose robe had fallen apart to reveal one pearly breast. The background was as dramatic as the figure, a kaleidoscope of shapes and colours in red, gold and green.

'If that's not a Klimt, then I don't know anything about art,' murmured Don, seriously impressed.

'You *don't* know anything about art. She'd hardly own a Klimt, they cost zillions, and if she did, she'd hardly bring it down with her in a car just wrapped in a rug, would she? It's probably one of those reproductions you buy as a student. Even I had *The Kiss* on my wall.'

'Did you?' Don sounded surprised. 'I didn't realize you were that much of a romantic.'

'There's lots you still don't know about me,' she smiled back.

'I suppose that's quite good after thirty-five years. Anyway, I'm worried about this Mrs Lal.'

Claudia was worried too but she wasn't going to admit it. 'Just remember, we couldn't have done it without her money. I just can't think why someone that rich ended up in Laura's spare bedroom.'

'To embarrass her son-in-law, according to Laura. Remind him he couldn't afford to put her up in the style to which she was accustomed.'

'I'm surprised she thinks *we* can. Hey-ho. I suppose she'll add a bit of spice.'

'Now who's culturally stereotyping?' Don laughed.

Claudia couldn't think of a clever reply so she tickled Noah's bare feet instead. He giggled appreciatively. What a pity life got so complicated as you grew up.

'By the way, where's Vito?'

They looked round for their dog, but there was no sign of him.

'We didn't leave him behind, did we?' Don asked anxiously.

'No, he was definitely in the back.'

They both ran upstairs.

Their double bed had already been assembled in the master bedroom, all made up beautifully by Bella.

'I think it's important people see their bed looking all inviting as soon as they arrive,' she explained.

And right in the middle of the pristine white duvet cover, Vito slept angelically.

'At least someone's happy,' Don shrugged.

'Come on, you old moaning Minnie.' Claudia took his arm. 'Let's go and see who else has moved in. We might even say hello to rich Mrs Lal.'

'I think we're all packed up.' Olivia looked round the house that had been hers for so long.

Memories here were like a patchwork – some bright, some dull. She'd never wanted to accept the truth that she had a mental illness. Brought up to be tough, illness was for the weak, but there had been times when she'd been genuinely frightened she was going mad. The medicine, which she resisted at first, had changed her life. But nothing could stave off the other threat – old age.

The final straw had been the washing machine. Ridiculous really. All she had to do was phone and yet suddenly she'd longed not to have to summon the John Lewis engineer, or the electrician when things fused. When she'd last had to call Barry, the man who'd mended their lighting for years, she'd asked him a question. What do old ladies living alone do when something breaks? His answer had chilled Olivia. 'They don't do anything. They just ignore it.'

After today she wouldn't have to worry. Someone else would do it. She'd never become that old lady who sat in the dark because she hadn't got the money or the energy to call for help.

She turned to her husband. 'One thing I want to get clear. That thing' – she pointed at Hiro – 'doesn't come with us.'

'If he doesn't come,' Len replied mutinously, 'then I'm not coming either.'

Husband and wife of over sixty years stood glaring at each other, a three-foot manikin all that separated them from physical violence.

'If I might suggest a compromise?'

They turned round in unison to confront Hiro.

'Yes?' barked Olivia, surveying the little robot contemptuously.

'That you switch me off when I am not needed to provide Leonard with companionship.'

Olivia knew that her husband had changed. The malleable character she had married had become more intractable, especially since this metal monstrosity had appeared in their lives.

But like the issue with the washing machine and the plumber, she hadn't the energy to fight him.

'Why are you smiling, Leonard?' Hiro asked him in a quiet voice as they fetched the last of his belongings.

'Because I won.' His impish smile had returned, making him seem suddenly years younger. 'I need your companionship all the time.'

Rose, with characteristic panache, had brought in the Homes Editor from the magazine she and Sal had worked on to design her apartment. 'I've got as much design sense as a colour-blind cabbie,' she announced. 'Besides, the secret of my success has always been to delegate to someone more talented than me.'

'But I loved your room at *New Grey*,' Sal had protested when Rose told her, remembering Rose's chintz paradise which had struck her as less an office, more a vicarage designed by Colefax and Fowler. 'It was so *you*!'

'That was because the Homes Editor designed that too!' Rose announced, roaring with laughter.

The result was, anyway, reassuringly Rose. Vintage standard lamps, Aubusson-style rugs, long drapey silk curtains, painted furniture and wallpaper decorated with birds of paradise. Somehow it looked instantly lived-in even though it was brand new.

Rose, restored to health, sank into a deeply cushioned sofa and declared that it was so comfortable she might never leave it again.

Bella, with her usual perceptiveness, plus a dash of self-preservation, decided to let Rose discover the features that would make ageing easier for herself. She could well imagine that introducing Rose to a loo that washed and dried you might end up with Bella being pushed down it. She would certainly get an ear-bashing about planners going mad to insist on such nonsense.

Sal stood staring out of their arched cottage windows at the swimming pool which was only a few yards away.

'Terrific!' Lou asserted. 'Now I only have to get out of bed and plunge in. I'll be doing a triathlon in no time, just watch me.'

'Isn't it a bit cold?' asked Sal the city softie.

'Nah. I'm used to it. We Brooklynites are tough.'

Sal had to admit he seemed genuinely enthused about the prospect of living with her friends, the eccentric Mrs Lal, his old friend Rose McGill, Claudia's parents and not forgetting Hiro the robot.

He caught her looking at him intently and slammed her against his well-covered chest. 'Yes!' he announced in a loud and definitive voice.

'Yes what?' asked Sal, trying to breathe despite being crushed in cashmere.

'Yes, I am happy to be here in this crazy commune full of decrepit seniors, so you can stop looking at me for signs of regret, horror and sense of impending doom!'

'Less of the decrepit if you don't mind. Was I looking at you for signs of regret?'

'Only every five minutes since we got here. Here I am in beautiful Surrey with the only woman I love.'

'Forgetting the previous three you actually married,' pointed out Sal, laughing.

'I'm an American, as you never fail to remind me. It's expected of us.'

Sal had been deeply relieved that when it came to doing up their cottage they turned out to have quite a similar vision, which Sal described as 'Shaker meets Arts and Crafts'. Lots of wood, simple but comfortable furniture, and a kitchen made by a firm who described themselves as 'English cupboard-makers'. The only sticking point had been that Sal demanded a bath with feet. 'I've wanted a bath with feet all my life,' she insisted.

'And I can see this is your last opportunity before the Grim Reaper comes to scrub your back,' Lou agreed, grinning. 'Okay,' he added. 'I'll trade you a bath with feet for a moratorium on cushions. I choose the cushions and there will be no more than six.'

'Six?' Sal squeaked. 'In the whole house?'

Lou nodded. 'It's generally assumed that men come from Mars and women from Venus due to their attitudes to sex, fidelity, remembering anniversaries and putting the trash out. The truth is actually cushions. Cushions are the essential difference between men and women.'

Sal shook her head, trying not to collapse with laughter. 'Six cushions it is then, but I'll choose them.'

'No pink satin?' he demanded, thinking of her bed in North Kensington, which had been piled with pink satin cushions.

'Positively no pink satin,' she conceded.

'Or any satin at all?'

'You're pushing your luck, Maynard.'

'Just think of that bath with feet when I bring you a glass of something chilled.'

'Okay,' she finally capitulated. 'No satin at all.'

Ella packed up the small bag of clothes she'd brought and looked around her. The cabin, which was really more of a summer house, had its own deck adorned with a white fretwork pelmet thing (there had to be a more technical word than that) which gave it a slightly French air. Funnily enough it reminded her of the summer house she'd had at the bottom of her garden in the big house she'd lived in for so long in London with her husband Laurence, but that had been a sanctuary from the city. This was deep countryside. Funny how people dismissed Surrey as commuter land, yet it could actually be as rural as Somerset or Shropshire. Ella, who had always seen herself as solidly urban, had surprised herself by loving it here.

Certainly it had been cold and frosty in the winter, but the stove had made it as cosy as if it had been centrally heated. She looked out at the quiet landscape, and listened to the silence, broken only by birdsong. She would miss the feathered friends who had sung to her throughout her time here.

You're actually talking to yourself about birds, a voice in her head intervened sternly.

Ella laughed. Just as well if she was moving into the mad Manor for the rest of her life. A sudden panic gripped her. Was she doing the right thing? It was fun meeting her friends once a month in The Grecian Grove, quite another to decide to live with them till she dropped dead. What if they loathed each other? What if one of them suddenly needed nursing? Would they be able to cope?

The lawyer in Ella told her they had gone into this too loosely. Okay, they had drawn up a trust document and it had a get-out clause, but actually exercising it would cause huge problems for the others. And then she remembered her terror when she'd thought she had dementia. At least she would have been among friends, not living alone, waiting to die or lying dead on the doormat for three weeks.

She looked around once more before deciding to pop into the pub for a farewell drink with the landlady to take her mind off her concerns.

'Your musical admirer's not in yet,' the landlady grinned.

Ella looked at her in surprise.

'He won't be long, regular as clockwork. Two pints. Never three. And again at six – well, you know that because you often come too. And good luck to you. Life's much better with someone else.'

Ella almost choked on her *glühwein*. They all thought she came in here deliberately to see Daniel. Jesus, why was she thinking she was getting to like the country? In London no one looked or cared.

But was it the truth? The question fizzled into her mind.

'You're not usually in here at this time,' said a voice behind her. 'Are you off on holiday?' Daniel pointed to her suitcase. He was wearing his usual outfit of jeans and cashmere sweater. A day's stubble blurred his chin.

Ella had to admit he was devastatingly attractive.

'No, no.' She shook her head. 'I'm finally moving up to Igden Manor with my friends.'

'Rather you than me,' he flashed his charming smile. 'I couldn't do it in a million years.'

'How's the choir going?' she asked brightly, wanting to change the subject. It was too close to what she'd just been thinking herself. Ella had found the best way out of any tricky situation in life was to ask the other person about themselves. It always worked like a dream.

'Pretty good as a matter of fact.' He took the bait as she'd thought he would. 'We've won another award actually.' He stood up. 'Just going for a refill. Would you like another?'

Ella shook her head. Her mind was swirling already.

It didn't take him long to get served. There were hardly any customers in the pub. Only the student Bella had cleverly hired to maintain the swimming pool, chatting to the gardener who kept the lawns mowed and the flowerbeds just about under control.

Daniel said hello to them then came back to Ella holding a pint and a large glass of white wine.

'Really,' Ella protested, attempting not to sound like a virgin trying to protect her honour, 'I can't manage all that.'

'Shut up and drink it,' replied Daniel, but with such a devastating smile that it took the sting from words which would otherwise have made her want to slap him.

Ella slugged it back quickly, suddenly wanting to leave Daniel and the mixed emotions he was invoking in her.

'So you're really going to do it?' he asked quietly. 'Sounds like a complete nightmare to me. Though who knows, if I start to lose my marbles it might be just the thing.'

'I really don't think so, Daniel.' Ella put down her glass feeling really rather drunk. 'Right. I'm off. See you sometime.' She picked up her case and concentrated on walking out of the pub in a straight line.

'Now, now, Daniel,' the landlady, who had clearly been listening to their conversation, remarked. 'They don't generally invite the fox to move into the henhouse.'

Seventeen

Laura sat looking out of the window in her new flat, suddenly realizing that all her friends, as well as her beloved daughter, were all in Surrey. Her son Sam was caught up with his new job and Calum had gone back to his wife. Ella was supposed to be coming back to supervise the sale of her cottage but she was taking her time. Ella, she supposed, still had more money in the bank than the rest of them after selling that huge house she'd lived in with Laurence.

The truth was, she was lonely. She laughed at the thought that Mrs Lal was determined to find her someone worthy of her, but Mrs Lal, back from India, was with the others and anyway, God knows what Mrs Lal's idea of worthy would be. Probably an accountant with no sense of humour.

She'd never resorted to dating websites as somehow they seemed too awful to her. She knew the young thought nothing of it and half of them met their partners that way, and anyway, she wasn't techie.

Nevertheless, she began to browse the web and stopped at a site called Out There. This made her laugh. It was a reference to that movie line she often remembered from *When Harry Met*

273

Sally when Carrie Fisher says to the man she's finally settled down with, 'Tell me I'll never be out there again.' And he holds her and says, very firmly, 'You will never have to be out there again.'

God, how many women had felt exactly that? The holy grail of finding some nice man who wasn't so boring he'd send you to sleep telling you about his stamp collection, or so ego-ridden he'd just talk about himself. Someone who would look after you and love you. It might sound unliberated and 1950s-ish, but it was still what most women wanted. Especially at her age.

Despite her better judgement, and her lack of tech savvy, Laura found herself registering for Out There.

No one would probably get back to her anyway.

'I know,' Sal suggested as they all gathered for the first time in the communal sitting room on the ground floor of the Manor. 'Why don't we have a party? We could ask the architects and the nice builders who've worked so hard to finish in record time. It would be a welcome-to-Igden party.'

Lou stood behind her, his gaze like a warm and loving shawl thrown over her in case she felt the cold.

Claudia watched him, trying not to feel just a little bit envious. It must be amazing to have someone who clearly thinks you're wonderful. After thirty-five years Don only noticed she existed if they ran out of toilet rolls or teabags.

'Great idea. I could make a chicken korma,' announced Mrs Lal, guessing this would be acceptable to British palates.

'I'm not sure my digestion would be up to that,' announced Olivia. Claudia tried to give her a quelling glance. It was clear that she and Mrs Lal were eyeing each other up as potential rivals. Her mother had been queen bee in Surrey for longer than Claudia could remember and she clearly wasn't giving up now.

'If we must have something Indian, then coronation chicken always goes down very well, I find.' Olivia smiled patronizingly at Mrs Lal as though this was an act of enormous cultural generosity.

'I think you will find,' Mrs Lal replied as if she were addressing a cack-handed scullery maid, 'that coronation chicken was the invention of the Cordon Bleu Cookery School for Her Majesty Queen Elizabeth's coronation. It has nothing whatsoever to do with India. In India we could never consider adding curry powder to mayonnaise.' She paused dramatically. 'Or to anything else. We only use fresh herbs and spices and consider curry powder to be the ingredient of the amateur.' She smiled benignly as Olivia struggled to find a suitably cutting reply.

'I'm sure the kitchen could come up with something delicious,' Bella intervened diplomatically. 'Why don't we put the idea to a vote?'

Everyone voted in favour except Olivia and Len, who was either doing it to keep in with his wife, or hadn't been listening anyway.

'A party it is then,' Bella smiled. 'How about next Saturday?'

'I may have to go to an urgent dental appointment,' insisted Olivia.

'How unfortunate for you,' commented Mrs Lal. 'And on a Saturday evening too.'

Claudia tried not to be discouraged. Their first communal vote and it left two people pissed off.

She just hoped Mrs Lal didn't bring her Bhangra music.

'We could decorate the room a bit,' suggested Sal, looking round. It was a very pleasant space with armchairs dotted around small tables with reading lamps in muted shades. 'How about a little Forties glamour? A bit of the vibe of *Casablanca*? Men in DJs, ladies in evening dress. We could download *Play It Again, Sam.*'

'Sounds great,' agreed Ella, thinking of the Forties-style sequin jacket she never wore.

'I might get out my tortoiseshell hairclips,' Rose seconded. 'Unless they got thrown away in The Great Clear-Out. I suppose we all had one of those?'

'Too right,' Ella agreed. 'Although I'd already downsized a lot to move to the cottage.'

'Giving away some things nearly broke my heart,' Olivia announced dramatically.

'But think how happy the charity shops were to get your stuff,' reminded Claudia. 'I'm sure it's done a lot of good.'

'Yes, but not to *me*,' was her mother's swift reply. 'And now I need to go. Leonard, come along.'

'Why don't you stay for a bit, old chap,' Len said to Hiro, sounding like an indulgent uncle. 'More fun here than another early night.' It took them all a moment to realize he was addressing the robot.

'Thank you, Len, I think I will do so.' Hiro turned to the assembled gathering. 'Possibly I could help at your party.'

They were all fascinated to know what he would offer to do.

'I could read poetry. Perhaps the sonnets of William Shakespeare?' He revolved in a complete circle and began to declaim: '*Can I compare Thee to a summer's day?*'

'That's terrific, Hiro,' congratulated Lou. 'A robot who knows Shakespeare. That's really something.'

'And I could do fortune telling,' announced Mrs Lal. 'I am quite famous for it in India, as well as the matchmaking.'

'Gosh.' Claudia was feeling a bit overwhelmed. 'That sounds fascinating.'

'Maybe I could ask Mum.' Bella was beginning to wish her mother Laura had joined in with all her friends instead of staying on in London without them.

Claudia glanced at her friend's lovely daughter. She was so glad that everyone had accepted Bella deserved a cottage for as long as she wanted to stay, after all her hard work. From what she said, Nigel loved his new job and it might be for a long time. Maybe she'd be able to start that business of hers. And she couldn't wait to have her daughter Gaby and nice son-in-law Douglas there too, who'd also given his all to get the manor finished. Of course they'd have to get their planning permission and the question of some kind of payment might come up. Fortunately she and Don had some over from their house sale and might be able to help. She did so hope it would be okay for them.

Later on, when they'd all gone back to their rooms, Claudia turned to her husband and put her head on his shoulder. 'Oh God, Don, I'm not sure what I've done here. All these egos battling.'

'It's only your mother and Mrs Lal. And anyway, if they don't like it, they don't really have to see that much of each other. Everyone has their own key and can come and go as they want. It's not some kind of care-home prison, it's just a way of giving each other a bit of support.'

Claudia giggled, feeling a bit more herself. 'Plus fortune telling and Shakespeare.'

'And why not? I like a good sonnet. I might even get out my Jew's harp.' At this Claudia collapsed completely. Don playing the Jew's harp was a source of wild family amusement.

She saw that Don was looking hurt. 'I'm sure everyone would love you to play it,' she insisted guiltily, but probably too late.

'So what are you going to wear?' This was clearly Don making an effort. He had about as much interest in women's fashion as Boris Johnson on a bad day.

'I'll have a look in my wardrobe,' replied Claudia, thinking it didn't really matter. There would hardly be any glamorous men like Humphrey Bogart arriving to sweep them all off their feet.

In her rented flat in London Laura was trying to resist the lure of Out There and failing.

It was just too tempting to get out her laptop and look at men rather like a menu in a restaurant, even if some of the specimens were more fish and chips than haute cuisine.

She decided, just for purposes of comparison, to browse some sites aimed at older people. Instantly a website popped up offering 'Free Russian Ladies'.

Laura giggled, wondering what entitled you to a free Russian lady. Did you get one as a gift free with a litre of vodka?

So far she hadn't created a profile on Out There, just done a bit of window shopping. It was clever of the dating sites, Laura noted, that you didn't have to pay just to sign up, but could just flick through the pictures and only go further if you saw someone you fancied and then pay if you wanted to find out more about them.

Tonight she'd gone a step further and put up a profile with her age, where she lived, the fact that she was a mother of two grown-up children and that her status was currently single. Then she panicked at the idea of putting up her photo. Instead, since she'd listed reading as one of her interests, she took a photo on her phone of a very beautiful book and used that as her image.

Laura went to the kitchen to get a glass of wine and when

she came back two of the men she'd been looking at had sent her a heart, which apparently meant they were interested.

Now, if she wanted to make contact with them, she would have to properly join Out There.

She studied the men closely. She could look at their profiles, their marital status, their interests, where they lived, etc., to see if they had anything in common, but she couldn't actually get in touch. Did she want to?

Laura looked at one of the men, Gavin, more closely. He was fifty-eight, slightly younger than her, with a full head of brown hair and the kind of smile you just had to reciprocate. He wasn't particularly tall, five ten, but tall enough. He described his size as average, which she found rather engaging. Mr Universe types had never been up her street. He had a degree and under income bracket he had put 'highest'.

He was also a widower. This really appealed to Laura. She always remembered the advice Ella, herself a widow, had given her. The best bet for a happy relationship was with a widower who had been happily married before, because people who had once been happy could usually be happy again. Like her, he also had grown-up children. The only downside of Gavin seemed to be that he lived and worked abroad. It wasn't very clear from this brief outline exactly where.

Laura was conscious of a kick of disappointment. What if it were Australia or somewhere like Singapore? And yet, if they were able to make anything of a relationship, maybe living abroad for a while would be exciting. After all, at his age it probably wouldn't be for that long.

So absorbed was Laura in staring at Gavin's warm brown eyes that she didn't hear the phone until it finally clicked to voicemail.

'Hi, Mum, Bella here. We're having a party on Saturday, A

Night at Rick's Café American, you know like in *Casablanca*, to celebrate that we're finally in the manor. Why don't you come down?'

Laura smiled at the sound of her daughter's voice. How lovely she was. But even more strongly than usual, Laura felt glad that she hadn't signed up with the others. She still had some living to do.

Especially now that Gavin had just sailed over her horizon.

She called Bella back. 'That sounds wonderful but actually I'm not feeling a hundred per cent.'

'Oh, Mum, poor you.' The love and concern in her daughter's voice made Laura feel a flash of guilt. There was absolutely nothing wrong with her.

It was just that an evening with the computer was suddenly more enticing.

Bella, with her usual energy and panache, forgot about her mother in her enthusiasm to make the party a success. She started by setting out with Noah in his buggy to trawl the thrift shops of Surrey, an excellent area for thrift shopping because its residents were so well-heeled that their throwaways came from Phase Eight or Jigsaw, unlike the usual Primark or Peacocks.

She spied a set of coloured cocktail glasses which were going for a song, a rather wonderful tuxedo which, with luck, she could force Nigel into, a beret which she could wear herself, just right for singing the 'Marseillaise', and best of all a rather dog-eared movie poster of Humphrey Bogart playing Rick.

Even better was the Chinese supermarket down a back street where they sold all manner of party decorations. Bella bought red, white and blue bunting, a couple of fake moustaches, the kind worn by bounders and con artists, dozens of tea lights for two pounds, and some lovely combs to put up her hair. They looked so good and were so cheap she bought a load to offer the others.

Afterwards she was about to buy a takeaway coffee but, disgusted by the price tag, she went into the second-hand record shop and bought a CD called *La Belle France* which featured songs by Charles Trenet, Jacques Brel and Edith Piaf. It wouldn't be in period but would at least be French and full of atmosphere.

'Boum!' she sang, realizing she didn't actually know any more of the words to Charles Trenet's famous thirties hit.

'Boum!' she improvised. 'My beating heart goes boum! The birds in the trees go boum!' That couldn't be right but Noah was waving his hands and kicking his feet in ignorant delight.

She even found him an outfit with a white shirt and bow tie. It was all going to be such fun!

Rose opened her wardrobe and took out the outfit she'd ordered online from a vintage shop. It was an exact replica of the belted tweed suit, white blouse and wide-brimmed hat with its distinctive black band that Ingrid Bergman had worn in *Casablanca*.

She was slightly ashamed not at how much it had cost but at her motive, which was to put Mrs Lal firmly in her place. She had been slightly miffed at Bella so enthusiastically agreeing to the ridiculous clairvoyant display the woman had offered. She'd probably come dressed up to the nines as a gypsy queen or Greek sibyl or some such nonsense.

Rose slipped the outfit on, grateful that the skirt was lined, though so it should be at that price. She'd been worried about the size but the whole ensemble fitted perfectly. Rose had even done her hair in the exact style of Ilsa.

She stood in front of her long mirror and added the hat.

The effect was just what she'd wanted. Subtle, sophisticated and classy. The next important thing was timing. If she'd gone to all this trouble, she didn't want to get overlooked in the crowd. She needed to pick the right moment to make her entrance. She could already hear the French tunes, interspersed with some Sam-style piano, coming from the lounge.

It had been due to start at seven and it was now half past so she decided to take the plunge.

She pushed open the door to find it was quite dark in the lounge, which was lit mainly by lots of tea lights in jam jars, dotted round the room, which was decorated with masses of bunting.

Bella at least turned to greet her. She was, for some reason, wearing a false moustache which, disturbingly, had the effect of making her a rather handsome man.

'Rose!' she exclaimed. 'That outfit! It's perfect! Where on earth did you find it?'

Suddenly Rose felt embarrassed about confessing to all the trouble she'd been to. 'Oh, this old thing! Found it in the back of the cupboard.'

She turned to find Claudia, Ella and Mrs Lal in a group talking to some of the young builders. They all, to a man, were wearing black, as if their foreman had issued one of those statements like 'No Hard Hats, No Work' but this time it was 'Only Wear Black', plus a fez on each of their heads. The result was they made Rose think of six Tommy Coopers about to break into a comedy routine.

There was no sign of Olivia and Len; she had clearly stuck to her word and made sure he did too. Poor old Len.

Lou Maynard was dressed as the disreputably twinkly Chief of Police and Sal, her new hair scrunched under a short wig and resplendent in a white tux, was a very unlikely Bogey.

Behind them Ella was wearing her statement black and had added hair combs to achieve a rather minimal Forties effect. Claudia had tried a bit harder in a taffeta jacket with padded shoulders and a slinky dress that had a hint of Hollywood glamour about it.

Mrs Lal had renounced the gypsy look Rose had expected and was wearing a long square-shouldered suit in white silk crepe material that managed to look discreetly classy while also clingingly suggestive at the same time. A large brooch adorned her left shoulder. Rose had to admit she looked stunning.

'Isn't Lalita clever?' Ella laughed. 'She's managed to find a copy of the suit Ingrid Bergman wore in the nightclub scene in *Casablanca*?'

Fortunately before Rose had the chance to respond scathingly Bella clapped her hands. 'Ladies and Gentlemen, I'd just like to announce that we have a mystery guest.'

'Humphrey Bogart!' suggested Ella.

'Hardly,' reproved Mrs Lal. 'He's been dead since 1957!'

Bella disappeared through the door into the next room. 'I'm sorry to have to hide you,' she apologised to Lord Binns. 'I just thought you ought to have a dramatic entrance, seeing as us being here is really down to you.'

'I'll wear a suit of armour if it would make you happy,' Murdo twinkled.

Bella decided again that she liked him. Of course he might just be happy because he'd avoided the embarrassment of his hotel going bankrupt and was enabling an exciting social experiment instead. Or maybe he was just a happy man.

She opened the door. 'Residents, architects, and those who physically changed Igden Manor from a hotel into a home for the rest of us, I give you . . . Lord Murdo Binns!'

Rose was so surprised she spilled her wine down her new suit under the infuriatingly amused eye of Mrs Lal.

Murdo worked his way elegantly through the crowds with a comment here and a handshake there worthy of a minor royal until he arrived in their corner.

'Rose, what a wonderful ensemble! You're Ingrid Bergman to the very life. I can already feel my heart breaking at the thought I will have to give you up in the cause of a higher duty.' He held up his glass and clinked with hers. 'Here's looking at you, kid!'

'Murdo!' Rose chided flirtatiously. 'May I remind you that you're not Humphrey Bogart!'

'A jolly good thing too!' Murdo's patrician tones rang commandingly through the room. 'Though I have been practising.' He suddenly drooped his shoulders and adopted an anguished gravelly tone: 'Of all the gin joints in all the towns in all the world, she walks into mine . . .'

The little group round him roared with laughter.

'And who is this?' he suddenly gazed admiringly at Mrs Lal. 'Another Ingrid Bergman if I'm not much mistaken.' He bent and kissed her hand as Rose seethed beside them. Surely at his age Murdo wasn't falling for that 'look up through the eyelashes' routine? Rose realized with deep irritation that was exactly what he *was* doing.

The soothing tones of 'As Time Goes By' tinkled unexpectedly from the piano in the lobby and they all turned to find that Daniel Forrest, looking astonishingly dashing in a white tux and bow tie, sat playing and crooning as if he were simply amusing himself.

'You've got a bloody nerve!' Don strode across the floor with all the repressed anger he'd felt about Claudia's flirtation with the man. 'You nearly broke up my marriage! How dare you come here uninvited!'

Daniel played on as if he didn't have a concern in the world.

'As a matter of fact' – he swung round and smiled at her provocatively – 'I came to see Ella.'

Ella flushed scarlet. 'Well I certainly didn't invite you!'

'When did you and Ella get to be such bosom buddies anyway?' Claudia demanded, trying to bite back the jealousy she shouldn't be feeling.

'In The Laden Ox. We were neighbours. Ella had her cabin in the woods. She knew I went to the pub twice a day and she'd pop in.'

'You didn't mention that!' Claudia flashed at Ella. 'You never told me you were involved with Daniel.'

'Because I'm not!' insisted Ella. The truth was, she had found Daniel attractive. Until today.

'Well, you're not bloody welcome here!' insisted Don angrily, taking a swing at him, which missed because Daniel ducked expertly, so that Don hit his hand hard on the piano casing and it began to bleed over Daniel's white tuxedo.

'Are you all right?' Claudia rushed over.

After that the party went with quite a bang.

'Well,' Rose said, beginning to see the funny side, 'this *has* been an evening to remember. To think I thought retirement would be boring. I think I'd better leave before something even more dramatic happens. A murder perhaps, or a virgin birth.'

'You shouldn't go yet,' coaxed Bella, eager to keep the party going since she'd been to so much trouble. 'We haven't had the fortune telling yet!'

Rose noticed Murdo kissing Mrs Lal's hand again before he

285

headed towards Rose. How could he be so stupid when he'd professed himself undyingly attached to her?

'Really, Murdo,' she couldn't resist jibing, 'you should be careful. You know what they say. "There's no fool like an old fool."'

Sensing the tension in the air was mounting to dangerous levels, Hiro appeared and began to solemnly declaim:

> 'Let me not to the marriage of true minds
> Admit impediments; love is not love
> Which alters when it alteration finds,
> Or bends with the remover to remove.
> O no, it is an ever-fixed mark
> That looks on tempests and is never shaken:
> It is the star to every wandering bark,
> Whose worth's unknown, although his height be taken.
> Love's not Time's fool, though rosy lips and cheeks
> Within his bending sickle's compass come;
> Love alters not with his brief hours and weeks,
> But bears it out even to the edge of doom.
> If this be error and upon me proved,
> I never writ, nor no man ever loved.'

They had all been expecting the rather hackneyed sweetness of 'Let Me Compare Thee to a Summer's Day', and Hiro's choice, so appropriate to all of them here, who, apart from Bella and the builders, had indeed found alteration and might quite easily find themselves at the edge of doom, had a startling effect.

Murdo Binns reached for Rose's hand and raised it to his lips.

Lou pulled Sal closer to him and repeated into her ear, 'Love is not love which alters when it alteration finds.'

'Just as well for you,' she whispered back, stroking his head which was bald as a billiard ball.

'Love's not Time's Fool,' Ella murmured, thinking of Laurence and all they'd missed due to his early death.

'The star to every wandering bark . . . well, that's certainly me,' Mrs Lal sighed. 'But no sign of love on the horizon.'

'I thought love was your business,' remarked Rose, feeling mean.

'Yes,' Mrs Lal agreed, suddenly humble, 'but it hasn't worked for me. I'm still alone.'

'You know.' Lou was watching Hiro, fascinated. 'I think we can be proud of ourselves. It's hard to believe that little guy isn't human. He has such extraordinary empathy. The one thing robots have lacked till now is empathy, and Hiro has it in spades.'

'Glad you liked it.' Hiro pirouetted on his metallic wheels. 'Time for me to remind Len to go to the toilet.'

Lou fell about laughing. 'And he certainly knows how to deliver a one-liner as well.'

'Do you know,' Mrs Lal announced dramatically, swishing her white Ingrid Bergman suit with all the old-fashioned glamour of a forties movie star. 'I think this is not the moment for looking into the future. Let us leave the last word to Shakespeare and wait until another time.'

Lou's eyes twinkled appreciatively as she sashayed out of the room. 'And she's not bad at making an exit either.'

'I wonder what happened to Mr Lal,' speculated Murdo. 'I mean, there must have been a Mr Lal if there's a daughter. Certainly in India.'

'She probably dumped him on a rubbish tip outside Calcutta

on her rise to TV stardom,' Rose speculated, just a shade too crisply.

'Now, now, Rose,' Murdo suggested naughtily, 'anyone would think you were jealous.'

As Laura wasn't there to correct them, no one suspected that it was Mr Lal who had dumped *her*.

Eighteen

'Oh God, that was pretty much a disaster!' Claudia slumped as they got ready for bed in the coach house. She'd decided it might be more diplomatic not to mention Daniel Forrest at all.

'Nonsense!' Don challenged. 'I thought it was an evening full of promise.'

'If you like ego clashes on an operatic scale.'

'Better than boredom. Who wants to go gently into the good night? Not me. I could have done without your fancy man showing up, though. Is he really involved with Ella?'

'God knows.' Claudia sat down in front of the mirror at her dressing table. 'She looked pretty stunned. Are you sure your hand's okay?'

Don grinned. 'It was worth it.'

Claudia got into her nightdress and opened the door of her bedside cabinet to look for her book. There was a crunch and the front of the cabinet fell off onto the carpet. 'Bloody MDF!' she shouted. 'And I thought the builders were so good. I hope this isn't just the beginning. Bella says we need a handyman and we forgot to put it in the budget, so God knows what we'll do.'

'Look no further.' Don, in blue stripy pyjamas, bowed to her formally.

Claudia, thinking of the shelves he'd put up which had promptly fallen down, taking her favourite Murano glass vase with them, found herself lost for words.

Her astonishment was to grow.

'I've been on a course.'

'When?'

'Every Wednesday from three till six. Clearly you missed me and my witty conversation.'

'But where?'

'Don't laugh. Organised by the Men in Sheds Movement, Godalming branch.'

Claudia stifled a giggle, feeling ashamed that she hadn't even noticed his absence.

'It was an Aussie idea originally but it's spread all round the world. Men, to be honest, mostly retired men, get together and learn new skills. Furniture restoring, car maintenance . . . I did DIY. Apparently it's good for our spiritual well-being and sense of self-esteem, all the things we used to get from work. Men need work for self-esteem and go downhill when it stops. I'm surprised you hadn't noticed.'

'I know another way to boost your sense of self-esteem.' Claudia pulled back the duvet invitingly. 'And it doesn't even need tools.'

'I wouldn't say that,' Don replied. And before her eyes Don's manhood rose obligingly to meet the challenge.

Ella lay in bed too angry to sleep. She had been attracted to Daniel, it was true. But the vanity of the man appearing at their party and implying she'd invited him! Had he come to stir

things up between Claudia and Don or because he genuinely
wanted to see her?

He had looked rather gorgeous in his white tux tinkling
away. She mustn't think like that. She tried to summon up her
beloved husband Laurence, dead for five years now, but that
didn't help. Laurence had been tweedy and reassuring. There
was nothing either tweedy or reassuring about Daniel Forrest.
He was a flirt. Anyone with half a brain could see that.

She wouldn't think about him. She would go to sleep
instead and hope he and his tinkling piano didn't invade her
dreams.

Laura tried not to think how much these photographs were
costing. She had decided to sign up for Out There at a cost of
£14.99 per month so that she could get full access to Gavin's
profile and he would be able to see hers. That was why she
needed a really good set of photographs. The advice on internet sites was to dress up and give it your best smile. That was
why Laura found herself in a photographer's studio in hip
Clerkenwell, in front of a beige background, with her hair
done and full make-up, wearing her favourite fluffy cardi and
tight blue jeans. She'd thought of putting on a skirt but she so
rarely did these days that she wouldn't feel natural.

With the photographer's encouragement she'd opened her
top button, feeling like a page-three girl with some old lag
shouting, 'Come on, darlin', show us what you've got!'

She was very conscious, as a matter of fact, that her cleav-
age might be as wrinkly as an old apple, but the young man,
who was not much older than her son Sam, assured her it was
very tasteful and attractive.

Part of her was screaming, *Laura, you are an intelligent, sane
woman, what are you doing?* But another part was reassuring her

that this was what intelligent sane women did nowadays, and how was she going to meet a nice man if she just stayed at home?

When she got back she started on her profile properly. What *were* her interests? The advice site said don't just say things like watching TV and films, it sounded too dull.

Laura sat back in her chair, taken aback because she couldn't think of a lot of interests. Her family had been her number one interest. A wave of longing for the soft downy head of her grandson Noah suddenly overtook her. She couldn't put him down as an interest on a dating website. Actually, why not? Laura thought about why she was doing this in the first place. The whole idea was to meet someone she was in sympathy with, so no point pretending to be someone else even if it was more attractive. She didn't particularly like walking or sport, or the life and *oeuvre* of François Truffaut or anything intellectual like that. She didn't even really like gardening. Anyway, she didn't have a garden at the moment. She did like browsing junk shops and creating interiors. She'd loved her family home, but that was all over now, husband Simon living somewhere else, Sam up in Manchester and Bella down at Igden Manor. Funny that her daughter should be living with *her* friends rather than Laura herself, but to Bella it was just a job and cheap accommodation. To Laura it would have been a prison.

She might as well be herself. So for interests she wrote 'my gorgeous grandson Noah, finding hidden gems in junk shops, restoring old furniture, listening to Sixties music and watching *Poldark*'.

She had only chosen her favourite photograph and uploaded it about five minutes ago when a heart came back from Gavin. This meant he wanted to talk to her!

Laura knew it was ridiculous but she felt as excited as a

schoolgirl going to her first party. She tried to calm herself by looking for a long time at the photograph he'd posted on Out There.

With his warm brown eyes and slightly too long wavy hair he really was quite devastatingly attractive.

But she wasn't going to jump right into anything. She was going to be sensible and take her time.

Until tomorrow at the very least.

Rose looked round her sitting room and sighed with satisfaction. It was south-facing and the sun was streaming in. She had opened her French window onto the small balcony and could hear a bird singing. A blackbird or maybe a robin, given the time of year. She loved robins, not only for their cheery Christmas-card appeal but because they sang so much of the year, even at night sometimes. Rose suffered from insomnia and it was often a robin she could hear when she got up to read for an hour in the middle of the night. The robin at Igden seemed almost like a friend.

That had been quite a drama last night, but like Don she didn't want to live in some ghastly place where everyone pretended to be nice, and where the staff displayed awful fake cheeriness. 'Come on, dearie, there's a good girl!'

She much preferred a bit of reality, even if it was a little uncomfortable. Give her *EastEnders* rather than *The Archers* any day, though even *The Archers* was fraught with drama these days.

She thought about Murdo for a moment. The truth was, she'd been deeply flattered that he still cared enough to make selling them the Manor dependent on her presence here. Mrs Lal coming along at the last moment, and Murdo's evident attraction to her, was certainly an irritant, but she believed

Murdo would have the sense to see that Mrs Lal would be trouble one of these days. At least she hoped he would. Perhaps she shouldn't have been so sharp with him.

She made herself her favourite tea in a delicate china cup and decided that unless things got a lot rougher here, it was a place she could be happy. And for someone who'd lived alone for years, she was actually enjoying the company much more than she'd expected. And the food, something that mattered a great deal to Rose, was excellent.

She'd done a good job in persuading the chef to stay on. It had only been the offer of free accommodation that had done it. But accommodation was one thing they had plenty of at Igden Manor.

With her unsettled state of mind, Ella decided to distract herself by thinking about what she would do with the gardens.

There was nothing like a bit of digging and weeding for calming the soul. Fortunately the main areas were already established so it really only meant improving the herbaceous borders and trying to ensure some year-round colour. Ella was excited to find there was a tractor lawnmower like the one Laurence had appropriated in their London garden. Now she would get a go.

She also rather fancied doing a bit of private planting around her own cottage, perhaps even putting up some unobtrusive fencing, something she could disguise with climbing plants so she could have a bit of privacy. It was Ella's little secret that she occasionally liked to sunbathe topless and she didn't want to frighten the horses by whipping her bikini off in the communal areas. Wrinkly boobs were best kept to yourself, in her view, but a nice row of hollyhocks which bloomed well into September and fast-growing roses should do the job if she were discreet about it. She even took her top off in winter

now and then if there was a bright enough day. *I mean, we all need a shot of Vitamin D, don't we?* she thought to herself.

Whistling happily, she started her tour.

'So where are all these young people we were promised?' Lou teased Bella. 'A student flat crossed with a kibbutz was the description that lured me in.' He looked lovingly at Sal. 'And that old crock of an Amazon over there of course.' He indicated Sal, who laughed back at him.

'I'm young,' protested Bella. 'And Noah's even younger. Douglas and Claudia's daughter Gaby *will* be here. It's just that getting planning permission for a new build on that land beyond the coach house is taking much longer than our renovations did.' She laughed back at him. 'I'll see what I can do.'

Bella put a protesting Noah into his buggy and pushed him round the grounds. She wanted to think. It was true real communities didn't just have one age group and they still had plenty of empty rooms. What about inviting students to occupy a couple, just for a short space of time, and seeing how it worked out? If it was ghastly, then there would be no long-term commitment.

There was a university not too far away that used to be a tech and had loads of practical courses. She could easily put a notice on their boards and see what happened.

Just in time she remembered she probably ought to ask Claudia first.

As it turned out, Claudia thought it would be fine, but no more than two of them and initially just for three months or a term, whatever worked for the students.

'Don could do with some help in his new handyman role and I'm sure Ella could handle some young people giving her a hand with the garden.'

'And talking to the residents,' added Hiro who'd just come into the room to get something for Len.

'Hang on,' protested Claudia. 'This isn't a care home and we're not gaga yet!'

'Olivia would like a young man to chat to,' suggested Hiro. 'She doesn't like me but she likes young men.'

'Right, Bella.' Claudia winked. 'Bear that in mind when you're interviewing.'

'Claudia,' Hiro added in a low tone, 'could you have a word with Leonard? There's something urgent he wants to talk to you about.'

Her father was sitting in his new shed, which had been created out of the old stable block, watching cricket highlights. The effervescent crowd sat in bright sunshine drinking beers and cheering.

'I wish I were there,' he stated. 'Everyone looks like they're having such a bloody good time, which reminds me: Claudie, you made me a promise a while ago.'

'What was that, Dad?'

'That if something nasty were to happen to me – heart attack, stroke, that kind of thing—'

'Dad—' she started to interrupt.

'No, listen, Claudie. You too, Hiro.'

'Dad,' Claudia replied more assertively this time. 'I'm sure Hiro won't mind me reminding you. He's a very good friend but he is a robot.'

'He's got a lot more damn sense than most human beings. Especially your mother. If I have a heart attack or a stroke I DO NOT WANT TO BE RESUSCITATED. Got that?' He handed her over a piece of paper. 'There you are. All typed out for you to make it official. What's more, I do not want to be taken to hospital and left to die on my own among strangers. I want to stay here. Is that clear?'

'Have you talked to Ma about this?'

'No. For the very good reason that she won't agree. She believes in the wonder of medicine and I don't. Besides, look.' He pulled an article from the desk behind him and announced with huge satisfaction: 'New Report from America says 88 per cent of doctors would opt for Do Not Resuscitate if they had a terminal illness.'

'Yes, but how would we know if you had a terminal illness?'

'Life is a terminal illness, Claudie. And I have had my fill. The good part is behind me, I don't want to hang on covered in test tubes. Promise?'

'Oh, Dad . . . I love you so much.'

She put her arms round him, feeling the frail brittleness of his bones. Her big strong dad.

'Dad, I can't.'

Len turned away, looking dashed. 'I'm sorry I asked you then. It was probably unfair of me. Off you go now. Our lot are batting again in a moment.'

Claudia turned away, feeling more torn than she could ever remember. She was letting her beloved father down. And yet how could she agree not even to call an ambulance?

Bella put her advert up on the student noticeboard. She had drawn a colourful design showing the manor and written *Free accommodation in luxurious manor house in exchange for some help with older residents in new-age old-age commune! Help required for thirty hours a month. Contact Bella Minchin, Igden Manor.*

She hoped it would be sufficiently intriguing to attract some bright young people.

*

Now that she had joined up for Out There, Laura was able to access Gavin's full profile and even get in touch with him on the app's website. Feeling very nervous, she sent her first tentative message: **Hello, Gavin, this is Laura. I'd love to hear more about you.**

A reply came almost at once. **Hello, Laura! I am fifty-eight years old, with brown hair** (his hair was obviously important to him, as well it might be, it was gorgeous), **I'm five feet ten tall** (she had a feeling she'd already read that on the website) **of average build** (good, not fat!) **and I have an outgoing personality. I like to play tennis** (well, she *had* played tennis a bit when she was younger) **and because I am living in Beirut** (wasn't that dangerous or was she out of touch with world events?) **I spend quite a lot of time outdoors, especially in my work as a civil engineer.**

Laura instantly googled Lebanon. It was above Israel, between Syria and the Mediterranean Sea. It wasn't really that far from Damascus and she instantly started to feel frightened for him, which was ludicrous and quite possibly deeply ignorant too. Laura began to wish she'd taken a bit more interest in Middle Eastern politics.

She wondered what kind of civil engineering project he was involved in. Of course she wished he was in England, but the Lebanon wasn't too bad compared with Singapore or New Zealand or somewhere really distant.

She dimly remembered there had been a girl at school with her – my God she hadn't thought of her in fifty years! – who had come from Beirut and said in those days it used to be the St Tropez of the Med, all yachts and casinos.

She realized she wasn't quite sure what civil engineers actually did. The Institute of Civil Engineers came up with an answer: **Civil engineers are creative people. They design**

the transport systems to keep big cities on the move. They create easy-to-build schools so children in faraway places have somewhere to learn. They use the sun and wind's energy to make electricity for our homes.

She liked the sound of Gavin being a creative person. Engineering had sounded a bit off-putting.

And then another email from Gavin popped up.

You say you have a grandchild. Do you have a husband?

I'm divorced from my husband. Laura sighed. She didn't know why she didn't like saying that. Millions of people got divorced and yet she still somehow felt a failure.

How long ago?

It seemed a slightly strange question, but why? **Fairly recently.** She wasn't going to be specific. She would have liked to ask him how long he had been a widower, but it seemed too intrusive. Instead she enquired **How old are your children?**

In their thirties. Amazing, isn't it? was the reply.

Yes, it's hard to believe, Laura replied cautiously. **What are you working on in Lebanon?**

A solar energy plant. They have a lot of sun.

Laura found herself laughing rather too loudly at this mild joke.

Rather like a first meeting in real life, she decided to reveal herself a bit more gradually. **Have to go now**, she added. **Hope you have a great evening.** Actually she had no idea of the time in Lebanon. Good old Google supplied it. They were two hours ahead of the UK in Beirut.

As a matter of fact, Laura's own evening spread out before her with absolutely nothing to do.

Gavin had one last thing to say before she went. **Why don't we get off this app? Do you have a number I could message you on?**

For just a few seconds Laura thought twice about giving out her private number. Then she thought of Gavin's warm brown eyes and lovely wavy hair and she typed it in.

'Ella.' Sal knocked on the door of Ella's cottage. 'There are some very peculiar people waiting for you in the lounge. Lou says he thinks they've come to the wrong place and must be auditioning for *Waiting for Godot* at some local theatre. One of them is holding some kind of vegetable.'

Ella hurriedly finished her coffee and rushed along the path towards the main building, her face glowing with pleasure. She had a strong suspicion who these unexpected visitors were.

And so it proved. In the lounge, looking entirely mystified at being addressed by a strange American as Estragon, Vladimir and Pozzo, were Bill, in his usual bobble hat despite the lovely weather, and Les and Stevie, who were standing nervously by.

'Ella,' Bill greeted her gratefully, as if she could rescue them from a dangerous lunatic, 'I think this gentleman has got the wrong end of the stick. He keeps calling us by some very odd names. Could you vouch for our identity?'

'Absolutely.' Ella hugged each one in turn which made Les turn the colour of a Scotch Bonnet pepper. 'These are my very good friends Bill, Stevie and Les.'

'We bought you these.' Improbably Stevie produced a battered Harrods bag dating from about 1954, and invited Ella to peer in. It was crammed full of assorted vegetables plus the seeds from runner beans, onions, garlic, peas, radishes, spinach and Swiss chard, all in separate envelopes marked in Pentel.

'We've brought some pegs and string to mark up the different sections in your new vegetable garden,' supplied Stevie eagerly.

'You know,' Ella said, trying to embrace them all at once, 'it's so bloody good to see you. Let me go and get you a coffee.'

'I'll go,' Lou offered.

'Actually,' Stevie said shyly, 'I'd prefer a Lapsang Souchong, if you don't mind.' They looked grateful not to be left with this small but strange American.

'Now, tell me.' Ella could hardly wait. 'How is life at the allotment? How are Sharleen and Sue, not forgetting Mr Barzani?'

'They all send their love,' Stevie replied. 'And Mr Barzani sent some of his special aubergine seeds. We were that surprised. He never shares them with anyone. Says they come from Cyprus before the Turks invaded. They're a little bit of home.'

Ella found she had to fight back a tear. It really would embarrass the Three Musketeers if she started blubbing.

As soon as the coffees and Stevie's tea arrived Ella suggested they go and have a tour of the gardens. She felt ridiculously happy to see them. Just like Mr Barzani's aubergines, the seeds they had brought for her would feel like a little bit of the allotment at the manor.

After a couple of hours of measuring and marking, they planted out some of the precious seeds. When they finally finished they were amazed to find it was late afternoon.

As she summoned a taxi and waved them off, Ella realized this what was what she'd needed to get over missing the allotment and finally feel settled here.

Lou braced himself for his early morning swim, leaving Sal luxuriating in bed, and reminded himself that it was good for him to take exercise at his time of life. He didn't want to get old, and he didn't feel like having a heart attack just at the moment. Strange that a born New Yorker, with ex-wives and children back home, should enjoy life in a Surrey mansion with a bunch of women, but oddly he did. And it was great being near his youngest daughter and her baby. He hadn't been the greatest grandfather. He'd been one for the large gesture rather than time spent at the coalface, but now he was doing his best and discovering the rewards too. And of course there was Sal.

At that moment he heard her calling him.

'What's it like in the water?'

'Great. Why don't you join me?'

Sal bent over with laughter. 'You must be joking. Anyway, hot news!'

'Tell me.' He pretended to splash her and she pretended to squeal.

'Mrs Lal is doing the fortune telling this afternoon at four in the lounge.'

'I can't wait.'

Sal smiled tenderly. 'Don't be such an old cynic.'

'Old is the operative word. When you get to my age anything a fortune teller predicts can only be bad news.'

'What, like meeting the love of your life at over seventy?' Sal pirouetted girlishly by the side of the pool.

Lou heaved himself out and hugged her, drenching her from head to foot.

'I've already met her. A fortune teller would only tell me she was going to leave me.'

'Hey, what happened to all that American optimism?'

'Who says I'm an optimist? You just called me a cynic.' He towelled himself enthusiastically.

'You've been married three times. I call that optimism!'

He pulled Sal into his arms.

'Get a room, children!' a voice called.

They turned to find Rose on her morning stroll to the local shop. 'They never have anything I want but I enjoy the journey.'

'Now if that isn't a metaphor for life, I don't know what is,' pronounced Lou.

'There, you *are* a cynic,' Sal tutted.

'I'm a professional cynic but my heart's not in it, to para-phrase your great British rock band Blur.'

'Oooh, get you, trying to get down with the kids. I suppose you have enough of them . . .'

Rose continued her walk, watching them fondly. It was such a special thing when two people you liked so much got together. And of course she could take the credit for introduc-ing them.

Rose smiled with deep satisfaction. Moving here was work-ing out quite nicely.

'Rose, you are coming this afternoon?' Sal called to her.

'What's happening?'

'Mrs Lal in the lounge with a crystal ball.'

Rose laughed. 'I'll have to remember my dagger,' she replied.

Lou watched her, his face creasing a little with concern. 'I knew she didn't exactly go for Mrs Lal, but a dagger?'

'You really are an American, aren't you? It's a reference to Cluedo!'

'What on God's earth is Cluedo?'

'A British board game. We used to have them before smart-phones and iPads.'

'Right.' Lou nodded. 'A bit before my time . . .' he said as Sal chased him back into their cottage.

'Oh dear.' Sal made a face once the door was closed. 'Rose has really gone off Mrs Lal.'

'Not surprising. Didn't you see the way she moved in on Murdo at the party? He didn't have a chance. The lady is a vamp.'

'I thought he was supposed to be in love with Rose, and that's why he sold us the manor. Frailty thy name is Man.' She shook her head at the general laxity of the male gender.

'Very good. I see you know your *Hamlet*,' Lou congratulated.

'Well, at least he isn't in love with his mother,' Sal replied, straight-faced.

Lou had once, many years ago, encountered the Dowager Lady Binns and could recall three chins and a gimlet eye.

'Yes, well, let's be grateful for small mercies. If she moved in here, I'd be on the next plane to JFK.'

Nineteen

The setting sun was slanting in through the windows of the lounge, giving it an appropriately other-worldly glow. Mrs Lal had allowed a fire in the inglenook and a small lamp next to her but no other light.

'Madame Arcati to the life,' whispered Claudia to Don as they settled themselves into the row of armchairs.

'I was thinking more Agatha Christie,' Don replied. '*Murder at the Vicarage* maybe.'

They were all there apart from Bella, since Noah was unlikely to keep quiet for the duration, and Olivia and Len. Olivia due to her snooty attitude to Mrs Lal and Len because he was more interested in watching the cricket.

'Who wants to be first?' Mrs Lal, in a smart suit that Sal suspected came from Yves St Laurent, looked round at them all as if she expected a stampede.

Instead there was a long pause, eventually broken by Rose. She stepped forward and sat in the chair next to Mrs Lal.

'Your hand, please,' she requested.

Rose held it out. 'For God's sake don't predict a long life. A

305

nice aneurism while I'm enjoying a large G&T would be perfect.'

'But Rose,' Mrs Lal replied sweetly, 'you have already lived a long life.' She studied the hand. 'As a matter of fact, you have many more years to come.'

'Oh bugger,' Rose replied laconically. 'Will I still have my marbles?'

'Your lifeline does not reveal that, I'm afraid.'

'Okay.' Rose got stiffly to her feet. 'Next cab off the rank.'

Lou jumped eagerly out of his armchair and replaced Rose next to Mrs Lal. She took his hand.

'Will I be handsome? Will I be rich?' he quipped, looking round at the assembled group. 'No, don't spoil it for me. I don't mind long life. In fact, I'm with Woody Allen on this one; "I don't want to achieve immortality through my work, I want to achieve immortality through not dying."'

Mrs Lal looked at him sternly, her charity shop earrings flashing in the fire light. 'You will live a long life. You will have even more grandchildren. There will be some family strife.'

'Of course there will be family strife. Have you met my family?'

'They are not sure about your decision to settle here.'

Lou looked at her narrowly. 'Of course they're not. They're missing my sparkling personality. Not to mention my sparkling money. They are wondering whether if I die, they can challenge the will on the grounds I have gone gaga and moved into a mansion with a bunch of strangers.'

'Lou!' Sal shook her head. 'I'm sure your family love you!'

'They do. Especially my ex-wives. My youngest daughter's the best of them and she only lives ten miles away.'

'Sally,' invited Mrs Lal. 'Would you like to be next?'

For a moment Sal looked reluctant, then told herself not to be a spoilsport. It was a load of tosh anyway.

'Fine. Come on, Maynard,' she hissed at Lou, 'move your bloomin' arse.'

'What a fine turn of phrase you British have.' Lou started to get up.

'Ignoramus,' she murmured to him tenderly. 'It's from *My Fair Lady*. Eliza shouts it to her horse at Ascot.'

'Okay, if it's only a horse . . .' Lou replied.

Sal held out her palm for inspection. Mrs Lal stared intently at her lifeline for just a shade too long.

'Right,' Sal announced decisively, tearing her hand from Mrs Lal's grip, 'let's skip the long-life bit, shall we? How about will I be happy?'

'Yes,' Mrs Lal smiled and nodded. 'You will be very happy.'

'Fine.' Sal was already on her feet. 'I'll settle for that. Come on, Claudia, your turn.'

But before she could sit down Hiro appeared holding out his metallic hand to Mrs Lal.

'I cannot tell the fortune of a machine,' she protested dismissively.

'Just as well Hiro isn't a machine then,' insisted Lou swiftly, winking at the little manikin. 'He's Len's soulmate.'

Mrs Lal shrugged as if they were all completely mad.

Her face changed as she contemplated his claw-like digits and she looked at him in surprise. 'Hiro, you are going to be a hero!'

An expression of what looked very like delight appeared on his artificially created features and he scooted back to join Len in his shed.

Claudia sat down. 'I won't ask,' she announced to Mrs Lal. 'You tell me the story.'

'You will go through a lot of worry . . .'

'That's through worrying how everyone's going to get on!'

'But eventually you will stop worrying and feel nothing but calm.'

'Probably because I'll be dead!' She heaved Don out of his chair and he lumbered reluctantly forward.

'You feel overwhelmed by women,' announced Mrs Lal.

'Too right,' agreed Don.

'But you will learn to stand tall and be a man.'

'Just like Johnny Cash!' Lou pointed out from the sidelines.

Ella was the last one remaining. She suspected after the other night's performance Mrs Lal would foresee some nonsense about romance with a man in a white tuxedo, but she was wrong. 'You are going to have a very difficult decision ahead that you fear may cost you a dear friendship.'

'Any more details?'

'I am sorry, no. But be on the lookout.'

Ella shrugged. All her friends were here anyway. Apart from Laura.

There was a pause and they were about to decide the show was over when a voice from the back boomed, 'May I join in too?'

They turned to find Murdo Binns had appeared in the room without anyone noticing.

Don happily surrendered his seat, feeling he'd got off lightly, if embarrassingly, and Murdo folded his long body into the chair.

Mrs Lal took his slender patrician hand in hers and stared intently into his eyes.

'Trussst in me . . .' whispered Sal naughtily to Lou in her best Kaa voice.

'Okay, what's ahead for me?' Murdo enquired.

'You will marry again,' she asserted. 'There will be another Lady Binns.'

'And she will be tall, glamourously seductive and quite possibly Indian,' murmured Rose.

'Your children will not be happy at you marrying again at your age.'

'My children are never happy. Fortunately they are all well provided for. Will there be more baby Binns?'

'That is not for you to see,' Mrs Lal replied sharply.

'She doesn't want a wife young enough to give him babies!' Rose whispered, starting to laugh.

Don got to his feet, sensing that this was getting a lot too personal. 'Overwhelmed as I am by women, I thought I would take the opportunity to say thank you to Mrs Lal for her very entertaining session this afternoon.' He started to clap and the others immediately followed.

Mrs Lal got huffily to her feet. 'My dear man, the truth is not entertaining. Revealing possibly, occasionally frightening but rarely entertaining. Remember that!'

Despite her dire warning everyone tried to repress their smiles and giggles. Except for Sal, who felt that on the whole the future was best left unexplored.

'We've only had one student declare any interest!' Bella was shocked at the youth of today. The free rent had been a large part of why she'd come to help at Igden Manor herself and she was surprised the offer hadn't led to a stampede.

'They're probably all put off by the thought of living with all us oldies,' Claudia grinned. 'Like moving in with your granny.'

The young man, when he finally turned up, was called Spike. Bella didn't need to ask him why. He had one of those

Mohican cuts popularised by Johnny Rotten of the Sex Pistols which was so retro it seemed quaint to Bella. But he had nice eyes and he was studying social work and actually seemed quite interested in the whole concept of their new-age old-age community.

'I might even make it my thesis,' he offered generously.

'You'd better see round first.'

Since he was a serious student Bella pointed out all the aids to ageing that they had installed discreetly in the manor and cottages.

'Loos that don't need paper. Wow, that must feel weird,' Spike commented.

There was also voice technology that could announce the time and also remind you when to do things. Handles every-where. Walk-in showers.

'We only have one communal bathroom. Unfortunately baths get very difficult to climb in and out of.'

'Do you have any of those mobile scooter things? I love those.'

Hiro took an instant dislike to Spike, especially when he said, very loudly, 'A robot. Cool. I got one of those from Amazon.'

'It will be nothing like me,' Hiro announced proudly to Bella.

'I'm sure it won't,' Bella reassured.

Spike then went off saying he would think about the idea of moving in.

'What was he like?' Claudia enquired.

'He might want to do a thesis on us! He's gone to think about it.'

'Generous of him!'

Actually, Claudia didn't mind too much. It was Lou who

thought they ought to have more young faces about the place. All in all Claudia thought things were going pretty well.

Little did she know.

'Have you noticed how that woman keeps colonizing the shared spaces?' Rose demanded in tones of controlled fury as Claudia and Bella were passing through the lounge to check on the menus for the week. 'Piles of DVDs all over the lounge. Old biscuits under the sofa! Doesn't she realize we're out in the country and will get invaded by mice?' Claudia could see the rivalry between the two women was escalating faster than North Korea and the USA. 'And the other day I saw her knocking back a vodka and tonic without putting anything in the honesty box.'

'Maybe she just forgot,' suggested Bella diplomatically.

'Twice?'

'Right. Well, perhaps she needs a gentle reminder,' she said, hoping to God that Rose didn't decide to give her one.

At that very moment Mrs Lal strode into the lounge, looking so angry the goddess Kali would have shuddered and taken cover. 'Mrs Warren, a word if you please. You will not believe this. Your dog—'

'Vito? He's a dear little thing. Gentle as a lamb.'

'He has been into my kitchen and left a pile of excrement in the middle of my floor!'

'Oh dear, I'm so sorry, that's not like Vito at all.'

'My dear Mrs Lal,' replied naughty Rose McGill, 'don't tell everyone. They may all want some.'

The look she gave Rose could have frozen the Pacific Ocean. 'And as for your friend Mrs Thompson . . .' As Mrs Lal paused dramatically, Claudia wondered what on earth Ella could have got up to. 'She has appropriated a section of the communal garden. And if that were not bad enough, she bared her bosoms in it!'

'What?' Bella tried to stifle a giggle. 'Maybe she's become a pagan. It could be the solstice or something.'

'Bare bosoms and dog poo, you have been having a morning!' Rose, catching Bella's eye, was struggling not to collapse in giggles.

'Really, Miss McGill' – Mrs Lal emphasized the *Miss* – 'at your age I would have thought you might have behaved better. No doubt it is because I am Indian. May I remind you that the British no longer rule India. In fact, Britain is a sad small offshore island while India is one of the fastest-growing economies in the world.'

The situation might have resolved itself if Murdo Binns had not walked in and, spotting Mrs Lal in full flood, taken her hand and apologized fulsomely for whatever had disturbed her, which she willingly reiterated to him. 'My dear lady, let me come and deal with the emergency. No doubt in India you have an entire caste devoted to such things. How appropriate that in this country a peer of the realm should step into the breach!'

'Thank you, my lord, you are good manners personified,' Mrs Lal simpered.

Rose watched their departure, smiling despite her intense annoyance. 'Say what you will, he can be a very annoying man, but Murdo Binns certainly has class.'

'And I didn't even give him a poo bag!' Claudia bewailed. 'I really don't know what's come over Vito.'

'I think he's shown quite a lot of discrimination.'

'Now, Rose, behave!'

'Believe me, it's nothing to do with the woman being Indian and everything to do with her being bloody irritating!'

*

Laura woke up feeling like she used to when she was a child on her birthday, and looked round for her phone. She knew there would be a wake-up message from Gavin wishing her good morning.

Ever since they'd made contact they'd started to exchange emails and messages about different aspects of their lives, sometimes with silly emojis or pictures of things that had made them laugh: what they were doing, their favourite foods, movies they'd enjoyed, little details of everyday life. Often it had been about being grandparents and how much easier it was than being parents.

It might only be a short time since they'd connected but Laura felt like she'd known him for years. She yearned to share her excitement with Bella or her friends but instinctively felt it better to keep things to themselves for now.

Sure enough, next to her the phone pinged. It was especially exciting to make contact first thing in the morning when she was still in bed even if, due to the time difference, he was already up.

Good morning. Hope you slept well. The sun is shining here in Beirut. Hope you can join me soon. Gavin

Laura read it again, almost breathless.

And then she replied: Good morning to you. It's raining in London. Sun in Beirut sounds wonderful. Laura

And then a message came instantly back: Laura, I think you could be the woman who could light up my life. Gavin

Should she be suspicious that Gavin was already talking to her so passionately? She knew her friends would say so, but she couldn't help herself feeling excited. And besides she *did* feel she knew him.

Very quietly she began to hum and realized the tune was 'Oh, What a Beautiful Mornin''.

And now, thanks to the messages from Gavin, it would be.

'Any problem, Leonard?'

Len had collapsed into his favourite armchair in front of the cricket looking pale and sweaty.

'No, no. Just a little breathless. Like there's an elephant sitting on my chest.'

Hiro was instantly in front of him. 'Shall I call Olivia?'

'Please, no. She'll only make a fuss. You know women.' He came up with a small smile. 'Well, no, I don't suppose you do.'

Hiro was silent for a moment. 'I have consulted my computer. Do you have a pain in your upper arm, fast heartbeat or exhaustion?'

'I am a wee bit shagged out,' Len confessed.

'Then I must find Olivia at once.'

'Hiro, do you remember the conversation we had about me not wanting to go to hospital?'

'Yes,' Hiro replied reluctantly. Robots, it seemed, had no option but honesty.

'Well, now's the time not to send me. Or fetch Olivia. Promise?'

'I am a machine, Leonard.'

'You're the smartest damn machine I've encountered. Ouch!' He grabbed his side, suddenly doubling over in pain.

If artificial eyes could look alarmed, Hiro's did now.

Fortunately for him Olivia arrived in the room. 'Leonard, what's the matter with you? I could hear you groaning next door.'

'Nothing at all, Olivia. Aaargh . . .' Another wave of chest pain struck him down.

'I'm calling an ambulance right now.

She reached for the landline just as Hiro seemed to trip on the wire and disconnect it. 'Oh dear,' he apologized. 'I'm sorry, Olivia.'

'Leonard, make him plug the phone back in!'

'I just need one of my pills, dear.'

Hiro produced it instantly. In a moment or two Les started to look better.

'You stopped me calling an ambulance!' she accused Hiro. 'That could be murder!'

'He's a machine, Olivia. I don't think you can send machines to prison.' A shadow of his usual twinkle emerged, lighting up the bleakness of the atmosphere. 'Besides, I told him not to under any circumstances.'

'So you'd die on the sofa with this lump of metal instead of me?'

The anger and hurt in her voice cut through his pain. 'It's how I'd want it, love. Test match on the telly, crowds cheering. I'm ninety-two. What better way to go?'

She turned angrily on her heel.

'Leonard, I am your friend but next time you must call Olivia.'

'But she'll only call an ambulance.'

'Maybe I'll tie her up.'

They were both laughing when Claudia arrived. 'I was wrong about the old men from *Sesame Street*.' She shook her head affectionately. 'You two are Wallace and Gromit to the life! By the way, what's the matter with Ma?'

'She thought I was having a heart attack and I didn't get her because she'd only call an ambulance.'

'My God, Dad.' Claudia knelt at his knees. 'Shall I call the doctor at least?'

Claudia took one of Len's hands in hers. It was bony and veined like rivers on a map. She held it to her lips.

He shook his head. 'Do you remember what I asked you to promise? Not to make a fuss but let me go the way I want to?'

'But Dad . . .' she protested.

'Hiro kept his word.'

'Hiro's not your daughter or your wife.'

'He *is* my friend.'

'That's different, Dad.'

'I know.' He squeezed her hand. 'And thanks for not saying he's just a robot.' Could you go and talk to your mother? Try and make her understand. I'm ninety-two and no bloody good to anyone . . .'

Claudia hugged him tight. 'You are to me.'

'Then let me go, love. The old live too long. I don't want to be kept going on some bloody ventilator just to make a statistic about longer lifespan. And remember, in the end it's *my* life.'

Claudia struggled to her feet, trying to hide her tears, knowing she would never persuade her mother that, for once in his life, her father wasn't going to do what he was told.

The newly cheerful Laura sat down with a ready meal and a glass of wine. She felt pleased with today. She'd been round the National Portrait Gallery and listened to a free lecture on the Lives behind the Tudor Portraits, which had been excellent. She'd always loved those paintings of Queen Elizabeth I and Henry VIII, so stiff and formal and yet almost as familiar as our own royal family. She especially loved a huge canvas like a cartoon which followed the life of a diplomat called Sir Henry Unton from his birth to his grave, all in different pictures. The guide told them it had been commissioned by his wife Lady Dorothy, the only woman apart from the Queen to draw up her own marriage contract. Go girl!

She'd even sent Gavin a photo of Lady Dorothy, but what a civil engineer in Beirut would make of an Elizabethan feminist, heaven alone knew. Be impressed with Laura's cultural breadth, she hoped!

Just as she finished her wine a text came through. How was your day? I thought of you all the time but this is the first moment I could tell you. I liked the lady in the ruff. Will text again before bed. Gavin

When her phone rang later she jumped, hoping it might be him, though they hadn't actually spoken yet.

But it wasn't. It was Ella.

'Hello, lovely Ella, how's life down in the sticks?' Laura laughed.

'My, you sound happy.'

'Yes, I am. How's my gorgeous and efficient daughter?'

'Gorgeous and efficient as ever. She's a gem.'

'She is, isn't she?' Laura asked proudly. 'And my even more gorgeous grandson?'

'He's gorgeous too. In fact, your family runs over with gorgeousness. But, Laura, seriously, I've got a bone to pick with you.'

'What's that?'

'How did you lumber us with the monster that is Mrs Lal?'

'You needed her as I recall,' Laura replied a shade defensively. 'Besides, she's really quite nice when you get to know her.'

'*Nice?*' repeated Ella. 'She's been causing nothing but trouble.'

317

'She probably feels a bit of an outsider with all you knowing each other so well.'

'Hmm, whatever you say. So how are the fleshpots of London treating you? Simon behaving himself?'

Laura sounded almost confused about who Simon, her ex-husband, was. 'Oh. Well, I never hear from him as a matter of fact.'

'And have you started looking for a permanent flat? The one you're in's only six months, isn't it?'

'Yes, I really must start looking,' Laura agreed absent-mindedly.

'And a couple of months have already passed.'

'Yes, amazing, isn't it?'

'Are you really okay, Laura? You sound as if you're on another planet. You haven't started taking drugs now you're back in the Big Stink?'

Laura laughed. 'Hardly. I never even took them in back in the day. I'm far too conventional. But yes, as a matter of fact, I am pretty happy.'

Slightly hurt, Ella got the impression that, happy though she might be, Laura couldn't wait for her to get off the line. 'Okay, great, well goodbye for now, honeybun.'

'Bye, Ella, love to all the others.' She didn't add that she missed them because miraculously, since Gavin had come onto her horizon, she didn't. They'd probably only disapprove and tell her to be careful.

Laura had a luxurious bath with her precious Jo Malone Lime, Basil & Mandarin bath oil, which cost so much she kept it for very special occasions, and poured herself another glass of white wine.

An hour later she realized she'd actually fallen asleep in the bath. A sudden stirring of desire, something she hadn't felt for years, flooded through her and her hand strayed downwards in the bath water.

By the time the next message arrived she hardly recognized this turned-on, eager version of herself.

Laura, it read, wasn't it a Laura who inspired Petrarch's poems? Tonight you are in my heart and I wish with my whole soul you were in my bed. Sleep well and dream of me. Gavin

A secret smile of delight spread across Laura's pretty features as she typed in her rather more modest reply.

Bella was surprised when Spike turned up with his suitcase the following week. What's more, the Mohican had gone, replaced by a style that revealed him to be surprisingly attractive. She almost commented that he brushed up well but thought better of it. To start with, it was the kind of thing her mother might say and secondly, it might give him the wrong idea.

The thought of her mother flagged a small worry in Bella. She hadn't heard from her lately and was quite concerned that Laura was living alone while all the friends she used to depend on were down here. She quite understood why her mum didn't want to join them but she was worried all the same.

Ella was passing at that moment and Bella introduced Spike to her.

'I see,' Ella replied robustly. 'You've been brought in to chat to the old people. Are you planning a reminiscence hour when we all talk about the war?'

'Now, Ella, you weren't even born then,' Bella reproved.

'How about the Swinging Sixties then? We could have a singalong to the Grateful Dead.'

'You look pretty alive to me,' commented Spike.

Ella looked at him over the new half-moon reading glasses she'd acquired which Bella thought made her the spit of Jenni

Murray at her sternest. 'Thank you. I can still walk and talk at the same time, amazing, isn't it?'

'Actually,' Bella explained, 'it was Lou's idea. He wanted some young faces about the place.'

'How's your digging, young man?'

'Spike.'

'How's your digging, Spike?'

'I don't know. I'm studying social work and psychology.'

'Important psychological fact: there is nothing like digging to restore equilibrium to the troubled mind.'

'Right. I'll try it sometime.'

'Where are you living?'

'That cottage over there,' Spike replied warily, pointing to an area near Lou and Sal, and imagining himself being dragged out of bed on a freezing morning and ordered outside to dig by this Valkyrie in bifocals.

'Welcome to Igden, you bring the age down significantly. Of course there is Noah.'

'Who's Noah?' Spike was clearly imagining an old man with a beard given to predicting heavy rainfall.

'Noah is Bella's baby. Actually, while you're here . . . Bella, can I enlist Spike to help me with a little repair job?' She indicated the chicken wire fence she'd erected round a little bit of garden near her own cottage, cleverly disguised with climbing plants. 'Someone's been doing a bit of sabotage.' They all inspected the large hole in Ella's fence. 'Wire cutters.' Ella shook her head. 'It's Greenham Common all over again. Except this time I'm the enemy instead of nuclear weapons.'

Bella stared, appalled. 'My God, who could have done that?'

'Somebody who minds very much that I created my own garden.'

'Jesus.' Spike shook his head. 'I thought it was like an Agatha Christie when I walked in. Now I know it is.'

'No one's dead yet fortunately,' Ella shrugged. 'Now let's get on with replacing the chicken wire.'

Laura woke the next morning feeling uneasy and somehow dissatisfied. She realized it was because it was already eight and she hadn't had her wake-up message from Gavin. He'd said he had a job in the desert; no doubt he'd had a really early start and maybe even no signal.

His wake-up and goodnight messages were always her favourites, the highlights of her day. Today she was glad she was going to LateExpress for one of the occasional days she still worked for Mr A, mainly to give her life some structure. And of course the money was useful.

She must stop checking her inbox every ten seconds or people would think she had OCD. But she couldn't help looking at his photo. Maybe it was a bit weird of her but she'd photographed it and now she had it on her phone and could look at those warm brown eyes, with the laughter lurking just behind, whenever she wanted.

Which was quite a lot.

'Mrs Minchin.' Mr A launched himself on her with a beaming embrace and twice his usual exuberance. 'Top of the morning. You are looking so much better! Like a light has gone back on if you do not mind me saying. Mrs A and I were quite worried about you! But now I see we can relax. And how is my esteemed mother-in-law getting on in Surrey living with your very good friends?'

Mr A had been overwhelmed with gratitude that the demanding Mrs Lal had opted for Igden Manor and a safe distance from himself and his wife.

321

Laura instantly thought of Ella's call about the trouble she was causing. She wouldn't mention that.

'Fine, I think. A few settling-in problems.'

'Nothing serious, I hope?' She could hear the panic in his voice at the thought of Mrs Lal, in full vengeful goddess mode, returning to London and blaming him for dumping her with such unsuitable companions.

Laura decided to quickly change the subject. 'So, what would you like me to do today?'

'I am very sorry as it is not an interesting occupation, but could you flatten boxes for recycling? I have not liked to give offensive weapon to the class of helper I have been having.' He took a sharp knife from his belt and handed it to her. 'They are not responsible people like you.'

Responsible and reliable Laura spent the next hour happily flattening boxes and every five minutes or so getting out her phone to check if there was a message from Gavin.

There wasn't.

She wondered if she should message him again, but something – pride or an inner voice that told her she was not a silly teenager – made her stop.

By the end of the working day there was still nothing, leaving Laura with such a sense of abandonment than she felt physically sick.

How was it possible, she asked herself, that she could feel this intensity for someone she hadn't met or even spoken to? And yet she felt she knew him, that the true Gavin had come through in the messages they'd exchanged, and that he was warm and empathetic, and absolutely nothing like her ex-husband Simon.

The strength of her feelings scared her, but she was aware that fairy tales could be true: she'd been a kind of Sleeping

Beauty and now she felt alive and awake, and she knew it was thanks to this.

She wished she'd planned something for that evening instead of spending it alone. Even watching a DVD of her favourite film couldn't take her mind off the echoing silence.

Slowly she got ready for bed and cleaned her teeth. Maybe that was it then. Just a brief connection which for some reason, work or personal, he'd had to sever.

And then just before midnight her phone, which she kept by the bed, beeped with a new message.

> Laura, my heart, I am coming to London. At last I can meet my soulmate, the woman who haunts my dreams. Will you meet me, Heathrow Terminal 5, in two weeks' time?

Laura, who had been halfway down the road to believing it was over, sat down on the edge of the bed and almost wept with joy and relief.

She was going to meet Gavin at last. And the stupid incomprehensible thing was, she'd never felt like this – the wild, crazy joy, the sudden troughs of despair – for anyone before, not even Simon.

Ella stood at her window with the binoculars she'd bought to watch the birdlife at the manor, which was surprisingly varied. Apart from the usual robins, blackbirds, wrens, blue tits and the occasional mistle thrush, since she'd hung a fat block in her new garden she had spotted a green woodpecker and a family of goldfinches.

But today it wasn't the birdlife she was studying but her neighbour, Mrs Lal. The bloody woman had just come out of her cottage and was walking suspiciously in the direction of

Ella's garden, glancing around her as if she were about to shop-lift, but Ella suspected her real goal was Ella's garden fence.

She had just got something out of her Prada handbag and was leaning towards it when Claudia emerged and greeted her. She stuffed whatever she was holding swiftly back into the bag.

'Morning, Mrs Lal,' Claudia remarked as she was on her way to see Ella. Ella stood watching from her upstairs window. 'Prada for gardening? I usually use a trug myself.'

Mrs Lal smiled with an expression of surprisingly engaging mischief on her perfectly made-up face. 'Shh, I am about to steal some of Mrs Thompson's clematis.'

Claudia had been about to reply that she was sure Ella would willingly give her a cutting when a window opened and Ella herself leaned out.

'Morning, Mrs Lal,' Ella greeted her merrily. 'If you're after my clematis, you don't need to use wire cutters, you know.'

Underneath her pan stick the elegant Mrs Lal turned redder than her Christian Louboutin rouge lipstick which Claudia had seen for sale in Selfridges for £70, and shot inside her cottage like a frightened rabbit.

'What on earth's up with her?' Claudia enquired, stunned, when Ella appeared at the front door.

'She was only trying to cut a hole in my fence with bloody wire cutters! She's already done it once. What are you going to do about it?'

The usually even-tempered Ella, who they all often took their problems to in the Coven, looked so angry that Claudia was worried she might be about to pursue her quarry into her sanctuary.

'To be honest, Ella,' Claudia replied injudiciously, 'it was a bit naughty of you to pinch a bit of the garden without asking. We are supposed to be a community.'

'I hate bloody communities!' Ella stormed. 'I thought we'd agreed that this place could only work if we all had our privacy, and all I was doing was creating mine. I happen to find having my own a garden is vital to my happiness.'

She slammed the door and disappeared.

Claudia stared at the closed door, lost for words. So much for peace and harmony in the country.

Ella stood in her pretty bedroom wondering if she'd made the most godawful mistake moving here. Maybe your best friends were the last people on earth you should try and live with.

Claudia, feeling as if she had been attacked by an animal she'd thought was friendly, could see Rose McGill coming towards her and raised her hand in friendly greeting. But Rose was in no mood for pleasantries.

'That bloody woman!' She nodded furiously towards Mrs Lal's cottage. 'She's only gone and insulted the chef! Criticised his signature dish and now he's talking of packing his bags and going home to London!'

'Maybe he isn't serious,' Claudia offered, wishing she were anywhere but here. 'Chefs are always threatening to leave.'

'Yes, but they don't usually order a minicab to pick them up in half an hour and take them to the station.'

'Oh goodness, I'd better go and see if I can pacify him.'

Ella stood at her window watching with grim satisfaction as another crime was laid at the door of Mrs Lal.

It was Friday and she'd just decided to pack a bag and head for London too. She could probably stay in Laura's spare room; failing that, with her daughter Cory, though Cory always seemed to be working. Ella thought she'd worked hard as a lawyer but young people these days seemed to have to give up their entire lives to work and be available twenty-four hours a day. It made her worry about Cory but of course if she ever said anything, she was told gently but firmly to mind her own business.

If she stayed with Laura they could go and have a drink in a wine bar like the old days. Maybe even the good old Grecian Grove. And at least Laura would be pleased to see her.

Twenty

'Have you seen the injection of youth you asked for?' Sal teased Lou as they wandered through the grounds from their cottage. 'His name's Spike and he's actually quite attractive. If I wasn't the age I am and already in love with you, I might be tempted.'

They both studied Spike who was wearing a singlet and tracky bottoms as he limbered up outside the main building, despite the cold weather.

'Hi there,' he saluted them. 'I was just wondering if anyone might be interested in a fitness session for older people? Only I did a course on it and it seems a pity not to use it.'

'Sounds great. I'll ask around,' Lou said, 'and let you know.' He dipped down and murmured in Sal's ear, 'I've survived thus far without being described as an "older person" and I don't intend to start now.'

He saw Don walking past holding a Stanley knife and looking very intense. 'Don, my friend, don't go near any blondes in the shower with that thing.'

'Blondes in rather short supply round here,' Don replied, 'in the shower or otherwise.'

'Don,' tutted Sal, 'that is definitely an ageist observation.'

Don just laughed.

'You're American, aren't you?' Spike asked Lou, when they passed him trying unsuccessfully to persuade Claudia to sign up.

'Smart boy. New Yorker in fact. Most people don't count that as America.'

'I've never been to the US,' Spike confessed wistfully.

'Really? Why is that?'

'It's not because I don't want to,' he grinned. 'Just never had the dough-ray-me, if you get me.'

'You'd better tell us more about these sessions you're offering.' Lou decided he liked Spike. He was so very unsophisticated.

'It's called Fitness for Old Farts.'

Lou, who was fitter than any man had a right to be at his age, cracked up with laughter.

'It'll be like that Yoga for Oldies thing I went on,' Sal remarked. 'The moment we all lay down it was Who Can Fart First?'

'All right, I'll sign up,' Lou offered. 'And so will the little lady here,' he added, winking outrageously.

'Hey,' Sal protested, 'less of the little lady, please.'

'Okay, two old farts to go on your list.'

Spike went off whistling to try and enlist a few others.

'I wouldn't try the Indian lady,' Sal called after him. 'I don't think it's really her scene. On the other hand, I don't know what is – apart from sabotaging fences, offending chefs and some rather unreliable fortune telling.'

'What the hell am I going to do about Mrs Lal?' Claudia slumped into a chair in their bedroom as Don stood in front of her, naked as Adam before The Fall. 'I can't believe that Laura could have dumped her on us and then decided to stay in London. Maybe dumping Mrs Lal was her way of getting out of the guilt of not joining us.'

'To be fair,' Don reasoned, apparently unaware of his complete state of undress, 'Laura never showed any interest in coming here. She offered us Bella, who has been a total wonder, and as far as I know never even entertained the idea of living here herself.' He delved into his knicker drawer for clean boxers.

'Watch out!' Claudia responded crossly. 'Those have all been ironed!'

'I really don't need ironed underpants,' Don responded, further irritating Claudia who, weird or not, found ironing underpants soothing.

'Besides,' Don continued blithely, 'I thought you needed Mrs Lal's money. You hardly invited her out of the kindness of your heart.'

'Yes,' Claudia conceded, 'but Laura said she was okay, and she's clearly a complete nightmare. No wonder her daughter and son-in-law were so thrilled to see the back of her. And you still haven't answered my question.'

Don looked thoughtful as he pulled on the old blue jeans he wore for chopping wood, his favourite task at the manor house.

'I see you're wearing your lumberjack outfit. Mind you check with Ella before you chop anything down. She's turning into Gertrude Jekyll.'

Don whistled cheerfully.

'So you haven't got anything useful to contribute?' Claudia knew she was sounding horrible but Don could at least have understood how stressed she was.

'If I were you, I'd consult your mother.'

'My *mother*?' Claudia looked at him as if he'd metamorphosed into a dangerous lunatic.

'Yes, your mother. Have you forgotten it was your mother who saved our daughter's wedding?'

On the other hand, tact and people skills weren't exactly up Olivia's street. Claudia decided she'd have a go at talking to Mrs Lal first.

Rose McGill looked out of her window at the early morning unfolding beneath her. Mist still hung on the trees like a white chiffon wrap on the shoulders of a yawning debutante. A pheasant, the finest but stupidest of birds, strutted across the lawn displaying his finery and croaking away to his mouse-brown mate.

If she were younger, she might even think of having a swim, but her rheumatism pained her. It always seemed to take longer and longer for her joints to ease up in the mornings these days.

She was just about to go for a bath when she spotted Murdo Binns, looking as guilty as a condemned man, slip out of Mrs Lal's cottage, glance both ways and head for the back route to the car park. It really was too much when he'd made such a song and dance about being in love with her. But then Murdo had always been weak and easily led. She put it down to his Gorgon of a mother. That had been why, all those years ago, she'd refused to marry him.

She wished she were more mobile and could dash down the stairs and pursue him but by the time she got down he'd be in Godalming.

So much for only selling this place to them if she were part of the package. Stupid sod. But then, in Rose's experience, men *were* stupid where sex was concerned. They ran after it like some shiny toy and couldn't see that the toy they already had might actually be more precious.

Since Murdo was eighty, Mrs Lal probably seemed like a younger woman even though she had to be seventy at least. Maybe Indian women kept at it longer. All that Kama Sutra stuff.

She saw Claudia, looking distinctly nervous, heading towards Mrs Lal's door. Knowing she'd never get down in time to head her off, she opened her window and called down instead.

'Morning, Claudia. Beautiful day. You couldn't pop up for a coffee and a chat?'

Claudia's heart sank. Rose McGill wasn't the type to waste time on chats unless she had something important to say.

Rose, still in her dressing gown, was filling a cafetière. 'Can't be arsed with those little machines that need pods like we had in the office. You always seem to run out of the ones you like and be left with the *Fortissimo* when you want the *Arpeggio*.'

'Sorry, Rose,' Claudia replied, 'I don't speak Nespresso.'

Rose was so irritated she didn't even laugh. 'You know the chef's actually gone. Not just threatened, *gone*.'

'Oh dear.'

'And I've just seen Murdo Binns creeping out of Mrs Lal's cottage. Don't you think there ought to be rules about overnight guests?'

'Rose, for goodness' sake. We're all grown-ups.'

'He might have a heart attack on the job.'

Claudia had to stop herself from laughing, though a relationship between Murdo and Mrs Lal was very annoying, she could see that.

'So what are you going to do about the chef? Order meals on wheels? We're certainly old enough.'

Claudia had absolutely no bloody idea. Maybe she would talk to her mother after all.

*

Ella walked through the barrier at Waterloo station and felt a kick of disappointment. Laura had said she'd meet her if she possibly could. Of course, it was easy enough on the tube but there was something special about being met. It was human instinct to hope someone was there waving to you even though logically you knew there couldn't be. She headed for the giant tube map on the wall just as a figure leapt out from behind a large white noticeboard announcing delays on the line.

It was Laura, looking incredibly pretty in a pale yellow cardigan with a silk scarf tied round the neck and blue jeans, clutching a bunch of pink asters which she thrust into Ella's arms.

'Surprise!' She hugged her friend. 'I am SO glad to see you. I can't tell you how weird London is without you all. I mean, I know I'm supposed to be an old lady sitting by the fire in her slippers with no expectations but in my head I'm still nineteen and wanting to go out on the razzle!'

'The razzle it shall be. Well, a nice pub or wine bar anyway.'

'We could go to The Grecian Grove, for old times' sake.'

Ella put her arm round Laura, her pull-along suitcase in the other. 'Brilliant! That's just what I was hoping! Now, or shall we go to your place first?'

'It's six p.m. Already wine o'clock. Let's go now.'

Ella studied Laura for a moment. There seemed to be something different about her. There was no longer any hint of the abandoned wife or the guilty granny; she seemed to have an inner glow, just like the beauty companies offered you but never actually provided. If she could bottle it, she'd make a fortune.

'So,' Ella enquired as they sat down together in front of the familiar fading nymphs painted on the walls of the wine bar that had been their headquarters for so long, 'how come you look so amazing?'

'Do I?' Laura asked innocently.

'You must know you do. Have you won the lottery? Got an ace new job? Fallen in love?'

Laura just laughed. 'I'll tell you about it later. For now let's take a selfie of us with these boozy Bacchae and send it to Claudia and Sal. They'll be so jealous!'

Laura held up her phone and snapped as they toasted each other with Pinot Grigio.

After the next glass with just a few meze of deep-fried calamari and a dish of black olives, Laura was feeling a bit light-headed and daring. She got out her phone and showed Ella the photograph of a very handsome man with luxuriant wavy hair and melting brown eyes that somehow managed to look friendly and sexy at the same time. 'Wow! Who's that?'

'His name's Gavin.'

'Where did you meet him?'

Laura laughed again, with a slight hint of self-consciousness. 'On a dating site called Out There. I joined up so I could get to know him better.'

'Right. So tell me about him. Where does he live? Was he married? Does he have children?' Ella studied his face again. 'And is he really as knockout as he looks in the picture.'

Laura's back stiffened almost imperceptibly as she poured the last of the wine from the bottle into their glasses.

'The thing is, I know this probably sounds weird, but I haven't actually met him. He's an engineer and he lives in Beirut working on this big solar power project. But I'm just about to. He's coming to London in a couple of weeks.'

'How exciting! So you've just been chatting on the phone so far?'

'Well, actually, we've just been emailing and messaging all the time. We started out on the app and then, maybe I shouldn't have but I just knew he was trustworthy, so I gave him my mobile number.' Laura stared into the last of her wine and smiled. 'By now I really feel I know him. You can't believe how romantic it is. He sends me a good-morning message every single day, as well as messaging me to say sleep well, and some of his messages are just a little bit sexy . . .' She found an example and showed it to Ella.

> I long to spend the night with you and watch the sun come up lying in your arms. Laura, you are the woman of my dreams. Gavin

'Good heavens.' Ella tried not to sound too dampening. 'How can you be the woman of his dreams when you haven't even met him yet? He could be a sex maniac or a serial killer!'

'I knew you wouldn't understand.' Laura looked so wounded that Ella wished she'd spoken more gently. Laura had had such a bad time with horrible Simon.

'All the same, do be careful,' Ella added. 'Where are you meeting this chap? Somewhere very public, I hope, and you really mustn't take him back to your flat.'

Laura just laughed. Ella could see that somehow Laura really did feel she knew this man quite intimately already. 'Don't worry, I won't do anything silly. I'm just so excited to meet him at last.'

'Yes,' Ella replied, torn between worry and pleasure that her friend seemed so happy. 'I can see you are.'

She just hoped that this man was all right. She knew that lots of people met online these days and the whole business of apps and websites was another world to her. Maybe she was just old-fashioned and out of touch.

Claudia decided she'd better get Bella to see if the situation with the chef really was beyond rescue, and if so, find a temp to fill the post. What the hell had the bloody woman actually said to him? One thing she'd learned since they'd all set up home here was that the plumbing could be problematic, the cleaning patchy – but you couldn't mess with the food.

She was nearly at Bella's door when her father and Hiro overtook her on their way for their lunchtime visit to the pub, where Hiro beat Len at Scrabble and her father drank a half pint of Theakston's Old Peculier every day at 12.30. This meant her mother would be on her own. The ghastly carer, Mrs O'Brien, had been given her marching orders when they moved, thank God.

Claudia found her mother making a cup of tea and staring disconsolately out of the window. 'All right, Ma?'

'It's your father,' Olivia replied irrationally, 'he's so bloody *happy* these days. With that mindless lump of metal tagging along he doesn't need human company.'

Claudia didn't like to point out that Hiro was hardly mindless and that when Len had been available to chat with his wife, she had totally ignored him and preferred the company of the carer.

'I suppose it was him you were looking for anyway,' Olivia commented. 'You and your father always were thick as thieves.'

'As a matter of fact, it was you. I need a bit of advice.'

'From *me*?' Olivia demanded incredulously. 'You need advice and you came to *me*?' Her mother looked like a hare with a broken paw who found it was suddenly being splinted.

'I thought you and your friends all saw me as an interfering busybody.'

'No, Ma, not at all. Don was just reminding me how you rescued Gaby's wedding.'

Olivia sat down at the big dining table, hardly ever used now, but which had featured so often in Claudia's childhood. She had lost a lot of weight, Claudia noticed, and her clothes seemed suddenly baggy. Her terrifying mother, who could put you down with a lift of the eyebrow, looked suddenly pathetic.

'It's Mrs Lal who's the interfering busybody.' Claudia sat down next to her mother. 'The chef's left because of her and now Rose thinks she's trying to snatch her beau and become the next Lady Binns.' She sighed gustily. 'But Laura insists it's all a front and she's quite nice underneath it all.' Claudia laid her head on her mother's shoulder. 'Oh God, Ma, the whole thing's falling apart and it's all my fault. I was the one who got everyone to move here.'

'Come on, dear, pull yourself together. Why don't you throw a little drinks party?'

Claudia almost laughed. 'Because at the moment no one would come and if they did, they wouldn't speak to each other.'

'Even with some nice canapés?'

Claudia felt hysteria rising. It would probably end up as blinis at dawn between Rose and Mrs Lal.

'All right,' Olivia reasoned, 'now what do you think she's actually good at?'

'Apart from putting people's backs up on an Olympic scale? She claims she's a brilliant fortune teller and you've heard her boasting she's a famous matchmaker as well.'

'We've had quite enough of *that*,' Olivia huffed, 'what with that Daniel chap turning up the other night and flirting with Ella.'

'Why do you ask anyway?'

'When Dad and I were living in Dubai there was this lady who couldn't keep her silly nose out of anyone's business. I thought she might end up murdered and her body washed up in the Persian Gulf.'

Claudia listened, fascinated. Her mother so rarely talked about the days when Dad was successful and she was a company wife.

'Then I found out she was a whiz at bridge. We got her to start a bridge club and she taught all the veiled ladies who lived in the royal palace how to play and got really quite important. We never heard a peep out of her again.' Her mother looked thoughtful. 'I see there's a vacancy in one of the charity shops in the village. Do you think your Mrs Lal would consider it?'

'Goodness, she's frightfully well dressed, though Laura did mention she picks up all her jewellery in Oxfam.'

'Caramba! Do you want me to have a chat with her? She'll never be nervous about a poor old dear like me bending her ear. She can patronize me all she likes.'

Claudia grinned. Anyone patronizing her mother would certainly be underestimating their opponent.

'Would you, Ma? She can only bite your head off!'

'Not if I tell her about the cache of costume jewellery hidden behind the counter.'

'*Is* there a cache of costume jewellery hidden behind the counter? I didn't think that was allowed.'

'Not yet there isn't,' Olivia replied, looking like a witch who'd defied the ducking stool. 'But there jolly well soon will be!'

*

'Shall we go and eat in your local hostelry, seeing that the chef's absconded?' Lou suggested to Sal. 'Rose is still hopping mad.'

'I'm not surprised,' Sal grinned. 'Rose is very fussy about her food. And then to find Murdo corridor-creeping from Mrs Lal's cottage . . .'

'To be fair it wasn't a corridor and no one knows if it was her bedroom. He might have popped in for a cup of coffee. You Brits are so moralistic.'

'I thought it was Americans who were moralistic. All those Puritans going over in the *Mayflower*. Besides, old Murdo was carrying his shoes in his hand so as not to make any noise.'

'Hmm, a tad incriminating, I'll admit. So what about a light supper in The Laden Ox?'

Sal smiled at him lovingly. The truth was, she'd been feeling rather devastatingly tired lately, and didn't want to think about possible causes. 'Why not? Get one of their steak and kidney pies down you and you'll never want to live in Brooklyn again.'

'That good, huh?' Lou had noticed that Sal had taken to sleeping more, even in the afternoons, which she'd never done before, and it worried him too.

'No, it's just they'll immobilize you for the foreseeable future.' She held her hand up tenderly to his face. 'Do you know, I might just go and lie down for five minutes before we set out for the pub.'

'You do that. Would you like a cup of tea in bed?'

'You really are starting to get the hang of the British character.'

The next day Ella and Laura went shopping.

Laura wanted to buy something new for Gavin's visit. To

Ella's amazement the previously prim Laura stopped outside Victoria's Secret and stared longingly in.

'Do you think my boobs are too big for one of those balcony bras?' She indicated a skimpy black number with non-existent matching knickers. As far as Ella knew, Laura had never had any interest in such things when married to Simon.

She had been with her friend more than twenty-four hours now and witnessed her excitement waiting for the next message from Gavin, and noted the sheer number the man sent. How he had time to develop solar power when he spent most of it on the phone sending Laura intimate messages morning, noon and night, she couldn't fathom. Yet Ella was beginning to see how her friend could be feeling so loved-up and intimate with the man via this long-distance courtship.

But it wasn't courtship. That was what made Ella feel vaguely uneasy. It was the sheer persistence of the man. To Ella it smacked almost of control, though Laura would never see it like that. She was simply basking in the attention after being married to a man who hardly noticed she existed. Ella found herself wondering if this was the way the men in Rotherham groomed their victims, and then felt shocked at the thought.

Even though Laura was blooming like a rose that had withered and was suddenly flourishing again, Ella wished she'd met a man through more conventional means.

Laura had decided against the balcony bra and was dragging Ella into a boutique in South Molton Street where they sold off-the-shoulder black dresses to the wives of rich Russians and despite living in a two-bed rented flat, Laura was clearly going to buy one.

Laura caught her expression. 'Look, I've got my half of the money for the house in the bank. One little dress isn't going to bankrupt me!'

'That money's for your new home as soon as you find one.' Ella knew she sounded like a spoilsport parent. Or her own disapproving daughter Julia.

Good Age, the charity shop two doors down from The Laden Ox, had never seen anything quite like its two new volunteers when Olivia, with a somewhat reluctant Mrs Lal in tow, arrived the following Monday.

'My God,' decreed Mrs Lal, looking round in disgust. 'We would never allow such a down-and-out retail outlet at home!' She sniffed roundly. 'And what is that terrible smell?'

Olivia breathed in. It was the instantly recognizable charity-shop aroma: clothes stored in musty attics, shoes which ought to have been thrown out decades ago, spiced with the remotest suspicion of ancient pee. But she wasn't going to admit that to Lalita.

'That, my dear Mrs Lal,' announced Olivia, hoping not too many people could hear, 'is because this retail outlet is in need of someone to take control, someone with taste and vision.'

Mrs Lal's fine black eyes began to sparkle with enthusiasm at the challenge. 'Indeed!' She regarded the two seventy-plus ladies who were watching her with a mixture of admiration and fear, much in the way hitherto unshepherded sheep stare at a new sheepdog, as they opened the newly arrived bin bags of kindly donated items.

'The first challenge is to make the space look like an attractive shopping experience.' She eyed the ladies with their bin bags clutched to their cardiganed chests. 'Here,' she commanded, 'give me one of those!' She began to scatter the contents in the middle of the floor. 'How *dare* people offer such rubbish in the name of a good cause? No one I know would wear such things.'

Olivia guessed that Mrs Lal's familiarity with the concept of the charity shop was decidedly limited. 'It's quite different here, Mrs Lal. Lots of people use thrift shops, especially young people. They don't call it second-hand, they call it vintage.'

'I will stay on tonight,' Mrs Lal announced as if volunteering for the Charge of the Light Brigade. 'And tomorrow you will see something different.'

'I'm not sure you can do that,' protested one of the cardiganed ladies whose name turned out to be Flo. 'I don't know what the manageress would have to say.'

Mrs Lal turned to her. 'I will deal with the manageress.'

Flo knew what authority sounded like when she heard it. 'All right,' she agreed nervously, 'but perhaps you'd better phone her first . . .' She began scrabbling around behind the till for the number.

Olivia had always wondered what a gimlet eye was. Now she knew.

'That will not be necessary,' Mrs Lal assured them firmly. 'I have found in life that bureaucracy is the enemy of creativity.'

'Would you like some help?' Olivia offered, wondering what she had unleashed on an unsuspecting Minsley.

'No thank you,' Mrs Lal insisted. 'I always work better alone.'

Without further hesitation she removed her Stella McCartney overcoat and looked around her.

Olivia tried not to smile as she reassured Flo and her friend and got them to write down how to shut up the shop, whereupon they waddled off like two tough old turkeys trying not to think about Christmas.

Ella stood in the queue for Costa Coffee at Waterloo station trying not to think about Laura and the mysterious Gavin. One train had just departed and irritatingly the next wasn't for twenty minutes. At least at this time of day she'd get a seat.

'How about something stronger?' suggested a voice behind her.

Ella swung round to find Daniel Forrest watching her and smiling.

'You've got a nerve,' Ella replied, turning back to the counter.

Somehow he insinuated himself into the queue. 'Look, that was a stupid thing to do the other night. I'm really sorry.'

'Too right. You managed to really upset Claudia and Don.'

'I thought that was all water under the bridge. Claudia and I just flirted a bit, shared the odd kiss, it never went further than that.'

'Maybe it did for her. I gather it almost wrecked their daughter's wedding when Don found out.'

'Yes, well, he was up to no good himself. Even if it was only online, which seemed pretty weird to me.'

She was about to say that at least online was better than actual betrayal, but thought better of it as the memory of Laura flashed uncomfortably into her mind again.

'Look, I'm really sorry. Do you think I should apologize to Claudia?'

'Absolutely not. Just don't show up at the manor again.'

'What other penance could I do? Offer myself as a human sacrifice to the outrageous Mrs Lal so she can practise her matchmaking skills?'

'Daniel,' Ella replied severely. 'I think that would only cause more trouble.'

'I'm not Casanova, you know.' Ella had to admit his smile was very charming and had to shake herself mentally.

'Nothing I can think of at the moment, I'm afraid,' Ella said firmly.

'Well, if you do think of anything, let me know.' He handed her a business card.

'Very formal.'

'I thought formal was what you wanted.' Ella decided he was attractive and exasperating in equal measure. And definitely dangerous.

Anyway, she didn't need romance in her life, the pain and the worry of it. Besides, she was too set in her ways. And look at what it was doing to Laura. She was shining like a star at the moment but what if it ended in a black hole?

Once she was on the train she ordered a G&T from the trolley, opened her iPad and began browsing 'The Dangers of Online Dating'.

Maybe she was overreacting, but better safe than sorry, surely? Whether Laura would agree with her, she wasn't at all convinced.

Twenty-One

'Come on, Claudia dear,' her mother Olivia chivvied the next morning. 'I can't wait to see what your Mrs Lal has done with the charity shop.'

'She's not my Mrs Lal, she's Laura's if she's anyone's. Besides, I'm busy looking at temporary chefs with Bella and they all seem to either be working in schools or on work experience from their FE Colleges. Hardly Rose's style.'

'Does she really care that much about food?'

'Yes!' chorused Bella and Claudia. 'Rose was adamant we had a proper cook and somewhere to eat together. Civilized living demands it, according to Rose. I think she's right, even if it is an extravagance. Eating together *is* important. And she's not the only one. We've been having a lot of mumbling since Mrs Lal drove the chef out. Wretched woman.'

'I must admit,' added Bella, 'I haven't been able to detect this heart of gold that's supposed to lurk beneath the tough exterior.' Noah distracted her by tugging at the toggle on her vintage Afghan dress.

'I was just explaining to Mrs Lal how young people like you consider second-hand to be quite trendy,' Claudia commented.

'Pre-loved,' stated Bella with a grin.

'Sorry?' Olivia shook her head and made a face.

'Pre-loved. That's what the Americans call second-hand.'

'Really,' Olivia opined. 'Americans are such extraordinary people. Do you know they all think our road sign for deceptive bends is terribly funny? And guess what they call their own? Dangerous curves. I mean, I ask you!'

'Lou's all right, though.' Bella picked Noah up and put him on her knee.

'He's practically one of us,' agreed Claudia. 'I mean, fancy preferring Lower Minsley to Brooklyn!'

'I went to Brooklyn once,' Olivia announced. 'It was closed.'

The others looked at her strangely.

'It's a joke! A parody of WC Fields.' She on put quite a convincing imitation of the great man's double-chinned stature. '*I went to Philadelphia once. It was closed.* You see how I put in Brooklyn instead . . .'

'Yes, Ma, we both got it.'

'Well, you didn't laugh. No sense of humour, your generation.'

Claudia grabbed her arm and led her off as Bella stifled her giggles.

'*Now* she gets it,' announced Olivia with satisfaction. 'A bit slow, I must say.'

Olivia then insisted on stopping at the baker's and bought rock buns plus three takeaway coffees.

'She'll never be there at this time, Ma,' Claudia said. 'If she really did stay on for ages.'

'You wait. I saw the look in her eye. Besides, we can always give them to Minnie and Flo or whatever their names were.'

'The thing is, though,' Claudia said gloomily, 'even if she has tarted up the shop, I can hardly see her *working* there alongside dear old Minnie and Flo . . .'

She stopped in her tracks transfixed by the sight of Mrs Lal standing in the window of Good Age, her immaculate hair in dusty rat's tails round her face, wielding a paintbrush and completing the last of a colourful honeycomb of wooden boxes, in orange, blue and yellow.

'That's the last bloody box!' Mrs Lal announced triumphantly, falling on the rock cakes as if she'd never seen food before. 'I remembered seeing a pile of them outside the wine merchant and just managed to pick up paint and brushes before the hardware shop closed.'

'But what are they *for*?' Olivia asked.

'I'm going to put vases and some pairs of shoes and that cake stand in them' – she indicated a rather pretty glass-topped object – 'to catch the eyes of passers-by.'

It was at this point they noticed the cardiganed volunteers, Minnie and Flo, who were struck dumb at the transformation as they arrived for work.

And what a transformation it was. Mrs Lal had sorted all the random dresses, tops, blazers and skirts into areas of colour that somehow managed to echo the boxes in the window. Particularly eye-catching was the orange section with a row of similar-toned handbags, shoes and other orange objects on the shelf beneath it, next to a section of blues, which morphed elegantly into greens, yellows and purples with all the impact of a kaleidoscope.

It really was stunning.

'Goodness,' remarked Olivia.

'Bloody hell,' echoed Claudia. 'I can hardly believe it's the same shop!'

'I wonder what Vera will say,' mumbled Flo.

'I'm not sure she'll like it,' Minnie announced nervously.

'And who is this Vera?' enquired Mrs Lal scornfully.

'The manageress,' chorused Minnie and Flo.

'Then she should look and learn,' Olivia pronounced.

'I must admit,' Flo said, putting her hands into her cardi pockets and pirouetting in admiration. 'It is very nice. Pity we're too late for Best Charity Shop.'

'And what is Best Charity Shop?' Mrs Lal seemed suddenly to recover her energy.

'The forms came in the other day. Vera put them in the bin.'

'In *this* bin?' Mrs Lal delved into a metal bin behind the cash desk and pulled out some pieces of paper triumphantly.

'Yes, I suppose so,' replied Flo, visibly losing her nerve. 'The prize is a thousand pounds and lunch with Mary Portas.'

'She has always been my heroine,' announced Mrs Lal reverently. 'That haircut. The perfect colour red.'

Claudia marvelled at modern global media that Mrs Lal in India could follow a show about the revival of the British high street.

Mrs Lal took out a gold Parker pen from her Prada handbag and began to fill in the form.

'I'm not sure Vera's going to like this,' announced Minnie again.

'Then Vera,' pronounced Olivia in her best cut-glass tone, 'can take a running jump.'

'Thank you, Ma,' Claudia whispered as they waited for Mrs Lal to come back to the manor. 'You've saved the day again.'

Olivia picked up her coffee, a small smile of satisfaction just visible as she bent down.

'Would you like to come to my house for a cup of tea?' she asked Mrs Lal.

'I'd prefer something stronger.'

'What a very good idea,' agreed Olivia. 'Are you coming too, dear?' she asked her daughter.

'Why not?' Claudia nodded.

They were all laughing when they pushed open the door to her parents' apartment on the ground floor of what had been the main hotel building. It always amazed Claudia how her mother had achieved exactly the same look and feel here as she'd had in their old house: country house with a touch of shabby chic before anyone decided to call it that.

'I wonder if your father would like to join us?' Olivia surprised Claudia by enquiring, as she led them all out to the shed to ask him, then stopped, suddenly frozen.

On the sofa sat her husband, still as a statue, his eyes closed, a glass of whisky next to him on the coffee table, today's crossword, always done in competition with his robotic companion, just completed at his side. Hiro sat next to him.

Olivia knew at once that he was dead.

'When did it happen?' she asked Hiro quietly.

'Half an hour ago. I came to look for you.'

The words 'Not very hard!' were on her lips, but she didn't say them. Len had told her often enough that this was the way he wanted to go.

'Oh Dad, no!' Claudia flung herself onto her knees and kissed his hands.

'My dear lady, I am so sorry for your loss,' Mrs Lal put her arms around Olivia and to Claudia's amazement her mother, who hated to be touched, returned the embrace. How wonderful it would be if Mrs Lal could fill the role of comforter. Relief flooded through Claudia as she realized that her mother wouldn't be alone having to face an empty house, now she was part of a community of friends.

Claudia tried to hold herself together for her mother's sake. She supposed they had better do something, but felt paralyzed by grief.

In the silence they could hear Rose McGill, who had just arrived back from her walk. 'Has anyone seen the charity shop in the village? It looks absolutely amazing.' And then, sensing the stillness of the figures gathered around the shed door, she came over.

'It's my father,' Claudia explained in a low and anguished voice, 'he's just died. Probably a heart attack.'

'Oh my God, Olivia, I'm so sorry. Shall I call for the doctor?'

'Thank you, Rose,' Olivia replied, standing even straighter than usual to try and contain the grief that was threatening to fell her. 'That would be most useful.'

Choosing the hymns and readings for the funeral seemed to offer some consolation to Olivia, as it often does to the people left behind. 'Leonard loved a good funeral,' she announced to Mrs Lal. 'He always said they were for the living, not the dead. At our age they're the number one social event.' She smiled nostalgically. 'His old friend Bill said there were so many of them dying it wasn't worth going home, really. They might just as well stay in the cemetery.'

'And will it be a burial or cremation?' Mrs Lal enquired.

'Oh, burial definitely. He said he liked to think of the sun still shining on him, even if he was six feet under.'

'Perhaps he might prefer a Parsi burial where the body is consumed by vultures?' Mrs Lal suggested enthusiastically.

'Do you know, dear, I think he'd prefer C of E.'

Claudia and her daughter Gaby made sure that their adored father and grandfather got a funeral he'd have enjoyed going to himself. All his favourite hymns, especially 'Plough the Fields and Scatter', funny and tender evocations of the man they all remembered, a vicar who actually got his name right.

To their surprise there was an unscheduled addition. Hiro suddenly moved on his mechanical wheels and declaimed:

> '*He is not dead, this friend – not dead,*
> *But in the path we mortals tread*
> *Gone some few, trifling steps ahead . . .*'

and returned to his pew.

Ella threw a comforting arm round Claudia's shoulders. 'That was very sweet.'

'I know it seems a bit far-fetched since Hiro isn't mortal at all, but they really were good friends.'

'Well,' Sal added in a low voice just for Claudia's ears, 'if you're going to exploit artificial intelligence it's a lot better than a sex doll.'

'Sally Grainger!' Ella rebuked her, shocked. 'And at her father's funeral too.'

'Dad would have laughed and asked where he could get one for Hiro,' Claudia smiled, wiping away her tears for the father she'd loved so much.

'So what's going to happen to Hiro now?' Ella asked. 'Your mum hates him, doesn't she?'

'I have no idea. I'd better ask Lou. Technically Hiro belongs to him and he's spent a fortune developing him.'

'What are you going to do with Hiro, Lou?'

'I would be happy to find a use for him in the shop if you

were agreeable,' chimed in Mrs Lal. 'I'm sure he would be a considerable attraction.'

'So it is you behind the shop transformation?' Ella replied, impressed. 'I have to say it looks absolutely amazing.' She'd only just got back from London and was behind with the gossip.

'I'll talk to Hiro,' Lou replied cagily. 'And see what he wants.'

Mrs Lal moved off in the direction of Murdo Binns just as Olivia arrived with a tray of canapés. 'Eat up. It was always the food that Leonard most enjoyed about funerals. I think he would have particularly enjoyed this one.'

They all fell silent, thinking of the irony of this statement. Finally Ella spoke. 'We were all discussing the amazing window Mrs Lal's created in the charity shop.'

'I know,' Olivia nodded. 'And the two volunteers were convinced Vera the manageress was going to go ballistic. What fun. We haven't had excitement like this since Mr Benson's rampant goat got out and terrified all the womenfolk.'

'Mrs Lal does seem to create excitement wherever she goes,' commented Rose acidly as she joined the group.

'That's why we're trying to contain it,' Olivia replied, 'rather like nuclear fission, for the benefit of all mankind.'

'As I recall' – Rose watched Mrs Lal simper as she accepted a glass of white wine from Murdo – 'nuclear fission can cause a lot more danger than it does benefit.'

In the corner by the bar Claudia finally managed to tie down her mother for a moment. 'Are you all right, Ma? Really?'

'I suppose it hasn't really hit me properly.' Olivia sat down next to her daughter. 'I don't suppose it will until all the hoo-ha has died down and everyday life reasserts. At least there's one good thing. I'll be able to get rid of that revolting robot.'

Claudia put her arm round her mother. She could see her husband Don the other side of the room and beckoned him over. 'Why don't you take over handing out canapés and give Ma a break?'

'Delighted.'

'No, dear,' Olivia insisted, 'I prefer to be doing. But thank you all the same.'

'She can't wait to get rid of Hiro.'

'She was obviously jealous of him, and then embarrassed about it. She'll miss your dad.'

'Even though her main communication with him was through nagging.'

'I don't think he paid a lot of attention.'

'I wonder who she'll decide to nag next,' Don grinned. 'I do hope it isn't me.'

'Hey.' Claudia knitted her arm through his. 'I thought that was my job.'

Laura couldn't remember last feeling this excited. Gavin was actually coming next weekend and they were going to meet at last. She looked at the photograph she had of him that she kept on her phone and noticed that he'd sent her another three texts since lunchtime. It must be a slow day at the solar power installation. The messages were getting sexier and sexier too. A sudden terror came over her again that he'd be disappointed with her. He was five years younger and maybe he hadn't really taken in how old she was. She looked into his warm brown eyes and willed a message to him that she couldn't wait to see him. She needed Sal's chutzpah or Ella's calm confidence or even Claudia's feeling that women were just as good as men. All her feelings of rejection by Simon for a younger woman flooded back.

She began to worry that this meeting she'd been looking forward to so much, and the secret belief she'd allowed herself that Gavin would turn out to be someone she could love, maybe for the rest of her life, was stupid and unfounded. That he might take one look at her and go back to Beirut.

She went into her bedroom and opened her wardrobe. For about the third time that week she riffled through her clothes trying to pick the outfit that made her look youngest and prettiest.

His newest text didn't exactly help.

My Laura, I can't wait to be next to you with your lovely body next to mine. It can get so lonely out here in the desert. Your Gavin

Funny, she didn't think Beirut was in the desert but no doubt that was her geography again. She wasn't remotely techie enough to find where a message came from and thought for an instant of asking her daughter, Cory, who was good at these things. But of course Cory would tell her to be careful, so that was out.

Ella was due to go and have supper with Claudia and Don and Claudia's mother Olivia a few days later to cheer her up a bit after the funeral but she had a spare couple of hours first so she made herself a large mug of tea and got out her laptop. She had mixed feelings about what she was about to do – genuine affection for Laura and also a sense of guilt from the past, remembering how betrayed Laura had felt by her when she'd blogged about the collapse of Laura's marriage. She hadn't used Laura's name but Laura had instantly recognized the circumstances and been bitterly hurt all the same. She suspected

Laura would feel the same about this. And yet Ella had an uneasy feeling about this mysterious Gavin which she couldn't shake.

She started by googling online romance and of course a hundred dating apps appeared – Match.com, which seemed to be the biggest, the wittily named Plenty of Fish, Elite for professional singles, who all no doubt thought they were worth it, Our Time, aimed at the over-fifties, Tinder of course – she'd encountered young people who'd met on that – Happn, which showed you photographs of people you'd crossed that day in the street who might be interested in meeting and even one called Three-Ender, apparently aimed at setting up threesomes. It was such a different time. No more drinking six ciders and getting off with someone at a disco.

Ella sipped her tea, reeling from the shock of how far this world was from the one she'd grown up in when she'd met her husband Laurence at university and they'd got married five years later. Since Ella was doing well as a lawyer they'd delayed having children until her mid-thirties and had an extremely happy marriage until Laurence had been killed in a train crash on an average Tuesday afternoon five years ago.

She put down her mug and conjured his face, sad that it was becoming more indistinct. Would she have ever thought of putting a toe into this unknown world of online dating? She shuddered, grateful that she had given up all that and come here instead, though she could see Laura's circumstances were very different to hers.

The next thing she moved on to was dating scams. Ella was amazed at just how much there was on this topic. One thing she noticed were the constant references to something called 'catfishing'. Catfishing, it seemed, was deliberately using a fake profile, often using a photograph stolen from someone's Facebook page or other social media, to dupe innocent people, sometimes cheating them of quite large sums of money. There was even a TV show in America where the host confronted one of these catfishers on camera.

Ella felt a horrible cold shadow of apprehension, the kind of feeling she hadn't had since she'd seen a uniformed policeman walk up her front steps in London on the day of Laurence's death, and had known there was something terribly wrong.

One article actually listed the most common things to look for. Usually they had a job which meant they had to travel a lot – pilot, soldier based abroad, engineer. Quite often they said they were in the SAS or the Special Boat Service, adding a dash of James Bond glamour to their profiles. Ella could remember Laura saying Gavin worked abroad, but she couldn't remember his actual job.

They were very eager to get you off the dating websites, which it seemed were monitored for dodgy behaviour, and onto messaging or email. They often employed the technique of 'lovebombing', sending you loving texts many times a day. Very often they became intensely passionate even though you had never met.

And then they asked for money.

There were countless stories of victims, nearly all of them middle-aged women, who had been taken for a ride. 'I am neither stupid nor naive,' asserted one rather attractive woman who had given away thousands of pounds to an unknown scammer. 'I just happened to be very lonely.'

Ella looked at her watch. She would find all this riveting if she wasn't so worried about Laura. But it was time to go.

Ella turned off her laptop reluctantly. Bloody hell, she was getting pulled into this weird and addictive world herself! No wonder Laura, raw and wretched after the end of her marriage, had been easy game.

But was she? Maybe Gavin was a perfectly normal man who happened to be a long way away and was feeling lonely himself. Maybe he was just what Laura needed.

Whatever kind of person he was, they would soon find out. He was due to arrive at Heathrow Terminal 5 in less than a week.

Ella was surprised to find that Mrs Lal had been invited to supper at Olivia's request, and that she and Olivia were behaving almost like old school friends, but they ought to be grateful as it was clearly proving a comfort to Olivia. Just as surprising was that Don had cooked the meal, and it was delicious.

'It's this Men's Shed thing he's joined,' whispered Claudia, looking as stunned as anyone. 'It's amazing. Not only is he now the King of DIY, but he's moved on to cooking!'

'I don't suppose he could be the new chef,' Ella ventured.

Mrs Lal, looking elegant but decidedly overdressed for a kitchen supper in the country, immediately took offence.

'Rose McGill is convinced it was I who caused the cook to go. But all I did was suggest a different way of cooking steak I had enjoyed in a French restaurant. Why would the man object to that? In India it would be a compliment that I was interested.'

Nobody could think of an answer to that, so Claudia swiftly changed the subject. 'This really is delicious, love.' She pointed to the tortellini with homemade ragu, amazed that Don had actually made his own pasta.

'I enjoyed it.' He winked at Mrs Lal. 'But I'd appreciate it if Mrs Lal didn't give me a better recipe for the filling. Hey, we can't go on calling you Mrs Lal. What is your first name?'

How strange we all call her that still, Ella thought.

'Lalita,' announced Mrs Lal as if she were presenting a precious gift.

'That's a pretty name,' Claudia acknowledged.

'Thank you,' conceded Mrs Lal graciously.

'Anyway,' intervened Olivia gleefully, 'you've seen what Mrs Lal has done to the Minsley branch of Good Age? She's utterly transformed it!'

'Yes,' Ella agreed. 'I was stunned when I saw it. But equally amazed they just let you go in and do it.'

'Yes,' Mrs Lal admitted, 'I was rather naughty, but the large sum I have donated will help calm things down, I can assure you. But wait and see what happens next. When I have finished it will be better than Selfridges. Perhaps not Harrods, but it is a mistake to be unrealistic.'

Claudia, who always found Selfridges rather dauntingly full of stylish things she couldn't afford, nodded.

'We're going to win the Best Charity Shop UK,' announced Olivia proudly.

'Starting tomorrow,' endorsed Mrs Lal. And they suddenly embraced each other like Bush and Blair deciding to invade Iraq.

Good Age clearly didn't know what was going to hit it.

Spike, the lone representative of youth (if you didn't count Bella and Noah), smiled to himself that he'd enlisted more people than expected for his oldie exercise class. His friends all laughed at him for living here, but he rather liked it. A city lad by birth and upbringing, the countryside was new and exotic. He got free food and lovely, comfortable lodging and all he was supposed to do was organize a few classes, help Ella with the gardening, and generally inject a sense of youthful liveliness.

Actually, he was a bit stuck here because it wasn't as if the people living here were really old, more his grandparents' age, and thinking about it, he didn't actually talk to *them* much. His gran talked to him, non-stop. But what about? He was suddenly struck by the fact he'd never asked his gran or granddad anything about their lives. She'd spent most of her life cleaning doorsteps or placing endless minimum bets at the bookies.

He walked past an open window where music was blaring at maximum volume, just like one of those cars with their speakers booming out rap music so loudly the whole town can hear it. Faintly, beneath the deafening music, Spike could hear the sound of a Black & Decker drill, and even worse, someone singing along.

'Too loud for you, is it?' asked a voice, straining to make itself heard over the music.

'Don't you have rules about this sort of thing?' marvelled Spike. 'I mean, you're supposed to be some new-age community, all peace and love, not heavy metal at eleven a.m.! Surely it's a nuisance?'

'It's just Don building some shelves in the lounge,' Lou grinned. 'You young people, you should go to more live music. We all grew up standing next to the speakers at Rolling Stones gigs.'

'But Lou,' protested Spike, 'it's Status Quo!'

'Point taken. Why don't you go and ask him to put on someone else?'

Spike wasn't sure if confronting an angry Status Quo fan holding a Black & Decker was really such a good idea.

Sal emerged with a worried expression she was trying to hide behind a smile, and began to belt out 'Whatever You Want'.

Lou turned round, smiling hugely.

'What a voice!' He opened his arms to her. 'You sound like Janis Joplin. Spike here can't take the volume. He wants to know why we don't ban it in our new-age community.'

'Spike, haven't you worked it out yet?' she asked naughtily. 'We're just a bunch of old rockers!'

'What?' Lou instantly batted back. 'Even Mrs Lal?'

'Mrs Lal is a law unto herself. How do you know, in the privacy of her own home, she doesn't do levitation while chanting *Om* to the sound of Iron Maiden?'

'Now, now,' Lou chided, 'don't insult the sacred mantras of Eastern religions.'

'I hope you're not a load of wackos who're going to arrange a mass suicide one of these days,' Spike muttered.

'Actually, that's not a bad idea,' Lou nodded seriously. 'I've always thought we live far too long. What's the point of living till you're a hundred when you've got no fucking idea what day of the week it is? Good thinking, Spike. I'll definitely look into it.'

'Come on, Lou,' Sal said with unusual abruptness, 'that really isn't funny.'

He looked at her, suddenly concerned. 'Hey, are you okay?' He had to shout over the deafening Phil Collins that had followed Status Quo. 'There isn't anything you're not telling me?'

'Come on,' she replied. 'Let's go into the village for a coffee. I want to look at this famous window of Mrs Lal's.'

'Oh,' Spike shouted, suddenly smiling, 'speaking of the devil, I may have found you a chef.'

They exchanged glances. A chef that Spike knew would probably be a just-graduated catering student or someone who'd lost their job from a gastropub.

'Oh, well, if you're not interested,' Spike shrugged. 'He's my uncle as a matter of fact, but he's more your age than mine. He's thinking of retiring and I thought maybe if you offered him a house here he might consider it.'

'Right.' Lou winked at Sal. 'Where's he been working till now?'

Spike repressed a grin and shouted, just as Phil suddenly broke into 'You Can't Hurry Love', 'At the Ritz, as a matter of fact.'

And he walked off, confident that Lou and Sal would be standing stock still watching his departure.

Laura was grateful today was one of her days at LateExpress. Mindlessly stacking shelves was just what she needed. Also, she admitted reluctantly to herself, she could do with the company.

Of course she had Gavin, and the wonderful texts he sent her to read in bed. It was amazing to be welcomed into the day by someone who told her he loved and desired her rather than her surly ex-husband who'd blundered silently out of bed and to the loo without even acknowledging her existence for twenty-five years. Simon had not been a morning person.

Perhaps that had been part of their problem. She liked going to bed early and waking with the light. Simon stayed up half the night on his computer and only stumbled into bed at two or three, wondering why he was bad-tempered in the mornings. Anyway, she thought comfortingly, he wasn't her problem any more.

Another text arrived an hour later.

Are you dressing now? I would love to watch you slipping into your lacy underwear. And even more, watching you take it off. Till Saturday. Gavin

Thank heavens she'd bought some new stuff; her usual was beige M&S. She could have worn a leather thong and tassels on her boobs and Simon wouldn't have noticed.

As she walked to the bus, the feeling of shyness came over her again. What if her body was a disappointment? She knew she'd aged well but that couldn't undo the fact she was over sixty. Sixty might be the new forty with your clothes on, but when you took them off it was a different story. He might make his excuses and get on the first flight back to Beirut. The cruel truth in the dating game was that men could choose women twenty years younger and women her age were lucky to even get answers to their ads.

No, she told herself firmly, she wasn't going to think like that. She and Gavin had so much rapport, had become so intimate so quickly that it was bound to be all right. Wasn't it?

Mr A was his usual cheery self. 'Mrs Minchin,' he greeted her warmly, 'always a pleasure to see you. And how is my mother-in-law getting on in the ashram?'

'It's not really an ashram . . .' Laura began.

'I know, I know, dear lady, only teasing,' he twinkled. 'Has she offended all the other ladies again?'

Laura had to admit that, according to Ella, this was always on the cards. On the other hand, she hadn't had any crisis calls lately asking how she could have foisted such a monster on them, so that had to be good.

'I think they're all getting to know each other slowly but surely.'

Mr A smiled. 'You are a very diplomatic lady. Anyway, thank you from the bottom of our hearts for finding her somewhere congenial. We are now having a normal life again. My wife in charge and me doing what she says. When her mother was here my wife became very docile and even did cooking and washing-up.' He paused to convey the full drama of this revelation. 'Once she even sewed a button on my shirt.'

'I can see that would be a change for you.'

'Now we are okay again,' he concluded merrily. 'Whenever she treats me very badly there is always a reward in the bed-room.'

Laura nodded attentively. It was fascinating to see how other people's marriages worked, though she was pretty sure this wasn't a pattern she wanted to emulate. 'I'll go into the stockroom, shall I, and unpack today's deliveries?'

'That would be most kind. So you mustn't worry when Mrs A is exceptionally rude to me, you see.'

'Absolutely,' Laura agreed and disappeared through the plasterboard door behind the cigarette and lottery ticket sales area. That was as much revelation as she could deal with today.

Her phone vibrated in her pocket. She carried it round with her at all the time since Gavin had appeared in her life. Even into the bath and loo.

Only a few days now. Maybe she should make a calendar like she had at school and tick off the days till he arrived.

She looked at the message that had just appeared.

Darling Laura, it read, I have a big problem. I have lost my job. You are not allowed to use your phone for private calls in my company and this arsehole made records of how many times I messaged you. So now I am fired. I have no money in the bank so I'm afraid unless I can get hold of 5,000 US dollars, I will not be able to come. Gavin

The double shock felt to Laura almost as though she had been kicked. The fear he would not come, followed quickly by a streak of anger that he was asking her for money, and then the comforting if contradictory realization that she still had most of the money from her house sale so she could help him out of this hole.

This was Gavin, she told herself, and he had lost his job, partly because of her. Five thousand US dollars was a large sum, but if it meant she would still meet him after all this time, surely she had no choice but to give it to him? And, after all, if he'd lost his job maybe he would think about making a new life here.

Twenty-Two

'Mrs Lal ... Lalita ... why don't you give us a proper tour of the charity shop? We only had a moment before and I'd really like to see it again,' Claudia suggested, partly as a distraction for her mother who had been sitting staring into space lately, and only the plans for Good Age seemed capable of cheering her up. To be truthful, Claudia knew how she felt. She was missing her dad dreadfully too. How much worse it would have been for Olivia if she'd been on her own in an empty house after sixty years of marriage instead of having people all around her. Their mad commune had unexpected benefits.

They both graciously agreed and they all trouped down to Little Minsley together.

The village was much fuller than usual. Claudia noted not one but two grey-haired couples holding hands. Good God, it seemed to be catching! One couple particularly caught her eye: an elegant pair, probably nearer seventy than sixty, she with sleek silver hair, wearing black trousers and a beige jacket, he, patrician and slightly stooping, in beige trousers and a black jacket. They looked like a chess board designed by Calvin Klein. And to top it all there they were, bloody holding hands! The next were a much sloppier pair, smaller, squatter, cheerier, and they were at it too. Claudia shook her head in disbelief.

After a while they noticed the small crowd that seemed to have gathered outside Good Age. There seemed to be some kind of scene going on inside which was clearly entertaining enough to stop and watch.

Inside the manageress was shouting at her two cowering assistants.

'What I can't understand is how you let this happen!' she screeched at Flo, who had her hands deeper in her cardigan at every accusation. 'I mean, you let some complete stranger come in here, take the place over, actually daring to throw away some perfectly usable clothes donated – donated, mind, by people who are trying to help the cause of the elderly in this country – and you let this woman chuck them out.'

'She was with Mrs Warren,' Flo defended herself. 'And we know her, don't we, Min?' Flo was finding it hard to account for how the tsunami that was Mrs Lal had swept into the shop.

Minnie was getting a bit of her nerve back. She'd never liked Vera anyway. A little Hitler in a flowery dress, who didn't think twice about creaming off the best stock for herself. Probably even that dress she was wearing now. She was no better than they were. 'As a matter of fact,' Minnie said, stopping slouching and drawing herself up to her full five foot three. 'We think she's got a gift for it, don't we, Flo?'

'What has she got a gift for?' The manageress screeched. 'What are you going on about?'

'Style, that's what she's got! You'd never even know this

place since she put her stamp on it! All the customers have said so, and we've had double the numbers popping in.'

'Thank you, dear lady.' Mrs Lal imposed herself on the scene with all the authority of Catherine the Great. 'I greatly appreciate your kind words. And what exactly is the problem?'

'You!' responded an incandescent Vera, her voice rising several octaves. 'You aren't even connected to the organization and you sweep in here . . .'

'Ah, but as a matter of fact, I am,' Mrs Lal replied patiently as if addressing a particularly thick teenager. 'I have actually become a Good Age gold-star donor, so I think I have a perfect right to lend you any practical improvement I can.'

Vera was temporarily silenced. A gold-star donor was someone who had given the organization a very large sum of money.

'In that case, I resign! Perhaps you might like to take over managing the place yourself since you seem suddenly to be so devoted to our cause!'

Mrs Lal rose to the occasion. 'If I might count on your good offices, Olivia, to help me out with your advice and wisdom.'

'And experience of being old,' added Olivia, smiling.

'And the assistance of these two good ladies,' she gestured to Minnie and Flo rather like the Duke of Wellington reviewing his troops before the Battle of Waterloo. 'I think we might make something of this shop.' She delved in her voluminous bag and pulled out two pieces of paper. 'And even win Charity Shop of the Year! It was not too late to enter so I have done so.'

'What Head Office is going to make of this . . .' Vera spluttered.

'I talked to them yesterday,' Mrs Lal replied sweetly. 'I am surprised they haven't been in touch. I suppose they must have had more important things to do.'

At the suggestion she wasn't important enough to bother with, Vera picked up her handbag and made for the door.

Flo, emboldened by Minnie's defiant stance, put her oar in too. 'Goodbye, Vera. Sorry you won't get the chance to buy your wardrobe here on the cheap.'

'Did you really talk to Head Office yesterday?' Olivia asked Mrs Lal in a low voice.

'Of course not,' Lalita smiled mischievously; even Claudia had to admit this new Mrs Lal was delightfully disarming. 'Silly woman. Yesterday was Sunday anyway. Of course I will do in due course. I will explain that I was carried away by the shop's possibilities. They will smooth things down, explain I am a very rich and eccentric donor who doesn't understand how things are done here, find her another shop. Do you know, ladies' – she turned to include all of them – 'I think we're going to have a whole lot of fun!'

That night in bed, Claudia put out a hand and stroked her husband's back. He looked at her in surprise.

'Thank you for the lovely lasagne.'

'Tortellini,' he corrected. 'But thanks accepted.'

'What are you making this week at the shed?'

'Ah, you've decided to take an interest, have you?' Don commented wryly. 'Bread and butter pudding using Panettone instead of bread.'

'Mmm. Count me in. And thanks for all you're doing round the manor. You're becoming rather indispensable.'

He turned back to her and took off his pyjama top. 'That's a relief,' he replied with a smile that made him look engagingly boyish. 'I suspect you've been wondering what I'm for.'

She returned his smile and lay back invitingly on the pillows. 'I haven't quite forgotten as a matter of fact.'

As he leaned towards her, Claudia thought how much better life had become since they'd moved to the manor and how – thanks to her mother's ingenuity – Mrs Lal had stopped being a nuisance and was becoming really rather fun. Even Don was surprisingly happy now that he'd found a role as the man to call in a crisis. Maybe – and she hardly dared think it – she'd done something rather clever in getting them all to come and live here.

Sal stood in front of the bathroom mirror trying not to break down. Despite the check-up a few months ago, there was a distinct area of redness on her remaining breast and the nipple was inverted. She wondered whether to call Lara, the natural daughter she'd given away as a baby and only been reunited with for such a short time. Lara had been so brilliant when Sal had had cancer before and hidden it from everyone, even her best friends. How angry they'd been with her, especially Ella, for not sharing her worries with them. But Lara was in Norway with her husband and three children. Sal didn't want to worry her for what might prove to be nothing. But Lou was a different matter. He already suspected something was up. She could feel him hovering about her like an anxious budgie, which was very different to his usual style. She knew she had to tell him, but it was so much the news she'd been dreading that she was putting it off. If she didn't admit it, it wasn't real. Stupid when that was at best perverse and at worst dangerous.

She must go and see the specialist who treated her last time. And she must let Lou go with her. After all, sharing was the American way. All your dramas became Oprah-ified in the US. And Lou was also capable of being a huge comfort.

She was furious and terrified at the same time. Things had been going so well for her. For the first time in her life she felt loved, happy and secure. And now this.

You'd almost feel the Almighty had it in for her. Maybe for being a rank unbeliever. And yet if she was such an unbeliever, how come she thought things like that in the first place?

She pulled up the bra she'd had since her mastectomy. It covered the scar across the left side of her chest, which had faded from livid red to faded raspberry. She had decided not to have a breast replacement and yet still – miraculously – Lou had fancied her and called her his Amazon.

What if she had to lose her other breast as well? How would he feel about making love to a woman with no breasts at all?

Ella was almost as keenly aware as Laura of the mysterious Gavin's imminent arrival. She bumped into Bella, pushing Noah round the grounds in his buggy, and decided to broach the subject discreetly with her.

'Hello, Bella, what a lovely morning!'

The air had a clarity you could almost taste and the sky was a bright happiness-inducing blue.

'I know, it's on days like this I'm so glad we left London!'

'Speaking of which, how's your mum?'

Bella's pretty face clouded a little. 'I don't know. I do worry about her there without all of you lot. She's gone rather quiet lately. Maybe I'd better give her a ring. She certainly jumps on her phone and answers at once these days, almost as if she's waiting for your call.'

Ella suspected it wasn't her daughter's call Laura was waiting for so eagerly. Should she mention Gavin?

'How's her love life? Any handsome swains on the horizon? Or even bald and paunchy ones?'

Bella laughed. 'She wouldn't tell me if there were! Daughterly disapproval is one thing she can do without.'

'Would you disapprove?'

'Depends on the man. Last time I talked to her she seemed a bit obsessed with internet apps. Funny it should be her rather than me, when I'm part of the digital generation. Yet since I moved here I hardly ever even go online.'

'And has she met anyone?' Ella asked tentatively.

'Not that she's told me about.' Noah intervened lustily, clearly deciding there had been enough chit-chat between the grown-ups.

'Better get him his breakfast. See you, Ella.'

So Bella didn't know any more than she did; less actually. Ella sighed, not wanting another rift to open up between her and Laura. Maybe she'd just give her a ring later.

She walked on into the village, past Mrs Lal's amazing shop window, to the bakery and cafe. She quite often went there for breakfast. With its vintage furniture and French signs it had the air of a cafe in the south of France in the fifties. Extravagantly she ordered a hot chocolate with a croissant to dunk in it.

She had only been sitting down a minute, staring absently into space, dipping the flaky pastry into the steaming chocolate, when a voice interrupted her reverie.

'Very French. I've only ever seen chic Parisians dunking with quite such confidence and flair.'

Naturally it was Daniel Forrest.

'You get around. The Laden Ox and now here.'

'I'm not much of a homebody. Self-catering isn't exactly my thing.' Again the charming, slightly untrustworthy smile.

Out of the blue she suddenly asked, 'Have you ever tried online dating, Daniel?'

'Never needed to, darling,' was his instant reply. 'Actually, that's not quite true. I had a rather disastrous encounter with a beautiful young Russian. I thought she was after my body but it turned out it was my bank account. When she discovered how empty that was, she dumped me.' Underneath his usual debonair smile there was, a touch of unexpected vulnerability. It made him seem much nicer.

'How did you find out?'

'A friend of mine checked her out on social media. Apparently my sweet Maria had quite a lot of names. Svetlana. Ekaterina. Katya. I never found out which was real. After that I avoided the temptations of click bait.'

'And stuck to the ladies in your choir.' The words had slipped out before she thought about them.

'Indeed,' replied Daniel crisply, before picking up his paper and walking out.

Ella hadn't really meant to offend him, but maybe it was for the best.

All the same he'd given her an idea. But first she'd just ring Laura and see how she was. If she'd got it right, Gavin was due in tomorrow.

'You're never going to believe it!' Bella could hardly contain her amazement as she broke the news to Claudia and Don. 'But Spike was telling the truth. His uncle *is* a chef at the Ritz. He's quite a charmer actually, considering what despots chefs are supposed to be, and he's prepared to come and see the manor and talk to us about what the job would actually involve.'

'So you won't be needing my newly acquired culinary skills after all?' Don made a clown face of mock disappointment.

'You can save them for me.' Bella noticed Claudia's smile and thought *Hmmm . . . things are going better at the coach house.*

'So when can he come?'

'Next Monday so we'd better start thinking what we could offer him. Get Rose involved, she's the foodie queen.'

'Good idea. She'll be thrilled. All that pâté de foie gras.'

'Not on our budget,' Bella grinned. 'It's generous but not that generous.'

Rose was indeed thrilled. The possibility that they might have a chef who made life delicious almost got her over her irritation at the sudden rise of her rival, Mrs Lal, as heroine of the hour.

'Have you heard?' Rose asked Ella when she bumped into her on her way from the bakery. 'We might be getting the chef from the Ritz. He wants to semi-retire and a free cottage plus cooking for a bunch of oldies who go to bed early might just appeal.'

'Speak for yourself,' Ella replied. 'I stay up till at least ten o'clock.'

Back in her cottage Ella saw the red message alert blinking on her phone. It was a message from Laura asking her to call.

Laura had been wrestling sleeplessly with what to do since early morning and ringing practical, calm, down-to-earth Ella had seemed like a good idea. That was when she left the message. Then she remembered the blog Ella had written using the details of her marriage breakdown and she felt angry and betrayed all over again. True, Ella had been abjectly apologetic, but deep down it still rankled.

She decided to make up some story when Ella rang back and make her decision alone.

Should she lend the money to Gavin or was she being completely naive and stupid to trust a man she hadn't even met, but only messaged? It struck her again that it had been odd that they hadn't even talked on the phone. Certainly they hadn't known each other long and Gavin had always had a valid excuse for not being able to call. But still.

And then another text came through.

> My darling, I can't believe fate could be so cruel to stop me holding you in my arms at last. And I will have to pay for the British Airways fare anyway as it is too late to cancel. Your Gavin

Housewifely Laura suddenly couldn't bear the idea of a wasted fare. She came to a decision before the smile had even left her face and rang her bank on the spot.

There, it was done. She messaged him back the details and ran a bath, dreaming of the new underwear she would put on, and the look on his face when they finally ran into each other's arms.

Ella took a deep breath and dialled Laura's mobile. When her friend answered there was an odd, dreamy note to her voice.

'You're not taking Valium or anything, are you?' Ella asked, only half joking.

'Oh, Ella, of course I'm not. Actually, I'm incredibly happy.'

'So, tomorrow's the big day.'

'Yes, yes it is.' Was that a note of anxiety creeping into Laura's voice?

'Well, good luck with it all. Let me know how it goes.'

'Ella . . .' Laura began. Should she confide her worries in Ella after all?

'Yes?'

'Nothing.' No, she wouldn't. She knew Ella would advise caution, and really it was too late for that. 'Bye. Love you.'

'Love you too. Bye.'

Ella put the phone down. Somehow she wasn't reassured at all.

Ella had always been someone who felt better when she took action. In one of the articles she'd read about internet scams a simple solution was suggested. It might not work, but it could provide the answer as to whether this Gavin was genuine.

The only thing was, she needed a photo of him and the only way she could think of was to grab that screenshot Laura had on her phone. But how?

There was only one thing for it: she'd have to go to London and see her. And if Laura worked out what she was doing, it might well cost Ella their friendship forever.

'Hello, nice to meet you.' Claudia held out a hand to Spike's Uncle Bill and welcomed him into the lounge where Olivia, Bella and Rose were already sitting. Fortunately for all concerned, Mrs Lal was taking her new duties very seriously and was at the shop full-time.

'Call me Billy, everyone does.' Billy turned out to be a grey and grizzled version of Spike, fortunately without the Mohican, and even shared his nephew's barrow-boy charm, though in Spike's case it was tempered by a college education. 'I expect you'd like to see my CV.' He handed them over a single sheet of paper. 'I don't believe in embroidering.'

Rose had to admit his disarming grin was very taking, but

she was far too old for such things to be of interest. What she really cared about was the food.

'Fine. Well, just tell us briefly about yourself,' she suggested.

'I was crap at school, failed at everything. The only thing that interested me was cooking. That was considered about as normal as being a ballerina. This was before all these TV chefs, Gordon Ramsay effing and blinding all over the shop. My dad thought I'd gone off my head. But I got an apprenticeship at fifteen in a big London hotel.' He laughed hollowly. 'That was tougher than the army, I can tell you. Survival of the fittest. But I watched and learned and I felt part of something at last, with people who got me.'

'And what did you do after that?' prompted Claudia.

'Moved to another big hotel. Assistant pastry chef.'

Rose perked up. She loved a pudding.

'The kitchen was hot as hell. We had to change our jackets three times a night and most of us got chef's arse.'

'What on earth is that?' demanded Rose, unshocked as usual, as Bella struggled to repress a giggle.

'It's the perspiration. Makes your skin raw, a handful of cornflour down your trousers helps.'

'I'll bear it in mind,' replied Rose, somehow staying deadpan.

'After that I worked my way up to the dizzy heights you ladies see me at today.'

'And now, Spike says you might be ready for a quieter life?'

'Too bloody right. My back's giving in. The body can't take it. Spike mentioned your chef here had thrown in his cards and that I might like the set-up. I'm not a hippie,' he added defensively. 'Always thought they were a bunch of middle-class wankers. All that peace and love on Mummy and Daddy's handouts. More of a Metallica man myself.'

'I might have guessed you would be,' Rose nodded.

'So what's the deal here?'

Bella outlined the offer they had discussed between them.

Billy nodded. 'Okay. Could I see the accommodation now? And do you have any rivers nearby? I'm a bit of a carp fisherman in my spare time.'

'I'm surprised you have any,' Bella smiled as she got up to show him.

'Oh, er, Billy . . .' Rose began. 'Do you have a wife – sorry, partner – or any children who might live with you?'

'Two exes. Cheffing and marriage don't go, to tell you the truth. And a terrific son. But he's all grown-up now and he didn't make the mistake of following in my footsteps.'

While Bella showed him round the cottages that were still available, the others discussed him.

'What do you think?' Claudia asked.

'I liked him,' Rose answered at once. 'Quite a colourful character, but honest. Of course we'd have to try his food.'

'You don't think we've got enough colourful characters?' Claudia asked.

'You mean Mrs Lal?' jumped in Olivia. 'She'll be all right. She just needs occupying. And anyway, you can't have too many colourful characters. Take it from me, the enemy of old age is boredom. Well-meaning bloody carers asking if you're all right, dearie, and how are your bowels today? Give me rough and ready Billy any day.'

'Well, that looks like the answer then,' Claudia nodded. 'We'll ask Bella what she thought too and see what the man himself has decided. I just hope our rivers are bursting with carp.'

They all left the lounge at the same time, just as Bella and Billy were returning and Murdo Binns had appeared from nowhere.

'Murdo,' Rose twinkled mischievously, 'meet Mr Williams. Mr Williams this is Lord Binns.'

'Not another bleedin' aristo,' Billy commented cheerfully. 'Thought I'd be getting away from your sort.'

'Right,' replied Murdo, looking mystified.

'Mr Williams, Billy, we'll email you over something this afternoon,' Rose said. 'What sort of notice period do you have to give?'

'I handed my notice months ago. Spikey said I'd end up with a heart attack at my age if I didn't leave soon.'

'Absolutely,' Rose agreed. 'And don't forget the other condition.'

Billy looked at a loss.

'When you have to put cornflour down your trousers.'

This sent him off into guffaws as Bella showed him the way out.

'Curious chap,' Murdo opined. 'Bit of a rough diamond. Who on earth is he?'

'We're rather hoping he's going to be our new chef.'

'Ah. Where is he based now? Army camp? Open prison.'

'Actually,' Rose replied, enjoying herself hugely, 'he's coming to us from the Ritz.'

She would treasure Murdo's look of astonishment for quite some time.

As it was such a sunny day, Olivia decided to go and visit her husband's grave and make a final decision about the headstone. Len had only wanted his name and dates, but somehow that didn't seem to do justice to a man who had so enjoyed life

'I miss you, you know,' she found herself saying out loud. 'I bet you'd be surprised how much.' She was about to turn away, taken aback at what, from anyone else, she would have described as sentimentalism, when she caught the sun gleaming off a three-foot-tall metal manikin.

'Hiro! What are you doing here?'

Olivia reminded herself for the hundredth time that Hiro wasn't a person but a machine.

'Lou lets me come. I don't think he's sure what to do with me.'

'Are you missing Leonard too?'

The large artificially blue eyes looked at her. 'More than I could have imagined. Except that robots don't really have an imagination, so maybe it's just habit.'

Despite herself, Olivia felt touched. Hiro was like an electronic Greyfriars Bobby, the Skye terrier who spent fourteen years guarding his dead master's grave until he died there himself.

'Me too.' A beat of silence passed when they both looked down at the recently turned turf.

A thought occurred to her, but maybe it was too ridiculous. She would talk to Lou Maynard and see what he thought.

'I'm trying to think what to put on the stone.'

Hiro raised a metal arm in salute. 'How about "Bowled out at 92" or just "A good innings"? He loved cricket so much.'

Olivia smiled. 'Thanks, Hiro. You could be on to something there.'

Ella rang the bell of Laura's flat, her arms full of flowers and holding a bottle of champagne. She'd been feeling terrible for the entire train journey and had almost turned back but loyalty to Laura – even if Laura didn't see it that way – made her feel it was her duty to try and protect her friend, especially as she was so vulnerable after her divorce.

She'd emailed ahead and Laura was expecting her, though not the presents. 'What's all this?' Laura asked as Ella pressed them into her hand.

'To wish you luck for tomorrow.'

'Yes. He arrives at midday.' Was that the tiniest quaver of uncertainty in her voice?

'I thought these would make you feel festive.'

Laura laughed, looking ridiculously young and happy. 'I don't think we should waste champagne on men. They usually prefer beer. Let's you and I have it.'

She went off to the kitchen to get glasses.

Her iPhone lay between them with the photograph of Gavin as a screensaver. Ella quickly grabbed it and photographed it, then just as quickly put it back, feeling like Judas with the fateful kiss.

Laura poured the fizz into two flutes and held up her glass. 'To friendship. As we've often said, "husbands come and go, but friendship lasts forever!"'

Sal sat down in the reception area of the Princess Mary Hospital's imaging department, just as she had when she'd first been diagnosed. She knew the ropes very well. She would be asked to go into a cubbyhole, lock the door, remove her top and put on a hospital robe. Her remaining breast would then be placed on the good old salami slicer, aka the mammogram machine. Very likely she would have to go and have a core biopsy when a needle would be inserted to remove cells to examine under the microscope. Then she might have to wait a week – *a week!* – before she got the results.

An hour later, she came out of the hospital just as lonely and desperate as she had been last time. Why the hell hadn't she told Lou after all?

'I thought this is where I'd find you,' said a voice behind her. 'I was so worried I called Ella and she guessed you might be here when I explained why I was so concerned about you.' She whipped round to find Lou leaning on the door of a waiting taxi. He opened his arms and she ran into them. He held her very tight as she began to cry helplessly.

'Sally Grainger, my beloved girl, you're not a very good actress, you know. I don't suppose you're aware you glance downwards continually and feel your breast when you think no one's looking. You've been looking like Marley's ghost for at least a week now. It was just a matter of when you deigned to share your misery with me.'

'Oh, Lou, it's just so bloody unfair when finally I'm happy! I'm so sorry I didn't tell you.'

'Love is never having to say you're sorry.' Lou quoted the famous line from *Love Story*. 'What bollocks!' he added. 'That's one British word I do love. Love is continually having to say you're sorry and hoping the other person is big-hearted enough to forgive you. Fortunately I'm famously big-hearted and I do forgive you.'

Sal sniffed. 'Thank God for you, Lou Maynard!'

'And for you, Sally Grainger. Come on, we can get through this together. And don't forget, I'm an American and an optimist.'

Finally she grinned. 'And for once I'm really glad you are!'

'Well, there you go. Now how much longer are we going to keep this taxi waiting?'

Sal climbed into the back and put her head on Lou's shoulder as they drove back to the manor. Sal tried not to think of the extravagance, still amazed she was with someone who could afford a taxi all the way to Surrey and who had loved her enough to come and find her.

Life wasn't so terrible after all.

Twenty-Three

Laura arrived at Heathrow two hours before the flight, but then she loved the drama of airports, the reunions and the farewells, the tiny children rushing to meet Dad back from some trip abroad. It made her feel quite Richard Curtis – soppily sentimental and inclined to read happy endings into the most unpromising of circumstances, quite possibly including her own.

She had dressed carefully without overdoing it in a pretty blouse and soft fluffy cardigan, wrap skirt and her knee-length, high-heeled, confidence-inducing suede boots.

She sat in Costa coffee just near Arrivals trying to guess from people's clothing where their flights had come from. This was easy with the Aussie ones where tired but happy holiday-makers wore their shorts and T-shirts, even though it was winter at home, to try and prolong that holiday feeling just a little longer. The New York flights were a mix of smart business types and baggily dressed ordinary Americans. The Indian flights were her favourite: with their apprehensive grannies in crumpled saris terrified of having come to the wrong destination, love and relief lighting up their faces at the sight of tiny grandchildren racing towards them with bunches of wilting daisies.

She looked at her watch for the tenth time. Not long now. The BA flight from Beirut was bang on time. She was conscious of feeling almost sick with excitement mixed with apprehension. Was she completely barking mad to be falling in love with a complete stranger at her age? She determinedly pushed the five thousand dollars to the back of her mind. She was sure he'd give it back to her sometime. Besides, it was only money. Even if she couldn't really afford it.

At last a stream of passengers who looked as if they were from Lebanon started to emerge and make their way through the gate, anxiously watching out for family, friends, colleagues or taxis that had arrived to meet them.

Several hundred passengers passed by until finally the stream began to thin out. There was still no sign of Gavin. She decided to message him, but for once got no reply. How odd. Maybe his phone was switched off from the flight.

There was still no word from him when the passengers from the next flight began to arrive. Had he missed his flight? But if so, surely he would have got in touch with her?

Squashing down her rising panic, she decided to go and ask the BA information desk, feeling obscurely comforted that the flight was with a British airline.

The girl on duty was charming and eager to help. 'Right. Your friend's Christian name is Gavin. What's his surname?'

Laura drew a complete blank. Ridiculous, as his name must have been on his original profile with Out There, but that seemed such a long time ago.

'Foster!' she suddenly remembered.

'Fine,' the girl said, smiling reassuringly. 'I'll just put Gavin Foster into my system.'

She deftly typed away on her keyboard. There was a pause that seemed to go on forever. 'That's strange,' she commented as Laura's stomach began to turn to liquid, 'I don't seem to have a Gavin Foster. Are you sure that's the right name?'

Laura shook her head, all the fears she'd repressed beginning to surge back and engulf her in a tidal wave of horror. There was something very wrong here.

Slowly she turned away and walked without glancing behind her towards the tube station.

Mrs Lal looked round at the revamped shop and felt deeply gratified, like God when he had created the world in seven days and saw that it was good. The truth was, she had been feeling at a loss since she'd arrived in England. Her daughter clearly found her presence overpowering, she was frankly fed up with matchmaking and the fortune telling was one step up from a parlour game. But this! Here she could use her talents and make some money for the charity at the same time. Helping other people was a new sensation and one that could grow on her, she felt. Of course she'd quite like to win the award at the same time.

She had a good business brain, as well as a well-developed fashion sense, and she didn't see why she couldn't bring them together here.

'What is the weekly turnover in the shop?' she asked Minnie.

Minnie jumped. 'Vera never mentioned. We just stick labels on things. Vera did the cashing up.'

'But you must have an account book? Some kind of record?'

'I suppose it would be by the till.'

Eventually they found a letter to Head Office mentioning £950.

'Good God! That's peanuts. Let's try and double it this week. If not treble it?'

Flo and Minnie exchanged looks that conveyed something between 'Is she barking mad?' and 'She'll be bloody lucky!'

'I don't see why everything should be second-hand,' Mrs Lal persisted. 'The big brands must have lots of stock they can't sell. I will approach them and offer to relieve them of it.' She made this sound like a fantastic act of generosity. 'For now we need an immediate injection of class and style. I will be straight back.'

They watched her retreating back, enthralled. 'Well, I must say,' confided Flo. 'She's a breath of fresh air after Vera.'

An hour later a taxi stopped outside and Mrs Lal emerged, assisted by a young man who appeared to be wearing gym clothes. 'This is Spike. He has very generously helped me out. Now' – she clapped her hands imperiously – 'can you both go and find me some hangers. Nice wooden ones, not those bent dry-cleaner efforts.'

An hour later the window was filled with a selection of Mrs Lal's own Catherine Walker collection, together with a large photograph of Princess Diana wearing her own Catherine Walker outfit. 'That should bring them in. Nothing wrong with exploiting a little shallow sentimentalism in the name of a good cause.'

Minnie and Flo shook their heads in blank incomprehension. The frocks were nice, though, and they both loved Princess Di.

Mrs Lal stepped back, glowing with her newly discovered altruism. *Move over, Mother Teresa, you wrinkly old prune, there's room for more than one modern saint, and let's face it, you weren't even really Indian.*

*

Feeling like a wife checking on her husband's affair, Ella sat down at her laptop and switched it on. She searched through everything she could find about spotting catfishers and scammers, suddenly struck by one piece of advice from the experts: 'Be extra wary if you are recently divorced or bereaved. Scammers are quick to pick up the signals from anything you tell them.' The next note of caution was about strangely stilted grammar being used or inappropriately sexual messaging. These messages were often not written by one individual, but by teams of catfishers working round the clock from Albania to Accra.

The scale of the industry, totally unknown to most normal people, and the speed with which it had sprung up, took Ella's breath away.

And then the final piece of the jigsaw fell into place. 'If you wish to check that the photograph you have been given is genuine, this can usually be done by Reverse Image Search.'

Not only was there a whole industry in fleecing people online, there was also a parallel industry in catching them. Her breath almost stilled. Ella transferred the photograph of Gavin she had stolen from Laura onto her laptop and selected Reverse Images from her browser. The identification was almost instantaneous.

The brown eyes, warm smile and wavy hair that Laura had found so alluring belonged not to an engineer called Gavin currently working in Beirut but to a male model called Patrick Johnson who lived in Huddersfield.

Claudia was on her way to meet Bella and find out if they'd heard back from Billy, the potential new chef, when Spike stopped her.

'You look knackered,' she commented, noting his red sweaty face.

'It's Rose McGill. She may not be young but that woman is lethal! And she looks like such a harmless little lady. When she joined our class I thought, *Oh good, another old fart for the group*, but she's got more energy than I have! Forget Miss Marple, she's Jane Fonda on speed.'

Claudia tried to picture Rose in leggings and Lycra and grinned. She hoped it wasn't going to be bad for her heart.

'By the way,' Spike added. 'A message from my Uncle Billy. He thinks you ought to sample his wares before you finally commit yourselves.'

'Do you think he's really interested then?' Claudia asked, delighted.

'Yeah, I think he really is. Did you know you've got the best carp lake in the south of England right on your doorstep?'

'As a matter of fact, it had passed me by,' Claudia acknowledged. 'Fishing actually makes cricket look like a fast and exciting sport to me.'

'Tsk tsk. Fishing is the sport of philosophers. Haven't you heard of Izaak Walton?'

'I'll take your word for it. So when would he like to provide his mouth-watering temptations?'

'The day after tomorrow if that's all right with you. Then he's going to head off with his rod afterwards.'

'I'll tell the others. We must turn this into a grand occasion. Candles and white linen at the very least! Ask him to talk to the wonderful Bella. She'll sort it out.'

'She is rather wonderful, isn't she?' Spike echoed dreamily. 'She does so many different things and all of them brilliantly.'

Claudia watched him head back to his old farts. Hilarious that he couldn't keep up with Rose. And was that a little *tendresse* he was developing for Bella? Nigel had better watch out. She wondered whether to mention it to Laura. Such a pity Laura hadn't wanted to join them all here. Still, she was probably having a terrific time in London. She certainly deserved to. They must invite Gaby and Douglas too. Douglas had put in so much hard work beyond the call of what he was being paid for. She so hoped they would get their planning permission. How wonderful if it went ahead and Gaby had a baby! Claudia stopped herself. Too many people she knew had a bad case of Gagging to be Granny and she knew it wasn't fair.

Sal was having a lie-in and being brought tea in bed by Lou who had finally mastered the art of making a British cuppa. 'It's only taken me fifty years,' he conceded. 'With coffee you want the water off the boil, with tea it needs to be still bubbling.'

'I knew you weren't really an American,' Sal teased. 'Even though you can't stop getting married.'

'It's probably my British accent that fools you.'

Sal spluttered into her tea. Lou's accent was broad Brooklyn with a dash of uptown Manhattan when he wanted a smart restaurant booking.

They were both surprised when Olivia knocked on the door.

'Having a lazy morning?' she asked Sal. 'Ooh, and tea in bed, how nice.'

'Just feeling a bit queasy.' They hadn't decided yet when to tell the others.

'Not morning sickness, I hope?' Olivia joked heavily.

'So,' Lou intervened. 'What can we do for you?'

'It's about Hiro.'

This surprised Lou since Olivia never used his name, only called him 'that damn robot'.

'Yes. I ought to come and get him. When would suit you?'

'Well, that's the thing. I wondered if I could borrow him for a while.'

'To do what?'

'Talk about Leonard. I miss him more than I can possibly say.'

'I thought you loathed Hiro,' Sal pointed out.

'Even I can be wrong,' Olivia stated with something which for her almost sounded like humility. 'I've come to realize he's a nice little chap. Besides,' her voice took on the ragged tone of genuine emotion, 'I know I bluster a lot but I'm actually quite lonely.'

'By all means keep him then,' Lou agreed.

'Thank you. I promise I'll be nice to him.'

When she'd left Lou turned to Sal. 'I think we've just witnessed the awesome power of artificial intelligence. Even Olivia is starting to think of Hiro less as a machine than a companion in her loneliness.'

'You bet. She'll have him judging flower shows next, mark my words.'

Rose showered and changed into her more usual outfit of neat beige blouse and well-cut slacks. She had greatly enjoyed astonishing that nice young man with her unexpected energy despite her operation. It was in the genes. All her family had been hill-walkers and could keep it up mile after mile.

She was just looking out of the window to see if the postman was coming when she caught sight of Murdo Binns ringing the bell to Mrs Lal's part of the house. He was holding a red rose which was so out of character in Murdo that Rose was suddenly struck by the conviction that he had come to ask Mrs Lal to marry him.

And of course she'd obviously accept. Being transformed

into an actual British lady would do wonders for her matchmaking business, and how could she resist becoming chatelaine of the multi-turreted, if ramshackle, Binns Hall?

Perhaps she'd been a bit withering to Murdo, but that was because he was being so stupid. Give an old man a bit of flattery and look what happened. No wonder she'd never married. Look at that blonde floozy Anna Nicole Smith who married the oil man of eighty-nine in America. And he thought she was in love with him. Honestly!

Disappointingly for Murdo, there was no reply. Rose took a wicked delight in shouting across to him that if he was looking for Lalita Lal, she was down at the charity shop in the village.

Murdo looked temporarily dumbfounded, then, with characteristic British resolve, clearly made up his mind to go and look for her.

Rose decided this was too good a spectacle to miss.

She slipped her trainers back on and strode off discreetly in his wake.

It was quite hard to keep up. Murdo might be old but he had a long lolloping stride which reminded Rose of the giant from her favourite children's book.

She got there just in time to see him approach Mrs Lal with a determined look in his eye.

Rose hid behind a clothes rail of winter outfits just as he dropped down on one knee and held the rose out towards Lalita.

'Dearest lady . . .' he began.

Rose couldn't help feeling this was a little over-formal. Surely 'Darling Lalita' might have better encompassed his unquenchable passion?

'I offer you my hand and my heart. Would you do me the honour of agreeing to become the next Lady Binns?'

A muffled giggle escape from Flo or Minnie, it was hard to tell which.

Mrs Lal turned to gaze at him as if he was a slightly irritating distraction. 'My dear Murdo,' she replied. 'I am deeply honoured but I'm afraid I have at last found my calling. I am going to be the Mary Portas of charity shops!'

'But I thought Mary Portas occupied that role herself,' he replied, confused and visibly disappointed.

'It is time she shared her role,' Mrs Lal announced with spirit. 'Just like Mother Teresa. The Empress must make room for a Queen!'

'I'm afraid I don't follow you,' Murdo replied, understandably thrown by Mrs Lal's logic. 'What on earth has Mary Portas got to do with Mother Teresa?'

'They are both selfish in their unselfishness. I see more shops, Murdo, all making double or treble the money for Good Age.'

'And you don't think a title would help you in your fight for charity world domination?' he suggested rather pathetically.

'I'm afraid it would only be a distraction!' Lalita announced with truly Shakespearean grandeur. 'I have found my true role at last!'

'In that case I bid you good day.' He summoned every ounce of dignity he could as he strode from the shop, refusing to acknowledge the delighted whispering from behind the till.

Everyone loved the idea of a full-blown feast with Billy's generous donation. Bella went to hunt in the wine cellar since a few bottles, some rather old, still survived from the manor's days as a country house hotel.

Rose produced some gorgeous gold-edged china and Olivia added the silverware and glasses. Claudia had the brainwave of using white hotel sheets on the huge dining table as no sign of a damask tablecloth could be found. Mrs Lal completed the final touch with candles from the shop which she made a grand show of paying full-price for to assert her superiority over the recently departed Vera.

Ella was just changing into an evening frock in honour of the occasion when her front door was flung open and a tear-stained Laura tumbled straight into her living room.

'Laura! What on earth's the matter?' Ella asked, although she had a pretty strong suspicion.

'Oh God, Ella!' Laura threw herself into Ella's outstretched arms. She looked pale, exhausted and her eyes were glittering with unshed tears. 'I turned up at Heathrow and there was absolutely no sign of Gavin! What the hell do you think can have gone wrong?'

Before Ella could decide whether to tell Laura now or to make up some comforting story before softening her up gently for the truth, two of the others arrived to drag her off to the dining room.

'Laura!' Claudia screeched. 'How absolutely brilliant! I had no idea you were even coming! Are you here for the meal our potential new chef's sent?'

Ella put an arm round her protectively. 'She doesn't know anything about Billy yet. Are you sure you're up to a big dinner in the dining room? If you like, I could pinch us a bit and we could eat it quietly here?'

Laura visibly shook herself. 'No, no, I don't want to spoil your evening. What happened to the old chef?'

'He walked out after a difference of opinion with Mrs Lal over the right way to cook a steak or some such thing,' Claudia replied.

'Oh dear, is Mrs Lal still causing trouble?' Laura asked anxiously. 'I hoped she would have settled down by now.'

'Trouble and entertainment value in equal measure,' soothed Claudia. 'Anyway, this new chef is Spike's uncle. Spike's our intern student who lives here rent-free.'

'And complains about our loud music,' giggled Ella. 'Especially Status Quo.'

'I don't blame him.' Laura grinned. 'I can't stand them either. They were Simon's favourite band. And is his uncle a good cook?'

'He bloody well ought to be. He's coming to us via the Ritz!' explained Ella.

'And he's brought us a bang-up spread just so we can all see the kind of thing he'd offer.'

'But if he's cooked at the Ritz, why on earth would he want to come here?' Laura insisted, beginning to look a bit more cheerful.

'For a bunch of wrinklies who'll soon need their food put in a liquidizer, you mean?' Claudia enquired.

'He wants to semi-retire,' Ella explained.

'Plus he loves carp fishing,' Claudia added knowledgably. 'Did you know we have the biggest carp lake in the south of England a mere two miles away? We've offered him a free cottage and he's very nearly said yes.'

'So from now on it will be pastries that are perfection, and meat that is mouthwatering, and hors d'oeuvres that are heavenly . . .' Ella began to list.

'And a free ambulance to A&E when we all have a heart attack . . .' Claudia added crisply.

'Well,' Laura smiled at last, her pinched face visibly relaxing. 'I've obviously chosen the right day to turn up unexpectedly.'

'We've all missed you so much, Laura!'

Laura's smile wobbled before she pinned it deliberately back on. 'Let's go for it then!'

The dining room looked wonderful. Someone had discovered the vast arrangement of dried hydrangeas in gorgeous Renaissance hues of dark aubergine, faded blue and sea green that once adorned the hotel lobby and plonked it in the middle of the table. Candles flickered on silver and glass and lit up the amazing feast Billy had provided.

As they each got themselves a glass of champagne Ella hoped Laura would forget all about what had happened until they were alone and she could break the news to her gently.

But whether it was the bubbles in the wine or the safety of being among old friends that emboldened Laura, Ella had no idea. So when Sal asked her why she'd gone off their radar for so long, Laura looked coy and told them she'd met an amazing man.

'He's called Gavin,' Laura boasted. 'He works abroad and we were due to meet up today and then he must have missed his plane.' She got out her phone and passed the photo of Gavin round for them all to look at admiringly.

'Oh, poor you!' Olivia sympathized. 'He looks very charming and attractive.'

Without being able to help herself, Ella murmured, 'For a male model from Huddersfield!' under her breath.

She took a sip of her drink. But Laura had turned on her, eyes blazing. '*What* did you just say?'

'Oh, nothing,' Ella replied, angry at her own indiscretion.

'I heard you perfectly clearly. You said, "For a male model from Huddersfield". What exactly did you mean?'

'Laura, let's talk about it later. Why don't we just have a good evening?'

'No, Ella, you can't say something like that and let it go.'

'Let's have a chat outside then.' Ella didn't want to humiliate her friend in front of everyone.

'No, Ella, it's perfectly okay here.'

'I looked him up on Reverse Images.'

'Who?'

'Gavin.'

'But you didn't have a picture of him.' Laura paused, understanding beginning to dawn. 'You stole it from my phone.'

'I didn't steal it, I just photographed it.'

'Wait a minute. You came all the way to London just to get that picture,' she accused furiously.

'He's called Patrick Johnson, Laura. He really is a male model. You could probably meet him if you wanted.'

Laura stood up, knocking over her wine as she got to her feet. 'I can't believe you'd do that! Steal a photograph of him from my phone!'

'I was trying to protect you.' Ella attempted to stop her leaving. 'It's really common to be scammed after you're widowed or just divorced. They specifically warn you about it!'

By now everyone round the table seemed to have understood what was going on.

'Surely, Ella, that was an invasion of Laura's privacy . . . ?' began Rose.

'I think she was right to do it,' Lou disagreed. 'Internet scammers can be dangerous people.'

But Laura was halfway across the room.

'Laura, Laura . . .' Ella stood up and began to follow her. 'I couldn't bear to see you hurt again!'

'So you got in first and hurt me yourself!' flashed Laura as chaos took over and everyone began to accuse each other.

'Stop it!' Sal had got to her feet and shouted all of them down. 'Just stop it right this minute!' They all turned to look at her pale and angry face. 'You might as well find out now, it's as good a time as any. I think my old mate cancer's back again in my other breast.'

For a beat of a second silence engulfed the room, before Sal climbed onto a chair, with Lou looking on anxiously.

'And if you lot don't stop arguing,' she shouted as loudly as she could manage, 'I won't ask any of you to be my brides-maids!'

Twenty-Four

'Sal, you're getting married! How absolutely bloody wonderful!' Claudia was the first to pounce on her friend and embrace her in delight. She knew sympathy for her revelation would be the last thing Sal wanted.

Ella followed her cue. 'I'm so incredibly happy for you both. You couldn't have found a more perfect man.'

Laura, still reeling from shock, followed. 'And you as well, Lou, millions of congratulations. I know you'll be really happy.'

'I am so utterly thrilled,' Rose beamed. 'You are very special people in my life, both of you.'

'But this frightful illness, Sally,' Mrs Lal interjected with all the subtlety of a double-decker bus, 'how long have you known about that?'

'I was thinking of keeping it to myself,' Sal replied, looking embarrassed. 'Crazy, I know, after last time but at least until the diagnosis was certain. And then Mr Interfering Busybody here' – she grinned lovingly at Lou – 'worked it out and turned up at the hospital in a taxi.'

'What a very sensible man,' endorsed Olivia. 'I do think a taxi improves most situations.' The others tried not to smile at the idea of how improving it might have been to go to the guillotine in a taxi instead of a tumbril.

'And you're sure it's really serious?' Mrs Lal persisted, despite black looks from Rose.

'I'm focusing on the not entirely reassuring words from my consultant: if you must get cancer, then breast is best.'

'And you will definitely let them chop off your breast if it is?' Mrs Lal ploughed on, entirely impervious to the desperate signalling from the others.

'Lalita!' Even her new ally Olivia decided enough was enough. 'This is supposed to be an engagement celebration.'

'Absolutely! Come with me, Mrs Lal.' Bella linked her arm through Lalita's. 'Let's go and look for some champagne!'

They managed to find two bottles amongst the few remaining in the hotel cellar and Lou popped them with all the panache of a lifetime's experience.

'So when's the wedding going to be?' Ella enquired, passing round the glasses.

'Cancer waits for no man – or woman – so hopefully next week,' Sal replied. 'As long as my daughter Lara and family can make it over from Oslo. I can't go ahead without them. And Lou's daughter, of course, and a couple of his ex-wives maybe.' She raised her glass at him, grinning.

'I don't have that many and you know I wouldn't ask them. You make me sound like Bluebeard.'

'No, just an American.'

'Ms Grainger,' replied Lou affectionately. 'You are going to have to get over this absurd prejudice against my countrymen.'

This time she kissed him. 'I'm working on it. I like you and that's a start.'

'Where will it be?' asked Laura.

'We wondered about the town hall, but amazingly it's booked up.'

'Wait a minute.' Bella was looking thoughtful. 'I'm sure they had a licence for weddings here at the manor. They were bound to really. Lovely country hotel, pretty grounds. Half the hotels in the country only survive with weddings.'

'This one didn't,' pointed out Rose. 'I know, let's ask Murdo. I'll phone him now.'

As soon as he heard the news Murdo arrived straight away with two bottles of vintage Ruinart which meant the party could keep going.

'I'd been saving them for another occasion,' he announced meaningfully, his eyes on Mrs Lal.

'Murdo,' Rose replied briskly, ignoring the tactlessness of this admission, seeing as he had previously been pursuing her, 'I've become very fond of dear Lalita here, but the idea of you and she settling down together is about as likely as a monsoon in the Isle of Wight. She's a force of nature and you like a quiet time.'

'I suppose you're right,' he conceded, brightening visibly. 'You wanted to know about a wedding licence at the hotel. Indeed there was one. And it's still valid, I checked.'

'That's brilliant!' Sal sipped her champagne with delight. 'I can't think of anywhere I'd like to get married more!'

'The only thing is,' Murdo added, 'the pretty pagoda where they held the weddings started to rot and has fallen down.'

'I'll rebuild it!' They turned to find Don beaming from the doorway. 'It can be my contribution to your wedding.'

A slightly strained silence ensued.

'You don't think I'm up to it!' accused Don. 'Ah, but that's because you haven't heard of Men in Sheds!'

'I certainly have,' Olivia corrected. 'Leonard used to spend his whole life in one.'

'No,' Don explained patiently, 'Men in Sheds is the organization I belong to, so I won't be doing it single-handed, though it's great to know I'm getting such a vote of confidence in my new skills,' he added in a wounded voice.

'Don, that sounds absolutely wonderful,' Sal announced, repressing the question on the tip of her tongue about whether it might make more sense to get married in the lounge rather than a flimsy pagoda since it had been raining for days.

'Sally, I have been thinking,' announced Mrs Lal ominously. 'It is very kind of you to invite me to be a bridesmaid and believe me, I am very moved, but do you not think it should just be your closest friends?' She indicated Ella, Claudia and Laura. 'After all, they are old but we are even older!'

Rose and Olivia both nodded in agreement.

'And you have your daughter to consider and maybe your little granddaughter as well,' Rose insisted. 'It's a wedding, after all, not a freak show with ninety-year-old bridesmaids!'

'I don't give a flying fuck about whether it's a freak show!' protested Sal robustly.

'Spoken like a true English lady,' congratulated her fiancé.

'Look at it this way,' Don put his oar in. 'I'm a mere bloke but just having the Coven as your bridesmaids does have a certain emotional rightness. You've been there for each other through thick and thin.'

'Sometimes very thin,' Laura endorsed, thinking about Simon and now the whole of the Gavin fiasco.

'I agree with Don,' Olivia said, slipping her arm round her daughter Claudia. 'You girls have something really special. I wish I had a friendship like yours.'

Claudia hugged her back, realizing it must have been very

lonely for her mother, especially with the episode of bipolar she'd suffered, and all with no women friends to share in the worries.

'Is it going to be a white wedding?' Mrs Lal enquired.

Sal looked at Lou. 'Well? What do you think?'

'I think it should be whatever kind of wedding you want,' Lou smiled at her lovingly.

'Classic male,' Sal replied, returning his smile. 'Too scared to get off the fence. I would like a fabulous, colourful, outrageous wedding with lots of fun and as many clichés as possible.'

'In that case,' beamed Mrs Lal, 'I could be in charge of sourcing your dresses.'

'From Good Age?' Claudia couldn't resist asking.

'No. I'm not sure that would be appropriate. I was wondering, since you want to go for colour, what you would feel about an Indian wedding?'

'Well, that makes perfect sense, seeing as neither of us has any connection whatsoever with India.' Sal laughed, looking enquiringly at her husband-to-be.

'Oh, what the hell,' Lou replied, holding Sal next to his side and winking at her. 'It'd certainly make a change from my previous outings.'

Sal pretended to scratch his eyes out, while Don managed to squeeze the last drop out of the Ruinart.

Later when they finally dispersed for bed, Ella persuaded Laura to come back to her cottage before she headed off to her daughter Bella's to sleep.

'Laura, I just wanted to say, I'm really, really sorry if I've been an interfering bitch. It's just that I was so worried about you.'

'Come on,' Laura suggested, 'call me an old soak, but let's have one glass of white wine before bedtime. With what I've been through, I need it.'

Ella produced two glasses and sat down next to her on the sofa.

'I don't know why I can't just admit it.' Laura's voice shook with suppressed emotion. 'I was conned. Gavin didn't exist. And there's worse.'

She put down her wine, suddenly convulsed with sobbing. 'I gave him five thousand dollars! What kind of stupid gullible pathetic idiot hands over five thousand dollars to some man she's never even met?'

Ella held open her arms. 'Lots of people,' she said softly, holding Laura tight. 'I read the cuttings about all the people who'd been scammed. There was even an Oxford professor who'd lost hundreds of thousands. It's not about being naive, it's about how you're feeling when they hit on you. You were raw and hurting after Simon and then Calum . . .'

'And now Gavin. I seem to be an excellent picker.'

'Laura don't. You're so lovely.'

'I don't want to tell Bella and Sam. I can't bear for them to know I'm that stupid and naive. Is that just as crazy?'

'I quite understand, but Laura, it isn't really such a big sum.'

'Or, my God, Simon. He'd go mental. One good thing has come out of it, though.'

She smiled wanly through her tears. 'God, I look like a panda with hay fever. If there's a cottage free, I've decided to come and join the Coven.'

'Laura!' Ella's voice rang with delight and relief that Laura wasn't going to cut her out of her life. 'Everyone will be absolutely delighted!'

'Even if Bella moves on and develops her own business, at

least I'll get a little while with my grandson. After all, you never know how long you've got, do you? Look at Sal.'

They grabbed each other's hands.

'Let's hope her consultant's right,' Ella said in a low voice. Neither of them could imagine a world without Sal.

'And you lot do seem to be rubbing along together somehow or other down here,' Laura smiled.

'With occasional eruptions from the volcano that is Mrs Lal.'

'Speaking of my grandson, if I don't go back soon, I'll miss seeing him tonight.'

At the door of the cottage Ella gave her one last hug. 'I really am thrilled you're thinking of joining us. And so will the others be.'

'Well, living in London, just me and the dating app, it wasn't that much fun without the rest of you.'

'If you take to dating again, you'd better try Mrs Lal. I thought she was going to fix you up with someone who deserved you.'

'I think I'll leave well alone, thank you very much.'

'A wise decision, I suspect. Especially if Mrs Lal is involved.'

Laura waved goodbye, relief flooding over her. They were all going to be together again. The future, living with her family and friends all around her, suddenly seemed brighter.

The deputation from Men in Sheds arrived the very next day, with Don obviously loving being in charge. Wonderful Bella had discovered a photo which featured the wedding pagoda and the four-strong team happily bickered about how to reconstruct it until one of them who had sat quietly down at a table produced a workable sketch.

'Mike, that's amazing,' congratulated Don.

'Actually,' the one called Mike confessed modestly, 'I pinched it off Pinterest.'

'I don't care if you personally requested it from Xi Jinping,' Don persisted. 'It looks doable to me and that's enough.'

'Who the hell's this Xi Jinping?' demanded one of the others. 'Is he from the Guildford branch?'

'President of China, mate,' replied Mike with an engaging grin.

'Oh, I see. He knows a lot, Don, doesn't he?'

Before the admiration went to his head, Don and Mike sat down to make a list of the materials they were going to need to reconstruct the pagoda.

Don studied the photo again. 'The back and sides can be normal wood but how do we get that fretwork effect for the front?' He looked at the sketch. 'And that curvy roof looks a bugger to me.'

Mike calmly reached for his laptop again. 'I saw some trellis with fretwork a bit like that in the posh new garden centre. The roof's a bit trickier. I've got a pal who's a boat builder, I think we might need to get him involved.'

'On our budget?'

'He'll do it for mate's rates. Keep him out of the pub.' He laughed as though this might be doing his pal a favour.

'But could he do it for next week?'

'I'll have to ask him.' He picked up the photograph together with his laptop. 'Why don't you lot all go down the builders' merchants and start with the rest of the stuff, then we could at least get cracking on the base and sides tomorrow.'

The other two leaped to their feet while Don looked mutinous. They all knew that Mike had quietly taken charge, but none of them would admit it. Least of all Don.

Claudia, Ella and Laura, sitting in the lounge having a

coffee, witnessed this masculine interchange and tried not to laugh.

'I love men, don't you?' Ella grinned. 'Adam and Eve would never have survived on their own in the Garden of Eden. Men need other blokes to play power games with.'

'I just hope Don doesn't sulk,' Claudia grinned. 'Or I shall have to go out there and remind him it's for a higher cause.'

'I thought this organization of his was all about building self-esteem.' Ella shook her head. 'They looked as if they were point-scoring to me.'

'Maybe that's how men build self-esteem. They take it in turns to point-score. Next time it'll be Don's turn.'

'Mike seemed nice,' Laura shrugged as the others started giggling. 'Oh, stop it, all of you! Women are supposed to support each other instead of scoring points, remember?'

In a rare outbreak of sensitivity, egged on by her new friend Olivia, Mrs Lal decided that Sal should be allowed to choose her own wedding dress.

She arrived with a carful of rainbow-coloured saris in which bright red and shocking pink seemed to have the starring role.

'So,' Ella enquired. 'What colour would the bride like to wear?'

Mrs Lal held out a beautiful and surprisingly tasteful coral-coloured length of fabric, heavily encrusted with pale gold, plus large golden earrings and a ruby drop to be worn in the middle of the forehead. 'I thought perhaps this was the one.'

'It's beautiful, Lalita.' Sal held it up against her in the mirror. 'Can I try it on?'

'Only the sari. Bad luck to try all together before the morning of the wedding,' Mrs Lal pronounced grandly.

'And what about the bridegroom?' Sal enquired. 'What exactly will he be wearing?'

'He will be even more resplendent than the bride,' Mrs Lal announced reverently. 'In the costume of a rajah.'

'The perfect ensemble for a property developer from Brooklyn,' Sal laughed.

Spike's Uncle Billy had generously agreed to provide the food, as long as it wasn't Indian as well. After great consideration, and much to the amusement of all, Mrs Lal had generously consented.

Excitement mounted when Lara and her family arrived from Oslo and joined in the sense of general anticipation.

'Just whose wedding is this?' Ella was moved to demand when her plans for tasteful flower arrangements were abandoned in favour of Mrs Lal's more ambitious ones.

'Christ knows,' Sal hid her head in her hands, laughing uproariously, 'but I love it all!'

Reassuring sounds of hammering could be heard from outside. Don had taken control once more as the pagoda began to be reconstructed.

At least the concrete base had survived and wouldn't have to be replaced.

Despite the rain the back wall went up with impressive speed, then the fretwork sides, sourced as Mike had suggested in the upmarket garden centre. The trellis looked surprisingly effective.

Ella stood at the lounge window watching the construction. 'Correct me if I'm wrong' – she began to get a serious case of the giggles – 'but isn't a pagoda supposed to be Chinese?'

Giggling being as infectious as yawning, by now they all

joined in when Mrs Lal, followed by Olivia, reappeared in the lounge. 'Are you ladies all right?' she demanded testily.

'Oh yes,' Sal reassured before another wave overtook her. 'Everything's hunky dory, thanks.'

The pagoda construction continued apace. Mike's boat-building friend was happy to create the roof from some old bits of hull he had lying about.

Things were moving so fast that Sal had hardly a moment to worry about anything else. At least she still had her hair. A bald bride would test anyone's sense of optimism, especially the bride's. 'Have you noticed how many cups of tea Laura's been making for that friend of Don's?' she whispered to Ella. 'If he drinks any more, he'll explode!'

'Not to mention all the nice warm towels she keeps giving him in case he catches cold in the rain,' Ella grinned.

'Now, now, ladies,' Don intervened, overhearing them. 'As a matter of fact, Mike's been asking me what Laura's current situation is.'

Once the pagoda was finished, Don proceeded to paint it in shades so bright they might outshine the saris.

'Well, you did say you wanted a colourful wedding,' he reminded Sal.

The pièce de résistance was when Mike went out to buy nails and came back with a Nepalese wedding arch he'd discovered in the antique market in Godalming.

'Now all we need is one of those lucky cats that wave their paws in Chinese herbalists,' Claudia pointed out, trying to keep a straight face at the increasingly over-the-top nature of the celebration.

'Don't be such a cynic,' Ella chided. 'I think it's all wonderfully global, especially as the celebrant's a humanist from Walling-ford.'

'That's all it needed.' Claudia shook her head.

But there was one more surprise Mother Nature had up her sleeve for them yet.

Twenty-Five

When they all woke for Sal's wedding day the persistent rain had changed to hail, with hailstones as big as tennis balls.

'Hailstones in summer!' Ella pressed her nose against the window to get a better look. 'I bet you don't get this in India, Lalita?'

'Nonsense!' Mrs Lal corrected. 'Haven't you ever heard of the Himalaya Mountains? They have avalanches!'

'I hope we're not going to get one those in Surrey.' Claudia joined Ella at the window.

'Do you think it's Jehovah telling me to change my mind?' suggested Sal, joining them.

Mrs Lal left them to it and went off to help Lou get dressed.

'Come on, sir,' she encouraged the rather reluctant Lou. 'Enjoy yourself!' She patted his broad shoulders. 'What would your Colonel Flashman do on his wedding day?'

'Run off with all the bridesmaids, from what I've heard of the guy!' was Lou's instant response. 'Actually, I'm an American, and Flashman was a Brit. Of course I'll do my best to behave badly.'

After that he submitted quietly to being dressed in the

ornate white outfit she produced. Once she had finished he surveyed himself in the long mirror, from the tasselled head-dress to·the wreaths of white flowers she placed round his neck. 'Liberace on speed!' he pronounced. 'Where's my best man got to?'

Don appeared rather sheepishly, also clad in white cloth which forcibly reminded Lou of upholstery fabric. 'Don't sit down or I won't be able to tell you from the couch,' he counselled.

'I'm doing this for you, Lou . . .' Don replied, wounded.

'I know, I know, and as the only other example of living, breathing manhood resident here I'm deeply grateful to you.'

'There was always Hiro,' Don grinned.

'He's agreed to be the ring bearer.'

They both laughed as Mrs Lal appeared with a fortifying brandy for each of them.

'Bridegroom's nerves,' she announced as she handed them over.

'I thought it was the bride who got nervous,' Lou replied, knocking back his courage-inducing snifter.

'From my observation,' Mrs Lal corrected, 'it is far more often the bridegroom who disappears to an unknown destination.'

'Don't worry,' Lou reassured, 'I certainly won't be doing that.'

In the coach house, which had been designated as changing room for bride and bridesmaids, all was happy chaos.

The bridesmaids, assisted by Olivia, were busily winding themselves in saris and trying to reveal as little bare middle as possible.

'These bloody things go on forever,' protested Ella.

'The whole nine yards as a matter of fact,' Laura laughed. 'I looked it up on Google.'

'Oh well, it'll make a nice tablecloth afterwards,' pronounced Olivia.

'*Three* nice tablecloths,' corrected Ella.

'Ladies!' Mrs Lal, who appeared to have the knack of being in two places at once, suddenly emerged from the corridor. 'Champagne!'

'She certainly thinks of everything,' murmured Laura.

'This is a very special wedding!' They were relieved that for once she didn't suggest that the bride might not make it through the honeymoon. 'To the wonder of women!'

'I'll certainly drink to that,' conceded Ella, holding up her glass.

Sal's daughter Lara and her children came into the room, happy and laughing.

She held Sal at arm's length and studied her. 'Sally . . . Mum . . . You look amazing!'

At the word 'Mum' Sal began to dissolve into happy tears. 'I just never thought I'd hear that word applied to me, that's all.'

'And soon you'll be hearing another unfamiliar word,' Lara teased, holding her close. '*Mrs* Maynard.'

'And believe me,' Sal wiped her eyes, 'I'm going to use it on every bloody occasion I can. Fuck Ms . . . oops, sorry, girls . . .' She turned to her granddaughters and pretended to put her hands over their ears.

'Don't worry about that, Granny,' piped the older one. 'Mum called her boss a bastard the other day!' She studied her mother's embarrassed face.

'Well, he is . . .' Lara began, before she stopped herself.

'What good English you speak, girls!' Sal rescued her. 'Do

411

you know, I think it might be time for me to go and get married!'

'As excuses go,' Lara murmured to her, 'I don't think I've ever heard a better one than that!'

Mrs Lal stopped them at the doorway. 'Let me just go and check. You may be very modern but I still don't think you should arrive before the bridegroom. It would spoil the drama if nothing else!'

'Do we need any more drama?' Claudia asked, peering outside. 'Oh my God, it's stopped! Look, everyone!' The hail had disappeared and in one of these dramatic shifts that makes us talk about nothing but the weather, it had been replaced by a bright blue sky. 'It's brilliant sunshine!' She turned to Sal. 'Jehovah's changed his mind. He says it's fine as long as you marry someone Jewish from Brooklyn!'

'Go on, tell me there's a rainbow!' Sal smiled.

'Don't push your luck, Grainger. One miracle's enough.'

They stepped gingerly out, holding up their saris. Ella held a large umbrella over Sal in case Jehovah had a rethink.

All the way across the garden from the lounge to the new Chinese pagoda Mrs Lal had laid a carpet in exactly the right shade to complement the bride's ensemble. Just outside the pagoda, under a couple of parasols improvised to ward off the worst of the hail, sat a small group of musicians playing what could only be described as Indian lift music, designed not to offend anyone's cultural sensibilities.

Inside the pagoda stood a beaming Lou, Don at his side looking almost as delighted. The only other guests were Olivia, Rose, Bella with Nigel and Noah, Douglas and Gaby, Sal's daughter Lara with her lovely family, Lou's daughter plus her husband and baby, Spike and Uncle Billy, Lord Murdo Binns and Hiro.

412

Mrs Lal had got it absolutely right. These were the people who meant most to Sal and Lou, and to be frank, no one else could possibly fit in the pagoda.

The ceremony was short and sweet. There was no need for vows that promised loyalty in sickness and in health because that was already happening.

Hiro appeared at exactly the right moment, beaming and bearing the ring, and didn't even declaim any Shakespeare.

After they were pronounced man and wife and the rose petals had been beautifully strewn, the happy couple kissed and the party began. Then they went inside to eat a wonderful meal of foie gras to be followed by rare roast beef provided as a gift from Uncle Billy.

By some matchmaking sleight of hand, Laura found herself sitting next to Mike from Men in Sheds, with whom she happily swapped photos of their grandchildren.

Ella was delighted and relieved that dangerous Daniel Forrest was nowhere to be seen.

'Well done,' Claudia congratulated her husband, 'you look lovely in white.'

'Sarky cow,' Don responded.

'*Excuse me?*' Claudia replied, nettled.

'I like sarky cows as a matter of fact. I find them quite a turn-on.'

'Don! We're at a wedding!'

'Where better?' He looked in the direction of Sal and Lou. 'I think they'll be happy, don't you?'

Claudia looked at her friend of more than forty years. They had lived through excitement, loneliness, success and failure – in other words, life, together. And it wasn't over yet. Not by any means.

Now that the foie gras with black truffle had been cleared,

Sal was clapping for silence. With all the outrageous nerve that came from sixty years of living, she clambered onto the table.

'Okay, quiet, the lot of you! I've got something to say. I never thought I'd be a Mrs. In fact, to be honest, I much preferred the idea of being a Ms, but that was before I met this man.' She waved her champagne glass at her new husband, who was beaming his approval – tempered with slight alarm at her precarious position – from his seat next to hers.

'So, everyone here, my beloved and much treasured people, a toast!' They all raised their glasses in readiness. 'To Mrs Henry Louis Maynard the Fourth! In other words, ME!!'

'Come on down now before you break something, you crazy broad!' Lou held his hand out to her, his face full of love and happiness. 'If there's one thing I'd change about you, it's your propensity to climb onto tables. By the way, isn't someone supposed to be toasting the bridesmaids?'

Don had already leaped to his feet. 'You're quite right, Lou. I think that's my job. I would indeed like to toast the bridesmaids, and one of them in particular, my wife Claudia. I know there've been times when we've all felt moving to the Manor was a godawful mistake.' Rumblings around the room confirmed this to be no less than the truth. 'But recently things have been begun to change. No one said growing old would be sweet – or even bittersweet. In fact, most of us denied it was going to happen at all. But through some hideous accident it *has* happened, and maybe, just maybe, we've found a better way of facing it, with each other, among friends and family. So I'd like to raise a toast to all the bridesmaids but especially Claudia who dared to bring us here. So Claudia, my wife, my love, we'll be blaming you when it all finally goes wrong. To the bridesmaids, and above all, Claudia!'

All round the room people clapped and banged their feet on the floor as they seconded Don in his toast.

The next course arrived, followed by a beautiful chocolate wedding cake which Lou and Sal, in yet another global cultural reference, cut with a Scottish sword.

And Mrs Lal was on her feet to announce the dancing.

'It is very naughty of me to hijack this wonderful occasion,' she said without a shred of visible shame, 'to announce the news that we're through to the next round of Best Charity Shop at Good Age!'

Tumultuous clapping followed. 'And now,' she continued, beaming, 'Mr and Mrs Maynard will have their first dance in the lounge!'

The bridal couple took to the floor to launch their married life with the original version of 'Lovely Day' sung by Bill Withers. 'When I look at you,' Lou sang along to Sal, 'I always know it's going to be a lovely day.' And then he added, 'He's not much older than me, you know.'

'And not nearly as sexy,' she whispered back.

'Now that is a compliment. He's one of the sexiest bluesmen of all time.'

'I rest my case.'

Most of the furniture had been removed from the lounge, and it left just enough space for everyone to dance.

Laura found herself really enjoying the company of her new friend Mike. After they'd shared six dances, Don discreetly signalled to her.

Pretending to need the loo, Laura followed him to the table that had been set up as a bar.

'Laura, I thought I just ought to warn you about Mike . . .' Don's face was bleak with foreboding.

Laura's chest tightened. Not another shit. She really had a talent for picking them. 'Yes,' she replied curtly, her face hardening in anticipation. What was this one going to be? A wife beater or just terminally unfaithful?

Don's face broke into the widest of smiles. 'Mike's a really nice bloke. Just thought I'd let you know.'

'Thanks for the warning,' she said at last, not knowing whether to hug him or kick him. 'I think I could cope with that.'

Before she could get back to him, Bella had started to make another announcement.

'I didn't think Sal and Lou would mind if I shared some news.' She put her arm round her huge husband. 'Nigel and I are having another baby!'

Everyone cheered, especially Laura.

'That is wonderful news,' Mrs Lal's voice boomed out. 'Now we have births, marriages and—'

'Lalita!' Olivia descended on her before she could finish her sentence. 'Come and cut me a slice of that marvellous chocolate cake!'

It was a wedding few of the guests would ever forget.

Lou and Sal weren't going on a honeymoon but they were still cheered and whooped as they set off on the extremely brief journey back to their cottage where, unknown to them, Mrs Lal had lit fifty tea lights and strewn rose petals all over the bed, to celebrate their wedding night.

'Thanks for the speech,' Claudia acknowledged, as she and Don walked back through the gardens to the coach house. She stopped suddenly, pointing upwards. 'Look! Do you think Mrs Lal arranged that too?'

Above them a full moon had just appeared from behind the

clouds, illuminating the whole landscape in incandescent white light.

'No,' Don replied modestly, 'I ordered that. You deserve it after all your hard work.' To her surprise he was holding out a hand for her to take. 'Maybe it's time we joined the hand-holding brigade.'

With the reflection of the moonlight his face somehow looked thirty years younger.

'Okay.' Claudia glanced round the scene in case of witnesses. 'Thirty seconds max.'

Don took her hand in his and squeezed it tightly.

'Actually,' he smiled, pulling her towards him in the clear night air, 'I was thinking more of ten.'

Read on for an extract of

An
Italian
Holiday

a story of romance and friendship
on the Amalfi Coast . . .

Claire was the first to wake; she'd always been an early riser and often leapt out of bed leaving Martin to sleep. She padded over to the window and threw open the shutters. The sun hit her eyes with such force that she had to stand back and shade them. But as soon as she was accustomed to the sunlight she leaned out of her window. The vista unfolding in front of her took her breath away with its loveliness.

The terrace beneath her window was decorated with urns overflowing with pale pink geraniums which gave way to trees of bright, new spring green and below that a dazzling cobalt blue sea. A single fishing boat ploughed its way across her vision, heading inland with its overnight catch, leaving a white trail from its motor.

Claire looked at her watch. Only seven. No one else would be up. And she knew she just had to be outside.

She quickly changed into jeans and a T-shirt, scrabbled around for her trainers and sneaked out through the silent house.

In the gardens that tumbled down the hillside it wasn't just the light that amazed her but a heady perfume she didn't recognize. As she rounded the corner at the side of the house she came across a pergola, half hidden by a mass of purple wisteria, with two chairs placed underneath it. She sat down and breathed in the glorious scent, but it was too lovely to sit for long. At the back of the house almond, cherry and apple trees waved their pink and white blossoms in the morning breeze and she could hear the sound of bees buzzing from one flower to the next.

On the next level down, a small fountain trickled beside a half-hidden grotto with a fresh-water pool built into the rock face. Claire almost clapped her hands in delight. On the edge of the pool a life-sized marble nymph kneeled, staring into the water, an expression of longing on her face. The quality of the carving was extraordinary. This was not the work of some local stonemason. It had to have been chiselled by the hand of a master.

An irresistible temptation overcame Claire. She glanced furtively around, then, satisfied that she was alone, stripped off her clothes down to pants and bra. Oh what the hell, she thought, the nymph is naked, why not me too?

The water was icy cold and clear as gin, but country-bred Claire just held her breath until she got used to it.

She found a small ledge where she could support herself and stared again at the statue. 'Is it your lost lover you're searching for?' she enquired of the stone maiden. 'Banished under the water by some jealous goddess?'

The only answer was a laugh.

Claire swung round to find Giovanni pushing a wheel-barrow, his shirt undone even further than Simon Cowell's, though Giovanni's chest could not have been more different.

'*Due ninfe.*' He smiled with that sly sexy smile that seemed so characteristically Italian. Two nymphs. One nymph and a crone might have been more appropriate. Casually Claire slipped an arm across her breasts, conscious that if she let go of the ledge to protect her modesty she would disappear under the water. She must carry this off with confidence as if English ladies took naked dips every morning. The terrible thought struck her that Giovanni was looking straight at her body through the crystal-clear water.

'*Febbre di primavera*. The fever of the spring,' he stated as if this was a perfectly acceptable explanation for finding a nude woman in a fountain. 'Nobody can resist.'

And then he walked onwards, whistling.

Claire waited until he was safely out of sight and then climbed out. She didn't even have a towel. She pulled her T-shirt on over her wet body, realizing it only drew attention to her freezing nipples, and scrabbled into her jeans, the dampness of her body making her almost fall over as she tried to yank them on.

She glanced back at the pool.

From where he was standing with the sunlight illuminating the water, she would have seemed as naked as Lady Godiva minus her famous hair.

She wondered for a moment how Martin would have reacted if he'd come upon her nude in a pool. Probably wouldn't have noticed. Or maybe he'd have said: 'For God's sake, Claire, what the hell are you doing? You'll catch your death.' Certainly not called her a nymph. To give him his due he was from Cheltenham.

Angela drew back one of her extravagant devoré curtains and stepped out onto her large balcony, so large that it was really a terrace. For a moment she didn't notice the beauty of the day, still preoccupied with the fact that this was Stephen Charlesworth's house.

She remembered when they'd said goodbye as clearly as if she were still in the moment. He had been so kind when the father she loved so much had died and had even driven her home in his ancient black Austin Healey to take care of her mother. They had both been grateful that for once it hadn't broken down. How he'd loved that car.

And then he'd kissed her goodbye and they'd both promised to keep in touch, but she'd known it was a lie. He was twenty-one and had just found his feet at Oxford. He was attractive and, now that he'd lost his initial shyness, charming. He would be devoured alive by some clever, pretty girl who came from a background like his own, not a council house in Nottingham.

Angela had tried not to resent her mother, to accept that she had always been fragile, but there had been some small part of her that thought if she had been in her mother's place she would have done anything to avoid ending her daughter's brilliant university career before it had really begun.

Of course she had heard of Stephen's enormous success since that day. His name often came up in the financial pages, which Angela read avidly, or at least had done until now. The ache, just a dull background pain, suddenly roared out at her. She'd lost her business to the Tuan Corporation of Singapore and when she was twenty-one she'd lost Stephen.

At last the beauty of the day struck her and she almost laughed. It was as if some piece of grey rain-soaked scenery had been rolled away and another rolled into its place of bright blue sea that matched the sky, with small puffy clouds and a child's yellow sun.

She turned back to her room wondering what to wear.

Seen in daylight the room was truly spectacular, like the bridal suite in some grand hotel. The unfamiliar thought struck Angela that perhaps it had been a little selfish of her to simply co-opt the best room. She was so used to fighting for what she'd achieved that it didn't leave much room for considering others.

She remembered the other rooms that Sylvie and Monica had been left with and shuddered. Sylvie didn't even have her own bathroom! Maybe she'd wait a few days and then offer to swap. There was a good chance that by then they'd be settled, thank her for the kind offer, and stay put.

Sylvie climbed out of bed and stretched. There was hardly room to swing a cat in. What a stupid expression. Had anyone, apart from in *The Beano,* ever tried swinging a cat? Today she'd find another room even if it was the bloody stables.

She did her five minutes of Pilates, boring as hell, but it did seem to help once you'd reached the big Six-Oh. Not that Sylvie ever admitted she had.

She brushed her springy hair and selected one of her silk tops. She had these in countless colours which she matched with jeans and sandals and she was ready to go. If she had to dress up it was ankle-length silk, which she also possessed in endless different shades. This was Sylvie's look, known to everyone in the decorating world, almost as familiar as her colourful interiors.

She opened the shutter and closed it almost at once. Too bright. With her naturally olive skin and Middle-Eastern appearance the sun meant less to her than most people since she never needed to sunbathe. She was glad the rain had stopped for at least one reason. It made her hair go frizzy. In

Los Angeles they even had a hair-frizz factor on the TV weather. Sylvie greatly approved.

She checked to see that the purple Chanel nail varnish she always wore on her toes hadn't chipped, remembering all of a sudden that it was called Vendetta – which, for some reason, made her think of Angela.

OK, so Angela Williams was an uppity bitch but if they were both going to stay in the same house, maybe she'd make a slight effort to be friendly. At least give her one chance and take it from there.

There was a small chip on her third toenail and it almost undid her.

Tony used to paint her toes. It was a jokey ritual of theirs. She would be the haughty duchess and he the humble but sexy manservant. It often ended up in bed with her nail varnish all smudged, but she'd never minded.

She wondered what he was doing now. Had Kimberley's family accepted him as the prospective son-in-law even though he was probably older than her father?

She found the thought only made her want to cry more and she told herself sternly to pull herself together and go and have some breakfast.